Praise for *On the Threshold*

"… gifted and inspiring. The storyline has stayed with me."
~Eva Marie Everson,
best-selling author of *The Cedar Key* novels & *Unconditional; The Novel*

"… real women who write stories about real life."
~Bonnie Leon,
author of *The Alaskan Skies* Series

"With a writing style that flows gently between generations, this mother-daughter team has tackled a tough subject of grief at many layers."
~Jane Kirkpatrick,
award-winning author of *One Glorious Ambition*

To Ginny

On the Threshold

Sherrie Ashcraft

&

Christina Berry Tarabochia

Ashberry Lane

This book is available in print at most online retailers.

ISBN 978-0-9893967-1-4

Cover Design by Miller Media Solutions
Author Photo by Nicole Zena Photography

Dedications

Sherrie

~ my husband, John, who believed in me and my writing when I no longer did
~ my son, Mark, who brings me joy as I watch what God is doing in his life
~ my daughter, Christina, who has made the job of co-writing a wonderful experience
~ my parents, Glenn and Shirley Smith, who have set the bar in showing what it means to live a life of joy in the Lord

Christina

~my husband, Dave, who frees me to be who I am meant to be
~my mom, Sherrie, who got me into all this in the first place
~my kids, Austin, Andrea, Tanner, Joshua, and Liliana, who cleaned and cooked and minded themselves occasionally during the making of this book
~my dad, John, for a grammatically correct childhood

And most of all, to the Father, Son, and Holy Spirit. May this book draw others closer to You.

...As to a light shining in a dark place,
until the day dawns and the morning
star rises in your hearts.
2 Peter 1:19

Chapter One

Please let there be a heartbeat. This time.

Beth Harris stopped. One more step and the automatic hospital doors would sense her presence, open wide for her to enter. One more step, and she'd be swallowed up. It would be better not to find out. She could continue holding onto hope. But if the news were bad … "Keith, maybe we should reschedule. I'm sure the doctor wouldn't mind if we waited a few more weeks."

Her husband pressed his hand into the small of her back, urging her forward. "Beth, you shouldn't worry. Everything's fine."

She sidestepped out of his reach and onto a sunny patch of lawn. "How do you know that? It wasn't okay last time."

He settled his shoulders. "Think of how sick you've been. That's a great sign."

At the mere mention of sickness, Beth's stomach threatened to rebel.

"God has His hand upon us, sweetie. I feel it in my gut. This baby will be a blessing."

A couple of scrub-wearing women threaded between Beth and Keith, making their way into the hospital.

His words were meant to comfort, but he wasn't the one waiting to feel the first flutter, the one physically connected to the little life. He wasn't the one who feared stillness, feared being unable to carry a child. She didn't break eye contact with her husband. "And His hand wasn't on us six months ago?"

"No, that's not …" Keith blinked. "You know it was, but—"

"But what? What did I do wrong? Why didn't He give us what we wanted?" That was the real question—the one she'd been too afraid to ask until the threat of a repeat of the experience forced it out of her.

Keith closed the gap she'd put between them. "Don't be scared, Beth. This isn't like you." He tipped her head against his chest and kissed her hair. "Where's my optimistic wife? Where's the woman who won't let anything steal her joy?"

Beth drew back, but wove her fingers through his. "You're right." She forced the edges of her mouth into the semblance of a smile. "I'm probably making a fool of myself. The appointment will go fine and then you can make fun of me."

"That's better. You were starting to sound like your mother."

"Keith!" Beth followed her husband through the doors. A trickle of sweat from standing in the summer sunshine made its way between her bony shoulder blades. Despite the circumstances, she'd lost several pounds. "And what's wrong with my mom?"

"Suzanne's a glass-is-half-empty kind of person." Keith looped an arm around her shoulder and steered her toward the lobby desk.

Beth gave the receptionist her name and settled into the waiting room chair next to Keith. She glanced at the women's bathroom. "And I'm a bladder-is-full kind of person." If only she could pee …

"Beth Harris?" A pink-shirted escort waited by the check-in desk.

They rose and trailed behind the guide through a maze of hallways. Beth slowed as the lady indicated a room.

Nudging her forward, Keith whispered, "Do not be afraid, for the Lord your God is with you."

A young technician waited inside the darkened room. "Come on in. I'm Courtney." She shook their hands and patted an examination table. "Lie back and I'll get you a pillow."

Beth stared at the table. The last time …

Keith grasped her hand, helped Beth up, and stood to the side.

The crackling of the paper beneath her, the hum of the machine, the blank screen …

Stay in the moment.

She brought herself back to the room, focused on the atmosphere. The scratch of the paper towels as Courtney tucked them into Beth's waistband and slid her shirt up. The warmth of the gel applied to her belly. The lingering scent of clean as Courtney stepped over to the sonogram machine. The supportive twinkle in Keith's eye.

Nothing to be afraid of.

Beth relaxed, her long hair tickling her arms as she laid them flat.

"Are you ready to see your baby?" Courtney flashed a grin at Beth.

The ultrasound technician had no idea what she was asking. Could a woman ever be ready to— "Yes." Beth swallowed against the catch in her throat. "I'd love to see this baby."

Please let there be a heartbeat.

A shape formed on the screen: a tiny head perched atop

fan-shaped ribs.

She squinted, trying to make out more than the outline.

Keith leaned across the examination table. "That's the baby?"

Courtney moved the wand over the gel. "Yes, there it is." She clicked a button on the machine and a black and white image printed out. "And here's the first picture of your child."

Keith took the paper. "I think it has your nose, Beth."

"Better than yours." She smiled up at him.

The technician angled the instrument, varying the pressure while keeping contact with the same spot. "How far along are you?"

"Ten weeks."

A long minute passed. Tiny lines of concentration spread across the technician's forehead, her gaze fixed on the image of the baby. "Did your doctor schedule the ultrasound today?"

An alarm tripped in Beth's mind. *Please, God, please. I can't handle this again.* She reached for Keith's hand. "No, just a routine appointment. Why? What's the matter?"

The technician tilted her head and short dark curls bounced around black-rimmed glasses. "I haven't been doing this very long, so sometimes it takes me awhile to get a good angle." Restraint dampened the young woman's easygoing tone.

Keith's voice sounded gruff. "Something wrong?"

Silence was the only answer.

Beth stared at the monitor, at the pale circle floating in the grayness of her womb. Cool hospital air whispered over her heated skin. The walls of the room closed in. "What's wrong?" She choked out the words. "What's the matter with our baby?"

"Mrs. Harris, I'm sorry. Our instructors drilled it into us, class after class. We're not allowed to talk about what we see. That's your doctor's job and we're only lowly techs. That said, this is *your* baby. If I see the heartbeat, I'll tell you. And, if I don't ..." Courtney glanced at Keith, then Beth.

There had to be some mistake. Courtney was inexperienced—by her own admission. She must be misreading the machine. They could all see the baby on the screen.

The picture rotated as Courtney tried angle after angle. Time passed in stark silence. Courtney put the wand down and slipped from the room.

Beth continued to stare at the empty screen. *Please let her be wrong.*

Courtney returned with an older man, gray hair flirting with his temples.

He moved toward the table. "I'm John. Mind if I have a look?"

Beth nodded. "Please do." The wand, in John's capable hands, would wield magic and the screen would show the difference.

John found the same spot and transmitted the image to the monitor.

Keith stroked Beth's hand, drawing her attention his way. Eyes large, he looked like he wanted her to ask more questions, to have the man explain what was happening.

No way was she missing the first white pulse of heartbeat. She turned back to the screen, willing the baby's heart to pump, pump, pump. Then sighs of relief would drown out the ominous quiet.

Keith breathed heavily.

She hardly breathed at all.

"Courtney," John said. "Call their doctor and have him fit these folks in as soon as he can."

Her eyes drifted shut, hope killed by reality. Why wouldn't anyone give voice to the obvious?

Someone wiped the gel off and pulled her shirt into place.

Keith lifted her head in his sturdy hands and kissed her cheek. She kept her eyes closed as he helped her sit up and slide off the table.

Was it really gone? Again? Another baby they'd spent the last two years planning for? She would never be able to walk into the freshly painted nursery, pass the unassembled crib, or touch the soft onesies accumulating in the dresser drawer.

"Beth, honey." Keith drew her into a hug, brushed her hair to the side, and placed another kiss on the nape of her neck. 'Honey, I—"

Beth snapped her eyes open, grabbed the ultrasound printout, and crumpled it. "I don't want to talk about it. Not yet." She dropped the picture into the trash on the way out.

Chapter Two

"Well, isn't this the cutest thing?" The woman's soft, southern accent melted into Suzanne's thoughts like a pat of butter on steaming grits.

She turned toward the customer, who held a wooden plaque with a carved beaver attached to it, and pasted on a smile. "Those are made by a local man. He finds driftwood along the river and carves unique figures from each one." Forget the question of why someone would want a beaver doorknocker with *Beaver Falls, Oregon* burned into the wood.

"Hmm."

Not quite an enthusiastic response. Suzanne moved from behind a distressed antique farm table, its surface rich with the sheen of polish and the stories of its past. "Go ahead and try it. We've got a special this week—ten percent off." She'd tell her boss about the special after the sale.

The lady lifted the beaver's tail and let go. Wood slapped wood. "Still kinda expensive, though." She set it down and drifted to another display.

"Have you seen our line of homemade candles?" Suzanne pointed toward the wooden crates tipped along the wall. "My favorites are the cinnamon and the orange cream."

Even a ten-dollar sale would help the store. The rumored closing of the nearby lumber mill made for slow business. Who wanted to spend hard-earned money on knick-knacks, let alone heirloom furniture, when they were unsure of how many more paychecks remained? But a tourist might sink a few dollars into the local economy.

The woman lifted a candle to her nose, sniffed, and set it back into the crate. “Maybe I’ll come back tomorrow and show my husband what y’all have.”

“We’d love to see you again.” Suzanne folded a handmade scarf while she followed the woman to the door. “Thanks for stopping by.”

As the woman left the shop, the back alley door opened and Nancy Benson—best friend first, boss second—entered the shop.

Suzanne smiled. Things should liven up.

“Hey, I brought you a double shot Mocha Caramel Delight and a granola bar. I figured they’d cancel each other out.” Nancy plucked the coffee bean from the whipped cream mounded on top of the drink before passing the cup to Suzanne. “How’s business today?”

Suzanne shook her head. “The usual. A couple lookers, no buyers.”

“That’s what I was afraid of.” Nancy grimaced, her expression highlighting reddened eyes. “I’ve got to hole up in my office and go over some paperwork.” She closed the door partway, then stuck her head back out. “But feel free to disturb me if you can’t handle the flood of customers.”

As if that would ever happen.

The door clicked shut.

Why the bloodshot eyes? And shutting the door? Treating Suzanne like she was just some employee?

She snatched an antibacterial wipe from the cleaning supplies and ran it along the counter next to the office, ears straining.

Nancy’s voice came through the closed door, hesitancy

coloring the indecipherable syllables.

After a glacially slow day, Suzanne flipped the sign to CLOSED and locked the front door.

"Suzanne? Can you come in here, please?" Nancy sounded tense.

Stomach rolling, Suzanne headed to the back of the store. Something didn't feel right. "What's going on?"

Nancy clicked her manicured nails on the dark cherry desk. "It's over. I'm closing the store. Shutting it down."

"Wait a minute." Suzanne bounced her palms at Nancy in a sign to slow down. "Why don't we try one of those advertising ideas I emailed you last month? Then—"

"Nobody wants what we're selling. Ads in the gazette can't fix that."

"Actually, isn't that exactly what advertising does? Convinces people to buy things they don't need?" Her voice rose. How could Nancy be so blasé?

"It's too late, Suzanne. You can't talk me out of this one. I already signed on the dotted line."

There were few things in life Suzanne couldn't talk into going her way. This appeared to be one of them. She collapsed into the nearby chair as the fight left her body. "So you're really closing A Backwards Glance?"

Nancy's tone softened. "You know I'm not making any money. I've worked a deal with a woman in Salem for the inventory, and I got out of the lease on this space. A sporting goods store is coming in."

"So I'm out of a job and you're out of a dream?"

"I'm sorry, Suz. It's not the way I wanted things to go."

Suzanne ran a hand over her hair, smoothing wayward strands. Made sense. Instead of scented candles and furniture polish, the place would smell like fish bait and vinyl. The same men placing a freeze on their wives' spending would still need hunting equipment. Punching bags. Running shoes. Anything to keep them busy after they received pink slips.

"I can pay you for next week if you come in and help me get everything boxed up and ready to go."

"Nance, is there any other way? You love this store."

"I could keep going until we lose our house and declare bankruptcy." Nancy shook her head. "But somehow I don't think that's the best option."

"Why didn't you tell me sooner?"

Nancy sighed. "There was nothing you could do. Why make you worry?"

"What does Jim think?"

"He's disappointed for me, of course. He knows how much I wanted to make this succeed. But I think he's secretly glad I'll be around more." Nancy offered a tired smile. "Why don't you go home? I'll finish up and get the deposit ready."

"You sure? There's so much money, I'm not certain you're safe carrying it to the bank without an armed guard."

Nancy flapped her hand. "Take your purse and your sarcasm and go. Leave me to my misery."

Suzanne stood and gave her friend a hug.

φφφ

She fastened her seat belt and pulled into the little town's version of rush hour. A headache throbbing behind her temples, Suzanne fumbled in her purse for a bottle of aspirin. She popped the plastic top with her thumb and shook two tablets into her other palm, steering by holding the wheel between her knees. Jake would kill her if he knew, but it took only a moment. Both hands were back on the wheel before the last pill made its dry journey down her throat.

A thump against her front fender jolted her attention back to the road. Slamming on the brakes, she brought the car to a halt.

"Pay attention!" The angry voice of one of Beaver Falls police officers carried through her raised window.

What had she hit?

Ten feet in front of her, two cars were smashed together. Looked like the police had taken traffic cones from nearby construction and blocked off the right lane.

The policeman motioned for her to back up and pulled a crumpled cone from underneath the frame of her car.

She fumbled for the correct button and lowered the automatic window. "I'm so sorry, Officer." Pain in her head pulsed a crazy rhythm. "I didn't see it."

"Keep your eyes on the road. I don't need to deal with another accident."

"Yes, I'm so sorry." She waited until he crossed in front of her before pressing the gas pedal.

Unwanted tears threatened and she willed them away. What an awful day—pinning hopes on every customer, losing her job, watching Nancy forfeit her dream, and an almost literal run-in with the police.

No way could she cook tonight. The pork chops thawing in the refrigerator would have to wait for tomorrow. She'd stop at the store for deli meat and hoagie buns. Better yet, a big bucket of fried chicken and a container of potato salad. Jake could take the leftovers for lunch.

Her cell phone rang.

Not now. She didn't feel like talking to anyone except her husband … and maybe not even him. She checked the caller

ID.

Beth. Okay, make that anyone except Jake or Beth.

She pulled to the side of the road. “Hi, honey.” Suzanne forced a pleasant tone.

“Mom?” Beth sniffed, voice breaking. “I need you.”

Chapter Three

Officer Tony Barnett strode toward the brand-new red Saab convertible. The only thing worse than one inattentive woman driver was two. He planted himself at the driver's side. "Ma'am, please step out of the vehicle."

The black-haired female, approximately twenty years old, ignored him. "Daddy," she screeched into a cell phone. "It's not my fault! This old lady pulled out right in front of me."

Crooking his neck, Tony scanned the accident scene. The Saab's hood was jammed into the side of a 1950's Plymouth. June sunshine glinted off the broken side window. An EMT was helping an elderly lady out of the car. She appeared uninjured, but protocol insisted she take a trip to the emergency room.

"No!" The young woman wailed. "Daddy, how am I supposed to go anywhere if you take my car away?"

"Ma'am, hang up and step out of the vehicle."

She thrust a palm in front of his face. "It's nobody, Daddy. You're not even listening to me."

Tony reached into the convertible, gained possession of the phone, and snapped it shut. "Now open the door and step out of the vehicle."

"I'm not deaf, Officer. I heard you the first time." Jerking the handle up, the woman threw her shoulder against the door.

It flew open, jarring Tony's legs.

She got out and posed with hands on hips.

"License, please." Traffic, directed by another policeman,

snaked around them, exhaust fanning past his nose.

"Do you even know who I am?" She stalked back and forth. "My father is not going to be happy when he hears how you've been treating me."

Tony placed his body between her and the slow-moving line of rubberneckers. "The sooner you show me your ID, the sooner I'll know who you are."

She raised penciled eyebrows, reached back into the car, and hooked her purse strap on a taloned finger. "Here."

"Ma'am, I'm only going to give you one warning. Under Oregon statutes, unless you show me your identification immediately, I will need to place you under arrest."

His words seemed to pierce her bravado. She took the purse back, dug through it, and held out her wallet.

"Please remove your ID from the plastic sleeve."

She huffed, slid her license out, and handed it to him.

He flipped the card over. *Veronica Valdez.* Ah, the mayor's daughter. Other cops had run into her since she'd graduated from college and come back to little Beaver Falls, but Tony had escaped the pleasure. Until today.

"Miss Valdez, how did your car come to be parked in the middle of that Plymouth?"

She flipped a strand of hair over her shoulder. "The old prune pulled right out in front of me. She's probably senile. Way too old to be driving a car anymore, I'm sure."

"Did you come to a complete stop at the intersection?"

"I hit the brakes as soon as I saw her."

"I'm sure you did, as the skid marks behind your vehicle testify. But did you notice the stop sign?"

Miss Valdez flicked a finger toward the Plymouth. "She didn't stop, either."

"That's because she didn't have a stop sign, Miss Valdez."

"But … but she's old!"

Tony found a clean page in his notebook. "You'll be lucky to make it to her age if you keep talking on your cell while you're driving."

"I wasn't—"

"Before you make any statement to me about whether or not you were on the phone at the time of the accident, I'll remind you that cell phone records are easily obtained with a warrant."

She shut her mouth.

He took down the license plate number. "Last week, I extricated a seventeen-year-old boy from a rollover. Killed his younger sister. He'd looked away from the road to answer his phone."

The woman drew back. "The Fredrickson girl?"

At Tony's curt nod, her shoulders fell.

Miss Valdez rested a hand on the car. "I used to babysit her when I was in high school."

Tony stooped and copied the VIN from the dashboard.

She twisted a high heel into the asphalt. "My parents were at her funeral."

Meeting her gaze, he swallowed hard. "So was I."

The smell of hot metal, the moans of the boy, the limpness of the little girl—the accident scene came to life again in his mind. Tony shook his head, shrugging off the slo-mo replay. "Stay right here. I'm going to check on the other driver."

He hadn't had a decent night's sleep since he'd chanced upon the wreck on the side of the country road. A beautiful starlit night turned tragic. His knock pulling the parents from their bed, faces bleary with sleep. His words turning their expressions frantic with worry, crushing them with sadness.

Poor kid would have to live with the consequences of one moment of inattention for the rest of his life. He'd never be able to drive fast enough to escape the guilt.

How many more times in his career would he have to be the bearer of horrible news?

Chapter Four

Something was wrong—dreadfully wrong—in the tone of her daughter's voice, tucked behind the words she didn't say. A mother's heart knew these things.

Mom, I need you.

Suzanne pulled into her gravel driveway.

Jake stood at his car, withdrawing his backpack, which looked heftier than it had been this morning. Pity the summer school students. He must have assigned papers. "Professor Corbin" would have to spend the weekend grading them and Mrs. Professor Corbin would see little of her husband.

Jake waited at the edge of the walkway until she parked and opened her door. "Hi, Suzy. I'm starving. Been looking forward to pork chops and scalloped potatoes all day."

Suzanne grabbed deli bags from the seat beside her.

Savory smells wafted out and a look of disappointment ran across Jake's face. "I take it this means no chops." He hefted one bag onto his free arm and led the way into the house while she grabbed the smaller sack. "Did you get stuck behind that accident? I tried to call you to tell you to take a different route but my battery was dead."

"I almost became part of it."

"The accident?"

"Don't ask." She placed her load on the kitchen island. "Something's going on with Beth. I don't know what, but she called while I was on my way home. She sounded like she was about to cry." Suzanne dumped the bucket of chicken into a baking dish. "Here, put this in the oven, please, and turn it to low."

Jake took the dish from her. "Maybe it's her hay fever starting to act up."

"It's more than that. She and Keith are coming over to talk." Suzanne finished unloading the bags, took four placemats from the drawer in the hutch, and set them on the table.

He followed, arranging a dinner plate on each patch of fabric. "Hope it's not marital problems."

"Now why would you say that?" She rolled her eyes. Didn't he see how happy those two kids were together?

A sharp rap and the click of the front door opening meant her baby was home.

φφφ

The comfort of her parents' home wrapped itself around Beth like a cozy blanket as soon as she walked through the door. Her mom and dad had always provided a place of safety and security, a retreat from the restless world. If only they could do it again tonight.

She steeled herself as her mother drew her into a hug. She wouldn't cry, not yet.

"Honey, what's wrong?" Her mother led her into the dining room.

As Beth passed the kitchen, the odor of fried chicken hit like an iron fist. She moaned, swallowed several times. Too late. She bolted from the room and ran down the hall into the bathroom. No time to close the door behind her. No time to cage her grief. She dropped to her knees beside the toilet and gave in to the inevitable—retching and sobbing at the same time.

A gentle hand pulled her hair back, brought it out of her face. Her mother's voice whispered in her ear. "Oh, my sweet girl."

Several minutes passed before Beth was able to push away from the toilet and lean against the bathtub for support. Cold porcelain penetrated the back of her blouse as cold facts penetrated her heart.

Suzanne joined her on the rug and sponged Beth's face with a damp washcloth. "Are you feeling better?"

"I'll never feel better. I saw my doctor today. He said the baby—"

"You're pregnant again?" Elation peeked out of each syllable.

"Mom, it's not—"

"Honey, I know the morning sickness part isn't pleasant, but it's worth it. You'll see. Even when it happens at night, it's a sign the baby is growing well."

"No, Mom, listen." Beth pinched the bridge of her nose. "I *was* pregnant. I did everything I was supposed to—ate healthy foods, took my vitamins, got extra rest. Everything." She shifted her weight and nuzzled her head against her mother's shoulder.

"You lost the baby?" Suzanne's whisper was full of pain.

"The baby's still there, but it's dead."

"You're losing the baby?" Suzanne gathered Beth close and held her tight.

"We went for an ultrasound this afternoon, but there was no heartbeat. Just a snowy picture of a baby. And I didn't know it. You'd think I'd have suspected something was wrong, but I had no idea." Tears trickled down Beth's cheek.

Her mother wiped them away.

"I can't believe it, Mom. It's not fair. Keith and I wanted this baby so much. It's been hard to keep it a secret from you for all these weeks, but we were going to surprise you with the ultrasound picture." Beth rose and perched on the rim of the bathtub. "I'm never going to have a baby."

"Don't say that." Suzanne stood and leaned against the vanity. "You and Keith will make great parents."

"So when will that happen? I hoped for a day full of joy, and instead … It's not over, either. The doctor says I'll have a lot of cramping and bleeding. I can't stand the thought. How will I—"

Her dad appeared at the bathroom door, his eyes sadder than Beth had ever seen them.

She found herself wrapped in his arms before she knew it had happened. "Daddy, why?"

He shushed her and rocked from side to side.

φφφ

Beth rubbed her temples and stared at the red stoplight.

Keith drummed his fingers on the steering wheel until the light turned green. The driver in front of them was more turtle than hare and Keith laid on the horn, sped up, and changed lanes.

Beth grabbed her armrest. "Could you slow down a bit?"

"I don't know, can I? Why don't you ask your mother?"

Beth tightened her grip. "What are you talking about?"

Keith glanced her way before looking over his left shoulder and pulling into a 7-11 parking lot. He killed the engine. "Us. I'm talking about us. You shut me out from everything this afternoon. You went silent during the ultrasound and didn't say much after we saw the doctor. Then we get to your mom's and you talk with Suzanne like there's no tomorrow." Keith jiggled his knee and the keys shook, rattling against each other. "I don't know where I fit in the picture."

Had she forgotten his hurt was every bit as real as hers? That he needed consoling as much as she did? In the instant loss of her motherhood, she had become a girl again. A girl who turned to her mother for comfort instead of a wife who sought her husband's support.

"I'm sorry." Beth leaned toward him, as sobs reclaimed her body. "I should have opened up to you. I just can't believe we've lost another baby."

Keith unsnapped his seat belt and met her, as he always did, more than halfway. His embrace covered her. This man, and only this one, would share her life in ways her mother never would.

And he was the only one strong enough to help her through the uncertain days ahead.

Chapter Five

Fog hung close, droplets forming on her hot skin. The darkness was heavy, oppressive, but fear drove her on. A voice came from all sides, swirling, encircling her soul.

He called her name, again and again. "You'll never be able to hide from me."

Every syllable carried on the night wind, seeking her.

Suzanne sat up, wide-eyed, gaze probing dark corners of the room. Terror eclipsed the safety of the bed, and remnants of fog clung to her. She placed her hand on Jake's chest, which rose and fell, a smooth rhythm, like calm ocean waves. Her own breath rattled and caught.

She eased her way to the edge of the bed. Like a blind man tapping his cane, her bare toes found her slippers. She grabbed her robe, sneaked from the room, and pulled the door shut behind her.

Sidestepping creaky boards that lent the house its nighttime character, Suzanne tiptoed down the hall to the kitchen. She lit the gas under the teakettle, the flame mesmerizing, dancing orange and purple. She leaned her hip against the granite counter and bumped a notepad. A glance at the week's to-do list revealed only one item hadn't been crossed off—*organize hope chest*. Until her soul settled back into place, she could work on that.

She padded down the hallway to Beth's old room and

flipped on the light. Centered at the foot of the double bed sat the hope chest Suzanne had inherited from her grandmother. Gleaming mahogany blurred her reflection as she knelt before it.

She pushed the clasp upward and lifted the lid. Hinges stretched into place and the pungent scent of cedar filled the room. She rummaged through the chest and withdrew a dingy newspaper.

A hiss of steam escaped from the teakettle. She dropped the paper, hurried back to the kitchen, and intercepted the strident whistle. Squeaky floorboards were less likely to wake Jake than the scream of the kettle.

She carried a mug of Earl Grey back to the guest room, knelt again before the open chest, and twisted the cup into the uneven nap of the carpet. As she leaned forward, her knee crinkled the newsprint. A scarlet envelope peeked from its folds.

"Suz, what are you doing? It's the middle of the night."

She whipped her head toward the door, heart pounding. Her leg bumped the mug. Tea spread across the carpet and wet the edges of the newspaper. "Jake! Look what you made me do."

"All I did was wake up to an empty bed." Jake righted the mug.

Suzanne plucked the paper from the floor and dabbed the moisture off with a corner of the bedspread.

Ink smudged the cream fabric.

Fist clenched, she pounded the carpeted floor as hard as she could.

"What's wrong?" Jake stared intently at her.

"Isn't it obvious? I had that nightmare, and you made me

spill my tea and almost ruined our copy of the wedding announcement in the newspaper."

"The chasing dream? You've got to get over that."

Suzanne tossed her head back and exhaled. "Go back to bed. I'm not going to be good company right now."

He yawned, mouth gaping like a grizzly bear with hibernation on its mind. "Since you already woke me up clomping down the hall, we might as well talk about what's actually bothering you."

"Oh? And what's that? What's really bothering me?" She shook the newspaper at him.

The envelope fell from it into plain sight.

Jake sat, crossing his legs, and snagged the letter before she could reach for it.

"Jake, please don't."

But he was already lifting the flap of the envelope.

"Don't." She ripped it from his hands, shoved it into the pocket of her robe, and headed to the kitchen for carpet spray and a handful of old dishtowels.

Jake lifted his head as she walked back into the spare room and gestured at the envelope peeking out of her pocket. "It's okay to talk about it. I've been thinking about that baby ever since the kids left."

Shaking the aerosol can, Suzanne tossed the rags Jake's way. "You know I don't discuss that time in my life. And you're making assumptions." She sprayed chemicals over the darkened patch of carpet.

"Then what's going on?"

Bubbles formed as the foam thinned.

She wadded up a rag and scrubbed at the spot, gritting her teeth. "I lost my job. Business is too slow so Nancy's closing down."

"Is that all? You don't really need that job anyway."

Suzanne stopped scrubbing and looked at him. "I can't believe you. So, I need to find another hobby, like knitting booties for the grandchild we're not having?" Tears leaked from her eyes and she used a fresh rag to wipe them.

Jake scooted near and put an arm loosely over her shoulders. "They'll have another baby soon."

She shook off his arm. "But what if Beth can't carry a baby to term?"

"It breaks my heart, too, Suz, but there's nothing we can do about it."

Nodding, Suzanne sank into his embrace. Security. Her husband exuded it. She wallowed in it for a few minutes.

Jake's tender kiss met her lips. "I need to get some sleep. I'm meeting with Pastor Alan in the morning again. In fact … maybe you should come too."

"I see him once a week when Beth drags us to church. Isn't that enough?"

"He might have answers."

Couldn't her husband understand? "The answers he has aren't the ones I want to hear."

"Okay, babe. I won't push you." As he retreated down the hall, the peace evaporated, leaving Suzanne to her memories. Jake knew her far better than she did herself. Of course Beth's loss triggered her own emotions.

Running from the past changed nothing; acknowledging it might. Or at least it would settle her for tonight.

Suzanne's own handwriting splashed across the envelope's face. Remembering the excitement of penning it twenty-some years ago, she opened the letter.

Augusta, Maine
November 14
Dear Ellie,

Guess what happened? I was at the art museum looking at a painting—a knoll covered with yellow prairie grass, strands seeming to move like "amber waves of grain." A woman stood, bonnet blowing in the wind, arm wrapped around a young girl, looking to the horizon.

A guy behind me wondered aloud about the title— Completion. *We started talking about what it might mean and ended up having hot dogs on the steps of the museum. He walked me to the bus stop, paid my fare, and we hopped on. This guy was so charming and sincere, I didn't realize he was following me home. But when I did, I stopped talking. Mid-sentence.*

At first, he seemed confused. Then annoyed. Finally taking the hint that buying me a tube of ground-up meat by-products did not constitute a date, he moved to a vacant seat behind me. I hoped he would get off at the next opportunity, but he didn't. I decided to ride to the end of the line.

Imagine my surprise when he brushed past me at the college stop, turning only to thank me for "an afternoon of intrigue and disappointment." His blue eyes, which sparkled when we first met, were cold as flint. My heart fell as he walked away. I jumped off the bus, rushing after his long coat—the only thing I could see in the dusk.

I apologized, explaining I thought he was some sort of psycho art stalker following me home to kill me. He stared at me as if to judge my truthfulness.

Life flooded back into his eyes and he asked if he could

call me.

I nodded and watched him hurry into the warm light of the men's dorm. Trudging home under the gray sky, the hush of studying in the air, I suddenly realized he hadn't asked for my number. Of course, I sat beside my phone for hours anyway, skipping dinner, in case he'd call. He did.

Turns out, he sits behind me in Intro to Art. He got my number from a friend weeks ago, but lacked the courage to call. When he saw me at the art museum, he felt it was meant to be.

Amazing, Ellie! Already this guy, Jake, has made me feel something I never thought I'd feel again—after Dylan and that tangled mess.

Have you heard anything about him? Any news of my parents?

Your Best Friend, Suz

Suzanne had thrown out—or shredded and burned—any memorabilia having to do with Dylan except this letter. Such a small mention of him, but such a burden of regret entwined with it. How naïve she had been …

She tucked the letter back into its envelope, stashed it at the bottom of the hope chest, and closed the lid, closing her heart with it.

Chapter Six

In the morning sun, Suzanne's dream lost its edge. She breathed deeply, shoulders relaxing, and sipped her tea in the shade of the patio umbrella.

The door behind her opened and Jake set a glass of juice and a book on the table. A book that brought all the tension back.

"Why, Jake?" The sound of her voice surprised Suzanne. Thoughts shouldn't tumble from her mouth without warning.

"Because orange juice is full of Vitamin C." He pulled the onionskin pages of the book open with a thin red ribbon.

"No, you goof, why the Bible?" She pushed a strand of hair back from her face. "I don't understand why you find it necessary to go through this ritual every day."

Leaving his Bible open, Jake stood to readjust the protective umbrella. His movements were slow, deliberate. Couldn't he just answer? He finally sat. "We haven't talked much about faith," Jake began, "but—"

"There hasn't been much need." Her retort, simmering since he stood to fiddle with the umbrella, boiled out.

A meadowlark's joyful cry clashed with Suzanne's harshness.

"I want you to come with me to my meeting today."

"Why?"

Jake's gaze dropped to the table, his fingers rubbing at a spot on the floral tablecloth.

Last night she had jumped all over him, and now she was at it again. "Really, what makes you think I'd want to go?"

He still did not look at her. "Because I want answers, and I want you to hear the explanations with me. I only started studying the Bible because Alan challenged me to read it for myself, to see what I believe."

A quiver of unease ran along her arms. "You're not getting all fanatical on me, are you?"

Jake lifted his head. "Aren't you curious? Don't you want to know how Alan can say God loves us and wants the best for us when something like this happens? Beth's been into God since she was a teenager. Why is He allowing her to hurt?"

Suzanne shook her head. "All you're going to get is the usual platitudes: 'We can't understand God's ways.' Or 'He works everything for the best.'"

Jake drained the last of his orange juice. "You don't think those are true?"

"It doesn't matter. Life's life, and we're on our own for figuring this stuff out."

"I don't want to be on my own. Besides, Alan lost his wife to cancer years ago. I doubt he'll dispense generic answers." Jake sighed and took her hand. "Let's not fight. You know I love you. I'm grateful to wake up beside you each morning."

A peace offering. Suzanne clutched it, unsure of why she'd been so grouchy with him. "Sure. There I am with bad breath and mussed up hair. You lucky, lucky man."

"Yes, I am." He smiled. "We share everything and I want us to share this journey, too."

"I'm not interested, Jake. Do you want me to pretend that I am?"

His smile faded. "Of course not, but I'm going."

Suzanne stood, gathering her pen, notepad, and his empty glass. "I love you anyway." She kissed him, wanting to inject some lightheartedness. "A little something to remember me by."

"As if I could ever forget." He picked up his Bible again.

Really? Because it looked like he was already more interested in that book than in her.

When Jake came back three hours later, he moved differently, walked with confidence. He looked fresh and young, like the man she'd met at college. That meant trouble.

"What happened?" Suzanne folded the linen dishtowel and laid it on the kitchen counter. "Let me have it."

He strolled up and bowed. "This dance? But of course." He waltzed her out of the kitchen, past the breakfast nook, and into the great room.

The curtains, French doors, walls, and furniture swirled into a great kaleidoscope of greens and browns, speckled with white.

At last he released her and they collapsed, laughing, onto the love seat.

"I'm out of breath and dizzy, but you always do that to me, Jake." Suzanne giggled.

"Suzy, let's take a picnic to our spot by the river. I have some good news to tell you."

While making the sandwiches, loading the ice chest, driving to the river, she held back the question she wanted to ask. *Tell me what?*

They spread an old quilt under a birch tree.

Suzanne lay on her back, one arm wedged beneath her head, and watched the clouds float past.

The branches wove together, leaving gaps like keyholes to the sky.

She crunched a bite of crisp apple.

Was there a key to unlock the massive expanse of this world? To erase the past? To make Beth happy? To bring Jake back to her way of thinking?

A breeze swayed the branches and the peepholes disappeared.

“I’m a Christian.”

Suzanne rolled onto her stomach and took another bite. “Of course you are.”

Jake grabbed his egg salad sandwich and undid the plastic wrap. “No, this is much more than that. This is real. I surrendered my heart to God. I want to give the rest of my life to Him like Jesus gave His life for me.”

Suzanne’s appetite left, blown away on the breeze of his confession. “But you promised your heart to me.” She let the apple core drop out of her hand.

It rolled down the hill toward the riverbank.

“You’ll always have my love, Suzy-Q. And you know it.”

She closed her eyes and wondered.

Chapter Seven

Beth fingered the thin sheet that lay over her bare legs. Had the nurse asked her something?

"So you miscarried seven weeks ago?" The nurse held a chart in her hand, pen at the ready.

As if Beth could forget the date. "Wednesday, June eighth."

"And you'd lost one pregnancy before that?"

"Yes."

"Tell me more about the most recent miscarriage."

Why did this have to be so hard? Didn't they already have all this information? Was reliving those awful hours really necessary?

"The Friday before I lost the baby, I had my first ultrasound, at ten weeks along. There was no heartbeat. I didn't want a D&C, so Dr. Norman said to expect bleeding and cramping. If that didn't happen, I was supposed to come back in."

The cramps had wrenched her awake, coming in waves like the contractions of labor she'd read about in maternity books. Curled up in bed, crying, reality hit. Her baby was dead. The heating pad she held to her abdomen hadn't lessened the pain, yet it'd been a relief for her body to rid itself of the lifelessness it held.

The nurse tapped the pen against the edge of the chart. "So everything has been all right since that point? No fevers, prolonged bleeding?"

Beth tucked a corner of the sheet more securely underneath her. "No, but I was sick for a couple of weeks after the miscarriage. I'm tired and moody all the time."

The nurse laid the chart on the counter and reached for the blood pressure cuff. "Feelings of loss or sadness are normal. Do you think you're depressed?"

"No." Beth stretched her arm toward the nurse and tried to breathe evenly.

The nurse fastened the cuff and pumped.

Beth's veins throbbed and begged for the pressure to ease.

A moment later, the nurse ripped the Velcro apart, removed the cuff, and jotted a note on the chart. "Dr. Norman should be in soon."

The soft click of the door sounded as the nurse left, followed by the thud of her chart's sliding into the plastic holder outside the door.

After ten minutes of waiting, Beth stepped over to the magazine rack for the latest Newsweek. As she hopped back up onto the table, her chart scraped as it was pulled out of the plastic holder.

Dr. Norman knocked and walked in. The first time Beth had seen him, she'd had to stifle a laugh. Small ears perched high on the sides of his head. A few long wisps of hair crisscrossed to camouflage his baldness. His nostrils, which pointed straight out, flared as he spoke, while his jowls bounced. Beth loved his bedside manner and thoroughness, but his resemblance to a hippopotamus continued to catch her unaware.

"Morning, Beth. How have you been?" Which probably meant, "How are you dealing with your loss?"

Beth tossed the unread magazine onto a chair. "I'm not sure. I know I've been through this before, but it seems different this time. Harder to get over. Maybe because I was further along?"

"Could be. Each case is different." He patted her knee. "Miscarriage is very, very common, but it doesn't make it any easier to know that, does it?"

That needed no answer.

"Is your cycle back to normal?"

"Should it be?"

"In general, yes. Why don't we see what's going on?" He opened the door and signaled the nurse to join them.

Beth found the edge of the table with her fingers and slid down, putting her feet in the stirrups.

He examined her briefly before asking her to dress. "I'll be back in a few minutes to tell you what I think."

Beth stepped back into her loosest running pants. What might he have noticed so quickly? Did she lose the baby because something was wrong with her body? An early-stage cancer or some other serious problem?

Dr. Norman smiled as he reentered the room, nostrils flaring wider than usual. "We tested your urine sample and I confirmed it with that exam."

She held her breath.

"You're pregnant."

"What?" Unbelievable. It had to be some kind of mistake—leftover hormones messing with the test. "Are you sure?"

"Positive."

Tiny teddy bears and rainbows and nursery rhymes seemed to fill the air. Finally, she could stop thinking about the babies that would never be and plan for the one to come. God wouldn't let her lose another one … "We were going to wait until we got the go-ahead from you to try again. Do you think this baby will be okay?"

"No indication that it's not, but I want you to have an ultrasound so we can see how far along you are. I've freed up my schedule for the next half hour. If it's okay with you, I'll come downstairs and do it myself."

She loved this doctor. He knew she wouldn't want to end up with another Courtney telling her without words that something was wrong. If there were a problem with this baby, Dr. Norman would want to tell her himself. And if everything were fine, he'd want to share in her happiness.

Dr. Norman ushered her out of the room. "You should have had a follow up ultrasound to make sure you were okay anyway."

φφφ

Keith pedaled up to the picnic table, sinews snapping on his tanned legs, helmet covering his thick brown hair, sunglasses hiding his eyes from her view.

Beth got up from the park bench. "Hi."

Keith unbuckled his helmet and pulled it off, wiping his brow with his forearm. "Why'd you want to meet here?" He lowered the bike's kickstand and hung his helmet from the handlebars.

"'Cause it's a beautiful day. And I wanted to see your face when I told you." Once he found out, he'd be so far above cloud nine he'd need a telescope to see the earth.

"This had better be good." He grabbed her hands and smiled as if he knew it had to be.

"You'll never believe it. And you'll never guess."

Keith cocked his head. "Let's see, you went to the doctor and you sound happy, so I'm going to say we're pregnant again?"

"Yes."

Keith whooped and jumped into the air. "Beth, it will be different this time. I know it will. We'll have this baby. What, in March? April?"

Beth suppressed a smile and didn't say a word.

Keith studied her. "You said I wouldn't guess, but I did, right?"

"Nope, not all of it." Would the secret leak from her pores? She couldn't keep it in much longer.

"Twins? Triplets?"

She had wanted to be out under the hot summer sky to say the words, to give them room to fly. Indoors, their joy would have smashed through the walls. "The baby's due the end of December."

"December? That doesn't make any sense."

Beth fished a piece of paper from her purse. "It's crazy—it's absolutely insane—but there's a name for it." Dr. Norman's scribbles were difficult to decipher. "Vanishing Twin Syndrome."

"What?"

"We *were* having twins, but only one survived."

"I don't get it."

Beth rested a hand over her midsection. "We lost one baby, but the other has been developing this whole time. I'm four months pregnant."

Shaking his head, Keith fell back against a tree. "No way. How come we didn't see the twin at our ultrasound? You can't miss a baby."

"Actually, Dr. Norman thinks they did. Courtney was so new, and she and the other guy were so focused on finding a heartbeat on the baby in front, they didn't look for anything else." Beth laughed. "I feel delusional, like I'm making this up, but it's true." She revealed the photo behind the scrawled note. "Want to see the picture of our baby?"

Keith pushed off the tree and took the ultrasound print, a paper so small it fit in the palm of his hand.

How could something so little hold so much promise?

He blinked several times, as if fighting back tears. "It's a miracle, a true miracle."

Beth brushed a piece of bark from Keith's shirt. "What are we going to do to celebrate?"

Arms raised wide like a triumphant warrior, Keith spun around. "Everything, Beth. Anything. God gave us back what we lost."

She laughed as he drew her to him, lifting her off the ground.

He planted a kiss on her lips and lowered her feet back to the grass.

"Let's go home." Beth strolled toward the car as Keith followed with his bike.

Sounds carried from a game in the nearby baseball diamond. If they had a boy, maybe years from now, they'd be sitting in those bleachers watching him swing with all his might.

Or perhaps they'd have a girl. Girls could play baseball, too, couldn't they?

Beth paused for a moment, Keith at her side.

A batter fouled off a pitch and the ball jumped over the fence and into their path. The child took off for first and a sun-kissed ponytail stuck out from underneath her helmet.

Girls *could* play. A smile took over Beth's face.

Keith maneuvered his bike toward the ball, but Beth reached it first.

She palmed the baseball, right hand gripped the stitching of the ball, as the other hand drifted to her tummy. Cocking her arm, Beth whispered a prayer that she wouldn't make a fool of herself.

This was for her daughter.

Maybe.

Or to make a son proud.

The ball sailed over the chain link fence and into the umpire's waiting hands. He winked and gave her a thumbs-up.

Chapter Eight

The lady hesitated, giving Tony time to analyze her concentration during the baseball's release. A smile escaped as soon as the ball arced over the fence and into his ungloved hand.

Release? Escape? Can't I leave the cop-think behind for two hours?

Tony wiped his palm against his pants. Smarted a little. The sting echoed the tingle of catching the ball his senior year, securing the final out to win the league championship. That all-star mitt was safe at home, stuffed in the back of the closet beside his trophy and letterman's jacket. And somewhere in the pockets of that jacket, he'd tucked a letter informing him he'd not be playing baseball anymore.

Okay, it didn't actually say that. He could play, but why would he? If the minor league didn't want him, what was the point? Baseball wasn't a game built on second chances. Sure, a guy had the leeway of three strikes, but if the ump called him out, that was that. Out of there.

Like criminals. At some point, judges declared enough was enough, and sent prisoners off to do serious time.

"Hey, Umpire Barnett!"

Tony turned toward the dugout.

Parents congregated around the bleachers, but the two coaches stood waiting on him.

Tony jogged toward the men.

Coach and fellow officer James Noogan waved his cap in the air. “Stop thinking about that babe and start the game.”

“Yeah, Tony. Looks like she’s taken anyway.” A piece of ingenuity from Bill Katza, another cop. “Besides, aren’t you as good as married to Mandy?”

Rolling his eyes, Tony shook his head. Where had all this started? If Mandy had been talking again … “Coaches, have you exchanged lineups?”

Both Noogan and Katza nodded.

“Let’s play ball.”

The calls were easy. Eleven- and twelve-year olds learned skills as they played. Umping facilitated their learning process while keeping Tony involved in a game he’d loved since childhood.

By the fourth inning, pitches grew more and more erratic. If the home team’s pitcher didn’t take a rest, she would walk every single player.

“Time out!” Tony signaled her coach, Katza, to approach for a confidential chat. “She’s losing it. Why don’t you swap her out?”

Katza scratched his head and glanced toward the stands. “Her dad’s up there. He takes it personally every time I pull her. Like I’m discriminating against her gender.”

“So you want to leave her in?” What was this game coming to if the parents could intimidate the coaches? “Doesn’t seem fair to her. Or to the kids trying to get more batting experience.”

Katza grimaced. “I’d rather leave her until this inning’s over.”

“Your call, but if the kids don’t start swinging, the other team’s going to have a big lead on you.”

He shrugged and ambled back to the dugout.

A boy, hair longer at the top but faded into a near shave in the back, waited to the side, bouncing a batting helmet against his knee.

"Batter up."

Slipping the helmet onto his head, the boy stumbled forward with a smile on his face, dragging a bat beside him.

"What's your name, son?" Pale-skinned and wiry, he had an all-American look, like a young Prince William. Which was ironic.

The boy dug his foot into the dirt beside the plate. "Luke Winslow, sir."

Ah, the sweet sound of a good upbringing. "I've umped for you before, haven't I?"

"Yes, sir."

"Having fun?"

Luke broke into a quiet grin. "Yes, sir."

Tony rapped the top of Luke's helmet. "That's all that matters." At least at this age, according to the official motto of the league.

The boy took a careful stance. Once he got past the awkwardness of his age, he might shape up to be a pretty good player.

Tony bent, hands on knees, and signaled the pitcher to go ahead.

She threw a fairly straight ball, though it was slow, and Luke swung too early.

Strike one.

The next pitch went high and to the outside.

Ball.

The catcher scrambled in the dust, found the ball, and

lofted it back to the pitcher.

Jaw flexing, the pitcher readied herself, lifting her front foot several times before starting the rotation of her arm. The ball zinged across the plate.

Strike two.

Noogan called out to Luke from the sideline. "Eye on the ball, eye on the ball. Don't be scared to swing."

Luke twisted his foot into the dirt again and faced the field.

The pitch came as quickly as the last, but high and to the inside.

Tony lost sight of the ball as it zipped toward Luke.

Yelping, Luke dropped the bat, flipping his hand as if to shake pain away.

Noogan ran up and examined Luke's hand.

"He okay?"

Noogan nodded at Tony. "It needs to be iced."

"Send him to first when you're done." Tony walked along the edge of the field to Katza.

"Time to take her out."

"Okay, but I'm going to blame it on you."

He could handle that.

As Katza called her from the field, a man rose from the bleachers and headed toward the dugout. Maybe Katza wasn't such a coward. The guy could probably bench-press a semi truck. He bent over Katza and the girl.

When he turned toward Tony, muscles rippled down the man's neck and across his shoulders. "You got a problem with my girl playing?"

Tony's pulse throbbed in his neck as community-relations training kicked in. After all, officers umped and coached to endear the force to the public, not create problems. "No, no. She did a great job while she was fresh. After a break she can come back in. If Coach Katza wants her to."

A new pitcher, this one male, scampered out to the mound. He threw a few warm-ups and the game resumed.

The big guy glared from the dugout.

The next batter hit the second pitch just past the short stop. The short stop scooped the ball into his mitt and threw to second base. Luke, injured hand and all, tagged the plate an instant before the ball arrived.

Tony swung his arms horizontally in front of him. "Safe."

"You're kidding me. He was out!" yelled the hothead. "Don't play favorites because he's got a booboo."

Enough was enough. "Sir, I've got the better angle. I saw both the ball and the boy approaching the base." In as polite a voice as he could manage, Tony added, "If you think you could do a better job, by all means, volunteer." He waved the next batter to the plate.

The bodybuilder stepped onto the edge of the field and pointed a beefy finger. "Why are you here, man? You left after high school and we all watched you crawl back, dragging your tail behind you. You washed out. We don't need a loser trying to teach our kids how to win."

The batter's eyes widened.

The words—ones Tony had known were in the minds of the townspeople that sent him off as a hero and ignored him when he came back—stung. They didn't even know him, yet they judged him.

Tony stayed the batter. "Why don't you take a few extra practice swings?"

The kid stepped back into the warm-up circle.

Tony widened his stance, turning more cop than umpire. “Hey, no need to make this personal. I’m here for the kids. Like you’re here for your daughter. And if you’d like to stay, I suggest you go back to your seat and let me call the game.”

“I’m not going anywhere and you can’t do a thing about it.” He crossed his massive arms over his chest.

“Actually, I can. You can either return to your seat, or I’ll call an automatic forfeit and both teams go home.”

“You can’t do that.” But the man didn’t sound very sure of himself. He turned to the quiet parents behind him as if looking for someone to take his side.

“I can and I will. According to the official rulebook, it’s at my discretion.”

The lack of support, instead of deflating Mr. Testosterone’s anger, seemed to puff him up. “All right. Make me leave.” He charged onto the field and shoved Tony’s chest.

Tony ducked and twisted the father’s wrist behind him, clamping down on his bent fingers to discourage further aggression.

Katza joined them. “Need backup?”

A little late for that, wasn’t it? “Nah. I think this gentleman was leaving. Right?”

The muscle man nodded, sucked air through clenched teeth.

As Tony relinquished his grip, he anticipated a right hook to the jaw.

It never came. False bravado.

“Chief of police is going to hear about this.” The man swaggered off the field, yelling over his shoulder. “He’s a good friend, but I bet you didn’t know that.”

Great. They probably lifted weights together or

something.

Tony scanned the field. Kids hung their heads, stared at their shoes. This game needed salvaging.

"Let's have some fun, okay?" He clapped, jumpstarting the field back to life. Thirty minutes later, the game ended and he strolled over to the visitors' dugout to grab his bag.

"Nice show." Mandy, who couldn't ever keep her mouth shut about anything in this small town, stood behind the fence holding her daughter's hand.

Britney stuck her tiny fingers through a diamond of chain link and waved. "Hi, Tony. You stronger than mean guys."

They'd seen it all earlier, then. He squatted, captured her waving hand, and pressed a kiss onto it. "Sweetie, he wasn't being nice so he needed to take a time out."

Nodding, Britney scratched at her ankle. "I go right to my time outs."

"Yep. You're a good girl."

Straightening, he scrutinized Mandy. With tousled dirty blonde hair pulled into a ponytail, she looked like a teenager. The clothes she wore over-advertised her assets. No matter how much he tried to help her, she couldn't find her way to a good decision even if it were chained to her wrist. "Unlike your mother, who's in trouble."

Britney gasped, rounding her lips. "What did she do?"

Mandy snapped her gum "Yeah, Tony, what's the matter now?"

"You been talking to Katza again? Making us sound like something we're not? Yes, we live in the same place, but we're not 'living together.'"

Mandy smirked. "Who cares what other people think? I don't get caught up in all that stuff."

"My reputation's at stake. Don't do it anymore."

Mandy strutted away. Hard to do on tiny heels and tight jeans.

"Bye-bye." Britney skipped after her mother.

"Bye. I'll see you at home in a little bit."

"Yeah, see you at home." Mandy shouted over her shoulder.

Katza and Doogan hooted and hollered from the other side of the field.

Chapter Nine

Suzanne's hand hovered over the last roll tucked cozily in the breadbasket. Her waistline didn't really need it, but …

The doorbell rang.

"Who could that be?" Jake glanced at his watch. "Don't they know it's dinnertime?"

Suzanne folded her napkin beside her plate. "It's probably a neighborhood kid selling cookie dough, honey. I'll take care of it."

Jake chuckled. "Yeah, so don't spend more than ten dollars."

Laughing, she scooted her chair back. He knew her too well. She opened the door. Nothing but an empty porch. "Jake, there's—"

"Surprise!" Beth and Keith, holding hands, jumped into view from behind the bushes.

Gripping her chest, Suzanne welcomed them into the house. "Was this your idea, Beth? Kill off your mother to get an early inheritance?"

"Sorry we scared you." Keith pecked her cheek.

Beth giggled. "No, you're not."

Dinner roll in hand, Jake ambled into the entryway. "Come in, come in. We're almost done with dinner but you might be able to persuade me to share dessert. Or have you not eaten?"

Keith pulled him into a backslapping hug. "We couldn't eat right now."

"Were you passing by?" Suzanne resettled in the dining room chair.

The young couple shared a smug look.

"Yep," Keith said, "just passing by."

"But we brought you something." Beth thrust a brightly wrapped package across the table.

"How nice. You shouldn't have." She made a show of examining it. "Well, it's smaller than a breadbox."

"Yes, it is."

Was Beth glowing? Suzanne hadn't seen the two of them look so happy together in quite a while. Really, with Beth feeling under the weather so often, she hadn't seen them much at all.

"Just open it," Keith urged.

Suzanne opened both ends of the rectangular present and unwrapped the first layer of paper. "A copy of Dickens's *Great Expectations*. I've never read this. Thank you."

Beth and Keith grinned and stared at her.

She looked back down at the book. *Great Expectations.* Beth had always loved the older books, but—

"Oh!" She jumped up. "You're having a baby!"

φφφ

"Grandparents." Suzanne examined the wrinkles traversing her face. Too bad steam irons couldn't smooth skin. "We're much too young, aren't we?"

Jake took the jar of moisturizer from her hand and placed it on the bathroom counter. "Not sure about myself, but I know you most definitely are." He nuzzled her neck. "Umm … smells good. Too bad I'm so sleepy." He pulled her into the bedroom.

The red numerals of Jake's digital alarm clock showed

11:17. A late night for a man who would be up at 5:30 to go jogging.

With synchronized movements born from years of practice, they pulled the bedspread back, folded it over the quilt rack at the foot of the bed, and climbed in. She threw her side of the sheet off her body as Jake pulled the blankets over his shoulders. The old adage that opposites attract was certainly true in their case.

Especially with menopause looming around the corner.

She clicked off the lamp. Faint moonlight lit the room. "Remember when we first found out I was pregnant with Beth?"

Jake sighed. "It's going to be one of those late night conversations, is it?"

"So … what do you remember about finding out I was pregnant?"

He punched his pillow into place under his head. "Let's see … you thought you had the flu and went to the doctor as you couldn't seem to get over it."

"Good for you. I guess that's an advantage I have of being married to a history professor—you don't forget important events from twenty-five years ago. I can still picture the doctor smiling as he delivered the news. I was so surprised."

"So was I. Kind of like after Beth's announcement tonight." He found Suzanne's hand and gave it a squeeze.

She squeezed back. "Isn't it amazing about Beth and Keith? Not only being pregnant, but finding out about it halfway through the pregnancy?"

"Had you ever heard of this 'disappearing baby' thing before?"

"You mean Vanishing Twin Syndrome? No, but I can

understand how it happens. What's hard to believe is how the technician could miss seeing the second baby. I guess inexperience can be a dangerous thing."

Jake turned on his side to face Suzanne. "What a gift from God. How gracious of Him to save one of the babies."

She pulled at a loose thread hanging from a button on the headboard. "It's a medical phenomenon, that's all. These things happen occasionally."

"Oh, Suzy, it's so much more than that. God took something sorrowful and transformed it into joy. Like the verse that talks about God making everything turn out for the best."

She clenched her fists, fingernails digging into her palms. Why did everything always have to go back to God? "Jake, how can you say that? The best thing would have been for both babies to live. To think anything less doesn't make sense."

"I'm not saying I understand why this happened, Suzy. Twins would have been great. The Lord knows what He's doing, though. There's a reason for it."

A hot flash rushed from her chest to the top of her scalp. Suzanne groaned and reached for a piece of notepaper on her bedside table. She peeled the top of her pajamas away from her sweaty skin and fanned the gap. "What's God's reason for hot flashes? If He could put an end to them, I'd believe in miracles." Suzanne dipped her fingertips in a glass of water and flicked cool wetness onto her hot skin.

"Your hormones are about as out of whack as Beth's." Jake yawned.

The hot flash passed and goose bumps replaced trails of perspiration.

Pulling the sheet up to her neck, she absorbed the muted sounds of the night. The distant ticking of the grandfather clock in the living room. A barking dog on the next street over. Jake's body relaxed beside her as sleep captured him.

He was only inches away, yet he was out of reach, his mind already lost in a dreamy world. A world of which she was not a part. She was left behind to fend for herself, the curse of insomnia striking more often the older she got. Once she *did* manage to fall asleep, her rest would probably be tormented with unsettling dreams of someone chasing her.

But why dwell on that tonight? She was going to be a grandmother. No, that was too formal. She was going to be Grandma, or maybe Nana.

The realization of a surviving baby took deeper root in her mind. From what the doctor had told Beth, the loss of just one twin happened in as many as four percent of pregnancies.

How lucky they'd not lost them both. Luck. The hand of God. Whatever. It all boiled down to the same thing—a baby in the family. And in only a few months.

Jake stirred in his sleep. He mumbled something nonsensical and descended into substantial snores.

She'd be the ideal grandma if the baby were a girl. So many lovely things to do. Buying dresses in various shades of pink. Playing paper dolls and dress up. Tea parties, ballet, and baking. All the things she'd done when Beth was a child, but this time around there would be a new dimension, new meaning with the next generation.

Pity the child if it were a boy. What did grandmas do with one of those? Play in mud? Catch frogs? Thank God for dads and grandpas.

See? She thought about God. She believed in Him, knew

He had a list of rules for people to follow.

Jake's weekly meetings with Pastor Alan made her feel inadequate, as if she weren't woman enough to meet Jake's deepest needs.

She'd asked Beth and Jake not to discuss their new bond as "Christians" when she was around. If religion were something Jake thought he needed, she wouldn't stand in his way. So long as he didn't force it on her. She made her own decisions, controlled her own destiny.

But she believed all that stuff about Jesus, too. He was a good man, a great example. Why couldn't Jake leave it at that?

Chapter Ten

Keith unlocked the front door and held it open. "After you."

"Why, thank you." Beth batted her eyelashes as she ducked under his arm and sashayed into the house. Between her teaching seventh grade English and Keith's busy hours as the middle school counselor, childish chatter filled their days. At the end of the day, their quiet house became a haven.

She set her book bag down by a side table stacked with classics she had read over the summer: *Jane Eyre, Sense and Sensibility*, and *Middlemarch.*

A black nose peeked from under the table and a wet tongue licked her hand.

Beth pulled her hand away and wiped it on her hip. "Mizpah, what are you doing out of the laundry room?"

The puppy crawled from under the table and nipped at the leather strap of the bag.

"No." Keith nudged Mizpah away with his foot, then went rigid. "Beth, look at the house."

A throw pillow lay empty, shreds of stuffing strewn across the carpet. A pile of poop occupied the floor in front of the television. Black tape from the insides of old videos tumbled over the couch. And that was just the living room. What did the rest of the house look like?

"Keith, how did she get out? I know I shut the door after I checked on her at lunch."

"You're sure?"

"Yes, I'm sure, or I wouldn't have said that." Curling up in an afghan and grading papers would have to wait until she and Keith cleaned up.

Keith moved toward the laundry room. "Maybe the door didn't latch."

"Bad dog!" Beth glared at Mizpah, whose tail was threatening to shake off her rump.

And to think they'd gotten the lab to make life better, a warm little body to cuddle with after the miscarriages. Her name, which meant "hopeful expectation," came from a verse Pastor Alan had preached on a few months ago. He'd dubbed it the Mizpah verse. *May the Lord keep watch between you and me when we are away from each other.*

Beth shook a finger in Mizpah's face. "You, dog, are more trouble than you're worth. If we'd known about this other baby, we'd never have bought you."

Chocolate brown eyes stared up at Beth, begging for forgiveness.

She grabbed the leash from a hook in the entryway. "Let's go for a walk and see if you need to go potty again before we take care of this mess."

"I'll pick up while you're gone," Keith yelled from the next room.

The physical exertion of walking combined with the crisp autumn air drained the stress. Fifteen minutes later, mood leveled and mind calmed, she opened the door and urged Mizpah inside.

The sound of a cheering crowd and the high-energy voice of a sports announcer greeted her.

Keith's lanky body filled the length of the couch, taking his "game's on" position. He clasped an open can of soda in one hand. A bowl of salsa and large bag of tortilla chips rested on the coffee table.

Football.

Florida State Seminoles.

Tuned-in sports fan equaled tuned-out husband.

The ruined tapes had been pushed to the side, but tendrils of film still crept over the furniture.

Resisting the urge to yell, she walked over to the couch and stood between Keith and the television.

Keith shooed her out of the way with his hands. "Could you move? I can't see."

Beth moved, but only to turn sideways. Her protruding belly would further impede his view.

"What, Beth?"

"Did you disinfect the carpet?"

Keith sat up and moved to the foot of the couch where he could see around her. "What?"

"The pile that was here." She pointed with her shoe at the dry spot that had recently been home to Mizpah feces.

"Uh-huh."

"Did you use any disinfectant?"

A few seconds of blank stare later, the question seemed to pierce Keith's consciousness. He nodded his head and mumbled something about "after this play."

Beth went into the kitchen. Banging pans together or slamming cupboard doors would feel so good, but she was too mature for that. Did he think she was going to do all the clean up? The dog had been his idea in the first place.

She opened the fridge and stared at its contents, fingers beating out an aimless rhythm on the fridge door. Nothing looked appetizing. She shut the door with more force than necessary and bottles inside rattled against each other.

A peek through the doorway.

Keith's body was still glued to the couch.

She sighed. Might as well check the rest of the house. She tromped upstairs, each footstep hitting a riser with angry energy. Towels from the racks in the bathroom lay on the linoleum. The stench of urine confirmed they had been piddled on. She chucked them into the laundry basket, stomped into their bedroom, and emptied the hamper, fingers throttling each item as she threw it in the basket.

One of Keith's shirts had missed the hamper a couple days ago. She reached for it. Wait. Did he think she would pick it up? Well, he'd either have to wash it himself or wear it dirty. She was not his maid.

The laundry basket overflowed by the time Beth gathered all the dirty clothes. She carried them toward the bedroom door. As she passed the dresser, a sharp pain split her shin. "Ow! Ow!"

Towels, shirts, and underclothes scattered as the basket hit the floor.

She sank onto the carpet and yanked up her pant leg.

Drops of blood oozed from a small scrape.

Way to go, Keith. Leave a drawer open so your seven-months-pregnant wife can kill herself on it.

Beth limped to the bathroom and got a bandage from the medicine cabinet. Moisture gathered behind her eyelids, but she willed herself to fight it back.

She returned to the bedroom, put the spilled clothes back in the laundry basket, and hoisted it up to rest on one hip. Hand against the wall for support, she descended the steep stairs.

Keith looked up as she passed by. “Babe, you shouldn’t be carrying heavy things down those old stairs.”

Beth’s teeth ground. If she said what she was thinking, she’d regret it.

In the washroom, she separated coloreds from whites and started the first load of laundry. Stomach rumbling, she glanced at her watch. Apparently she was also the one designated to fix dinner tonight. All right, then. Hot dogs, Keith’s least favorite meal.

It didn’t take long to boil the frankfurters and open a can of pork and beans. Keith liked his beans warm, but tonight he’d get them straight from the can.

“Dinner’s on the table.”

Keith’s man ears, though they’d been able to ignore her stomping and flailing about upstairs, heard the announcement of food the very first time.

Beth poured a full glass of milk while he rummaged through the cupboard and brought out a new bag of chips.

“Selective hearing?” she muttered.

“What?”

“Exactly.” She pivoted to get the mustard and relish from the refrigerator and plunked them on the table.

Keith seemed puzzled.

Sure. Play innocent.

Keith took a bite of his hot dog and chewed a few times before swallowing. “I figured out how Mizpah got out. Want to hear?”

She shrugged.

“The inside of the laundry room is a levered handle. She must have jumped up, hit it with her paw, and out she went.”

The whirl of the washer ground to a stop.

Beth rose. By the time she put the clothes in the dryer, started the next load, and returned to the kitchen, Keith was gone.

His empty plate remained on the table, brown swirls of bean juice already beginning to dry. Dull thuds came from the garage.

The punching bag.

As if he had anything to be upset about.

The TV still blared in the living room, the noise compounding her irritation. She held her finger against the power button, but stopped as a commercial came on.

A man lifted a toddler into a safety swing, fitting her legs through the awkward holes. He pulled the swing toward his chest while walking backward. When he let go, the young girl squealed with delight.

Would Keith be the kind of dad who would take his daughter to the park? Delight in spending time with her? Or would he be stuck in front of the TV watching whatever sport was in season? She pushed the button and the picture shrunk into a gray square and disappeared.

Tears floated across her vision. She'd have to talk to him about his sports obsession, how it couldn't go on after the baby was born. She didn't want to raise a child alone.

An hour later, the house sparkled.

Beth carried a trash bag toward the kitchen.

Mizpah rounded the corner ahead of her. An instant later came the sound of a liquid stream hitting the floor.

Beth raced into the room and caught Mizpah peeing on the floor. "No! Bad, bad dog!" She sidestepped the puddle and yanked open the door to the garage. "Keith, get in here and do something."

Dripping sweat, he appeared with reddened knuckles. "Sounds like your Mizpah voice."

Beth blew a strand of hair off her face. "Take her. Right now her name stands for the hopeful expectation that I won't kill her."

Keith clipped the leash onto Mizpah's collar. "I'll run her ragged. Promise."

Ten minutes later, Beth made her last swipe across the kitchen floor, peeled off her rubber gloves, and sighed. Could it really only be 6:45?

She went into the utility room and hung the mop on its hook. Having mopped herself out of the kitchen, she could either perch on the washer and wait for the floor to dry or make her way around the outside of the house to the front.

The back door squeaked when she opened it, her past requests for WD-40 ignored. She stepped outside.

Cool October air soothed her heated mind. She breathed deeply. The night sky demanded her attention with its beauty. Wispy clouds caressed the moon's full face. Tree branches danced in the wind while fallen leaves played leapfrog across the back yard. Beth lowered herself onto a porch step, mind tumbling over itself like wind-tossed leaves.

The door squeaked again.

"What's wrong?" Keith's voice rose above the roar of a passing bus, the faint remnant of his morning cologne mixing with diesel fumes and fresh sweat from his run.

"Nothing."

"Can I join you?"

What had he really done? Nothing. She smirked. That was the point, though, right? "Sure." Even just allowing him to move close softened her heart.

Air stirred as he sat on the step above her, a leg splayed on either side. He turned her head and pressed her cheek against his chest, ran his hands up and down her arms. "You've got goose bumps. Want a sweater?"

Beth placed a hand over his. "No, just wrap your arms around me."

"Honey, I've got you wrapped in my heart." His whispered declaration warmed her as nothing else could, but was it true? Was it pretty words with no action to back it up? "I feel alone."

Keith tugged on her French braid. "I'm right here."

"Are you? I'm talking about the rest of our lives. It's a whole new thing to be parents, but you're acting like it's not going to change things. I'm scared, Keith. Scared I'm going to feel alone after the baby is born, too. You'll go on with your life as usual, and I'll be the one left to pick up the slack. We'll lose the 'us' we've had for years."

Keith brushed the spiky end of her braid across her neck. "I promise we'll raise this baby together. You won't get stuck with all the extra work."

She tilted her head, gazed into his eyes.

"I know I should have cleaned up more, but I selfishly wanted to watch the game." Keith kneaded her shoulders. "I'm sorry. And I promise to help more, but you're going to have to spell it out for me."

"So next time you want me to say, 'L-A-U-N-D-R-Y?'"

"Might get through my thick skull." He laughed as he pulled her closer. "Kiss and make up?"

She nuzzled his neck, drinking in his scent.

His leg brushed her back as he pushed himself off the step. "Let's go to bed. It's late."

It was, and nothing sounded better than following him up to bed and molding her body against his as best she could until drifting off.

But she had papers to grade.

She groaned. "Did you put Mizpah to bed?"

"Not yet, but I will. You go on up." Keith's hand pushed on the small of her back, directing her into the house.

"You left her inside alone?" Beth spun and searched Keith's face. Surely he was joking.

He grimaced. "It's only been a few minutes. What could she have done?"

Beth ran through the laundry room, avoided the wet patches on the kitchen floor from mopping, and stopped in the living room.

Mizpah lay on her back in her fleece-lined bed, ears flopped open, slack jaws showing little puppy teeth.

All was well.

"Keith, you're one lucky guy." Beth shook her head and smiled. "I'll see you upstairs." She reached for the leather strap of her bag, which had somehow moved under the decorator table.

The strap pulled free, bringing the bag into the light. Chewed papers scattered over the floor.

Keith gasped.

Anger coursed through Beth's veins. But she had already been there, done that. What had it helped? She threw up her hands and laughed. "I give up."

"I'm sorry, Beth, I really am." Keith looked back and forth between the sleeping puppy and the ruined papers. "Look at her. She looks like an angel. Who knew she was capable of such evil? How can you laugh it off?"

"I'm thinking of how tomorrow I'll have to stand up in front of the whole class and tell them my dog ate their homework."

Chapter Eleven

Tony bent his head and rubbed his callused fingers against the back of his neck. Maybe he should break down and make an appointment with one of those massage people to help with stress headaches. Pretty touchy-feely, but if the guys didn't find out, it might be worthwhile. Then again, perhaps the tension would work its way out in a day or two, especially since he had a few days off coming up. He'd sure earned them.

The workday had been filled with trouble, start to finish. Court in the morning, followed by responding to a drive-by shooting. Luckily, the victim was going to recover and the perp had gotten scared and turned himself in after the APB went out. The thought of gang activity creeping into sleepy Beaver Falls …

Tony lowered his head even more and snapped it to the right. *Crack.* There, felt better already.

He kept time to the country western music on the car radio, slapping his palm against the vinyl seat of his 1970 Nova, the same car he'd driven back in high school when all the girls thought he was a baseball star destined for greatness. They'd been wrong, but at least he still had the car.

He swung into a pizzeria parking lot and punched his dad's number into his phone.

His father answered on the third ring.

"Hey, Pop, it's me. I'm running a little late, but I'm on my way. Want me to grab a pizza?"

After negotiating topping choices, Tony ended the call and walked into the pizzeria. He ordered and sat on a bench against the wall. He hated to put his back to a window. He pulled out his pocketknife and ran the tip of the blade under his fingernails while his sausage and mushroom baked. Fifteen minutes later, he got back in the car and placed the warm box on the bench seat beside him. It felt like holding his stomach hostage not to dig in. Good thing his dad lived only a couple miles down the road, or Tony'd eat the whole thing on the drive over.

He signaled his turn and pulled off the highway, down the quiet street to his childhood home.

The lingering dusk softened the edges of everything it touched, filling the air with nostalgia. He could almost hear the voices of his friends as they played together among the trailers—Tag, King of the Mountain, and after-dark games of Hide and Seek. Too bad those carefree times didn't last. Happiness was elusive. Try to capture it and it would throw off its shackles and slip away.

Lester Barnett waited on the porch of the doublewide. A smile lit his face as he ambled down the steps and took the pizza from Tony's hands. "Tony, my boy, glad to see you. How's it going?"

A hard life, aided and abetted by cigarettes, booze, and late nights, had carved far too many wrinkles into his features for his fifty-plus years.

Lester held the screen door open and motioned for Tony to enter first.

"Not too bad, Pop." Tony scanned the room. The usual pile of newspapers, mail, and books cluttered the end tables hugging each side of the plaid couch. Decades of sunlight had faded the once vivid fabric. Tony had offered numerous times to haul it to the dump, but his dad had refused.

The TV was tuned to a crime show, closed captioning vainly attempting to keep up with the actors' lip movements.

Lester placed the greasy pizza box in the center of the dining table and seized the remote. "Don't need those fake cops around when the real deal's here." He grinned at Tony as the TV clicked off. "Want something to wash this down?"

"Sure. A diet anything will do."

"Some might think you a sissy, having something like that with pizza." Lester strolled over to the fridge.

"Let 'em." Tony accepted a can of diet Coke.

They settled at a dinette set as old as Tony.

He slid two slices each onto paper plates, passed one to his dad, and dug in. "How's it going at the mill?"

"The usual rumors that it's going to fold," Lester said around a mouthful of food. "Been hearing that for months, but nothing happening so far. Doubt it will. As long as there's an Oregon, there'll be lumber."

When the last string of cheese was scraped from the box, Lester stood up. "I'll be right back." He puttered in the kitchen and the flick of a cigarette lighter igniting echoed back.

Pop should quit smoking, but at least his dad tried to keep the toxic fumes to himself.

Lester reentered the living room, one hand behind his back, the other holding a saucer with a glazed doughnut in the center, lone candle aflame.

Tony couldn't hide a smile.

"Happy birthday, Tony. This seemed like the perfect cake for a cop." He brought his other hand from behind his back and handed Tony a package. "Hope you enjoy it."

And he'd thought his dad had forgotten what day it was. Once again, Pop scored points for pulling off a surprise. Tony blew out the candle, split the donut with his dad, and tore away the paper. Inside lay a five-piece gift edition of Louis L'Amour books. "Thanks, Pop. This is awesome."

The same well-worn titles already filled his bookshelf, but Pop remembered his favorite author. That was more than enough.

Tony could lose himself in the backdrop of a western sky peopled with the eternal conflict between good and evil. A man, his gun, and a horse—that's all he needed. Oh, and maybe a decent woman at his side. Things were simpler. Justice was swift.

Unlike nowadays.

"I need a smoke," Lester said. "Let's go out to the porch."

While Tony hunched sideways on the railing, Lester lowered himself onto a padded lawn chair and extracted a pack of cigarettes from his shirt pocket.

Tony hooked his thumbs through his belt loops and leaned back against one of the supports, keeping a foot on the ground for balance.

Dusk had grown to darkness, broken only by a crescent moon and shattered mosaic pieces of light falling from the windows of nearby trailers.

Lester turned his head away and blew a puff of smoke. "So, what's up with you and that Mandy girl? People are talking, you know."

"Oh, Pop, not you, too. Can't a guy help someone without a big deal being made of it?" Tony swung his leg down and paced the length of the porch.

In westerns, the gunslinger protected the downtrodden

woman and was considered a hero. In real life, the tones of suspicion painted the scene.

"There's nothing romantic going on, Pop. I wouldn't have taken her in if it hadn't been for that little girl of hers. Couldn't resist those big brown eyes." His sisters had eyes like that, eyes that took in more than what most people saw.

"All I'm saying is there's lots of talk at the mill about the two of you. And with a looker like Mandy, well, it's not hard to imagine what they're saying."

"I'd boot her out in a second if it weren't for Britney. I told Mandy I'd let them stay in the spare room for a couple of months, and that's long past, but she says she doesn't have any place else to go. Has no friends and ekes by on food stamps." Tony kneaded the base of his neck. The headache had returned. "I keep telling her to get a job, even if it's only flipping burgers or something. But she doesn't want to leave Britney in childcare. Says she has a God-given responsibility to take good care of her kid. Who am I to argue with that? I would have given anything if Mom had felt that way."

Lester snorted and knocked ashes into an empty beer can sitting on the porch. "Don't waste your time thinking about your mother, you hear?"

Easy to say, but bitterness over his mother's betrayal hit hardest on days like Christmas or his birthday.

How could she have walked out of his life without another word or apparent thought for him?

At thirty he understood it no better than he had as a twelve-year-old teetering on the brink of manhood. He only knew he was unloved and unwanted, left behind by a woman who took his two young sisters and entered the future with another man, leaving her son to build a life with a man ravaged by demons of his own making.

Lester threw the stub of his cigarette on the cement walkway, stood, and ground it out with his heel. “Tony, you gotta get rid of Mandy. Word is she’s using meth.”

Chapter Twelve

Sunlight peeked around the edges of the bedroom curtains, painting a swath of warmth across Suzanne's cheek. She forced a stubborn eyelid open and looked across the bed at Jake. He slept on his back, mouth open, upper lip fluttering with each snore. The man sure knew how to enjoy his Saturdays.

When she'd met him at the art museum all those years ago, she'd never imagined how intertwined their lives would be. Jake had carried her away from a past of regret and pain into a place of love and acceptance. Of course, the euphoria did not last forever. Life interfered. But the passing years had only deepened their relationship, binding them tighter than she had thought possible.

Leaving Jake asleep, Suzanne went to the kitchen. Keith and Beth would arrive in a few hours for brunch. She pictured Beth, the evidence of her pregnancy growing larger. Only two months to go.

After a cup of coffee, Suzanne combined the flour and salt for creamed eggs and set the mixture aside. She pulled the cinnamon rolls from the fridge and sprinkled pecans over the risen dough as Jake entered the kitchen.

He reached around her for his favorite coffee mug and kissed her cheek. "You look especially cute this morning." He wiggled his eyebrows. "It must be the smear of flour on your forehead."

"I'll show you 'cute.'" Suzanne ran her hand through a dusting of flour on the counter and brushed her fingers across his face, laughing. Her antic left trails of white across his weekend stubble.

Jake grinned and grabbed her wrist, pinning her arm loosely behind her back. "Beg for mercy."

Suzanne groaned with mock pain. "I won't be able to fix your breakfast if you don't let go."

Laughing, he released her at once.

"I'm going to get ready. Can you put the rolls in the oven in about twenty minutes?"

He nodded.

She showered and did her hair and makeup before returning to the kitchen. "Jake, what did you do with the dress you picked up from the dry cleaner yesterday? I checked in my closet and couldn't find it."

"Forgot all about it. Sorry. Do you need it today?"

"No, for church tomorrow. But how could you forget? I left a reminder on your office message machine."

"You have about a hundred other dresses."

She turned her back to him, rinsed the sink with the spray nozzle. "That's not the point, Jake." She reached into the lower cupboard for the cleanser, pushed the door shut with her knee. "You said you'd pick it up, but you conveniently forgot. It's a matter of dependability and—"

"For crying out loud, I said I was sorry. You can pick it up Monday. It's not the end of the world."

The doorbell rang.

Jake moved to answer it. "You on your cycle, or something? Everything was fine a little bit ago, and now you're all bent out of shape over a simple mistake."

Suzanne flung a furious look at Jake's retreating back. How could she love him so passionately and yet get so infuriated with him when they looked at things from completely different angles?

According to their pattern, after being married this long, they'd talk it through later in the day, both apologizing for their behavior. It was just a matter of time.

She had only seconds to bring her emotions under control before Beth sought her out. Breathing deep, she pasted a smile on her face as Keith came around the corner of the kitchen.

"Good morning to my favorite mother-in-law." He kissed her cheek.

"And your only." She pushed him toward the table.

"Boy, it smells good in here. Wish I could wake up to a hot breakfast every day."

"You could, Keith." Beth swatted the back of his head and took the seat next to him. "If you were able to cook in your sleep."

Suzanne barely paid attention to their banter. As she waited for the rolls, she lined a skillet with strips of bacon. When the timer dinged, she frosted the cinnamon rolls and brought them to the table, ignoring Jake's offer of help. She wanted to wear that blue dress to church tomorrow and it was his fault she couldn't. And she wasn't ready to admit she'd blown his forgetfulness out of proportion.

The bacon sizzled as the cast-iron skillet heated.

Suzanne tonged the strips onto a pile of paper towels and dabbed the grease off them before setting the platter on the table, beside a plate of toast and a tureen of creamed eggs.

The aroma of cinnamon and bacon fat mingled in the air. Conversation swirled around the room, garnished with bits of laughter. As far as she could tell, neither Beth nor Keith had picked up on the underlying tension between her and Jake as they ate.

Suzanne offered the last roll to Keith. “Have you two decided what you’re going to do about work after the little one comes? I’d be the perfect one to take care of the baby. I’ve already been thinking that I could turn the guest room into a nursery. You could drop the baby off on your way to the school each day.”

Beth licked some frosting from her fingers and glanced at Keith before responding. “That’s nice of you, Mom, but we’re not sure yet what we’re doing.”

Keith swallowed a massive bite of roll. “She’d like to stay home, but we don’t know how we’d manage without her salary.”

“I’ll get back to you once we’ve made a decision,” Beth said.

Suzanne rose and began clearing the table. Why hadn’t the kids been more enthusiastic about her offer? Free childcare? What could be better than Grandma doing the babysitting? It seemed like such an obvious solution.

Jake pushed back from the table. “What do you guys have planned for the rest of the day?”

Beth balled her napkin up and dropped it on the table. “Nothing much. Do you want to shop for baby stuff with me, Mom?”

So she could buy stuff for the baby, but not look after it? Suzanne loaded a plate into the dishwasher. Fine. She’d take what she could get. “I’d love to. Let me get things straightened up and then we can go. I’ve got some great ideas for decorating the baby’s room.”

Jake rinsed out his mug before sticking it in the top rack. "How about some golf? Seems a shame to waste a nice day sitting around the house while the women spend our money." He put an arm around Suzanne's waist.

She side-stepped out of his grasp, reaching for the skillet as an excuse to escape.

"Sure, but don't expect me to be Tiger Woods. I haven't played all summer."

"That's why I like to play against you."

Even Suzanne laughed at Jake's ulterior motive.

"Actually, I'd be satisfied to play like Tiger on one of his off days." Jake assumed a broad stance, hands grasping an imaginary club.

In the hushed tones of a golf commentator, Keith provided words to Jake's pantomime. "Struggling to maintain his lead, Jake Corbin hits one down the fairway. It looks to be his longest shot yet—all of fifty yards."

Beth smiled. "Okay, you guys, get out of here. What time will you be back?"

Jake shrugged. "Don't know. Depends on how many balls Keith has to hit out of the sand traps."

Suzanne wrung water from the dishcloth and draped it over the sink divider. "Can you be back by six for dinner?"

"No later than six," Jake promised. He turned to Keith. "I'll call for a tee time, get my clubs from the shed, and meet you at the car. We'll swing by your place and grab your things." He hesitated on the threshold of the back door and blew her a kiss. "See you later, Suzy."

Suzanne gave a half-hearted wave as Jake closed the door behind him. By the time he came home, she'd be ready to apologize.

Beth straightened Keith's collar. "Do you have sunscreen?"

"I'll put it on in the car. And I promise to wear my baseball cap, too, Mommy."

Beth took the red Trailblazer hat from Keith's grasp and set it backward on his head. "I don't want to hear you whine about a sunburn, that's all. Might as well practice my mothering any chance I get."

"Speaking of, take good care of my baby while I'm gone."

Beth snapped a salute. "Yes, sir, Mr. Dad."

"For that, you have to kiss me good-bye twice."

A series of honks came from the garage.

"Gotta go." Keith hurried out the door.

Beth clasped her hands and stretched her arms above her head. "If he comes home red as a cherry, it's his own fault."

"What would we do without them though?" Suddenly, she wanted to run after the car and apologize to Jake, tell him how ridiculous she'd been and send him off with a proper kiss. She held the dishtowel tighter until the urge passed.

Chapter Thirteen

The town of Beaver Falls flashed by Beth's window as Suzanne drove. The rain would begin within a few weeks and the nights would grow colder, a sign of more change to come with the next flip of a calendar page, but today a ripe Indian summer stained the landscape with bold brush strokes of school-bus yellow and pumpkin orange. Smoke from the neighbor's wood stove infused the mornings and the unmistakable aroma of burning leaves bordered the afternoons.

Suzanne broke their silence. "How are you managing teaching and being pregnant at the same time? Are you basically exhausted?"

Beth rested against the back of the seat and adjusted the seat belt under her belly. She rubbed both hands over her abdomen and her breath caught as an apparent foot pushed against her palm. "Yeah, pretty much. Keith's doing more at home. And I have great classes this year."

The foot kicked again.

"If I need a break, I sit on the edge of my desk instead of walking around the classroom like I used to."

Suzanne steered the car into a parking place near the store entrance. "You tell me if you start to get tired, and we'll head back home."

Beth waved to a student crossing the parking lot. "I'm pregnant, Mom, not an invalid. I'm supposed to exercise every day. I'm hoping shopping counts." Beth kept her voice light.

Her mother's concern could overwhelm. She said things out of love, but she held onto Beth with a suffocating grip. Some days Beth gritted her teeth and let things pass. Other days …

The greeter pushed a shopping cart toward them after they entered the store. The gray-haired man smiled as Suzanne buckled her purse strap into the child seat. "Have a nice day, ma'am."

Aisle after aisle brimmed with the necessities of motherhood. Beth brushed a soft fleece blanket against her cheek. "Imagine how snuggly my baby will feel wrapped in one of these."

Suzanne fingered it. "Feels like a cloud. Keep that one in mind." She pushed their cart past the displays of highchairs and car seats and an entire wall of disposable diapers spread out, stacks of squares forming a plastic quilt made from each brand's different colors.

"Sure a lot more choices than when you were a baby. I used cloth diapers back in those days. That's an option for you too." Suzanne touched a tiny comforter draped over a playpen display. "Oh, look at this bedroom set."

"Hi, Mrs. Harris."

Beth glanced up from examining a maple crib. Amber, a girl from last year's class, stood before her.

She grinned, her eyes on Beth's belly. "You're having a baby, huh?"

"Yes, in just a few months." She tugged her maternity shirt smooth.

"That's so cool. Call me if you need a baby-sitter. I'm reasonable." The girl handed Beth a homemade business card with her email address and cell number on it.

Beth took it. "Thanks. I'll be in touch if we need you."

"Cool." She pranced away, ebony hair swinging behind her.

Suzanne tsked. "You wouldn't leave the baby with a teenager, would you, Beth? Like I said, I'll be glad to watch my grandchild anytime you need me to."

Her mother's care was like a thick, soft blanket … wrapped around her head. Breathing space. All she needed was a little breathing space. Maybe Keith had the right idea. Moving to a nearby town might be a good thing. Somewhere close enough to be able to see her parents often, but with enough distance to feel she and Keith were truly on their own. As her due date grew closer, the wiser he sounded about being farther away.

"No, Mommy. I don't wanna!" A young child's voice burst out from the next aisle.

Suzanne smiled at Beth. "That's what you've got to look forward to, you know."

"I don't think you'd want to watch a grandchild who acted like that, Mom." Beth inflected a teasing tone to hide the sting of truth in her comment.

Apparently it worked, as her mother simply moved to the end of the aisle. "Beth, look at this adorable Noah's Ark bedding. Your teddy bear theme is cute, but don't you think this would be better?" Suzanne held up a crib-sized quilt.

Beth turned away. "It's not what I want, Mom."

"No? Why not?"

A little girl, barely older than a toddler, careened around the end of the display, bumping against Beth's legs.

"Whoa." Beth braced the girl's shoulder, stopping her from bouncing backward. "Honey, slow down—"

A young woman whipped around the corner, brushing her dishwater blonde hair out of her eyes. “Britney, you naughty, naughty girl. I told you to stay right by me.” She jerked the child away from Beth.

Britney squirmed.

“Thanks for stopping her. She can be such a brat.” The woman’s fingers tightened around Britney’s arm, her voice more and more distressed with each syllable. “You’d better start obeying. I’m not going to put up with your whining anymore.” She dragged the child away.

Beth started to follow, but Suzanne’s words halted her. “It’s really none of our business, Beth. I’m sure she’ll be fine.”

Maybe so, but something didn’t feel quite right. As a teacher, she’d learned to pay attention to the unsettling feeling in her gut. She hadn’t been wrong yet. The situation usually turned out to be neglect or abuse at home. Or lack of food. Or a lack of love and feeling of family.

Something about this little girl called out to her.

Beth walked past the Noah’s Ark bedding and around to the next aisle. Britney sat, crisscross applesauce, on the utilitarian flooring, her back to Beth, head bent, long hair falling toward the front of her body.

Beth looked up and down the aisle. No sign of the woman.

Beth’s tennis shoes squeaked on the floor as she approached.

Britney spun on her bottom, turning huge brown eyes toward Beth. The girl’s lower lip stuck out and quivered as she gulped shallow breaths and wiped the back of her hands across each eye.

"Oh, sweetie, what's wrong?" Beth hunkered down beside the child and stroked her hair. The mother could bear down on them at any minute and tell her in no uncertain terms to leave the child alone.

The girl burrowed her head into Beth's side, as if seeking a safe hiding place.

Beth lifted the girl's chin and inspected her face. "You're Britney, right?"

A barely perceptible nod.

"How old are you, sweetie?"

One at a time, three fingers stood at attention.

"Is the lady who was with you your mommy?"

"Who are you? Are you a stranger?"

The husky voice almost made Beth tumble back. "I'm a teacher, Britney. I take care of kids all day long."

A tremulous smile rewarded her answer.

"So, is that lady your mommy?"

Britney nodded. "She losted me." New tears began their short trek down her cheeks.

Suzanne joined them and knelt beside Britney, wiping the little girl's tears with a tissue. "What's your mommy's name?"

"Mommy. Or sometimes Mama."

Suzanne clicked her tongue. "Oh, you precious little girl. I'll find your mommy. You stay with her, Beth."

As if she would leave her alone.

At least five minutes passed before Suzanne returned with a young woman. "Beth, this is the manager. She wants to take Britney up to the customer service desk and make a public announcement. There's no sign of her mother anywhere."

Beth struggled to her feet and hitched her maternity pants up to a more comfortable position. How could any mother simply walk away from her child? The more she thought about it, the more she couldn't wait to give that irresponsible woman a piece of her mind.

Holding Britney's hand, she trailed after her mother and the supervisor.

After three announcements and no response, the manager picked up the phone. "We need to call the police."

Chapter Fourteen

Tony approached the tight knot of females gathered around the customer service desk. A vested one—a store manager he'd spoken with before when dealing with shoplifters—faced him. Two women, one of them pregnant, were moving in on a fourth who was partially hidden behind the manager.

The pregnant one, dark-haired and flushed, waved her arms wildly. She seemed familiar. "—and I can't believe you're saying it happened any differently."

From the midst of the gaggle, a little blonde girl broke free. "Tony!" She rushed toward him with arms wide open.

Out of context, it took a moment for the girl's identity to register. He'd gotten a radio call about a young child found in the store, no parent or caretaker around. They had been talking about Britney? Then where was Mandy?

He lifted her and stepped forward. "Brit, how's my girl today? Are you shopping?" From this angle, the fourth person was obviously Mandy.

The group turned as one to face him, heated emotions obvious in their expressions.

Britney stayed in his arms, fiddling with his badge. Her weight pressed his stiff bulletproof vest into his side.

"What seems to be the problem?" Though holding the child and ignoring Mandy, he injected authority and detachment into his voice.

One of the women stepped forward. "Thank you for coming, Officer. I'm the manager. The child was left in the store by her mother. Are you, I mean, is she your daughter?"

This did not look good.

He set Britney down, but she clung to him, rubbing her thumb along the black tuxedo stripe of his police-issue pants. "No, ma'am. She's not my daughter. I'm just a friend of the family."

Mandy met his gaze for a second before she ducked behind the store employee.

"You four ladies wait here while I have a little talk with Britney. Can you do that?"

Heads nodded all around him.

"Nobody leave, understand?"

More nodding.

He scooped Britney back up into his arms and carried her a few feet away to the miniature carousel. "That lady said your mommy left you. What did she mean?"

Britney crossed her arms. "I was bad. So Mommy left."

"She left you by yourself?" Finding his arms tightening with fury, he exhaled and lowered his shoulders.

"Yep." Britney rubbed her fist on her mouth. "Axually, she was bad to leave me. Nobody was there and I—" Her hand muffled the words.

"Don't suck your thumb, baby. I need to hear what you're saying. How long was she gone?" As if a three-year old had any perception of time.

"Forever. Tony, I alone forever." The thumb popped back into her puckered mouth.

"Brit, want to ride the horsies?" Tony fished a quarter out of his pocket. "You ride while I talk to all the ladies, okay?"

"You going to leave me?"

He tickled her side, fingers bumping over her ribs. "No.

I'll be right over there, by Mommy, if you need me." Tony let her drop the quarter in and waited until tinny music cranked from the lone speaker and the ride moved Britney up and down.

Time to make Mandy face her own music.

He moved toward her, heat boiling up and flooding his chest.

Be professional. You're in uniform.

But inside the brown and black uniform was an outraged human being. Mandy was lucky there were witnesses around.

"Mandy, why did you leave Britney alone in the store?"

The manager and the other two women backed away, parting like the Red Sea, allowing his interrogation to reach the target.

"Wait." Mandy stuck a shaky hand out in front of her. The other gripped a cup of coffee. "You've only heard one side of the story. Do you really think I'd leave her in the store?"

"No sane person would do such a thing. But your mental abilities aren't looking too good right now."

The manager covered a smile.

He needed to remember he had an audience. Her other issues could wait. "Okay, Amanda, tell your version." He rested his right hand on the butt of his weapon.

"Brit wouldn't leave the aisle. She was all whiny and falling on the ground. Well, you know I don't put up with sass, so I said I was leaving and I walked away for a minute."

Tony raised an eyebrow.

She spoke faster. "But I came right back and she wasn't there anymore. I looked everywhere. By the time I found her, they'd already called the police."

"How long were you gone?"

Placing her hand across her chest, Mandy said, "Just a minute, I swear."

"You're lying!" The pregnant woman who'd been gesturing when he'd first arrived broke in. "We waited with Britney for at least five minutes."

Mandy glared at her. "This really isn't any of your business."

The woman stepped between Mandy and Tony as if to break the path of lies. "I'm Beth Harris. My mother and I know this woman abandoned her daughter."

"I did not."

"We talked to Britney for a little while before we brought her up to the customer service desk. The manager made *three* announcements before calling you guys and *still* she didn't come."

"And who are you? Mother of the year?" Mandy stalked over to the customer service counter and kicked a display of the latest Barbie movie.

Tony followed her. "Did you hear the announcements?"

"No." Mandy's eyes darted to the side.

"Why not?"

She scanned the ceiling before answering. "I went outside to check if she was by the car. Like maybe she thought I would really leave her and she'd tried to find me." A triumphant smile crept over Mandy's face.

"She's lying."

"Please be quiet, Mrs. Harris." He turned back to Mandy. "So you were looking for Britney the whole time?"

"That's what I said."

Tony rubbed his chin, pushed at the throbbing pulse at his

neck. “Is it fair to say you were worried? Desperate to find her?”

“Of course. She’s so little and everything.”

Tony pointed to Mandy’s left hand. “So, while you were frantically searching for Britney, you had time to stop by Starbucks for coffee?”

Mandy glared at the cup as though it had scalded her. For a moment, she was silent. She set the cup on the counter. “It’s old, Tony. I bought it before we even started shopping.”

“Wow, Mandy. Amazing.” He growled the words, reached for the cup, and lifted the lid. “I can’t believe it’s steaming after all that time.”

At least she had the decency to look embarrassed.

“I’ll talk to you when we get home.” The way that sounded made it his turn to be embarrassed. If it weren’t for Britney, he would walk away from Mandy and claim he’d never known her.

After interviewing Beth and her mother, Tony noted their addresses and phone numbers on both the report and in his personal log. The little black book kept extra details and he always reviewed them before testifying in court.

Formalities taken care of, Tony took Britney by the hand. “Where’d you park, Mandy?”

“Out front.” She brought the coffee with her, but didn’t drink it as they walked to the car.

Once they arrived at the car, Tony grabbed the car seat from the back. “She’s riding home with me. You follow in your car.”

Without arguing, Mandy did as she was told.

Tony managed to control his temper until Britney was surrounded by catalogs, blunt-tipped scissors, and tape in her mother's bedroom. He had asked her to make a book of all the things she thought were beautiful. What he needed to deal with was ugly.

He found Mandy in the kitchen, loading dirty dishes into the dishwasher. Did she really think doing a little housework would show she was worth keeping around?

No sense tiptoeing around the subject as he had two months ago when his father told him she was into drugs. At that time, he'd bought her excuses, believed her rationale of the town and its excessive gossip. Now, he would tear the truth out of her if he had to. "Are you using?"

Mandy lifted the dishwasher door, slid the lock, and started the machine. Suddenly, she'd turned into Little Miss Homemaker. "Live with a cop and do drugs? I'm not that dumb." Hurt flecked her hazel eyes.

Could she be telling the truth? Was there any other explanation for her behavior? He wanted to believe her for Britney's sake. As a sworn officer of the law, he couldn't sit back and allow Mandy to get away with illegal activity. How could he not see signs of drug use? Was he blind to it?

His radio crackled.

"I'll be off in a couple of hours. I'm bringing home a drug kit and you're going to take the test."

"Whatever."

"And you're going to tell me what's going on or I'm kicking you out of here."

Mandy shook her head. "You wouldn't do that to Britney."

"Who said anything about her?"

Chapter Fifteen

Tony rolled down his window, relishing the bracing wind beating at his face. Mandy made him so hot, but not in the way she wanted to.

His dad, the force, his friends—everyone thought there was something romantic going on between them. Why didn't anyone believe he was merely trying to be a nice guy, give her a little help in rebuilding her life?

Why? Because she wanted the whole world to believe they were together. He could see that now. But it was long past time to plug her into services and get her out of his life. Still, it had been the right thing to do, giving her a chance.

One chance. Which she had blown.

He would not give her another.

Stomach growling, he detoured by a drive-thru window and ate a burger in the car. A whole lunch break wasted on dealing with Mandy, which forced him to eat in a rush.

Britney had a mother, though she wasn't much of one. Kinda like his mom, who had abandoned him, chasing after some man who apparently could give her something his father couldn't. He had no idea where his mother was, or how her situation had turned out, but he hoped she'd not ended up alone. If she was, then her exit was worthless and all his pain and loneliness counted for nothing.

For a guy who didn't like dealing with emotional junk, he sure had spent a lot of time thinking about it lately. He needed to get his mind off women and the problems they brought.

He steered the patrol car onto the shoulder of the highway and parked facing the road. This particular location lent itself to speeding; a slight turn at the crest of a hill where the speed limit dropped to forty. He'd catch more than a dozen drivers maintaining the fifty-five miles per hour, or higher, well into the speed trap. Constant distraction. Before he knew it, work would be over.

Sure enough, he ticketed three drivers over the next hour, each time returning to his spot and repositioning for the next one. He busied his body, sidetracked his mind.

A steel rectangle appeared at the crest of the hill, quickly rising up to form the top of a bright blue semi-truck. A puff of exhaust erupted into the fall sky.

Tony clocked the vehicle at forty-six. Today though, with Tony's mood, six miles per hour over the speed limit earned a driver a ticket.

They could all thank Mandy for that.

Tony flipped on his lights as he pulled the police cruiser, siren wailing, onto the highway behind the truck.

The semi swerved across the double-yellow line, then straightened. Was the trucker driving under the influence?

Tony reached for his radio.

A boom, trailed by a metallic grind, jerked his attention back to the road.

He screeched to a halt behind the now-stationary semi. With the trailer blocking his view, he couldn't see any cause for a sudden stop in the middle of the road, but that crunching sound meant trouble.

Adrenaline pumping, Tony shifted into park and left his lights flashing as a warning for traffic behind them. He opened his door and ran around the side of the cab.

The semi was planted diagonally into the driver's side of a golden Buick.

Tony groaned. Even after years of arriving first on accident scenes, he still felt like a rookie. Unsure of what to do. Cautious of the unknown. Intimidated. Wanting another officer to survey the scene and make the decisions before each image became potential fodder for Tony's dreams.

He grabbed his CPR mouthpiece from the pouch on his belt with one hand, raised the other to his shoulder, keying his mic. "Dispatch, I have a 12-16, two-vehicle, unknown injuries. Highway 41, milepost 13. Looks serious."

As he approached the driver's side of the semi, the dented door opened and a man tumbled out.

Tony ran to him and held the man's arm as he found his footing. "Sir, are you okay?" The guy was large. Tony couldn't support him for long.

"Huh?"

Tony maneuvered the limping trucker away from the wreckage and eased him to the ground.

"Meh lick." The trucker groaned, fumbled at his shoulder. A welt from the seat belt crossed the man's neck.

Tony made a mental note of it all. He might be called upon in court to describe each detail of the accident. "Sir, are you all right?"

The man nodded loosely. The odor of alcohol emanated from him.

It triggered Tony's neck pulsation.

A cursory check took less than twenty seconds. Eyes barely followed his finger and the trucker pulled at his lips when Tony asked the man his name. Hammered. The guy was driving truck—a twenty-ton weapon—while hammered.

"Sit down and don't move. The ambulance crew will be here in a minute."

Tony ran to the car. Music—jarringly upbeat sounds from an otherwise silent car—rose from the compacted vehicle, its front accordioned into the truck's bug-covered grill.

The driver's side lay crushed beneath the semi.

Tony moved toward the passenger side door and peered through the shattered window.

A young man sat motionless, bloodied head fallen back. Parts of the hood hid his lower body. His chest appeared to be intact.

Tony stuck his hand into a gap of the metal frame and reached for the carotid artery.

The man's head flopped forward.

Tony jumped.

The man murmured.

Tony pulled on the door handle, but there was no way the folded metal would open. He flipped through training scenarios in his mind. It was impossible to perform CPR unless the body was laid out flat. He needed an open airway. He would have to wait for the Jaws of Life to extract the man.

Tony leaned through the broken window across the passenger to confirm his assumption of the driver's death. His fingertips again searched for a pulse.

Nothing.

Acid burned the back of his throat at the sight of the driver's bloodied face. Tony pulled his hand out and wiped it on his pants, returning his gaze to the passenger.

The man's eyes fluttered. The victim's erratic breathing signaled his struggle to stay alive.

"Hang in there." That's all he could think to say, over and

over. He gripped the passenger's shoulder. The guy was about his age.

The scream of the ambulance neared and he ordered the few onlookers to stay back.

He fought the urge to pray. Why would God want to hear from him now when it had been so many years? His priest had promised that God was a Father who loved him, who would never leave him. But if his mother could abandon him, anyone could.

White-coated EMTs relieved Tony, freeing him to deal with orienting other officers and reporting what he'd witnessed.

Turned out the truck driver's name was Slim Hardy.

Slim—though he was anything but. If he hadn't killed a man, or possibly two, Tony would have laughed. The first ambulance had taken Slim to the hospital for examination and observation. He'd be placed under arrest after his release.

"Katza!" Tony shouted to catch Bill's attention. His friend looked up, closed his notebook, and met Tony in the middle of the road. "Did you do the Breathalyzer yet?"

Katza flipped his notebook back open and scanned the page. "The driver blew a .06 about half an hour ago. But you didn't hear it from me."

"And what else do you have?"

Katza shrugged.

"Stop playing games. I saw the accident happen and I have every right to know what's going on."

Trees rustled. A drop of rain hit Tony's bare forearm. Black clouds melded into a ferocious-looking sky.

"Maybe you should handle the traffic."

"Look, we need to work fast to gather evidence before the

rain destroys it all."

"Hey, Barnett, it's not my call. Looks like Chief wants to talk to you anyway."

Trotting over to the chief, Tony mentally reviewed what he had seen and heard.

Raindrops pelted his uniform, leaving marks on his light brown shirt. The world darkened as the storm grew.

After briefing his boss, Tony ran back to his car under orders to get his observations down on paper. He would write the whole thing up in the dry, lit vehicle. His home away from home.

The cruiser's door, left ajar for the past hour, sparkled with moisture in the illumination of the dome light. Tony slid onto the seat. He ran the truck's license first, its registration confirming Mr. Hardy as the driver on record.

Next, he entered the Buick's plate into his laptop. The registration information came up. Jake Corbin on Sycamore Lane. Something about the name and address seemed familiar. He yanked his notebook from his back pocket and found the day's entries. No way on earth." He punched the dashboard. What were the odds?

"Chief! Chief!" Tony burst from the car. "I've got something you need to see."

Chapter Sixteen

"Who knew a simple shopping trip could hold so much excitement?" Suzanne glanced at the grandfather clock in the living room as she dropped an armload of bags on the floor next to the couch. "We'll have to hurry to get dinner on the table before the men come home."

"I still can't believe that Mandy woman." Beth added her packages to the pile on the floor. "I need a drink of water to wash the bad taste from my mouth." She walked into the kitchen, grabbed a glass from the cupboard, and filled it from the tap. "I mean, there ought to be a law against a woman like her being a mother." She took several gulps, refilled her glass, and placed it on the countertop.

Suzanne opened the fridge and withdrew a package of hamburger from the meat keeper. "I was proud of you today."

"Really? Why?" Beth scooted out of the way as Suzanne reached into a lower cabinet and brought out a steel mixing bowl.

"You knew how to handle Britney. How to make her feel safe. And you certainly didn't take any guff from that woman." Suzanne grinned at Beth and pointed to the pantry. "Can you get me an onion and some tomato sauce?"

Beth found the can and brought it to Suzanne. "Did the policeman look familiar to you?"

"I'm sure I've seen him someplace. Maybe just around town."

"Wait, I think I went to school with him. He was a big

shot, tons of girls after him all the time."

"Hmm." Suzanne cracked two eggs into the bowl, plunged her hands in the cold ground beef, and mixed as Beth gathered the rest of the ingredients. Beth had acted like a she-bear—and it wasn't even her cub. Imagine how her daughter would react if her own flesh and blood were involved. She would be a good mama.

She dumped the meat into a baking pan, shaped the mixture into a loaf, washed her hands, and stuck the pan in the oven. A clap of thunder drew her attention outdoors.

A brisk wind spun the patio umbrella in its stand, twirling the floral canvas like a kaleidoscope.

"I'd better grab the umbrella before the whole table blows over." Dust and leaves blew up to meet her as she slipped out of the sliding glass door. Squinting and blinking against the gusts, she struggled to close the umbrella.

The bright blue tarp that covered the woodpile tumbled past. She ran to capture it before it flew into the neighbor's yard. The wind attempted to snag it from her fingers, but Suzanne folded it haphazardly and stuffed it between the woodpile and the garage before hurrying to the shelter of the house.

She closed the door and rested against it to catch her breath. "Last time this happened, your father called it a trade wind. Anything not tied down gets traded between neighbors."

Beth laughed. "Come here, Mom." She tipped Suzanne's head down and plucked several twigs from her hair. "Looks like you're building a nest."

"I'll get it." Nudging her daughter's hand away, Suzanne pulled back. "I wonder how your dad and Keith are doing. Hope they were off the golf course before this storm struck."

"I'm sure they're fine. I'll drop Keith a text."

Six o'clock arrived, but the men did not. Keith hadn't texted back yet, either. She and Beth sat in the living room, leafing through magazines, reading snippets to each other.

Half an hour went by. The minute hand took another lap around the face of the grandfather clock, jumping over each second as if it were a hurdle.

Beth's stomach rumbled. "I'm so hungry. Can we eat without them?"

"They'll be here soon."

"Maybe they were so involved with the game they didn't notice the weather any more than we did. I can see the headlines. 'Golfers Struck By Lightning on the Eighteenth Hole. Bodies Found With Big Smiles On Faces.'"

Suzanne swatted her daughter with the rolled up *Good Housekeeping* she'd been thumbing through. "Beth, what a thing to say."

"You know I'm kidding. Dad's too smart to get caught in a storm. I'll call Keith's cell again and see what's going on. He better answer this time."

Suzanne massaged tense neck muscles and stared out the front window. The Buick would pull up any minute, windshield wipers slashing across the glass, headlights warm and reassuring. There was no reason for this tension to crawl under her shoulder blades and burrow beneath her tendons. Maybe after she and Jake made up tonight she could talk him into giving her a back rub.

"Strange. It keeps going straight to voice mail. I'll try again in a few minutes." Beth shut her phone. "He's in big trouble for being out of touch this long."

"When Jake and I were first married, living in Houston,

he drove those terrible freeways to work. If he were more than ten minutes late getting home, I'd begin to panic."

Beth worried a hangnail. "I do the same thing sometimes. Start to think of all the horrible things that could happen. It was bad enough losing the babies. I don't know what I'd do if something happened to Keith."

A shudder skipped along Suzanne's spine. "You're so morbid tonight."

"I'm just thinking out loud."

"Well, stop. It can't be good for the baby."

"And keeping the worry inside is great for the baby. Gotcha."

"Don't be silly." Tightness crimped Suzanne's voice. She went into the kitchen.

Beth followed her. "So what *would* you do if something happened to Dad? Do you ever think about it?"

"No. If you dwell on negative thoughts, negative things will happen. If you focus on positives, life will be fine."

"I don't think it's as simple as that, Mom." Judgment reverberated through Beth's dismissal, making Suzanne's beliefs sound wrong, even stupid.

Suzanne counted to ten under her breath while she pinched the baked potatoes. Not overdone yet. She returned to the living room and lifted her favorite family photo from the mantle.

A seven-year-old Beth stood with a toothy grin in front of a lopsided sandcastle, an ocean wave surging toward her in the background. She hadn't even known what was coming until her castle washed away. Jake knelt in the background, being crazy, a seashell held to his ear.

"Beth." She set the frame back on the mantel top. "Why

are we discussing this?" She reclaimed her seat on the couch and placed a pillow behind her back.

Beth sprawled across the love seat and twisted a strand of hair around her finger, a sure sign she was deep in thought. "Because life happens. God allows things we don't necessarily like."

She checked the clock again. Was the minute hand even moving? "You know, honey, I think you're feeling uneasy because of what happened this afternoon. It unsettled you."

Beth's foot swung back and forth against the edge of the love seat. "I guess. But life can change so quickly. One minute everything is great, and the next—"

"Enough is enough, young lady. We're not talking about this anymore. The worst thing that's going to happen tonight is the trouble the guys will get in for being so late without calling."

The sound of crunching gravel on the driveway brought her to her feet.

"Finally." She hurried to the kitchen. "Dinner will be on the table by the time they wash up."

Two car doors slammed, one after the other.

She took the meatloaf out, turned the oven off, and stuck in a baking sheet of brown-and-serve rolls brushed with melted butter and sprinkled with herbs.

The doorbell drew her up short.

Beth started to rise from the love seat. "Did you lock the door?"

"Of course not. I don't understand why they wouldn't walk right in." The moment the words left her lips, a sense of déjá vu washed over her.

After their first fight as newlyweds, Jake had driven off in anger, returned forty minutes later, and rang the doorbell. When she answered, he was standing on the stoop, a huge bouquet of yellow daises clutched in his hand. "I'm so sorry," he had said.

Funny she'd think of that now, but she was certain that's what the guys were up to. Might as well beat them at their own game.

"We forgive you." The words burst out the door as she flung it open.

Two men stood in the glow of the porch light, quizzical looks on their faces.

Their hands held no flowers.

Chapter Seventeen

Chief had cornered Tony as the last body was removed from the vehicle. "You've had contact with a family member earlier today? Then you'll be breaking the news to the family," the chief had said. "And take someone with you."

Tony had chosen Katza, much to his friend's chagrin. Tony needed backup on this mission. Not because he feared being overpowered or having a weapon pulled in his face, but for dealing with all the emotions.

Crying women, orphaned children, forlorn parents. Families took bad news differently. How would the women he'd seen at the store react?

Gravel scattered as he turned the police car into the driveway of the ranch-style home. Light blazed from the front windows. If the occupants knew what lurked outside, they'd kill the lights, pull the blinds, and cower in a closet.

Part of him was glad no one had answered the door at the younger man's house. He dreaded repeating any kind of bad news. If luck were on his side, both women would be at this residence. He climbed out of the cruiser and the slam of Katza's door echoed his own.

Pressing the doorbell, he visualized what someone would see when they opened the door. Two men in brown uniforms standing on the stoop. Strangers with serious expressions shadowed by the porch light.

The older woman answered the door. "We forgive you." Jake's wife, Suzanne. Curiosity danced across her face, soon replaced by anxiety.

What? Tony flashed his badge. “Good evening, ma’am.”

“Sorry. How can I help you?” She gripped the door as she spoke. “Oh.” Her hand loosened. “This is about the little girl, isn’t it?”

Her relief almost disarmed Tony. “No, ma’am. I don’t expect you to remember my name, but I’m Officer Barnett and this is Officer Katza. We’re here on behalf of the Beaver Falls Police Department. There’s something we need to discuss. May we come in?”

“Of course. I’m sorry.” She moved back from the door. “Can I get you anything to drink? Coffee?”

Coffee did sound good, but this wasn’t a social visit. “No, thank you.”

Stepping over the threshold, Tony rubbed his hands together.

Beth Harris moved toward the door. “How’s Britney doing?” The pregnant woman’s voice held concern.

“She’s fine. Thank you for helping her earlier. I really appreciate it.” Could he let her have the soft look in her eyes a little while longer?

Katza fidgeted with his radio.

“Unfortunately, this isn’t about what happened at the store earlier.”

Tony couldn’t wait any longer. “I’m afraid your husbands were involved in an accident.”

Suzanne gasped. “What happened?”

“Mrs. Corbin, why don’t you sit down?” He helped her past the entryway to the couch as Beth followed.

Katza shifted from foot to foot.

“The accident was very serious.” The words stuck in his

throat. “I’m so sorry, Mrs. Corbin. Your husband died at the scene.”

Suzanne wilted. “No, that can’t be. He’s going to be home for dinner any minute.”

“What about Keith? Where is he?” Beth’s voice broke under the strain.

“He’s still alive, Mrs. Harris. He’s been airlifted to St. Andrew’s Hospital in Portland.”

Beth’s eyes widened, but she remained standing. Feet planted on the carpet, she clasped her belly between her hands like Britney clutching a beach ball to keep the wind from ripping it away.

Katza ducked into the kitchen, returned with two glasses of water.

Beth gulped hers.

Suzanne set her glass on the coffee table, mouth tight.

“What happened?” Beth turned toward Tony. “They were only going golfing.”

Suzanne sat up. “Officers, thank you for stopping by, but I think you have the wrong address.” Smoothing her slacks, she nodded. “Yes, you have the wrong place. So why don’t you go on now, and find the right house.”

Katza stepped forward, always eager to set the facts straight. “We found Mr. Harris’s identification in the wallet in his back pocket. Mr. Corbin’s wallet was found on the floor in the back of the car. We’re sure we have the right people, the right address.”

Suzanne collapsed onto the couch.

Tony glanced at Beth. Would she argue the identification issue too?

She closed her eyes. “Dad puts his wallet on the

dashboard when he drives. He hates how it feels to sit on it. It's so thick, with everything he could possibly need shoved inside of it. Phone numbers, business cards, every single one of my school pictures …" Beth's chin trembled and tears coursed down her cheeks.

"No, no, no," Suzanne mumbled, rocking back and forth.

Katza touched Beth's shoulder. "Is there someone you'd like us to call?"

Her eyes wrenched open. "Keith needs me. I've got to get to the hospital. St. Andrews, did you say?" Beth hurried toward the door and snatched her purse and keys from the bench in the entryway.

"You know … " Tony spoke as if he were coaxing a kitten out of a tree. "I'm not sure driving would be the best thing for you to do right now. Let's take a minute and think of someone else who could take you to the hospital."

Beth stared at her hand, which shook so much the keys clinked together. "Pastor Alan Kearn from Crossroads Community Church."

"Do you have his number?"

A typed phone number list hung on the side of the refrigerator.

Beth pointed near the bottom of the list.

Tony found Alan Kearn's number and dialed it.

The line rang twice.

"Hello?" A mellow voice, full of strength. Exactly what a man of God should sound like.

"Alan Kearn?"

"Yes?"

Tony ran through the details. "I'm sure it's a shock, but how soon can you come?"

After a slight pause, the pastor said, "I'll be right over."

Tony hung up the receiver and turned back to the women.

Beth stood behind him. "You think Keith's going to die." Fight, not sadness, filled her eyes. "But he's not. He's tougher than you know."

"The doctors can tell you what to expect. I'm no expert and I won't pretend to be."

"Please, tell us everything that happened."

He sighed. "I'm not sure you want to know."

Beth rubbed her belly. "Mom might not, but I need to know."

"Okay." Her calmness set him off balance. Her small frame held more strength than he would have guessed.

Beth sat next to her mother. "Go ahead."

Katza shot a questioning look Tony's way.

"A little after four this afternoon, I attempted to pull over a speeding semi. Instead of stopping, it crashed into Mr. Corbin's car. It's my belief Mr. Corbin died immediately and didn't suffer any pain. I stayed with Mr. Harris until medical help arrived. They got him out of the car as soon as possible and into the waiting helicopter."

Suzanne blinked rapidly. "Are you sure?"

"About what?"

"Jake being dead."

"The medical examiner made a declaration of death on the scene."

She sucked in a breath and leaned her head on Beth's shoulder.

"Why didn't the trucker pull over?"

"It was obvious he was—"

Katza jumped in. "We'll have to wait for the investigation

to be completed to know."

Beth ignored Katza. "What? It was obvious he was what, Officer Barnett?"

If Beth hadn't found Britney … if Beth hadn't argued so fiercely against Mandy's lies … if Beth didn't look so vulnerable with her pregnancy and her husband fighting for his life …

Sometimes people needed a reason to make it through a hard time. Katza didn't understand. "The driver was drunk."

"Barnett!" Katza dropped his forehead into his an open palm. "What are you thinking, man? Rumors get started when someone talks before they have all the facts."

"I know what I saw." Tony straightened up.

The information seemed to satisfy Beth. She didn't ask anything else.

When the pastor arrived, Tony met him at the door. "Thanks for coming so quickly. Mrs. Harris wants to see her husband right away. He's been taken to St. Andrew's and—" Tony lowered his voice "—Mr. Corbin's body is at Greenlawn Mortuary."

Alan's handshake was firm. "I'll make sure the ladies are taken care of." He handed Tony his card. "Here's how you can reach me if there's anything else."

Both women stood as Alan approached.

Beth reached out for him, but Suzanne held her ground.

Well, the hard part was over—for him anyway—but writing the report would take until midnight.

Once in the car, Katza punched Tony's shoulder. "Are you out of your mind? Telling them it was a drunk driver? Chief will tan your hide if he finds out."

"But he *was* drunk. I smelled his breath, you did the

Breathalyzer. They'll learn the truth sooner or later."

"It's your rear, buddy. She's cute, but I hope she was worth it."

"What's that supposed to mean?"

"I certainly can't picture you risking your career for some dried-up, old woman, that's all. Plus, she's carrying a lot of baggage. Seems to have settled around her middle."

"Her husband's in the hospital and you think I'm hitting on her?"

"Whatever, Barnett."

Couldn't a guy care about protecting and helping *any* woman without it always turning to ulterior motives?

Chapter Eighteen

Invisible claws pulled at the tire treads, slowing the car's progress toward Portland. Glare from oncoming headlights bounced off the sides of Alan and Suzanne's faces and dispersed into the darkness of the back seat.

Beth clung to the door handle as if she were a child being driven home by strangers, a child afraid to tell the adults they had made a wrong turn and were lost. As if reality had somehow become a slippery world of unfamiliar vinyl and broken seat belts.

She needed to escape, but couldn't open the door. Fresh air would help. Beth tapped the power button. As soon as the glass lowered enough, she could stick her head out into the night and vent the scream building inside her.

The window stopped halfway.

Beth groaned

"Want me to pull over?" Pastor Alan's eyes watched her from the rearview mirror.

"No, no. Keep going." Breathing out through pursed lips, she pressed her back into the seat. *Why aren't we there yet? Can't you go any faster?*

No one had told her anything more about Keith. He was injured, her father dead.

Dead? How could that be? She had talked to him today. Laughed with him at the breakfast table. What would she do without her daddy?

Pressure built in her sinuses and she pressed against it.

Those tears must wait. She needed to focus on the fact that Keith was alive. But how long would he live? Helicopters only flew patients with life-threatening injuries, didn't they?

She stared into the ebony sky. Was that pinprick of light his helicopter? No, he had to be at the hospital already, surrounded by seasoned professionals who knew how to repair his broken body.

Oh, Lord, be with them.

"Mom, will Keith be okay?" A stupid question. Mothers didn't know everything. The extent of their super powers seldom reached past elementary school.

Suzanne twisted in the front seat and extended a hand to Beth, spanning the gulf between them. A mantle of loss covered her face. "I hope so, Beth. I certainly hope so."

Neon lights flashed past as they approached the city. Pastor Alan navigated the turns to St. Andrew's Hospital and pulled into the first available slot in the parking garage. Moments later, he ushered them through the automatic doors of the hospital.

A lumpish, middle-aged man behind the information desk yawned as they approached.

"Can you tell me what room Keith Harris is in, please?"

If Pastor Alan hadn't been there to voice the question, how long would she and her mother have stood in silence?

The man brought the information up on his computer screen. "411. That's in the Intensive Care Unit, so you'll have to be buzzed through when you get to the doors up there. Do you know where it is?"

Alan nodded. "I've been here before. We'll find it." He led the women toward the elevator on the other side of the foyer.

Panic bubbled up in Beth, fear rising more rapidly than the elevator. This horror was real, the immediate future a gaping hole of unknowns ready to swallow her alive. She couldn't do this by herself. "Mom, I'm so scared," she whispered.

"Dear Jesus, be our peace. Be our strength." Pastor Alan's calm, quiet voice steadied her nerves, reminded her of who was really in charge.

Bible verses blew through her mind like skywriting on a windy day, hovering just long enough before the wispy letters dissipated in the air currents.

I can do all things.

I will never leave you.

My grace is sufficient.

Her mother at her side, Beth squared her shoulders, drew a deep breath, and broke the barrier of the heavy doors between life as she had known it and the ICU.

φφφ

An eternity later, a woman wearing green scrubs entered the waiting area and approached Beth. Strands of gray-blonde hair escaped her surgeon's cap.

The moment she made eye contact, Beth broke out in a sweat.

"Mrs. Harris? I'm Dr. Soren."

Beth pushed herself up from the couch. One of the hospital blankets the nurse had provided them during the wait fell to the floor. "How's Keith? When can I see him?"

"In about ten minutes. Why don't we go into the meeting room? I can give you some more information about his condition."

"Can my mother and pastor come, too?"

"That would be fine." The doctor escorted the group into a small room off the hallway and gestured for them to sit. "Mrs. Harris, we've spent the last few hours exploring your husband's abdominal cavity. I have to tell you, his injuries are extremely serious."

Beth cringed at the word "exploring." *Stay calm.*

Suzanne held Beth's hand.

The doctor grimaced. "The impact of the accident forced his legs to enter his abdomen as they shattered. Almost every organ in his lower body sustained damage."

Images from medical TV shows rushed through Beth's consciousness. This couldn't be happening to her husband.

"The bones broke into such little pieces that removing them is harder than looking for the proverbial needle in the haystack. It's more like trying to find all the shell particles in a mile of sand. And the ocean's tide keeps depositing more with every wave. Cuts from bone fragments are causing internal bleeding. Also, he's evidencing extensive brain trauma."

When would she stop? How many injuries could one man have? "What does that mean for Keith?"

Dr. Soren pulled off her cap and ran her fingers through her hair before answering. "It's not good, Mrs. Harris. We're not sure of his prognosis. Of course we'll be monitoring him, and I'll let you know if there's any change in his condition." She rose. "I'll ask a nurse to take you in to see him, but you can only stay for a few minutes. He's unconscious, but talk to him as if he can hear you. Maybe he can."

φφφ

Keith lay still, tubes and wires coiled around his body. Tape held a tube in place on his slack mouth. Eyelashes, so long and delicate for a man, created spidery shadows beneath his eyes. This was the face Beth loved. The face she wanted to see beside her as she fell asleep each night.

She stroked his cheek, bent, and whispered. “Keith, you can’t leave me. Fight. Fight with all you have. For me. For your baby. For yourself.”

Her hair fell across his mouth and the strands fluttered in his forced exhalations. He smelled of hospital-grade soap and antiseptic. Any sunscreen he’d slathered on before golfing was long-gone.

“Mrs. Harris, it’s time for you to step out. You’ll be able to return in about an hour.” A nurse eased Beth into the hallway before she could object.

Another hour and she could return. At least she wouldn’t have to suffer through this pain alone. Her mother would tend to the heartbreak, share the burden. Beth reentered the waiting room.

“So will you take me?” Suzanne pleaded with Alan.

Beth moved forward. “Mom, what are you talking about? Where do you have to go?”

Alan massaged his neck, stared at the floor. “Suzanne wants me to take her back to Beaver Falls.”

Suzanne nodded. “Because Keith’s okay.”

“I don’t think so.” Beth stared at her mom. “No, didn’t you hear a word the doctor said?”

“He’s alive.” Suzanne gripped the hospital blanket that draped her shoulders. “He’s going to be fine.” She took a step back, turned toward the door.

“Mom, what are you doing? Don’t leave me here alone.”

“Beth …” Her mother’s voice shook. “I need to go.” The blanket slid down her body, puddled around her feet. “I can’t stay here. I brought you to Keith, but now you have him and I have nothing." Suzanne's eyes begged for understanding.

"You have me. We have each other."

Suzanne spun toward Pastor Alan. "Please. Please take me back to Jake."

"But, Suzanne, it's late and—"

Her voice rose to a hysterical level. "I don't care how late it is. Jake's lying somewhere all alone and I need to be with him."

"I need you," Beth croaked. Wasn't a mother supposed to walk her child through difficulty and loss? To put herself second?

"You think Jake's in heaven. Wherever his spirit is, his body is here on earth. The same body I've slept by for so many years. The same hand that fits so well with mine. I need to see him, touch him. I hope you can understand."

Alan shook his head slowly but moved toward the exit.

Beth gripped the back of a chair as Suzanne and Alan walked down the hall and disappeared into the elevator.

She was abandoned. Her father gone forever, her mother headed in the opposite direction. A husband out of reach but for a few minutes every hour. Even the nurses were absent, busy with other tasks.

Prayer. She needed it, but couldn't find the words. A headache lodged behind her eyes.

She lay down on the institutional couch, wadded a thin pillow behind her neck, and pulled the cover up to her chin. Eyes closing, she stepped into a dream.

She walked through a makeshift hospital tent, dirty canvas stretched over hand-hewn poles. Moaning soldiers writhed in pain. Kerosene lamps hung from wooden posts and cast shadows into the murky sea of bodies.

She lifted her full skirt, stepping so as not to tread on any of the wounded men on the grassy floor.

In a corner of the smoke-stained tent, Keith lay sound asleep, wrapped in a blue wool blanket.

She fell to the ground at his feet, begging God to spare his life.

Keith awoke and draped his cover over her huddled form.

She looked up.

His eyes spoke of love, of promise.

Chapter Nineteen

Exhaustion seeped into every pore and pooled in the pit of Suzanne's stomach as she navigated through the parking garage and over the remaining steps to Alan's car.

He held the passenger door open.

She slid onto the seat and fastened her belt. The clock on the dashboard displayed an insane time: 2:37. No wonder the day seemed to have lasted forever—it had.

Alan backed out of the parking space and followed the huge arrows pointing to the exit. At each turn, the tires squealed like a dog howling in the middle of the night. The downward spiral through the parking garage made her head spin.

Alan waited for the barrier to lift and pulled onto the street.

Traffic was sparse, most people home in bed where they belonged.

"Suzanne, want to pick up something to eat?"

That's right, she should be famished. Brunch had been a lifetime ago, but the thought of food made her stomach lurch. She wrapped her arms around herself. "No, I don't think so. But you grab a bite if you want."

"You can't exist on coffee, you know." Alan's concern filled the space between them. "You've got some hard days ahead of you."

Hard days? What an understatement.

How could Jake do this to her? Walk out the door in the

morning and leave her to endure the rest of her life without him?

Alan stopped at an all-hours mini-mart and returned within minutes, a foil wrapped package in one hand, a large soda in the other. He clenched the package against his side as he freed a hand to open the car door, got in, and set the cup in the holder on the console.

Suzanne stopped him before he put the key in the ignition. “I want to see Jake.”

“I’ll call first thing in the morning—”

“No, tonight.”

He sighed. “I’ll give the mortuary a call and see if they’re open.” Alan reached for his cell phone.

Suzanne fumbled to recline her seat. A word from her college psych class came to mind. Disassociated. That’s how she felt. Removed from the circumstances around her, as if she were observing them from another world, unable to interact with the people involved. Scrutinizing their every move, but at the same time feeling no connection with their actions.

Alan snapped his phone closed. “Answering machine. They don’t open until eight.” He dropped the phone into the other cup holder. “I know that’s not what you wanted to hear, but this way you can get at least a few hours of sleep. It’ll do you good.”

She appreciated his concern, but she and Alan had no history to fall back on, no bond between them. Only this gruesome encounter orchestrated by Jake’s death.

“Take me to Greenlawn, please.” Her tongue refused to form the word *mortuary*. “Even if we can’t go in, I want to see where Jake is. Be close to him. I promise you can take me home after that.” Suzanne closed her eyes.

Alan didn't pursue more conversation. He'd probably had special training at seminary on how to deal with The Grieving, how to understand the importance of silence. Wait. He had experienced it firsthand when his wife died. Was he thinking of her right now? The last time he saw her body, touched her hand?

Within a few miles Suzanne surrendered to fatigue, the roughness of the road lulling her until she was caught in cross traffic on the corner of imagination and delusion.

A voice came from all sides, swirling, encircling her soul. He called her name, again and again.

"Suzanne, I'll never give up. You can never run far enough to get away."

Every syllable carried on the night wind, seeking her. She darted left and broke into a circle of moonlight. Fear clogged her lungs, strangling each breath. The moon's glow struck the silver crests of the waves and she blinked against the harsh contrast.

She couldn't stay exposed.

He would find her.

Digging her feet into the sand, she ran parallel to the ocean and back into fog. She splashed through a cold tide pool. A scream ripped from her throat as she plunged through tentacles of bulbous seaweed, sliminess grabbing at her bare ankles.

The voice resonated. "Suzanne, I won't hurt you."

Her body catapulted against the shoulder belt, jarring her awake. Heart racing, she braced both hands against the dash. "Why'd you do that? You scared me to death."

"A couple of deer ran across the road. I had to brake hard so I wouldn't hit them." The whites of Alan's eyes glowed in the pale light emanating from the dashboard. "Kind of a rude awakening."

They had reached the outskirts of Beaver Falls and their forced proximity would soon be over.

She'd call Jake's dad once the sun came up. No sense waking him in the middle of the night. He couldn't do anything for his son anyway. With the two-hour time difference between Oregon and Texas, he'd be rising soon enough. The loss would hit him hard, coming so soon after his wife's death last year.

Before Alan eased the car to a complete stop in front of Greenlawn Mortuary, Suzanne released her seat belt. She opened the car door, the chill of the deep-night air a refreshing change from the enclosed warmth of the car.

A row of pine trees lined each side of the moonlit walkway leading up to the glass doors of the red-bricked building. White pillars edged the portico.

Alan got out and stood next to her. "Want me to come?"

She gulped for her next breath, then shook her head.

"You don't have to do this."

"Yes, I do." She took the first step down the sidewalk, then another, each successive step like running a slow-motion gauntlet between the trees.

She climbed the two broad steps at the edge of the porch and peered through the glass door.

Blue carpeting. Winged-back chairs and potted plants. A coffee table covered with magazines.

And, out of sight, Jake.

Leaning into the door with the weight of her body, she

twisted the handle and tried to force it open. A whimper rose from her soul. She rested her forehead against the pane.

Jake was in there, and no one seemed to care they were separated, forbidden to be together.

She had so much to tell him, things she should have said every day. That she loved him with every fiber of her being. That he was the most important thing in her life and always would be. She longed to hold him in her arms, gather him close. She should be the one to tend to him, to wash his battered body and cover it with clean clothes. Wrap thick blankets around him to ward off the cold breath of oblivion.

She wiped at soundless tears, remembering the subtle strength in Jake's thumbs as he cradled her face in his hands and brushed tears from her eyes. She needed him. How could she cope with his death without him by her side? He'd been with her through life's difficult times—her secret, her parents' deaths, her miscarriages—but now had deserted her.

Alan approached, footsteps echoing in the empty air. "Come on, Suzanne, let me get you home. There's nothing you can do here."

He was right. She was powerless. She could either cling to the door until morning dawned and someone came to let her in, or she could walk into her empty shell of a home and wallow in thoughts of used-to-bes and might-have-beens, hide in her bed and pretend it hadn't happened.

"Goodnight, my love." She touched her fingers to her lips, then to the door, and retreated into the darkness.

Chapter Twenty

Tony rolled over, tangling in his sheet. What had awoken him? Cracking one eye open, he listened for the annoying beep-beep-beep of the alarm, but heard none. He dropped back onto the mattress and stretched.

At least today could not be worse than yesterday.

"Tony, me hungry." A little white face appeared over the edge of the bed.

Opening both eyes, he focused on it. "Huh?"

Britney blinked. "Ew! You have stinky breaf."

"Hey, don't come into my bedroom and insult me." He reached out and tickled her.

Britney giggled. "Make me food."

Tony reached for a pair of sweatpants. "Is that the right way to ask?"

"Please get me breaffast right now." She shuffled her My Little Pony slippers out to the kitchen.

Tony found her favorite pink bowl with the straw built into it and let her pick between Marshmallow Mighties and Crinkleberries. As soon as he poured milk over the cereal, she blew through the straw, forming translucent mountains of bubbles.

"No more, cutie. That's for drinking the leftover milk when you've eaten all the cereal."

"But it's fun." She scooped up a bite, tipping the spoon as she neared her mouth, managing to get half of the cereal in.

Tony handed her a napkin. "Why didn't Mommy get your

breakfast? Is she still asleep?"

Britney wiped a dribble of milk off her chin. "She's gone."

In the midst of plugging in the toaster, Tony froze. He placed the cord back onto the counter, strode to Mandy's door, and pushed it open.

Rumpled blankets piled on the bed. No Mandy.

"Cutie pie, when did she leave?"

"After night-night."

"Last night? When she put you to bed?" He had looked at the clock when he came in the door after midnight. Britney usually fell asleep around nine o'clock. She'd been left *alone* for three hours.

"Yep." Finished with her cereal, Britney slid off the chair. "I want cartoons."

Tony dropped to one knee. "If you answer all my questions, I'll put *Blue's Clues* on for you, okay?"

Smiling, Britney nodded.

"Did Mommy tuck you in and come out to watch TV?"

"Nope. She kissed me and said to go to sleep and I wasn't 'posed to get out of bed until morning time."

A chicken, that's what Mandy was. Afraid to talk with him about the episode of stellar parenting she'd displayed in the store. "She closed the door?"

"Uh-huh. She talked on the phone and went bye-bye." Britney's thumb inched toward her mouth. "'Fore she left, she peeked on me so I intended to be sleeping."

"How do you know she went bye-bye?"

"I sneaked to the window and saw her get in a big car." Britney stretched her arms up toward the ceiling. "A really, really big car."

A limo? “So you got back in bed, and when you woke up you couldn’t find her?”

“Uh-huh.”

“Good girl, Brit. Let’s start the movie.” He found the paw-printed DVD and inserted it into the player.

Tucked into a corner of the couch, Britney smiled at him, hair frizzing out on both sides of her head. The sun streaming through the window made her hair look like a halo.

He grabbed his cell and went into his bedroom, shutting the door behind him. “Pop? You going to be home in a couple hours?”

φφφ

They pulled into the trailer park a little before eleven o’clock. Tony held Britney’s hand as they climbed the steps.

Lester met them in the living room. “Come on in, you two. Britney, I’m going to make mac and cheese for our lunch in a little while. Sound good?”

“Uh-huh.”

The coloring books and markers strewn across the coffee table drew Britney like a stocking on Christmas morning.

“Where’d you get those, Pop?”

“The neighbors.”

The men stepped into the kitchen. Lester opened the refrigerator door and reached for a beer.

“Pop, I know it’s your weekend and all, but please don’t drink around Britney.”

Lester pulled one out anyway and handed the bottle to Tony. “It’s not for me. I was thinking you might need something to relax, loosen you up a little bit.”

“You can have one when I get back.” Tony replaced the bottle and shut the door. “Right now I’ve got to track Mandy down."

"I told you she was trouble. You should have listened to me. I got experience picking women that are trouble, eh?" Lester shrugged. "She was after you, I told you."

Tilting his head to the side, Tony snapped a few vertebrae into alignment. "You're not helping."

"I'm sorry, I'm sorry." Lester pulled out a yellow vinyl chair and sat. "You want to keep the girl?"

Tony looked over at the coffee table. A crooked rainbow arched across Britney's paper, primitive flowers parading underneath. "It doesn't matter what I want. Think they'd let a three-year-old girl live with a single man who's not even related? Not in this kind of world."

"Better not let them know she's with an old coot today."

Tony kicked at his father's foot. "Thanks for taking her, Pop. I want to make sure there's somewhere safe for her to go before I involve DHS. Maybe I can find her grandparents or something."

"Don't you worry. She'll be fine here. The next-door neighbors have a little girl about her age. We'll go to the park or something."

"I put a sweatshirt and some snacks in her backpack."

"Oh, is that hers? I thought you'd gotten real fond of Barbie."

Britney's barrette had slipped, sliding to one side of her head. Her hair didn't look anything like when Mandy did it. Now that he studied them, Britney's clothes didn't match too well either.

She raised her head. "I colored us, see?" Two stick figures, one larger with spiked hair, one with a red triangle of a dress, held hands between the flowers.

He'd never seen a more beautiful drawing. Or a more beautiful girl. How could Mandy keep walking away? Didn't she see the same Britney he did? Why did mothers leave their families?

He swallowed. "Awesome."

"It's for you." She folded it in half and slid the paper to the edge of the table.

"I get to take it?"

"Yep. You show it to Mommy when she comes back."

Chapter Twenty-one

Beth splashed water onto her pale face, dried it with paper towels, and applied fresh lipstick. The swatch of color looked garish under the florescent hospital lights, but it was Keith's favorite color. He had kissed it off on more than one occasion. She closed her eyes against the memory.

A nurse stopped her as she left the restroom. "You can see your husband again for a few minutes."

Beth followed the nurse into the ICU and to his room. Some part of her had hoped he'd be awake, able to talk.

Instead, he lay mute and helpless. A machine pushed breath in, sucked it out.

This nightmare lingered, worsened. Would Keith spend the rest of his life in a coma, unable to interact with her? A tangle of tubes his umbilical cord to life? Was this the "for worse" love she had promised in her marriage vow?

A rap sounded on the door and Dr. Soren entered. Her compassionate eyes assessed Beth. "You doing okay?"

"I'm more concerned about how my husband is."

The doctor perused Keith's chart. "Is any of your family here?"

"No. His parents are flying in this afternoon. Why?"

"I'd like to talk to you." Dr. Soren made a notation on the chart and returned the pen to the pocket of her lab coat. "I need to speak to the nurses, so why don't we meet in my office at the end of the hall in ten or fifteen minutes." She squeezed Beth's upper arm, then hurried toward the polished hallway, white jacket billowing behind her.

A sense of foreboding settled over the room and a rush of nausea flooded her body.

Lord, I'm scared. More scared than I've ever been. Be with me.

She lifted Keith's limp hand and moved it back and forth across her cheek, kissing it each time it neared her mouth.

Warmth radiated from his skin.

She leaned closer to absorb it. To hear the steady rhythm of his heart. "I've got to go talk with the doctor, Keith. I'll be back soon."

The door to Dr. Soren's office was open. She offered Beth a seat. Numerous photographs claimed the desktop. Framed diplomas littered one wall. Beth disregarded them and gave her full attention to the woman sitting behind the desk.

"Beth, we put Keith on a ventilator because he is no longer able to breathe on his own." Dr. Soren swiveled in the leather office chair and produced an artistic rendering of the interior of a body. "Your husband sustained a lot of injuries, the most troublesome of which was the trauma to his head. Immediately after the impact, his brain began swelling, which created intracranial pressure.

"The test results are not encouraging. We've seen nothing but declines in Keith's health. He flat-lined the EEG and the cerebral arteriogram showed no blood flow—" the doctor traced each side of the brain on the diagram "—to either hemisphere."

There was no blood going to Keith's brain?

Dr. Soren let the picture fall to the desk. "He also has no pupil response and isn't reacting to pain." Dr. Soren drummed her pen against the desk. "There's nothing we can do, Beth.

We can keep him alive on the ventilator for a time, but nothing is going to change."

Large medical words spun around Beth's mind. "What are you trying to say?"

"I'm sorry. I've already consulted with another doctor to be sure. Your husband is brain dead."

Beth looked at Dr. Soren without blinking. A blink would mean moving on to the next scene of life. "He's not just in a coma?"

"The intense trauma caused brain death. Some people call it an irreversible coma, though a coma and brain death are quite different. I'm afraid your husband will never regain consciousness."

Beth clamped the armrest of her chair. "But I see Keith lying there, looking like himself except for all the tubes and bandages and needles you've stuck in him, and you're saying he's already dead?"

"If he were taken off the ventilator, he could not sustain his heartbeat. All his other body systems would fail." Dr. Soren angled her head. "Keith is a registered organ donor. Were you aware of that?"

What a crude thought, to think of her husband as a bunch of organs stuck together. "Yes, but he's so injured. What could anyone possibly use?"

"His heart and corneas aren't damaged."

She had to share his heart with someone else? A stranger?

Dr. Soren leaned across the desk. "I've seen your love for him, and I wish I could tell you something different. But because of Keith's wish to be donor, we need to move quickly."

"I need to call my mom."

"I understand."

"Keith's parents will be here in about an hour. They just flew in."

"We can wait until they arrive and give you all a chance to say good-bye. I'll send the coordinator in to help you make the necessary decisions."

Back in the semi-privacy of Keith's room, Beth dialed her childhood number from the hospital phone as her cell was off limits. The phone rang, and she turned her back toward Keith.

How could she watch him breathe and think that ability would soon be taken away?

The answering machine played, her dad's voice booming an invitation to leave a message. Her father would have held her, helped her, but …

Beth choked up, pausing for so long after the beep her mother might skip the message. "Mommy?" She cupped her hand around the receiver to funnel the words away from Keith. "It's worse than when I talked to you earlier this morning. They say Keith can't make it. He can't breathe on his own, and the bleeding isn't going to stop. I need you to come back. Call me when you get this. And call Pastor Alan. Tell everyone to pray for us." She hung up and rested her hand on the receiver.

Her dad was gone, but her heavenly Father was there, right beside her, holding her up.

"Lord God, what do I do? If Keith is really gone, then he's already with you."

Taking Keith's hand again, she traced the blue lines of veins carrying blood back to his heart and lungs.

His heart pumping, blood racing … none of that could happen without a machine.

She got up, sat on the bed, and placed Keith's hand over her belly, pressed it to his child.

The baby kicked against the pressure.

Keith had made her a promise in the dream, had given her hope, but a promise of what?

A woman knocked at the door. "I'm with the transplant bank. Can we talk?"

Chapter Twenty-two

Tony stomped toward the back of the station. If he could find Mandy, then he could figure out what to do about Britney's situation, and Harold Olsen had a better nose for drugs than any K-9.

Or maybe Britney's account of her mother leaving voluntarily was inaccurate. Maybe he'd been stoking all this anger only to discover Mandy had been taken against her will. Far-fetched, but possible.

His dad would say to start with the obvious. Most likely, the rumors at the mill were true and Mandy was on methamphetamines. Sneaking around, somehow hiding it from him.

If so, she would have been buying speed under the cover of darkness, crashing and sleeping off the effects when he pulled long shifts of overtime.

Guilt clenched his gut. If he'd been home, Britney wouldn't have spent hours alone. Why hadn't she been more scared, more traumatized? Because it happened often?

Olsen sat at his desk, gnawing the tail of a pen, feet kicked up on the windowsill.

Tony knocked on the open door.

Olsen's feet hit the floor and he spun in his chair. "Wassup, B?" The pen bobbed in his mouth, his lips curled around it.

"Nothin' much, old man. Wondering who the big meth seller is these days."

Olsen jerked the pen out of his mouth. "You got something for me?"

"If you keep me in the loop. It's kind of personal, so I can't get too involved."

"You feed me, I'll scratch your back. Or something like that." Olsen grinned. "Sure, I'll play."

Tony slid into the room and closed the door. "Here's the story. About six months ago, I took in this girl and her kid. They didn't have anywhere else to stay. I thought I could help them out, but I think the mom might have started using lately."

"You know where she gets it?"

"Nope, I don't even know for sure that she's on anything, but there's been talk." He rocked back on his heels. "She's gone missing and I need to find her. Especially if she's getting high."

Olsen lifted an eyebrow. "If she's young and cute, I'd put money on Zach Martin. He trolls the bars looking for girls who want to party. Nothing he likes more than getting a fresh one hooked. But he's a slippery fish."

"What's he drive?"

"Why?"

Tony thought of Britney, probably skipping to the park with his dad, not a worry in the world, sure Tony would bring her mother back. "The person who last saw her reported that Mandy got into a really big vehicle."

"You could say that. Zach Martin doesn't believe in keeping a low profile. Drives a monster truck with flames painted down the sides, hydraulics, and green lights underneath."

"Do you have someone tailing him?"

"No, but I know where to look."

Tony scratched his chin. "I bet if you find him, you'll find Mandy, too. And I have a feeling you'll be able to pin something on him this time, though I might have to pressure Mandy to testify."

φφφ

They brought Mandy into the vestibule a few hours later.

Tony took cover in the office and watched the booking process. As soon as they snapped her mug shot, Tony brought it up on the computer. Matted hair, sunken eyes overtaken by dilated pupils, and sallow skin. How had he not noticed the changes happening to her? When he'd first met Mandy, she'd been fresh-faced, optimistic despite her homeless circumstances, grateful for anything he could do for her.

He peeked through the blinds.

The intake officer rolled Mandy's digits for prints.

So she had really run out on Britney, not been kidnapped or lured into a stranger's car.

Olsen walked past the office.

Tony opened the door a crack and dropped his voice an octave, hoping to disguise it from Mandy. "Olsen, over here."

The narcotics officer scanned the room, his height and long neck giving him the appearance of a periscope.

Tony waved him over.

As soon as Olsen drew near, Tony pulled him in and closed the door. "So you found them. Was she with Zach Martin?"

"Not exactly. Martin wasn't home, but Ms. Erikson answered the door and let us in. Your girl's buzzing."

"I can tell."

"They're searching the residence as we speak. Something else you might be interested to know. Some rich folks up on the hill reported a robbery last night. Lots of electronics taken. Found a few of the items in Martin's house. Your girl might be looking at more than simple drug charges. Possibly breaking and entering, theft." Olsen thwacked Tony's back and left.

Tony hooked his thumbs through the front belt loops of his jeans. If he never saw Mandy again, it would be fine with him.

And why was he hiding in the office? He hadn't done anything wrong. She should be the one ashamed, held responsible for her actions. She owed him an explanation.

He stepped out the door and crossed the pale blue tile, veering over the dark blue line meant to separate officers from arrestees. "Wow, Mandy. You're looking good."

She pushed a hunk of greasy hair back from her face. "You sic these guys on me? Like I'm some animal?"

"You're an addict who'll do anything to feed her next high. Sounds animal-like to me."

Other people waiting in the booking area watched the exchange. Why was it that conflict with Mandy always made him the center of attention?

"You don't know anything about me." Mandy sniffed, nudged her nose with the heel of her hand. "You think you're so good 'cause you're a cop? You're no better than me or anyone else in here."

"I know what you're becoming. I've seen it time and time again. Meth will eat your body alive. Your teeth are going to rot away, you'll go psycho, look like a skeleton, have panic attacks and nightmares. You won't even remember what normal felt like."

Mandy chewed at a nail. "I don't care."

"Never mind you. What about your daughter?"

Olsen came up on Tony's left, another officer on the right.

He ignored them. "What about Britney? Did you ever think about what could have happened to her? First, you leave her alone in a store where any depraved maniac could have snatched her. And, if that's not bad enough, you go out partying and leave her home alone. If there'd been a fire, she couldn't have gotten out. If something had happened to me, no one would have known she was at the apartment."

Olsen gripped Tony's arm. "Hey, let's go cool down for a minute."

He wrested out of Olsen's hold. "She's three, Mandy. There is *no* excuse for you to treat her this way. You're supposed to stay with her and protect her. Act like a real mother!"

"Enough, Barnett. You can talk to her later." Olsen pulled Tony back.

Mandy's gaze wandered, focused again on Tony. "I'll do better next time. I messed up, yeah, but I'm still a good mom."

Arrogant, ignorant woman. She lived in denial on every level. Britney deserved so much better.

Mandy's voice grew louder. "I love Britney, and she loves me. After I get out, I'll make it up to her."

"After you get out you will never, *ever* see your daughter again." Tony spat the words.

Mandy's head jerked back as if she'd been stunned with a Taser gun. She sprang to her feet, lunged across the few yards between them, and jumped, clawing at his face.

A fingernail gouged his cheek.

Her face loomed before him, teeth barred. "You can't take my daughter from me."

He twisted free and pushed against Mandy's rib cage. Her momentum too great for his limited balance, he fell backward. His skull hit on the floor, flares shooting across his eyes. "Get her off of me!"

Olsen was already grabbing Mandy's arms.

Someone else handcuffed her and dragged her away.

Chapter Twenty-three

"Beth, we're so sorry." Keith's mother hugged Beth, kissed her cheek.

"Yes, so sorry," echoed his father. "We came as soon as we could."

A wrinkled blouse hung from Linda's bird-like frame. Her coiffed, stylishly-gray hair seemed as perfect as ever, but weariness and worry dragged her expression down. "We rushed to make the plane."

Beth fidgeted. "How was your flight?" Banal, automatic conversation. Didn't mean a thing.

"A little iffy on the landing, but we lived through it." Linda winced after her last words and ran a finger under the strap of her purse. "The cab driver brought our luggage in and stowed it behind the desk in the lobby. That man drove like a—"

Walter placed a hand on Linda's shoulder, cutting off the flow of nervous chatter. "Are we able to see Keith?"

"Of course." Beth kneaded her forehead. How should she say it? "Before you see him …"

Walter's bespectacled eyes watered. "Beth, how bad is it?"

"I don't know how to tell you this." She crossed her arms, readying herself to admit it for the first time. "He's not going to make it."

"That can't be." Linda dissolved into tears. "He's so young. He's got his whole life ahead of him. And your baby.

Oh, Beth, your baby."

As her mother-in-law broke down, a new strength infused Beth. Putting an arm around Linda, she helped Walter guide her to the nearest seat. "I wish I'd been able to get hold of you sooner. Things changed so fast."

"How long does he have?" Walter checked his watch as if mere minutes of his son's life remained. He looked older already. Keith was their only child, one they'd waited long past the age of their peers to have.

"I've waited for you to be able to say good-bye. The sooner we let him go, the better the odds for successful transplants."

"He wanted that." Linda nodded and stood. "Take me to him. Take me to my son."

Swallowing hard, Beth walked over and pushed the button to be buzzed into the ICU. "I'll show you where he is and then let you have some time alone."

Linda patted her arm. "You're such a dear girl, Beth." Tears trickled down her papery cheeks.

φφφ

She couldn't stand the thought of watching his parents say good-bye. Instead, she rode the elevator to the ground floor and strode out into the misty afternoon. She powered up her phone and a voicemail message popped up.

Suzanne's voice, gravelly from crying no doubt, streamed into Beth's ear. "I got your message. I've just come in the door and checked the machine. Alan took me back to the …" Suzanne quieted. "I've seen your father. They made him look very natural. I couldn't even tell he'd been hurt, which kind of made me feel better as I kept thinking he'd be … Anyway, Nancy's going to drive me to the hospital. I'll be there as soon as I can. I love you."

Keith's life-and-death struggle sapped all Beth's emotions. She couldn't mourn her father when she'd only begun to grieve over Keith. Her mom's coming showed she was trying, but was that supposed to make up for leaving? Neither of them could truly be there for each other.

Beth shivered and turned back toward the hospital entry, bumping into a red-headed woman. "Sorry, I—Chloe?"

Her friend dropped the tote bag she'd been carrying and wrapped her arms tight around Beth. "I thought that was you. What are you doing out here by yourself?"

The warm embrace undid Beth. Silent tears coursed down her cheeks. "I'm so glad you're here."

Chloe drew back and offered her a tissue. "Pastor Alan called and told me what happened. Since you'll be spending a lot of time here as Keith recovers, he suggested Mizpah stay at their house, where his daughter can walk her everyday after school, and Alan will take care of her when he's home. I used my key to get her and pack some clothes for you."

"I hadn't even thought of the stupid dog. Did she make a horrible mess?" Beth dabbed the tissue against each eye.

"I took care of it."

"Chloe, that's so good of you. To drive all the way here, to think of all the things that have slipped my mind."

"What are friends for?" She grasped the handles of the bag and walked toward the door, pulling Beth by the hand. "I'll get your sub notes out tomorrow morning for whoever they get to cover your class."

"Wait." Beth pulled against her. "I don't want to go back in yet."

"Why?"

"Keith's parents are saying their good-byes."

Chloe dropped Beth's hand and turned to face her. "Good-byes?"

"Keith isn't going to recover, Chloe. They're taking him off life support within the hour, as soon as the transplant team arrives."

"No."

Beth nodded, tears cascading anew. "He's brain dead. Two doctors confirmed it. It's not like a coma, where he might wake up. When they unplug the machines, Keith's body won't be able to keep functioning."

Her friend offered her arms, and Beth spent what felt like hours emptying the bitter bowl of grief from her body.

φφφ

Leaving Chloe in the waiting room, Beth wound her way back to Keith's bed. She'd given his parents almost half an hour alone with their son, but she couldn't stay away any longer.

Linda, leaning over Keith's body, pressed her forehead against his.

Walter stood to the side, blinking back tears.

Beth watched the scene play out on the hospital bed: a mother stroking the face of her dying child. Why did it have to be this way? Where was God's hand in all of this? Was He trying to teach Beth a lesson she'd been too stubborn to learn in some other way?

Lord God, I don't want this pain to be for nothing, to be wasted. Whatever You're doing, don't let his death be in vain.

Linda looked at Beth, her sodden eyes reflecting the sad tones of a dirge. "Dr. Soren came by."

Walter blew his nose with a white handkerchief. "She told

us that everything is in place to honor Keith's wishes. We've said our good-byes." He tucked the square of cloth into his trousers. "We'll leave you to yours." Head bent, he trudged from the room, shepherding his wife into the hall before him.

Good-bye? How could she say good-bye to the man she'd pledged her life to? Beth placed her hand upon Keith's and their wedding bands clinked together. A hollow sound. She linked her fingers through her husband's for the last time.

The sheets, smoothly tucked around Keith, rose and fell with his chest. Two nights ago she had cuddled near him in bed and kissed his warm shoulder, slid into the crook of his arm, felt protected by his strength.

Now she had to be strong without his arms embracing her.

"Keith, I want you to do something for me. Tell God thanks for making you the other half of my heart. I want you with me for all of my life, but I'm going to trust …" A tear dripped from her nose and soaked into Keith's hospital gown. "I would never choose to lose you. But thank you for loving Jesus. If I thought we'd never meet again, I don't know what I'd do."

Needing to be closer to Keith, she squeezed onto the bed and draped his arm around her. She lay there, unmoving. How was she supposed to live without him? How could she mother a child who would never know its father?

She whispered her love, kissed as close to his lips as the tubing would allow, and laid her head on his solid chest. "Why? Why do you have to go?" She closed her eyes, emotions exhausted.

Tapping on the glass roused her. A nurse opened the door. "It's time."

Beth untwined herself from Keith's body, stroked his hair.

She lifted his hand to her face, his ring cold against her cheek. She twisted the symbol of their love from his finger and slid it onto her thumb. A treasure she could pass on to their child.

Within hours, Keith's body would join her father's at the mortuary.

She walked from the room.

Keith was gone.

And a part of her had died with him.

Chapter Twenty-four

The next day, Tony found himself praying he wouldn't have to work late.

Mister Lester, as Britney called his dad, expected Tony to pick her up before five. If Lester missed any of the pre-bowling-league gossip over hot dogs, fries, and beer, it would mean the sky had fallen on flying pigs.

And Tony still needed to come up with a plan for Britney on the days his dad worked at the mill.

As Tony headed to the vending machine, Chief called him into the briefing room. "Barnett, you're next on the list. Katza called in sick for swing. Says he's throwing up."

Apparently God hadn't paid attention to Tony's plea to evade mandatory overtime.

"Yeah, Chief, and you believed him? The big game's on in about an hour." Tony slid his reports across the counter. "I'm going to have to use a skip."

"That pretty much guarantees you'll be here for a double tomorrow." The chief flipped through the papers.

"I know, but I've got other obligations today."

James Noogan walked up. "You going to go see her?"

"Who?"

"Amanda Erikson. The woman who mauled you yesterday. Did you block the whole thing out already?"

Tony gingerly probed the damage around his swollen eye. "Every time I blink, I'm reminded. There's no way I'm getting close to her again." Looked like he'd been on the losing side of a fight—black eye, torn cheek, huge bump on the side of his head.

"Haven't you heard she's driving everyone nuts? You know her. You can make sense of her babbling."

"I don't care about her babbles."

"You're on her visitation list. The only name on there, actually."

"Noogan, she's not my problem. I should stay out if it, right, Chief? No personal matters at work."

Chief stroked his graying mustache. "The lieutenant called me about her. She's come down off the drugs, but she's wound up about seeing you. Says it's important and she won't talk to anyone else. Keeps yelling that she needs to get a message to you."

"She say what it was?"

"She said, and I quote, 'I'm not that innocent.' Why would she want to tell *you* that and not her lawyer? You know what she means?"

Tony scoffed. "She's crazy. But, yeah, I understand. She's talking about a Britney Spears song." Scary that he understood her little code, but she wanted to talk about Britney.

Noogan smirked. "Chief, why don't you order him to see her?"

"And why doesn't Chief order you to shut your mouth?"

"Boys, boys." Chief rapped the counter. "Barnett, I think it'd be best if you speak to Miss Erikson. She might have information about her dealer, or the robbery, or some other aspect we haven't considered. She trusts you, obviously. Won't talk to the rest of us."

Tony rolled his eyes. "I'll do it if you guarantee I won't

have to work late tomorrow." In case the neighbor couldn't take Britney on such short notice, he'd have fewer hours of childcare to cover.

"It's worth it," Noogan said. "At least we'll get some peace and quiet."

Chief nodded. "Just don't pass it around the whole department or everyone will start trying to make deals to get out of overtime."

"I'll put on civilian clothes, show her I'm not there in an official capacity." Tony headed for the men's locker room. He hung his uniform in his locker, grabbed a towel, and hit the shower.

The song Mandy referenced greatly resembled her recent life choices.

He threw the damp towel in the canvas hamper, pulled on a pair of Wranglers and a T-shirt, and took a look at his eye in the mirror. Did she think she could sweet talk her way out of this? Convince him she hadn't actually meant to leave Britney? Hadn't been higher than a jet stream in a cloudless summer sky?

He sat down in the first of the four visiting rooms. In all his years as a police officer, he'd never participated in the visitor's side of the ritual. The little room closed in as if he were the one in jail. He tapped his foot and glanced around, balancing on the metal stool.

Lipstick smudged the glass next to the wire mesh. At least she couldn't reach through and attack him again.

Behind the window lay the women's general population pod. An open area contained a half-moon of simple chairs facing a TV. Two levels of cells circled a central desk occupied by an unarmed female corrections officer.

As Tony watched, the officer grasped the radio on her shoulder and spoke into it.

Noogan must have called in the visitation request because the officer rose, went to a lower cell, and popped the door.

Mandy emerged. Wearing a lime green jumpsuit, she shuffled her way toward the booth. She sat and stared at him through the glass. Though her eyes were alert and her pupils normally dilated, she looked awful. “Thanks for coming.” Mandy’s hoarse voice evidenced her constant shouting. “Sorry about your eye.”

“What do you have to say about Britney?”

“Oh.” She smiled. “You got it. I wondered if you would.”

“Of course, I did. I’ve heard you sing that song a thousand times to Britney.”

“My grandma used to tell me how smart I was, how I was going to be somebody.”

“Hope she doesn’t know how wrong she was.”

Mandy flinched. “She died when I was sixteen.”

“Then she was spared the knowledge of what you have become.” Tony’s pulse quickened. He was allowing her to get to him after all.

Tears sprang up in Mandy’s eyes. “Exactly what do you think I am, Tony?”

“You don’t want to hear what I think.”

Mandy laced her fingers together, as if the tight weaving would hold her emotions in. “Actually, I do.”

“Okay, you’re an immature, thoughtless flirt who doesn’t care about anything other than having fun. I could go on and on, but that’s enough to give you the idea.”

“And a terrible mother, right?”

“That one’s the most obvious of all. I bet your granny

didn't let you dress like a prostitute."

"When my granny died, I didn't have anywhere else to go. CSD wanted to put me in foster care, but I begged a friend to take me in so I could finish high school in the same place, not have to jump around from home to home."

Tony leaned back, folded his arms, and tried to look bored. Which was hard since Mandy had never talked about her past. "Is that when you decided pop stars should be your role model?"

Mandy's nose twitched. "Will you please let me tell you this?"

"You can say whatever you want. It doesn't mean I give a rip."

"My friend's brother moved back in about the same time. Twenty-one and recently divorced. He told me how pretty I was, how I was mature for my age. When his parents were gone one night, he gave me some alcohol and we started cuddling and stuff."

"I really don't want to hear about it, Mandy."

"Britney's here because of that night. I woke up the next morning and couldn't believe how lucky I was to be his girl. But when I went downstairs for breakfast, his parents were waiting for me. Said I had to leave right away, that I wasn't going to trap their boy with my female wiles, or something like that. He told them I came on to him. They told the whole town. Everyone believed them, so I started acting the part. I mean, if they already thought that about me, what did it matter?"

He did know a thing or two about a town casting someone in a part he or she never wanted to play.

"After that, I crashed with whoever would let me.

Britney's kind of been along for the ride. One day I got sick of it and decided to move here. Beaver Falls sounded like the perfect little town."

"Mandy, you can't run away from yourself."

Slumping, Mandy dropped her head. "You think I'm hopeless, don't you?"

"I'm not going to feel sorry for you. We all make our own choices. You keep making bad ones."

Voice muffled, she said, "Tony, I tried. I tried to make better choices, but after a while even you seemed to think I was worthless."

"Not until you started neglecting your daughter." Tony shifted, leaned forward. "Listen, I didn't come to hear your life story. Why did you run off? Why did you leave Britney alone?"

Mandy sobbed into her hands. "Because she's better off with you."

Tony stood. "That's the first intelligent thing you've said."

Chapter Twenty-five

Suzanne drew a tremulous breath, paused at the doorway, and scanned the sanctuary. Crowded pews. Gentle music mixing with subdued hints of conversation. The scent of flowers so strong she could almost taste them.

"Are you ready, ladies?" Pastor Alan's quiet voice startled her. The lines by his eyes seemed to hold sorrow. At her nod, he offered an arm to both her and Beth, and the three began the slow walk down the aisle. Silence floated behind them like the soft train of a bridal gown.

Pastor Alan ushered them to their seats in the front row. Jake's father clasped Suzanne's shoulder from the pew behind. The moisture on his weathered knuckles told her he'd been wiping away tears.

Beth scooted close, leaving no space between them.

Pastor Alan continued to the pulpit as the music faded.

Suzanne raised her head and stared at the closed caskets. Candle flames reflected on the glowing walnut, twisting and writhing. A framed photograph of each man rested atop his respective casket.

Jake, I can't believe I'm here, and you're there. This is all so wrong.

She clenched the funeral program in her hand, rejecting the tranquil scene on the front. It would take more than a picture of a serene meadow and the words of Psalm 23 to bring comfort to her heart. She glanced over her shoulder at the pews packed with friends, church people, colleagues, and students. The few family members able to attend were clustered around her. A nice show of support, yet it didn't ease her misery.

Fragments of the service entered her consciousness, but the meaning behind the words never took root. An emotional fog created a barrier little could penetrate. Then came special music, eulogies, and an opportunity for people to speak about Jake and Keith. Through the lens of a broken heart, she drifted in a remoteness that was becoming as familiar as her skin.

Her mind stayed in neutral, unable to move forward to thoughts of the future, of how she would get through the next day, the next week, the rest of her life. Nor could it reverse and relive her past with Jake. Strolling through their years together would only bring intense loneliness and a realization of all that had been stolen.

If she really faced what was going on, and why, she would surrender to the wellspring of tears building inside. Once loosed, they would scour all dignity from her face, all pretense of control from her grasp. She couldn't allow that in public.

Nancy's husband, Jim, made his way to the podium. Though Nancy had been over several times in the last few days, Jim had stayed away. He stood still a moment before making eye contact with Suzanne. "There have been a lot of great things said about the two men we came to honor today. We've heard the impact they made in so many lives. Of the caring they both demonstrated in so many different ways." He shifted his weight, cleared his throat. "I'd like to share something a little different. A story about something that happened with Jake last Christmas. Somehow, I managed to finagle him into helping me hang Christmas lights."

Already chuckles sprinkled the crowd.

"We only had one ladder, so I convinced Jake to get up on the peak of the roof while I ferried lights up to him. The roof was icy. Jake leaned down for the string of lights and started slipping past me. He tried to flip around, but his legs got caught in the gutter, which bent under his weight. So he's lying there, cradled in the sagging metal, his hat—a furry, Russian thing—fallen to the ground." Jim chuckled. "And he looks at me and says, 'I'm so sorry for eavesdropping on you.'"

A gentle laughter swelled through the auditorium.

"That's the man I'm going to miss. That man with a great sense of humor and his son-in-law, who had the same." Jim returned to his seat.

A final prayer, and the service was over.

Ushers directed mourners as they dismissed a row at a time to pay their respects.

Suzanne closed her eyes, avoiding anyone's well-meaning, compassionate look. Tension built across her shoulder blades. Jake often gave her a massage when she felt like this.

But never again. Her head bent under the heavy weight of that truth.

When she next looked up, Jake's father and Keith's parents were leaving through the side exit. Only Beth and Pastor Alan remained in the room. Suzanne stood and let the funeral program fall to the floor. She'd keep no reminder of this painful day.

φφφ

Beth trembled, legs weak. The uneven ground of the cemetery made navigating with her high heels difficult. Her protruding stomach threw her off balance. She reached for her mother.

They linked arms like a pair of ice skaters.

Suzanne's breath warmed Beth's cheek. "It's almost over, sweetie. Are you doing okay?"

Beth blotted a lone tear with a tissue, half-afraid an icicle would form if she waited too long. An unexpected cold front had blown in overnight, bringing a raw, cutting wind. The weather had changed as quickly as their lives.

"I'm managing. I just want this day to be over." Beth stuffed the tissue deep into her coat pocket.

"We have to get through the meal at the fellowship hall before we can go home. You're spending the night, aren't you? Grandpa Corbin is leaving today, so you can have the guest room."

Beth nodded and glanced down the hill to where Pastor Alan leaned against the hood of his car, arms folded against the cold. Suzanne had asked him to wait while they spent a few minutes alone to say their last good-byes.

The women separated, each to her own husband's casket, but neither said a word. Beth spoke her farewell by the sign language of her hand's light stroke on the smooth, cold wood.

Astroturf sagged over the six-foot-deep holes, and bouquets stood like sentries guarding the caskets.

"I hate all these flowers," Suzanne blurted.

Masses of flowers could not hide the reality of death. They were only props. One night in the frosty air would steal their beauty, just as one night stole their husbands.

Chapter Twenty-six

Prowling wind whipped around the corner of Beth's childhood home, howling as it tried to climb through the windows.

She parted the bedroom curtains and peered into the blackness.

No moonlight, no porch lights at the neighbors.

This was her last night with her mother before returning to her own home. She dreaded the thought of facing an empty house, but it had to happen sometime. Keith's parents had returned to their home in Montana and Mizpah had surely worn out her welcome at Pastor Alan's. She and her mother both had to rebuild their lives, and staying alone at night would be a step they would each have to take.

Beth let the curtains fall from her fingers and slumped on top of the bedspread.

Keith and Dad were gone. Ever since her mother had left the hospital, she had closed Beth out. Even God seemed far away. Why? A few days ago, even though Keith had just died, God had been closer than ever before, as if He lent Beth supernatural power to make it through the painful time.

But tonight was different. God had allowed death and pain. Life wasn't supposed to be like this. She and Keith were meant to grow old together. Have passels of children and even more grandchildren. Help each other test hearing aids, unscrew prune juice lids, and care for each other well into their eighties. But now…

The baby gave a couple kicks, as if seeking more room in

its snug confines.

She rubbed her belly, offering the only comfort she knew to give. "Don't worry, little one. I'll take good care of you." As she spoke the words aloud, God's tender voice whispered the same thing to her heart. She, too, was a little child, needing a lap on which to climb and gentle arms to hold her tight.

Lord, You know that hurt and anger are threatening to overtake my heart. I'm blaming Keith ... my dad and mom ... even, yes, even You. The pain is almost more than I can bear. I don't like what You've allowed in my life, but I'm making a conscious acknowledgment that You have the right to do whatever You want. I will try to simply trust.

Not wanting to be alone any longer, she walked down the hall and lingered outside her mother's door before knocking.

Muffled sobs told their own story.

"Mom, can I come in?"

There was a slight hesitation before Suzanne replied. "Sure."

The room was dark except for the light streaming in from the hallway.

Suzanne turned on her side and switched on a lamp, threw a triangle of covers back, and motioned for Beth to join her.

The bed creaked as Beth slipped under the comforter. She lay facing her mother, looking into her sad eyes. "Mom, Keith's only been gone a few days, and I miss him so much. How am I going to get through this? He promised we'd raise our child together, but now it's not going to happen." Her voice faded as fresh tears signaled a new onslaught of grief.

Suzanne brought her hand to Beth's forehead and brushed her long bangs from her wet eyes. She cupped a palm around Beth's cheek.

Beth snuggled against it, waiting for words of wisdom.

Maybe there were no answers for times like this.

Suzanne turned to her other side.

Beth recognized the rasp of tissues being pulled from their box. “Hand me some, too, would you?” She struggled to a sitting position and leaned back against the headboard as Suzanne passed her a wad of Kleenex.

“Remember when your daddy was out of town and you’d sleep with me?”

Beth wiped her eyes and blew her nose. “I loved that. We’d play games and make brownies.” She threw a sodden tissue across the room toward the wastebasket.

It bounced off the rim and landed on the floor, glowing in the faint light against the dark carpet.

“Those were the only times I let you eat in bed.” Suzanne swiped at her nose. “I always had to change the sheets the next morning so your dad wouldn’t find crumbs when he got home.”

Beth stretched her legs, wiggled her toes until they cracked. “And remember what we’d do right before going to sleep? Use our fingertip to trace invisible words on each other’s back. See if the other person could figure out what we were writing.”

“Your worst problem was a fight with your best friend or not understanding your homework. Who knew things would turn out like this? Will life ever be normal again?”

Beth swallowed. “I’m not sure what normal is anymore. I know it’ll never be what it used to be, but I have to believe we won’t continue to feel this bad. I mean, sometimes I feel extremely close to God, and my heart is filled with trust. The next minute I feel incredibly sad and worried.”

"Why count on God at all? Why would He take Jake from me, especially after he'd become this 'born-again' Christian? You'd think God would want to leave him here to try to convert me." Suzanne shook her head. "This isn't the way for God to win me over. Nothing makes sense. All I can think about is how much I miss your dad."

What could she say to that? Even she had to admit it seemed something this devastating would only push her mother further away.

Maybe it was better to avoid that subject.

"Dad and Keith would have liked their memorial service today, don't you think? It fit them—had the right blend of celebration and respect. Sad moments as well as laughter. Like the story Jim told about Dad."

Suzanne smiled.

Beth's spirit gladdened at the sight. The sorrow of this past week had wrung all semblance of joy from her mother's face. It was good to see a glimpse of it again.

The grandfather clock in the living room announced midnight.

"No wonder I'm yawning. I'd better get back to bed." Beth started to throw the covers off, but Suzanne's hand stopped her.

"This bed has been awfully big these past few nights. Why don't you stay here with me? For old time's sake."

"I'd like that."

Suzanne switched off the lamp and a quilt of darkness settled over them. They lay in silence, but certainly her mother's mind was going down the same path as hers. It had been a strange day—the funeral and burial made the deaths official. There was a finality to it all, as if a judge had lowered his gavel one last time, pronounced a life sentence in solitary confinement with no possibility of parole, no time off for good behavior.

Her mother's hand touched her back. Fingertips wrote the letters B-A-B-Y.

Beth breathed a soft sigh and whispered, "I love you, Mom."

Chapter Twenty-seven

She couldn't stay exposed. He would find her. Digging her feet into the sand, she ran parallel to the ocean and back into fog. She splashed through a cold tide pool. A scream ripped from her throat as she plunged through tentacles of bulbous seaweed, sliminess grabbing at her bare ankles.

The voice resonated. "Suzanne, I won't hurt you."

Heart pounding, she fled along the polished beach. Her shin crashed into a chunk of driftwood; she tripped and fell to her knees. With every frantic heartbeat, her pulse echoed in her ears.

Run ... run ... run.

Scrambling to her feet, she scanned the vague horizon, searching for refuge. A hulking tuft of sand grass loomed before her. She dove close behind the vegetation. Stringy blades whipped her face, slashing at her tears.

He was coming.

Terror constricted Suzanne's airway, made her gasp for breath as she climbed out of the dream into reality. Of all times to have the nightmare again, the day after burying her husband would not have been her first choice. She deserved benign visions of happy days with Jake, not some phantom chasing her, calling her name in an unknown voice.

Burying her nose in Jake's pillow, she inhaled its everyday scent. She could almost imagine he lay beside her.

Instead, Beth's pregnant body sprawled next to her across

the queen-sized bed, forcing Suzanne to the edge of the mattress.

Beth. A young, vibrant woman left with the overwhelming responsibility of raising a baby on her own. Her marriage mowed down almost as soon as it began, leaving a gaping hole a husband should fill. Her child who would grow to adulthood without knowing its father.

At least she and Jake had shared nearly thirty years of marriage, built a life and nurtured a daughter. They'd had the chance to realize many of their dreams. But Beth and Keith would never have that opportunity, would forever be cheated of their life together.

Suzanne slipped from the bedroom and went into the kitchen. The sun had pushed aside the grayness of the previous day. She ran a listless hand along the clean countertops, searching for something to tidy up.

Nothing seemed to need her attention.

She opened the refrigerator door and stared at shelves full of carefully labeled containers, leftovers from the meal the churchwomen provided after the burial yesterday. Chicken casserole or spaghetti sounded as appetizing as foam packing peanuts. She'd send most of it home with Beth and stick the rest in the freezer.

A simple cup of coffee was all she wanted this morning. Soon the aroma of freshly brewed caffeine filled the room. She poured a cup and took it to the kitchen table.

No, that wasn't going to work.

Not with Jake conspicuously absent from his spot. His chair sat empty—as empty as her heart.

She moved to the patio door.

Two weeping willows stood in the backyard. Jake had

leveled the space between them in preparation for his latest project—a gazebo. She had hinted, then outright asked, for one. On her birthday last May, he promised to build it. His hopes of finishing it this summer were thwarted by the unexpected opportunity to teach summer school, but his detailed diagram lay on the desk in his office down the hall.

He would have finished it this winter.

For the first time since she met him, Jake would not keep his promise.

φφφ

The scent of frying bacon assaulted Beth the moment she opened the bedroom door. For some reason, even this late in her pregnancy, the odor made her stomach roll. A bowl of cold cereal held more appeal than the offering her mother was preparing, but it was the way Suzanne showed love—by giving what she thought people should want. Beth made a quick stop in the bathroom and joined her mother in the kitchen.

Suzanne stopped whisking the eggs. "Did you sleep well, honey?" She added a dash of salt and pepper to the dish.

"I did. Thanks for letting me sleep with you."

"Breakfast is nearly ready. Why don't you sit down?" Suzanne moved across the kitchen to the stove, poured the eggs into a pan, and scraped along the bottom with a spatula. "Your orange juice is on the table."

Beth tightened her robe around what was left of her waist and took a seat.

Her mother piled bacon, eggs, and toast on a plate.

Now that she saw the food, her nausea receded and hunger crept up. "Where's yours?"

Her mother pulled out a chair with one hand, held a full

cup of coffee with the other. “I’m not hungry. I’ll get something later.”

Beth sighed, picked apart a piece of bacon, and discarded the fat on the edge of her plate. “What are we going to do, Mom? When I look into the future, all I see is decisions that have to be made. I’m not ready for this. I’m having a baby in a few months. I have to figure out when to go back to work and get childcare lined up. It gives me a headache thinking about it.”

Suzanne sipped her coffee. “You know I’ll do anything I can to help. I presume you’ll want me with you at the birth, since Keith …” She set the mug down and rubbed her thumb on the handle. “Obviously, I can’t take his place, but I’d be more than glad to fill in.”

“I’d love that, Mom. It would be great to have you there.” Beth wiped her greasy fingers on the napkin. “I sure don’t want to go through it by myself. I’ve done enough ‘alone’ lately.”

“What do you mean by that?”

This wasn’t the best time to get into it. In spite of a good sleep, she had awakened feeling grouchy and out of sorts. Uncomfortable in her own skin. And she hadn’t been kidding about the headache, either.

On the other hand, what would be a good time? A part of her almost itched for a fight, for a way to release the tension that had been building over the past week and seemed stronger than ever this morning. Maybe it would be good to let her mother know how she’d let her down.

“I’m saying you pretty much left me high and dry at the hospital. I needed you with me, but you chose to be with Dad, though you couldn’t do a thing for him.” Beth turned sideways on the chair and crossed her ankles. “I don’t understand why you would do that.”

Suzanne stood and dumped the remainder of her coffee down the sink. Her body was rigid, eyes flashing when she faced Beth. “You think you have the right to question me? I did the best I could under the circumstances. I went with you to see Keith. I knew you could handle things. I didn’t think he would die. You were able to touch him, to talk to him. I needed to do the same thing with your father.”

“The mortuary was closed. You knew that when you left.”

Suzanne gripped the back of a chair with both hands, knuckles white. “You were lucky, Beth. You had hope, however small. You at least got to say good-bye to a warm body.”

“Like that made his death easier? Less painful?” Beth stood and gathered her robe around her again, sheltering her baby from angry words that seldom found life in this house. “I was lucky to spend those long hours watching a machine breathe for him? To pull the plug, dole out body parts? That’s real lucky, Mom.”

“But you don’t have to live with the regret that will haunt me the rest of my life.”

“You never regret anything because you are always right.”

Her mother crumpled into the chair. “Your dad and I had a fight that morning before you kids came for brunch over a stupid thing that really didn’t matter. But I got all bent out of shape about it and acted like it was a big deal.” Sorrow drew wet lines down Suzanne’s cheeks. “I knew I was wrong, and I planned to apologize when he came home that night. But I never got the chance. So every day I live with the knowledge that my husband's last memory is of me yelling at him. Which means I am extremely lucky, by your definition."

Her mother's sarcasm cut deep. Any empathy in Beth fell into the chasm of those bitter words. Her mother was back to thinking about only herself. Didn't she see how she had abandoned her own daughter? Made Beth not only fatherless, but motherless, too? "I think I'd better pack up and go home, Mom. This can't be good for either of us."

"Fine." Suzanne watched in silence as Beth brought her few belongings to the front door.

She stepped outside and turned back. She should say something to make it better. "I'll call you later, Mom."

Suzanne nodded and closed the door between them.

Chapter Twenty-eight

Tony's phone vibrated in his pocket as it played Miami Vice's theme song.

Last night, he'd fallen asleep on the couch watching *Who Shot Liberty Valance*. He wanted to be sure to hear Britney in case she woke up or had a nightmare, but he hadn't meant to sleep through the night in his jeans and sweatshirt.

He fished the phone out of his pocket and checked the number.

Work.

Tony hit *accept*, though *reject* sounded pretty good after being awakened from a deep sleep and dreams of baseball greatness. "Yello."

"Am I speaking with Tony Barnett?" The booking clerk projected a professional image of the office.

"Yes, Amber. Can't you recognize my suave voice?" He yawned and pressed his back into the couch, stretching his shoulders forward.

"You need to come in right away."

"Is there an emergency, or is Katza sick again?"

"Chief says to get your keister in here ASAP."

"He speaks, I obey. Maybe half an hour?"

"I'll pass it along."

Tony tossed the phone onto the coffee table and glanced over his shoulder at the microwave clock.

8:30

Britney would be waking up soon anyway. So much for a

supposed day off.

He jumped in the shower, dressed, and went into her room. "Wake up, baby girl. Time to go to Annie's house to play with Jacob again."

Britney sat up, rubbing her eyes. "I like Jacob. He's my friend."

"Good. Put these clothes on and come out for breakfast."

In the living room, Tony called his neighbor and let her know he needed childcare about an hour earlier than they'd agreed. After meeting with the chief, he might still have time to research where Britney should go. Maybe call the pastor—the one he'd met when telling those women that their husbands had been in the wreck. He'd read in the paper that the younger man had died from injuries sustained in the accident. How was his wife handling his death?

The pastor could answer that. And maybe he could recommend a family from his church that did foster care. There had to be a way to manipulate the situation, have control over where Britney ended up.

φφφ

Tony parked at the station, directly across from the jail. Somewhere in there, Mandy went about the business of being incarcerated. This meeting had better not be about her. If it were, he needed to draw a line for the chief—on one side, Tony's job; on the other, his life. The line should not be crossed or he would have no life at all.

Amber took him down the corridor and stuck her head in Chief's door. "He's here."

"Come on in, Tony." The chief perched on the edge of his massive desk.

Why call him by his first name? Everyone referred to

each other on a last name basis. Unless something was wrong.

"Hey, Chief, if this is about Mandy, I think I need to step back and remove myself from her situation."

"Have a seat."

Tony rubbed his hands along his jeans as he lowered himself into a chair. "So it's not about her?"

"I got a call from the local newspaper." Chief's mustache wiggled. "I really didn't enjoy our topic of conversation."

"What did they want?"

"The newspaper got a call this morning from an irate woman who finally got around to reading the paper's account of the crash."

"Why was she upset?" Tony's breathing quickened. What did this have to do with him?

"Her husband was killed on the scene, and she chewed the newspaper out because they failed to report that the driver of the semi was drunk."

Tony's stomach fell to his feet.

"Tony, Mrs. Corbin named you as the officer who told her the driver was drunk."

If he denied it, Katza would sell him out.

As if Chief read Tony's mind, he said, "I've already confirmed this with your partner on the assignment."

Tony groaned. "I did tell her, yes, because it was obvious. The guy was plastered. You read my report. He reeked of alcohol, he slurred words, and he could barely stand up."

"Did you read the accident team's report?"

"No, sir. I didn't feel the need to. I saw it with my own eyes."

"Mr. Corbin's car crossed the line. He drove into the path of the semi truck."

"No way."

Chief nodded. "Medical report matches. His right temple hit the steering wheel on impact. He was looking out the window, distracted by something, and didn't stay in his lane."

"Even if he didn't, it doesn't change the fact that the other driver was severely impaired by alcohol."

"About that …" Chief's words hung like a guillotine above Tony's neck. "Let's look at your report, shall we? You stated the trucker said something like 'meh lick' to you?"

"Yes, he did."

"Are you aware some diabetics are told to ask for milk if they are experiencing an insulin reaction called severe hypoglycemia?"

Tony gulped. "You're saying he wasn't drunk?"

"It's called gatherings the facts. Not making assumptions like the ones you fed Mrs. Corbin."

"What about the smell? The way he acted? The *fact* that he blew a .06?"

"The odor and the false result of the Blood Alcohol Content came from acetones on his breath. Slim Hardy was not drunk. And he never drinks because it plays havoc with his sugar levels."

The blade fell. "I'm sorry, sir. I shouldn't have said anything."

"What are you going to do to fix it?"

Squinting, Tony looked up at the chief. "Go back in time?"

"I've got a woman who believes her husband was killed by a drunk driver. Maybe she'll become a leading force in MADD, which isn't bad at all, but she needs to know the truth. And I've got a reporter nosing around convinced there's a police cover-up of the accident."

Nodding, Tony ran through various options and settled on the easiest. "I'll talk with Mrs. Corbin. I'll let her know about the inconsistencies in the report, and I'll ask her to call the paper off."

Chief raised a bushy eyebrow.

"And I'll apologize for providing her with wrong information."

"Do that."

Tony stood and moved toward the door.

"And Tony?"

He turned back to the chief. "Yeah?"

"I know about Miss Erickson's girl. If you don't start the proper proceedings to place her in a legal home, I will."

Chapter Twenty-nine

The peal of the doorbell echoed through Suzanne's quiet house. Should she ignore it? She wasn't expecting anyone and had no intention of buying magazine subscriptions from some kid trying to earn a trip to the nation's capitol. Nor did she want to listen to the mindless drivel of a religious fanatic trying to earn a trip to heaven.

She stood in the middle of the hallway. Maybe whoever it was would go away and leave her alone.

The doorbell rang again, persistent as the itch from a mosquito bite. Sighing, she answered the door.

A man stood on the stoop. He wore an unbuttoned denim jacket over a black turtleneck. The sun shone over his shoulder, making it difficult to discern his facial features. Though he was out of uniform, she recognized him immediately.

He moved to the side as he spoke. "Good morning, ma'am. I'm—"

"I know who you are, Officer Barnett. What do you want?" No squad car in the driveway, just an innocent-looking blue Nova. Must be his day off.

"I'd like to talk to you for a few minutes. If you're not busy, that is."

"About what?"

"May I come in?"

She opened the screen door and motioned for him to enter.

He removed his black baseball cap and brushed a hand over his short-cropped hair as he stood before her, while the other hand found the edge of his jacket and ran a thumb back and forth over the hem.

"Why don't you give me your coat and have a seat?" Her hostessing skills kicked in despite herself.

He shrugged out of his jacket and handed it to her as he sank onto the nearest couch.

She hung his coat over the edge of a chair.

He scanned the room in stereotypical cop fashion, as if he half-expected a criminal to be hiding behind the recliner. His gaze lingered on family photos arrayed on the mantle.

She walked over to the fireplace, picked up a framed picture, and joined him on the sofa.

The vein in his neck throbbed as she held the photo between them.

She turned it so he could see it. "This is one of my favorites. Beth and Keith so full of hope and expectancy on their wedding day. Pure joy. And to think it all ended so soon." She struggled to regain control of her emotions. "What is it you want?"

"Mrs. Corbin, I want to say again how very sorry I am about the loss of your husband and son-in-law. I hated having to be the one to come tell you about the accident."

"Let me tell you what I hate." She rose to replace the wedding picture. Hand on hip, she glared, daring him to disagree with her. "I hate drunk drivers. Guys that think they can get away with breaking the law, that don't think about the possible consequences of their actions. I also hate newspapers that don't report the whole truth or stand up for the innocent."

He squirmed. "That's why I'm here, Mrs. Corbin. I need

to explain some things. There's new information I've been made aware of, and it puts a different slant on the situation."

"What do you mean?"

"When I saw you right after the accident, I mentioned the driver of the semi-truck had been drunk. My coworker did a blood alcohol count on him out in the field. When he registered a .06, I naturally assumed he was under the influence. Plus, he couldn't talk right or pass any of the other tests. But it turns out Mr. Hardy wasn't drunk. Not even a little."

She sat down, thoughts swirling with the implications of his revelation. "I don't understand."

He stroked his hand along his chin, repositioning his body and looking her straight in the eyes. "I spoke in error that evening. Mr. Hardy was experiencing a diabetic problem, something called severe hypoglycemia. His blood sugar was extremely low, causing him to evidence the same physical problems as an intoxicated person. I'm sorry I indicated something different."

"So you're saying he wasn't drunk? That the accident happened because of his hypoglycemia?"

"Well, not exactly. It may have contributed to Mr. Hardy's slower reaction time—not being able to think as clearly as usual. But the accident report shows your husband was the one who lost control of his vehicle and crossed the line into oncoming traffic."

"No. No, that's not possible. Jake would never do something like that." She jumped up, hands clenched at her side. "We kidded him about being so careful. He doesn't speed. He signals his turns in parking lots."

Officer Barnett stood, baseball cap in his hands. "I don't

know what happened. Maybe he got distracted, lost track of his position in the traffic lane. Whatever caused it, you need to know he didn't feel any pain. The report shows his death was immediate upon impact."

What were Jake's last seconds like? Panic at the unavoidable hulk of the big truck bearing down on him, its grill drawing closer and closer until there was no place to go? Had he known it was his fault?

"Ma'am, I know it's hard to take in, especially if it's so out of character for your husband. All it takes is that one second of inattention." His eyes strayed again to the pictures on the mantle, the smiling faces a mockery of recent events.

She shuddered at the thought of what this meant. Jake was no longer a victim. Instead, his actions—or inaction—had directly led to his death, as well as Keith's. How would Beth react when she heard? "You're sure? This isn't an attempt at more cover-up?"

The officer shook his head, face solemn. "No, ma'am. It took a while for my chief to convince me, so I can imagine how you feel."

"No, I don't think you can. Jake's just another statistic to you, a traffic fatality."

He slipped his hat back on, curling the brim with his hand. "Your husband is not just a statistic to me, Mrs. Corbin. I truly am sorry about everything: the accident, the wrong information I gave you, and our conversation today. I wish none of it had happened."

Not as much as she did.

He picked his jacket up from the chair and slung it over his shoulder. "I need to ask one thing of you. I heard you called the newspaper and requested the editors correct the story to say the truck driver was drunk. Of course, now you and I both know that's not the truth. But some reporter down there thinks the police are trying to cover for Slim Hardy, and they're searching for a reason. I'll stop by the paper and let them know there's no problem, but I'd appreciate it if you'd give them a call. Let them know you're okay with their original story."

This was too much for her to digest in such a short time. He shouldn't be here, disturbing her silence, stirring up conflicting emotions about Jake.

She spoke quietly so he would pay careful attention to her words. "Another thing I hate is police officers who can't get their facts straight." She turned her back.

A few moments later, the door squeaked open and closed.

Chapter Thirty

Beth hit the speaker button on the phone as the line rang. She squished the herbal tea bag against the top of the mug with a spoon. "Please, answer the phone." Her ten-minute window to reach Chloe between classes was slipping away.

It rang again.

She pulled a chair out from the kitchen table and sat. Fatigue made her body heavy. Her huge belly, the funeral, the quarrel with her mother … had she been wrong to say how she felt?

Chloe answered on the fifth ring. "Beth?"

"Did you get my email about calling you now?"

"Yeah. I got out of second period late and my phone started ringing in the hall. All the kids looked at me like I should be expelled since they can't have any electronics at school." She blew out a puff of air. "Anyway, enough about me. How are you?"

"Can you talk? I mean, how many other teachers are in the lounge?"

"No one else yet. If it's secretive, you better talk quickly."

"It's not secretive. I just don't want anyone hearing your half of the conversation because they'll probably figure out who you're talking to."

"So, what's up? Spill."

"My mom. She's driving me nuts." Beth tightened her fingers into claws in the air. "I told her how I felt abandoned when she left me at the hospital, and she didn't get it at all.

We had a huge fight yesterday morning, and I haven't talked to her since."

Sure, she had wanted the fight, but regretted it as soon as she walked out the door. Why add conflict on top of everything else?

"Have you tried calling her?"

"No. She called me an hour ago. I let the machine pick up and she left a message saying she had something 'important' to talk about, but I can't handle another conversation with her right now. If it's so important, she should leave it on the message. I think she's just saying that to manipulate me."

"Beth, I completely understand how you feel. You were in a situation where you needed Suzanne's full support and you didn't get it. No wonder you're angry."

"Thank you." Validation. So why hadn't the unsettled feeling in her spirit gone away?

"I'm not done. Under any other circumstances, you would have been at your mother's side while she coped with the death of your dad. But you couldn't be there for her because you were with Keith. Maybe she felt deserted, too."

Conviction. There was a fine line between setting boundaries with her mother and being uncompassionate. She'd fallen into bad territory with her accusatory words. She groaned. "Why do you have to be right all the time?"

"It's a sickness."

"Without Keith's input, it's hard to know where the boundaries should be with her."

"I know." Chloe cleared her throat. "This is going to sound horrible, but I have to go. The bell's going to ring in two minutes, and I can't be late."

"Wait. What should I do?" She tightened her grasp on the

phone.

"Call her back. Give her extra grace. Let her know you care. Apologize if you're woman enough."

"Okay, Chloe. Maybe I'll ask her to dinner."

"Good idea." It sounded as if Chloe were gathering papers. "Got to go. Call you after school."

Beth hung up. Okay, she'd keep it short. Invite her mother out to dinner in a neutral, public place. Say they could talk then.

φφφ

Wide, curved steps rose and met the brick edifice, lending a grand air to Meriwether Lewis Middle School, the transitional building between William Clark Elementary and Beaver Falls High.

Beth climbed the steps and entered through the door posted with directives that visitors must check in at the office.

As she passed the office window, the head secretary, Jill, hurried out. "Oh, Beth, how's the baby doing?"

"Fine. Kicking up a storm."

"We're so sorry about what happened to Keith and your dad."

"Thank everyone for the flowers, will you?" Beth waved to the women in the back office, all of them wearing appropriately mournful expressions. "Did they appoint you as their spokesperson?"

"Well, nobody knows quite what to say, but we hope you know how much we care. It's been so strange—" She glanced from one side of the empty hallway to the other.

"What's been strange?"

"Oh, I probably shouldn't have said anything. Never mind." She touched Beth's arm and moved toward the office.

"No. Go ahead and tell me. I've wondered how the kids have been dealing with losing their counselor."

Jill tucked a fold of her starched white blouse into her plaid jumper. "That's what's been different. You know, I've worked here almost twenty years, and I've had the unfortunate experience of being with the school during the loss of faculty before, but we've never had this happen."

"I'm not following."

"The kids trusted your husband." Jill clasped her hands and held them against her plump waist. "The county brought in grief counselors from other schools, but the kids don't want to talk to them. They want to talk to Mr. Harris about Mr. Harris. It's hard for them to process."

"They did love him, didn't they?"

"He was a fine, fine young man. We'll miss him." Jill gave her a quick hug and let her continue down the hall.

How odd to walk past Keith's office and know he wasn't there. She'd have to work up the courage to remove his personal effects another day.

When she arrived at her classroom, she peeked through the rectangular window set in the door. That period's students, their desks lined up in rows of five, faced the front of the room. Black lines crisscrossed their faces from the window's design.

What was she doing here? School seemed orderly and structured, unlike her life. If she went in and spoke to her class, would she upset their learning environment? Maybe they didn't want to see her anymore; afraid, just like the grownups, of what to say or—more importantly—what not to say.

Betsy Larken, the girl who wanted to be called 'Elizabeth'

once she discovered Beth's first name, glanced toward the door. A smile burst onto her face and she gave a little wave under her chin.

Beth touched the doorknob. She'd been spotted—there was no going back.

Noise erupted as she opened the door.

"Mrs. Harris! Mrs. Harris! You're back!"

"I told you she was coming back!"

"You're late!"

Excitement winged around the room, each exclamation lifting Beth's spirits. "Thank you, kids. I'm sorry I wasn't here last week, but I'm glad you missed me." She closed the door behind her. "I see you're being well-behaved for your teacher."

Betsy scooted her chair back from her desk and popped up. "Are you going to be teaching us again? No offense, Mrs. Dannon."

The substitute smiled. "None taken, Elizabeth."

So the girl had won Mrs. Dannon over, even if the other kids still called her Betsy.

"That's a good question, and exactly why I'm here today. I know I've been your teacher less than two months, but each one of you is very special to me."

Luke Winslow, seated in the back row, dropped his head on to his desk, obscuring his face.

"As are all the students in my classes." She stared up at the ceiling. "Last week was extremely difficult for me, as I'm sure you all understand. You know my husband died." She scanned the class. How much did they want to hear? "I know it made you sad, and it made me very sad, too, which is why I didn't come to school. I talked with the principal and we agree

I will feel sad for a long time. Because I'm going to have my baby in a few months, and I was going to be on a leave of absence anyway, we thought it would be best if I took a little break until next semester."

One child groaned, but she couldn't tell which.

"I'm really going to miss you." She forced a smile. "Do you have any questions?"

Almost all of the twenty-five students raised their hand. All except for Luke.

"Okay, Jessica?"

The dark-haired girl leaned forward, elbows on her desk. "Will you tell us when you have your baby? And bring it in for us to see?"

"I can—maybe on the last day before Christmas break. Chad?"

"I was at Mr. Harris's funeral."

Several heads nodded.

"I saw you." Beth put a hand over her heart. "Thank you. I saw so many of you there, and it certainly meant a lot."

"Do you really think your husband is in heaven?" Chad blurted, cheeks tingeing pink. "'Cause that's what the pastor at the church said."

"Mr. Harris loved Jesus, so yes, I truly believe he's in heaven." With her dad. The two men she had loved the most on earth had gone on without her.

Mrs. Dannon, standing behind Beth, cleared her throat. Beth knew the rules concerning religion in a public classroom. She wasn't allowed to start a conversation about her beliefs, but she could answer direct questions from her students if she chose. Couldn't the substitute cut her some slack?

"Chad, we can know for sure if we're going to heaven. If

you," Beth's gaze swept over the whole class, "or anyone else wants to know how, you can ask me anytime. You can email, if you want. My address is on the first page in your reading journals, on the page we called a syllabus."

Mrs. Dannon exhaled loudly.

Beth turned, preparing to make her defense.

The older lady made the sign of the cross and grabbed for the Kleenex box on her desk.

Oh. She had a relationship with God, too.

"They told us he died in an accident, but what happened?" A girl's voice.

Beth faced the class. "Remember how we had the assembly on drunk driving and they brought in the wrecked car? That's kind of what happened to Mr. Harris." They didn't need to picture her dad's death.

Luke kicked his backpack out from under his desk and stormed up the aisle.

"Luke, where are you going?" Beth blocked his way.

"To the bathroom." He brushed past her and shoved the door open so hard it bounced off the outer wall and slammed shut.

Beth looked at Mrs. Dannon and whispered, "What's the matter with him?"

"Class, please start reading Chapter Three of *A Wrinkle in Time* and write down any vocabulary words you aren't familiar with in your notebooks. I need to speak with Mrs. Harris about your future assignments." The women walked behind the desk and stared down at the class calendar.

Beth followed her. "Mrs. Dannon, why is Luke acting so … unlike himself?"

"Funny you should say that." Mrs. Dannon ran her finger

along the calendar as if their conversation focused on schoolwork and lowered her voice. "He's been like that the whole time I've been subbing. Mr. Hyatt mentioned it was unusual."

Beth sneaked a look at Luke's empty seat. "I wondered why he was in the back row. He loves being in the front, raising his hand to answer every question. He's been one of my most earnest, enthusiastic pupils."

"Maybe he's having some problems in his home life? I've already talked to the principal about it, but Luke won't go see the new counselor."

"I'd be surprised if it's a family issue. His dad's a stay-at-home. He's awesome at volunteering in the classroom, PTA, and for field trips. Teachers fight over who gets to have Luke in their class. His mom works a lot, but she's very supportive."

"Well, there is something going on in that boy's head." Mrs. Dannon opened the top drawer of Beth's desk and pulled out a paper. "I took this away from him earlier this morning, but it's not the first I've seen."

Beth stared at the drawing.

A boy lying on the ground. Severed limbs in pools of vibrant red blood. In place of each eye, a forceful black *X*.

Beth swallowed back bile.

Chapter Thirty-one

Tony threw the comforter off and sat up. He'd blown it.

Mrs. Corbin made a great point—any police officer worth a badge would make sure he knew what he was talking about before opening his mouth. Not him, though. He just spouted whatever came to mind first.

Two in the morning and sleep escaped him. He punched the mattress. His hand glanced off the bedding and slammed into the headboard. "Ow."

Great. Now he needed ice. In the dark, he stumbled toward the kitchen and grabbed a dirty glass from the sink.

The automatic dispenser kicked on the door light, blinding him for a few seconds.

He dumped the ice onto a dishtowel, rolled the cloth over on itself, and grasped both ends in his palm.

Ice molded around his swelling knuckles, soothing the ache.

"Barnett, you're a stupid man." He didn't have to worry about waking Britney; the foster care system had absorbed her into its bowels about ten hours ago. She now slept in a strange bed, tightly hugging her little stuffed lamb, unfamiliar sounds and smells all around her.

He wanted to punch something else.

Had he given up too easily? Sold her out? No, she couldn't live with him. As much as he wanted to be, he was not her father.

They better not try to track her real father down or he'd

…

Or he'd what? Nothing he could do.

Mandy screwed up, and Britney paid the price.

He screwed up, and dead men's wives had to pay the price.

He thought again of Mrs. Corbin describing how meticulously her husband drove, how seriously he took the law. Signaling in parking lots? People never did that, though Tony often used it as a good excuse to pull over a suspicious vehicle.

What would distract a man like Mr. Corbin? Did he have a flat tire? A blowout? Tony didn't know any specifics, only what he had seen, and that limited knowledge had already proven to be wrong.

He needed to read the accident report.

φφφ

The tow yard opened at 8.

Tony walked into the office at 8:01. "Hey, Matt, I need to take a look at a car towed in last week. Pretty bashed up. Can you show me where it is?"

Matt glanced up. "Sure, Officer Barnett. I just need to see your badge and ID to make sure that's you under all those scratches and bruises." The kid cracked a smile.

"It's nothing. Really." Tony flipped open his wallet with one hand and showed his badge with the other. "You still going to college?"

"Yeah." Matt scanned the pictures. "I'm halftime right now 'cause I have to work to pay tuition, but I'm on the criminal justice track."

"Maybe we'll work together someday. You can be my partner."

Matt's smile grew as large as the Cheshire cat's. "That would rock, my friend." He held out his fist to bump Tony's.

Tony pulled the accident report he had copied earlier at the office out of his back pocket. He laid it on the counter, and pointed to the top of the paper. "Here's the license plate. I need to look through the interior."

Keys tapped in staccato as Matt searched the computer records. "Here it is. I'll show you which slot." Slipping on a Carhartt jacket, he headed for the back lot.

Tony zipped his regulation coat and stepped into the chill. Since he wasn't on duty, he'd gone back and forth about wearing his uniform, but doors opened more readily when he showed his badge. If anyone caught wind of his unofficial visit, he could explain it away as improving citizen relations.

"Here she is." Matt gestured.

Hard to believe the mangled piece of metal in front of Tony had ever been a car. During his response at the accident scene, he had worried more about the people involved than the vehicles. Now that he saw it up close, the extent of the damage was surprising. Not that a car ever came out on top when it wrangled with a semi truck, but he had assumed some of the Buick's front had avoided the collision. The car, though, was totaled.

Looking at the wreckage … how had the younger man managed to survive? Well, for a while.

The Jaws of Life had destroyed the front doors to remove the injured man for the helicopter and the dead body for the mortician. The front seat almost touched the dashboard. Blood and glass sprinkled the interior.

He ripped the staple out of the accident report he'd shown Matt and laid the papers in order across the trunk of the car, placing his radio, keys, and handcuffs across the tops as weights. The medical examiner's notes listed blunt trauma to the right temple as the cause of death. Jake Corbin hadn't felt a thing.

CART, the crash and accident reconstruction team, found the Buick to be traveling at thirty-nine miles per hour, a hair under the speed limit, while the truck, at time of impact, clocked in at forty-two. Nothing new there. Precise measurements, down to the half-inch, filled the report. Every item on the roadway had been tagged, measured, photographed, and collected. They had searched the car, also, but nothing stood out except two sets of golf clubs.

Something niggled at his mind. Hours before the accident occurred, Tony sat in his parked car with his radar gun looking the same direction Jake Corbin's head had turned before it crashed into the steering wheel. Closing his eyes, Tony conjured up the view: a hill rising higher than the road which curved around it, ferns and blackberry bushes covering the ground beneath tall timber, a few deciduous trees growing here and there. Nothing remarkable, especially to a man who must have driven the road often, as most of Beaver Falls did. Nothing to take Mr. Corbin's eyes off the road or to set him swerving.

They had checked his mobile phone records, and the son-in-law's, too. Neither man had been talking on the phone.

A section of the report explained Slim Hardy's medical issues. Tony skipped over it. Time to check the car.

The passenger side back door clicked open after a couple of tugs.

Aside from broken glass, the back seat was free of any trash, crumbs, or clutter. Not only did Jake Corbin follow the letter of the law, he also kept a clean automobile.

Tony leaned into the car, broken glass from the windshield digging into his knee. He surveyed the space under the seats. More nothing.

Maybe he was just a dumb cop after all. A failed baseball hero and an incompetent police officer.

Face the truth. Jake Corbin turned to his left and crossed the line. So what?

Tony walked around the car. Why didn't he buy the explanation? It was cut and dried. And, as his father said about everything, it was obvious.

He circled the car again, stopping at the driver's side. The floor had been smashed into nonexistence.

What was that? A steel ball lay trapped between the track of the adjustable seat and the bolt of the seat belt.

He rolled it in his hand. Less than half an inch across, it had heft, substance. Tossing it from hand to hand, a flash of familiarity hit him like an arrow to the heart.

Chapter Thirty-two

"Thanks for coming in." Attorney Spencer Chee reached over his desk and shook Tony's hand.

"I'm impressed you want to talk to me less than a day after Britney was taken. Placed, I mean."

"We try to meet with the concerned parties as soon as possible. Why don't you sit down and I'll explain exactly what will be happening."

Tony ignored the stare and the unvoiced question about his black eye.

Pictures of smiling children plastered the walls of Chee's office. An espresso machine hovered on the edge of the windowsill.

"Officer Barnett, I've been appointed as the child advocate for Britney Marie Erikson. My purpose in having you come in this afternoon is to find out as much as possible about her previous home environment. During the preliminary hearing this morning, temporary custody was granted to the state."

"When will you decide what happens to Britney?"

"The judicial settlement conference will take place in four to eight weeks. I'd like to tape our conversation today for use in the hearing. Are you comfortable with that?"

"Sure."

"Wonderful." Spencer smiled. "I'm warning you—I might sound a little aggressive."

Tony removed his jacket. "I can handle it."

Spencer flicked a button on a small hand-held recorder. “Officer Barnett, it is my understanding you have both a personal and professional witness to give in this matter. Is that correct?”

“Yes.”

“Let’s deal with the professional side first, then. Please recount what occurred on October 14 of this year.”

“I received a call from a store manager that a young girl had apparently been abandoned. By the time I arrived, the mother had returned.”

“And the mother was Amanda Erikson?”

“Yes.”

“Continue.”

“Mandy—Miss Erikson—said it was all accidental, a misunderstanding. But several witnesses I spoke to contradicted that.”

“To whom did you speak?”

“Mrs. Harris and Mrs. Corbin, the women who found the girl. And the store manager. When Mrs. Harris first saw—”

“They are on my list of witnesses I’m scheduled to speak with later today. Stick to what you yourself observed, please.”

“Right. Sorry. Britney seemed to be all right physically, but she was hesitant about being far away from me. She mentioned fearing I might leave her.” Tony bounced his leg. “I observed that Miss Erikson had recently bought a coffee drink that was only available across the parking lot and determined her story to be false. My professional opinion is that she left the child in the store to punish her.”

“How long have you known Miss Erikson?”

“We met about six months ago. She didn’t have a place to stay, so I offered the extra bedroom in my apartment. It has always been a strictly platonic relationship." Good to get that on record.

"While sharing an apartment, what did you observe about Miss Erikson's parenting?"

"For the most part, she paid attention to her daughter's needs. However, I don't know what happened while I was not there, and I work overtime frequently. On evenings when I was home, Miss Erikson would often ask me to watch her daughter while she went out dancing or drinking."

"Did you ever observe her drinking alcohol of any kind?"

"No, she never drank in front of Britney. I took Miss Erikson at her word for where she was and what she was doing."

With his forefinger, Spencer pushed his glasses back into place. "Do you allege any kind of illegal drug use?"

"There were rumors she was using methamphetamines. Until a couple of weeks ago, I didn't believe it."

"What changed your mind?"

"On the morning of October 15, Britney woke me up asking for breakfast. She told me her mother had left during the night before I got home. I tipped narcotics and they found her, high on meth, at a seller's house."

"Again, Officer Barnett, just what you observed."

Tony leaned forward. His forearm rested on his leg, pressing against the steel ball he had pocketed at the tow yard. "I observed her enter the jail booking area through the sallyport door, followed by the narcotics officer I had spoken with. I assumed by those observations that he had arrested her for narcotics use. Her mannerisms were consistent with drug use."

"Did you speak to her at that time?"

"I did, whereupon she attacked me." His English teacher would have been proud of that word.

"And you have proof of that?"

"Yes, several police witnesses."

"What, in your opinion, is in the best interest of the child?"

"That she be anywhere but with her mother."

Chapter Thirty-three

Rhythms of a mariachi band. Colors as vivid as exotic jungle birds. Spicy aromas that made the palate sit up and beg.

Beth drank it in as she and her mother followed the waiter to their table. The popularity of Su Casa was evident, even on a Tuesday night. The room brimmed with the buzz of conversations in both Spanish and English.

She accepted the menu from the waiter, though she didn't have to open it to know what she would order. Several months had gone by since she had eaten the restaurant's famous enchiladas. Mexican food might not be just what the doctor ordered for a pregnant woman with recurring heartburn, but she was willing to pay the price.

Suzanne flipped through the menu and set it down. "This was a good idea, Beth. It's nice to be talking again."

The waiter reappeared, saving Beth from responding, and took their orders, filling their water glasses before he left.

Beth sprinkled salt on a tortilla chip and scooped a chunk of salsa. "I went back to school today to talk to my classes and let them know what's going on. They were so sweet and caring. Even the boys." She wiped a drip from her chin.

Except for Luke, who seemed too uncomfortable with the situation to look at her, let alone make a comment or ask a question. His abrupt exit from the classroom was strange, too. He acted nothing like the boy who usually volunteered to help her file papers or make copies.

And that gruesome artwork.

"Beth, are you sure you should have done that? I mean, it's awfully soon after the funeral for you to go back in the classroom, to face all those curious stares. Did you break down in front of them?"

"I was able to hold it together. I answered a question about spiritual issues, so I definitely know I was supposed to be there and—" Tightness crept across her belly.

"What's wrong, honey?"

"Nothing, I guess. Maybe one of those Braxton-Hicks contractions I've read about, but it packed a wallop." She settled back into the booth as the pain receded. "I'm fine, really."

The Hispanic waiter appeared, two plates in his hands.

Beth caught her mother's eye and mouthed along with him. "Hot plate. Hot plate."

Beth brought her plate closer as the waiter moved on to another table. "That's the best part of Mexican dining. I mean, is there any other eating establishment that serves warnings with their food? You don't hear the wait staff at a steak house saying, 'Sharp knife. Sharp knife.'"

"At least some things stay the same." A smile lurked at the corner of Suzanne's mouth. "Have you decided what to do about work?"

"I told my students I was going to take a leave of absence for this first semester." Strings of melted cheese hung from Beth's fork. "I should have time to get everything sorted out regarding the accident before this little person arrives at the end of December. I plan on going back after spring break."

"Beth, my offer stands about taking care of the baby for you. I know you and Keith wanted to manage on your own, but I think you need me now more than ever."

"Let's see how it plays out." She sipped water, abdomen growing taut as it had before.

Suzanne added sour cream and guacamole to her chicken fajitas without glancing up.

"So, Mom, what was the important thing you wanted to tell me?"

Suzanne straightened in her chair. "You won't believe what happened this morning. Tony Barnett came by. The police officer."

Tony. She had pulled out her yearbook and found she'd been a few years behind him in school. Now the guy kept showing up. At the baseball field—she'd finally figured out where she'd first seen him—at the store, and at her mother's front door. Again.

"What did he want?"

"He found out some new information about the accident. The truck driver wasn't drunk. The police claim your father must have lost control of the car."

Beth wiped her mouth with her napkin. "No way. Dad wouldn't do that. Besides, the cop said he ran tests on the guy and he was drunk. Couldn't talk straight or anything."

"Well, now they're saying something different. According to the official report, it had something to do with diabetes, and the guy wasn't at fault."

"No, I simply can't believe it." Beth shook her head. "Dad's the one who lectured me about safe driving before I was ever interested in getting my license. 'Keep both hands on the steering wheel at all times. Constantly scan your rearview and side mirrors. Know where other drivers are.'" Her appetite suddenly gone, she forced herself to take another bite, tried to digest the implications of this new account of the accident.

Maybe she should talk to Tony herself, make sure her mom's bereavement was not affecting her ability to comprehend what had been said. Perhaps she had simply misunderstood.

Another pain gripped her belly. She stiffened, a soft moan escaping her lips.

Alarm spread over her mother's face.

She would have to offer an honest explanation as soon as the spasm ebbed.

"How often is that happening, honey?"

"I don't know. Four or five times an hour." A few more breaths and it was over. "I started having some after I left the school today. It's probably from the stress of everything."

"Maybe you should see your doctor. Or at least call him."

"I'm sure it's nothing to worry about, Mom."

Suzanne signaled a passing waiter and gave him her credit card. "I need to pay our check. Please see to it as quickly as you can."

He nodded and disappeared in the direction of the cash register.

"Mom, there's no rush. I'll tell the doctor what's happening at my appointment tomorrow. You can come along if it will make you feel any better."

"You're not going to buy me off that easily, Beth. How many contractions have you had since we've been here?"

"I haven't been keeping track, exactly." Beth clenched her knees together. "Several. Maybe quite a few. Another one's starting."

This one felt different. More intense, purposeful. Perhaps her mother's worry was justified. Dr. Norman would understand Beth's uncertainty. First-time mothers were often overly cautious, weren't they? Especially one who had recently lost her husband and father. The doctor would probably listen to her fears and reassure her that the baby was staying put for at least another month.

In the midst of the noisy restaurant, a gentle quiet settled over her soul, calmed her anxious heart. Whatever was happening, her Father was there, closer than any human could ever be.

Her mother gathered up her purse and coat.

“Mom, God has promised me this baby is going to be okay.”

“I don’t care what you think God promised. I’m calling your doctor.”

Chapter Thirty-four

Suzanne's heart fluttered when Beth excused herself to use the restroom. Maybe this was a false alarm, but what if it weren't?

She whipped her cell phone from her purse and went out to the lobby to make the call. A blank screen stared back, taunting her with an uncharged battery.

Wouldn't you know.

A pay phone glimmered on the wall.

The hostess counting a pile of bills behind the cash register looked up as Suzanne approached.

"Can I get a phone book? And change for a dollar?"

While waiting for the hospital operator to put her through to the appropriate nurse, Suzanne kept watch for Beth's return.

"Birthing Center. This is Laura."

"Yes, hi. My daughter's only thirty-three weeks pregnant, but she seems to be having contractions. I wondered if I should bring her in."

"How old is your daughter?" Deep concern colored her voice.

"Oh!" Suzanne blinked. "She's an adult, married and everything." And widowed.

"Is this her first baby?" Laura's voice sounded matter-of-fact.

"Yes."

"Is she in pain?"

"When she has a contraction? Yes, I think so. Not like with full-blown labor, but enough to get her attention. She's fine in between them, but obviously uncomfortable when one hits."

Beth returned to the dining area, and Suzanne waved her over to the lobby. Beth's face was paler than usual, the shadows under her eyes more pronounced.

"Sounds like it would be a good idea for her to come in. We can make sure everything's okay."

"Thanks. We'll be there soon." Suzanne hung the receiver in its cradle and handed Beth her coat. "Come on, honey. We're going to the hospital."

"Mom, what if we get there and they laugh at me because these aren't really contractions? One of my friends went to the hospital *four* times before she was in active labor. I don't want to be like that."

"The doctors and nurses are there to decide if you're all right or not. That's their job—let them do it. If nothing's wrong, nobody has to know we went." She led Beth out to the parking lot and to her car. "I'm driving."

Beth got in. Hands shaking, she struggled to fasten her seat belt. She closed her eyes and leaned her head back against the headrest.

Suzanne tried to keep her attention on the road instead of her daughter's face.

After a few minutes, Beth said, "These contractions are starting to hurt. While I'm having one, it's as if my mind can't focus, it's so preoccupied with my body. They're lasting longer."

"We're almost there. You want me to run this red light?" She asked in jest, but didn't rule out the possibility.

By the time they reached the turnoff to the hospital, Beth huddled over her stomach, whimpering.

Not sure where to go, Suzanne chose the emergency room lane and parked against the curb. She'd worry later about moving the car. There were more important things to take care of at the moment. She ran around to Beth's side, opened the car door, and grabbed hold of Beth's elbow. "Here, let me help."

They entered the hospital. The cacophony pouring from the ER waiting room assaulted her ears. A young man stood at the check-in desk, holding a bloody cloth to his head. The older woman next to him was yelling at the receptionist in a foreign tongue, her hands flailing as if gestures would help her be understood. A large group, all talking at once, filled the corner across the room.

"Let's skip this," Suzanne said. "We don't know whether you'll need to check in or not."

"Wait, Mom." Beth leaned into the wall and groaned.

"Breathe, honey. Just breathe."

"I don't know how. I haven't had a birthing class yet."

Suzanne rubbed Beth's shoulder and looked around for help.

An aide appeared at the end of the hall.

Suzanne waved her hand in the air to get his attention.

He snagged an empty wheel chair and hurried toward them. "Looks like we better get you to the fourth floor." He eased Beth into the chair and placed her feet on the footrests.

Suzanne answered his questions as they waited for the elevator.

A white-haired nurse, experience evident in her calm demeanor, took over for the aide when they got off the elevator. "Hi, I'm Laura. We've been expecting you." She glanced at Suzanne before squatting down to Beth's eye level.

"How are you doing? Still having those contractions?"

"Yes, but it's too early. I've got weeks to go."

"Well, let's get you in a gown and put a monitor on to see what's happening. If you *are* in active labor, we'll do our best to stop your contractions and give your little one more growing time. Do you know what you're having?"

"No, we chose not to find out."

Minutes later, Beth lay in the hospital bed, a Velcro belt holding the monitor against her belly.

Suzanne sat in a chair beside the bed, watching the ever-changing numbers of the baby's heartbeat on the nearby machine. A paper tape, spilling from the printer to the floor, tracked the intensity of contractions.

Laura examined Beth and studied the markings on the paper. "Your mom was right, Beth—you're officially in labor. I'll give Dr. Norman a heads-up and let him know you're here and dilating. He'll probably order something to stop the contractions, or at least slow them down. Could be a quick shot or some pills. Sometimes a simple IV works. I'll be back in a minute to examine you." Laura disappeared around the privacy curtain surrounding the bed.

Suzanne didn't want privacy. She wanted someone medical to stay in the room, able to respond to Beth's needs as soon as they arose.

"Mom?" Fear and pain made Beth's voice nearly unrecognizable. "I've got to use the bathroom."

"I'm not sure you're supposed to get up, Beth. Besides, you went a little bit ago."

"But, Mom ..." Beth's voice grew silent for a moment before becoming a wail.

A gush of liquid soaked the bed.

Suzanne sprang up and jabbed the call button.

The door burst open.

Laura shoved aside the privacy curtain. "What's happening?"

The sound of Beth's panting filled the room.

Laura washed her hands and pulled on a pair of latex gloves.

"Mrs. Corbin, could you step outside for a few minutes? I need to examine your daughter again."

"My mom … is staying." Beth sounded stronger, though her breathing was ragged. "I want her here."

Laura smiled and patted the back of Beth's hand before proceeding with the exam.

Suzanne watched the nurse's face, caught the flicker of concern before the flame of activity.

Laura ripped the gloves from her hands, stuck her head out the door, and hollered, "I need some help in here!"

Suzanne moved to the head of the bed, out of the way of the commotion around her. "It's okay, it's okay," she crooned, as much to herself as to her daughter. The situation seemed to be spiraling out of control, changing with every second.

The nurses tossed words back and forth. "Fully dilated." "Plus-two station." "Umbilical cord presenting."

Laura paused in the midst of the hubbub. "Beth, let me explain what's happening. Your baby isn't waiting any longer. We need to get the little one out as soon as possible, because the umbilical cord is in front of the head. Every time you have a contraction, the head presses on the cord, depriving the baby of oxygen."

A third nurse entered the room. "Dr. Norman is on his way."

"I hope he makes it in time," Laura murmured. "Get the O_2 going."

Suzanne moved aside as the nurse placed an oxygen mask on Beth's face and blotted beads of sweat from her brow.

Beth twisted on the bed, groaning, and grabbed her belly.

Suzanne's stomach clenched. Why hadn't they given her anything for pain?

"Don't push yet, Beth." Laura's voice was firm. She opened a sterile package and arranged the instruments on a metal tray.

"I … can't … help it," Beth gasped. Her hand wrapped around Suzanne's so tightly it prevented blood from reaching her fingertips.

Laura spoke from her position at the foot of the bed. "Listen to me, Beth. Everything's going to be fine. I want you to put your feet right here." She touched a metal brace on each side of the bed. "With the next contraction, you can go ahead and push. And Grandma, you help her lean forward."

Suzanne moved into place.

Laura glanced at the monitor. "Here comes another contraction. Tuck your head to your chest, Beth. Take a deep breath in. And out. And in. Now bear down."

Beth's shoulders shook as she grunted.

With a single push, the child entered the world.

Laura caught the bundle of flesh and the baby whimpered a raspy complaint.

"It's a boy!" Suzanne clapped a hand over her open mouth.

"Great job, Beth. He looks good." Laura laid the baby on Beth's abdomen, suctioned the baby's mouth with a rubber bulb, and cut the cord.

The baby's purple face wrinkled as if to wail.

Beth's fingers explored his slippery skin. "Is he okay?"

The curtain screeched along its track as a white-coated man yanked it out of the way.

Laura looked up. "Sorry, Dr. Norman, you missed the stork. Don't worry, though. I signed for your delivery."

He chuckled. "I've got to work on my timing." He laid a hand on Beth's propped up knee. "I apologize for not making it here soon enough, but you don't give a doctor a lot of leeway, do you?"

Another doctor entered the room, pushing a small baby bed. Two other medical people followed him.

Dr. Norman put a hand on her shoulder. "Beth, this is Dr. Reeser, the on-duty pediatrician. His team is going to take your baby for a thorough assessment."

Dr. Reeser whisked the baby from atop Beth's stomach into the tiny crib, his gaze fixed on the baby.

"Wait. Why are you taking him?" Beth struggled to sit up. "Is he okay? I want to hold my baby."

"I'm sorry, ma'am." Dr. Reeser pushed the bed toward the door. "If he's really seven weeks early, we've got to get him to intensive care right away."

Chapter Thirty-five

Laura passed her badge in front of the scanner, and the door to the nursery unlocked. "We'll need to wash before we see the baby."

Suzanne trailed her to the sink. Squirting soap into her palm, she studied the small neonatal unit. Curtains ran along tracks in the ceiling. Most were pulled out from the wall to form dividers and were left open at the front so the nurses could see the babies.

Only two of the nearby cribs were taken, as far as Suzanne could tell.

"Hey, Janet," Laura called out. "How's the new baby boy doing?"

A nurse popped her head around the farthest curtain. She walked up and set her coffee mug on the counter. A smile spread across her face. "Quite exciting for you, huh, Laura? I heard you delivered him."

"Can you believe it? I didn't really do anything more than catch him. This is his grandmother, Suzanne."

Suzanne had never expected her first introduction as a grandparent to come from one nurse to another in the middle of a nursery. "Nice to meet you."

"Oh, he's a beautiful boy." Janet tsked, two thick black braids rattling down each side of her face. "Right now, though, he is struggling to breathe. His retractions are pretty bad—chest near touches his backbone—but the docs want to wait awhile and see how he does since he's so big." She led them back the way she had come.

Suzanne's grandson lay under some kind of contraption on an open-bed warmer at the far end of the nursery. The blue information card taped to the incubator listed his particulars as four pounds, eleven ounces, sixteen inches long.

"I'm hoping your daughter was farther along than she thought." Laura studied the infant. "He might be a couple weeks older, gestationally speaking."

Suzanne gazed at him, drinking in the first real look at the next generation.

They had bathed him already. His body was filled out more than the gangly, frog-like form she expected of a preemie. A translucent box with a semi-circle cut out for a neck hole covered his head. Condensation made it difficult to make out his features.

Laura tipped the box back, revealing his dewy, purplish face. A creamy white substance had been spread over his closed eyes.

"What's that box for?" Suzanne grazed a finger along the bottom of his foot.

"It's like a miniature oxygen tent. Nice, hydrated, warm air for him to breathe." Janet touched his other foot, his pale toes curling around her dark finger.

His shoulder twitched.

"Aren't you adorable?" Laura cooed. "Janet, do you have a camera handy? His mom barely had time to look at him before Dr. Reeser took him."

Janet scavenged through a cupboard. "Too sad. That's one of my favorite parts."

Laura moved the oxygen box to the side. "What part?"

Janet handed Laura the Polaroid camera. "Putting the

child in his mother's arms for the first time. The instant bonding. The sudden weight of responsibility. Women transform into mamas right before my eyes."

"His mom will have that chance in a little while." Laura took a picture, the flash momentarily brightening the nursery. "When her son is breathing better."

The nurses talked, moving over to the desk, as Suzanne stared at the baby boy. "Hey, buddy," she whispered. "Your grandpa would have loved to be here for this. He always wanted a chance to love his own little boy. A grandson would please him even more, I think. He would have spoiled you rotten."

The infant's ribs jutted out like the frame of a covered wagon. Near his sternum, a concavity sank and rebounded with each breath. Monitors were stuck to his chest, wires snaking out of the bed and into several machines.

"I'm your grandma, but you can call me Granny, or Nana, or anything you want."

Dark hair peeked out from under a blue and pink striped hat.

She pinched the top of the hat and pulled. Brown wisps covered his firm little head. Cupping her hand beneath it, she grazed the fuzz with her thumb. "You're beautiful. So beautiful."

His eyes opened to slits, then spread farther apart to reveal deep blue. He searched for the sound of her voice, found her after a few squirms, and gazed at her. Hospital bracelets, an inch in diameter, bounced toward his shoulder as he brought a fist to his cheek and blinked.

"You found your face."

He extended his thin fingers and poked himself in the eye.

Arms and legs spread-eagled with a jump.

She laughed and slipped his hat back on.

Beth should be here.

Recent events had taught her that "shoulds" rarely happened. Instead, Beth lay alone in a hospital bed waiting for her mom to come back and report that the baby was fine.

She planted a kiss on his sweet hand. "I'll be back soon. You keep breathing and everything's going to be okay."

Leaving him, she hurried to the nurse's desk. "Can we take that picture to my daughter?"

"Of course." Laura plucked it off the desk. "I didn't want to rush you."

As they left the room, Janet called out as she replaced the oxygen hood, "Make sure and get his name for me as soon as you can. I want to start singing his song."

Suzanne turned left down the corridor. "Singing his song?"

"I'm not sure if it's a Native American custom or not, but if a baby's born while Janet's on duty, she sings a welcoming song."

Laura flapped the stiff photo a few times and handed it to Suzanne. The baby's features had appeared, emerging from the gray cloud of the fresh Polaroid. Though Janet had said it wasn't the same as placing a warm, swaddled babe in Beth's arms, the picture did hold a promise for the future.

A promise, not from God, as Beth would say, but from the medical advances of the last few years. Babies born much earlier in pregnancies turned out fine, so why wouldn't a strong, perfect boy like her grandson?

Laura knocked on Beth's open door.

"Guess what I have for you?" Suzanne offered the picture.

Beth grabbed the photo from her grasp.

"Look at your boy. Keith would be so proud."

Beth held the picture as if it were food set before a starving man. "You're right, Mom." Hair had fallen from her French braid in gentle tendrils around her face. "I think Keith's watching right now."

Laura moved up to the bed. "I'm going to check your blood pressure, okay?"

Beth flopped an arm toward the nurse, never taking her gaze away from the photograph.

Laura slid the cuff onto Beth's arm. "Have you got a name for him yet? The nursery asked me to find out."

Beth giggled. "Mom, should I name him Enchilada since I had him instead of finishing the one I ordered at dinner?"

Suzanne chuckled. The nurse had to be impressed by Beth's attitude.

Laura undid the cuff. "Your blood pressure's fine. I'll get you admitted properly and find you some food. In a little while, I'll wheel you over to see him."

"Thank you. All joking aside, I know what to name him." Beth glowed. "God promised him to me like he promised a baby to Sarah in the Bible, so his name has to be Isaac. Isaac Keith Harris."

Chapter Thirty-six

The sun's heat danced over Beth's face. The aroma of cocoa butter swam around her nose. Opening her eyes, she sat up and propped her elbows behind her.

Keith squatted beside her, unrolling a bamboo mat. Palm trees rose behind him. "You couldn't be farther from big land anywhere else on earth."

"What are you doing here? Why did you leave me?" Beth's voice drifted across the sand. How could she sound so calm when she should be furious? He had left her all alone and didn't seem to think a thing about it.

Keith grabbed her hand. "I've been swimming. Come see the fish."

Already, at his words, they were in the ocean, floating next to each other, heads submerged. Triangles of orange, slashes of red, and lines of blue flitted past. Keith kicked hard and shot deeper underwater, pulling her with him.

Beth couldn't keep up. Her hand slipped.

Air. She had to breathe. One finger at a time, she released his hand and struggled up, toward the haze of light.

She broke through the surface, gasping, and found herself in Keith's embrace. Water slid off her arms as warm air wrapped around her. Solid ground formed under their feet and other people appeared. Instead of her swimsuit, a flowered cotton dress hung from her frame.

The black sky held pinpricks of white light in place as music started playing. When the Hawaiian band announced the wedding song, Keith spun her across the dance floor under the enchanting night. Hundreds of newlyweds surrounded them, yet in his arms, they were separate, cocooned.

The song ended.

Keith draped a lei of yellow plumeria over Beth's neck and stepped back. "I'm sorry, I have to go now." He pressed his hand to his mouth and blew a kiss toward Beth.

The heady scent of the blossoms slowed Beth's response. "Wait. I have something to tell you, something important. You can't keep coming and going whenever you want."

She woke, clutching the hospital sheet to her chest, and used the fabric to wipe her tears. A faint glow lit the room.

On their honeymoon, Keith and she had done everything in the dream. Snorkeled hand in hand, tugging and pointing for underwater communication. Lolled on bamboo mats, soaking up the drying rays of sun. Slow danced as the sun fell into the ocean, creating sizzling reds and flaming oranges in its last moments.

They had done those things, but the memories had faded. How long until the things they had done shortly before his death hazed and disappeared?

Beth clenched her teeth and tried to remember more. She could imagine the picture of their silhouettes in front of the sunset, but could not evoke the emotions she felt looking into Keith's eyes. Or exactly what his eyes had looked like. She could recall sitting on their mats on Kaheliki beach, but had forgotten the feel of his hand as he brushed sand from her leg.

Even in the short time since his death, the reality of Keith eroded, drifting out of her mind like an expert swimmer caught in a rip current. No matter how hard she tried to hold on to him, he would slip away more every day. How could she keep him alive in her heart? And could she bear the hurt to peel off each day's callous to keep him alive enough so his son would know him?

Lifting her head, she felt under the lumpy hospital pillow and pulled out Isaac's picture. A beautiful boy, but something was missing. There should have been two babies cradled in the arms of their proud father.

Instead, she was on her own, arms empty.

"Beth?" A nurse stepped into the room. "I'm glad you're awake. In a few minutes, the doctor needs to talk to you about your baby."

"What time is it?" Beth placed the photo on the bedside table.

"Almost six A.M."

"How's Isaac?"

"I'm sure they would tell you right away if there were a problem."

"But it's so early."

"Babies are up at all hours, as are doctors." The nurse yawned.

Beth pushed herself up and slid her legs off the edge of the bed. "Can you help me to the bathroom first? I feel a little shaky."

She was easing back into bed when Dr. Reeser entered the room. "Good morning, Beth. I'm sorry to say it's been a tough night for your son. His size led us to believe he might have been older than you thought, but his lungs are definitely underdeveloped."

"Why didn't anyone wake me?"

"He's in no immediate danger, but he's been working too

hard for too long. Young babies don't have much of an energy reserve. I put in a call to St. Andrews in Portland. They sent an ambulance team which should arrive anytime."

"What will they do?" Beth crossed her hands over her soft, empty stomach.

"They are bringing some drugs and equipment that will help him breathe better. If you choose to keep him here, we'll administer the drugs and continue monitoring him, but I'd recommend letting the team take him back to St. Andrews."

Cobwebs of sleep clung to her thoughts. "Drugs?" They wanted to take Isaac to the very place his father had died?

"He needs at least one dose of surfactant. His lungs didn't have time to develop completely, so they aren't fully inflating. That means he has to work harder to get the oxygen he needs. The medicine will open up the smaller air sacs and increase his oxygen level."

She had seen Isaac the night before—stroked his cheek, counted his toes, and been amazed at God's creation. But she still hadn't really held him yet. Now they wanted to take him farther away from her?

Her stomach tightened and her chest throbbed. "Can I see him again before I make my decision?"

"Of course." Dr. Reeser held out a clipboard of various papers. "Here's the consent form for the ambulance." The doctor lingered at the bedside. "Laura told me you recently lost your husband. I'm sure this is hard, coming so soon afterward. I want you to know that if Isaac were my boy, I'd sign the forms right away. We're a little hospital and we do a great job with what we have, but we aren't well prepared to care for an infant of a lower gestational age than thirty-five weeks or so."

"You thought I was farther along? That's why you kept him here instead of calling St. Andrews right away?"

"We had hoped." Dr. Reeser checked his watch. "I'll meet you in the nursery when the ambulance crew arrives."

Beth pulled her hair back with the elastic band she'd worn the day before. She lacked clean clothes, makeup, and personal toiletries. Packing her birthing bag had not been scheduled for a few more weeks. But she had already bought an extra memory card and a going-home outfit in greens and yellows for the baby. The clothes would be much too big on his little form, and when would he get to come home anyway?

In this modern world full of convenience and gadgets to memorialize every event, she had no video and no digital pictures to email to the extended family. Isaac's birth had been reduced to a solitary Polaroid.

She tucked the picture in the pocket of the hospital-issued robe and shuffled to the nursery.

A new nurse on duty greeted her.

Beth didn't bother to look at the man's name tag. "I'm visiting my son, Isaac Harris."

Isaac looked the same as the last time she'd seen him. Wearing only a diaper, he lay on his back. He didn't seem to be suffering, though his chest sunk in so deeply it seemed to touch the mattress beneath him. Anger flashed down her arms to her fists. Why hadn't they believed her due date? Why had they made Isaac fight to breathe for the first eleven hours of his life?

Again, a loved one's life in the balance.

She forced herself to relax. "I'm sorry, baby. I'm going to let some people take you to another place so you can breathe better."

Dr. Reeser came in followed by five people in matching scrubs. They carried coolers, machines, and other gear.

Beth stepped in front of the bed.

"Mrs. Harris, these are the folks from St. Andrew's. What would you like them to do?"

"I'll sign the release for his transport."

Dr. Reeser nodded. "I think that's the wisest thing."

Her baby was leaving her and he wasn't even a day old. "Doctor?"

"Yes?"

Never mind that she was exhausted. Never mind that she had just given birth. She would not be separated from her son. "I'm going with him."

Chapter Thirty-seven

The morning's late autumn rain drenched the accident site. With each step, clumps of mud clung to Tony's boots, slowing his progress. He put a hand against the trunk of a Douglas fir for balance and scraped his foot along a fallen log, moss running down its back in a smooth velvet line.

A plane buzzed low overhead, cutting through the metal-gray sky. Clouds bulged in the west. A storm was brewing. Same as one had the night of the accident a little more than a week ago.

What was he searching for, anyway? Signs of whatever had happened had long been washed away.

Cries of geese and the answering bark of a dog sounded in the distance as he continued to wander. Would he know it when he found it? The elusive piece that would fill in the blank? A confirmation that the steel ball had something to do with the accident?

He wasn't sure, but years on the force taught him to go with his gut. Follow his instincts and not stop until he was satisfied. So here he was, walking around the accident site, searching for concrete answers to nebulous questions.

Mrs. Corbin's vehement objection to the findings of the accident reconstruction team rang in his ears. A normal reaction to the situation, a zip tie of denial holding together her grief.

Her argument that Jake Corbin was a safe driver hadn't meant a lot until Tony ran a background check that showed the guy never got a ticket. Not a one. And the medical examiner stressing the impact of the right temple on the steering wheel … it didn't add up. Anyone facing a semi would swerve to the right, try to find a way to escape the inevitable. Jake Corbin didn't sound like the suicidal type.

A logging truck rumbled by, downshifting to climb the hill with its heavy load.

Tony turned and made his way back to the edge of the rural highway. He stood beside the makeshift memorial, contemplating the various items surrounding the two small crosses erected in honor of each man who had lost his life. A short poem about angels taking flight from the spot; a sodden, dirty teddy bear; bunches of flowers, their petals battered by recent rains.

Enough of this Mr. Corbin, Mr. Harris stuff. Jake and Keith. He could call them by name. Two men had died, and he wanted to know why.

He stuck his hand into his pants pocket, fingered the round, smooth steel, the reason for his rainy-day tromp. It was so out of place in the wrecked car; something neither man would have been likely to possess.

Tony bent and grabbed a deflated rubber balloon attached to the bottom of a cross. As he cut the knotted string, his fingers snagged on a piece of dirty rubber tubing stretching up from one end of a muddy stick.

He pulled the rest of it out of the ground. A fork-shaped frame of a homemade slingshot.

No way.

The summer Tony turned ten, his dad had taken him to a meadow. As Timothy grass swayed around them, his father had handed him a bag filled with small steel balls.

Then handed him a slingshot.

Out in the field, Pop had taught him how to use the slingshot to kill birds that went after the fruit on the apple trees, something the animal rights activists would raise a stink about today—though if they knew what a poor shot he'd been, they would have saved their energy for something more important.

He could imagine a father and son engineering the slingshot he held. Finding the perfect kind of wood, shaping and sanding it, discovering the correct tension for the tubing to render a proficient shot. He flipped the weapon over in his hands, noticed a letter carved into the handle. Was it someone's initial? He wiped the mud off on nearby grass, inspected the mark again. No, not initials, but a single word: *Sorry*.

What did that mean? And why was it left here? Without a doubt, it was connected to the lone piece of ammunition he'd found in the car.

He slipped the slingshot into his back pocket, zipped his jacket up to his neck. A cold front was blowing in. Rain would soon arrive again, reinforcing the stereotype of Northwest weather. If he were going to look for more clues, he'd better hurry.

The urgency to scout for more evidence overrode his obligation to get to the station, and Tony crossed the road. A glance at his watch told him he needed to book it. No reason to make Chief upset by showing up late to work.

The terrain on this side of the road was steeper, more heavily forested. His foot caught in the tendrils of a blackberry vine and he pitched forward, breaking through an invisible spider web hanging between two trees. Great. Cobweb covered his jacket, mud splattered his pant legs. Very professional.

He hiked a little farther before stopping to catch his breath, scuffing the toe of his boot through the mix of oak leaves and pine needles covering the ground as he gazed down on the accident site. He was enclosed in a natural shelter formed by dried weeds intermingled with bushes of poison oak. Waist high, the undergrowth opened up, providing an unobstructed view of the highway.

Head down, Tony combed the ground, searching for the clue that had to be there. He worked his way in a widening spiral. Within a few minutes, he found it.

The small bag of steel shot lay on its side, balls spilling out as if they had been dropped at random with no further thought of the consequences. At least a hundred balls scattered over the area. He picked up the packaging of the Fly-True balls and read the label on the front. "Warning: A slingshot is not a toy. Adult supervision is recommended. Misuse or carelessness may cause serious injury or death."

Tony groaned. Something *had* distracted Jake Corbin and caused him to swerve into the path of the unsuspecting truck. A steel ball shot from a homemade slingshot striking the window, shattering the glass, would do the trick.

Carrying the bag down the hill, he anticipated the upcoming conversation with his boss. Chief would need to initiate a new investigation, and Tony would make sure he was part of it. Especially part of telling the widows their men did not die from Jake's recklessness after all.

When he got to his patrol car, Tony took the slingshot from his back pocket and placed it and the bag of steelies in an evidence bag. He unzipped his jacket, threw it over the back of the seat, and sought the protection of his vehicle.

Rain began to fall. The wind hissed through the treetops as it whipped branches back and forth like wiper blades on high. Yep, the storm was about to hit.

He could feel it in his bones.

Chapter Thirty-eight

Chief pushed his office chair back from the messy desk and clasped his hands behind his head. "So, Barnett, you think it's worth opening the case again, huh? Think you've got evidence against someone?"

"A slam-dunk. The steelie in the victim's car, the slingshot and ammo at the site. Seems pretty tight to me. Now I've gotta find the perp."

The chief stroked his mustache with an index finger, as if contemplating the worth of Tony's argument. "Well, I suppose I can assign somebody to the case. Might be worth looking into."

"Assign *somebody*?" Tony shot from his seat, placed his hands on the desk, and leaned toward Chief. He knew he'd been in trouble, but—"My name's *Somebody*, sir."

"I was playing you, man." The chief chuckled, reached for the mug on his desk and cringed as a swig of station coffee cruised down his throat. "Don't know why I keep drinking this stuff. It's thicker than tar and doesn't taste much better." He wiped the back of his hand across his mouth. "Okay, Barnett, you're on it. Let me know what you find."

Tony snapped a sharp salute in answer and strode out of the station to his car. The rain came down harder, wind howling. He slid behind the steering wheel, turned the key in the ignition, and punched the button for the heater as he contemplated his next move.

It took all of ten minutes to drive across town to the

middle school. He'd hit the high school next, then the elementary. Hunching his shoulders for protection, he pulled his hat low as he loped up the slippery brick steps. He brushed water from his jacket, wiped his feet on the large blue mat inside the heavy doors, and headed toward the school office, damp soles of his boots squeaking in protest. Good thing he wasn't trying to sneak up on anyone.

The dreaded odor of learning lingered in the hall, mixed with wet coats and dry-erase markers. Chalkboards had disappeared years ago, much to his dismay. School didn't seem like school without chalk dust hanging in the air. He sniffed, tried to catch a whiff of Tuna Wiggle that the lunch ladies served in the cafeteria back in the day. These kids didn't realize how lucky they were to have choices in the lunchroom.

The walk to the front office reminded him of the many he took as a student nearly twenty years ago. He made frequent visits to the inner sanctum of the principal's office after his mother left and he found trouble.

"Hi, Mrs. Corey, how's it going?"

The secretary jumped at the sound of his voice, then batted her eyes when she saw who it was. She left her computer screen and came over to the counter. "How many times do I have to tell you to call me Jill?"

Tony winked. "I just can't. Even after all these years, it wouldn't be right to be on a first-name basis with someone who used to escort me to detention."

"You weren't all that bad, you know. You needed a little extra care, is all. Some time to sort through what was happening in your life, things out of your control."

Their conversation halted when a young boy came in requesting a Band-Aid for his skinned elbow.

Mrs. Corey administered the needed first aid with a proper amount of concern and sent him back to his classroom. "So, Tony, are you stopping by for old time's sake, or are you here in an official capacity? I didn't forget about a D.A.R.E. program scheduled for today, did I?"

"No, I'm looking for some names and addresses and thought you could probably help me out."

"I wouldn't ordinarily give out this information without running it by the principal, but she's out of the office for the day. Our policy protects the students, you know. May I ask why you need it?"

"Would it make any difference if I told you it has to do with an investigation concerning Keith Harris?"

Her hand rose to her chest and tears misted her eyes. "Oh, bless his soul. His wife was in here yesterday, trying to be so brave." She grabbed a tissue from a nearby box and soaked up the tears threatening to fall. "We all feel so badly about the whole thing. What do you need to know?"

"I'd like a list of the kids who live ten to twenty miles out on Highway 41." If he were lucky, there would be only a couple youngsters living in that direction. People far from town tended to have big chunks of property with lots of elbowroom between neighbors. Should help him narrow his search.

Mrs. Corey stepped back to her computer. A short time later she said, "I'll print this out for you."

Tony smiled his thanks. Within moments, the list was in his hand. He scanned the paper—at least ten different addresses. It would take time to go house to house and conduct interviews, ask if anyone had seen something suspicious on the day of the accident.

"I appreciate your help, Mrs. Corey."

She pulled the edge of her sweater over her ample hips and glanced up at the large clock hanging over the door. "Almost time for the bell to ring for lunch, Tony. Sure you don't want to stay?"

"No, I'd better get working on this list. Maybe another time."

"I'd like that, I really would. And I haven't seen you at mass for a while. Are you doing okay?"

No denying she was right. It had been longer than "a while" since he had shown his face at church. Somehow he got out of the habit, decided he could do fine without it. Weeks, maybe months, passed without him giving a single thought to the faith he had once been a part of.

"I'm fine, Mrs. Corey, just busy. You know how it is. But maybe I'll surprise you and show up some Sunday."

A smile lit her face. "You do that, and I'll fix you a home-cooked meal afterward. It won't be the same as cafeteria food, but it'll do."

He waved good-bye and headed back to the parking lot. The wind and rain had let up. Reaching for the door handle of his cruiser, he thought of one more thing that would help with the investigation. He retraced his steps to the secretary's office.

Mrs. Corey seemed puzzled when he reentered the room. "Did you change your mind about lunch?"

Tony pulled the printout from his pocket and slid it toward her. "Could you look up the attendance record of these kids? Were any of them absent last week?"

"Not that I remember, but I can certainly check." She brought up the information on her computer screen. "Oh, of course. How could I have forgotten? Only one of them missed school all last week. I felt so sorry for him."

"Who was it?"

"Luke Winslow. He was out with a bad case of poison oak."

Chapter Thirty-nine

Heart in her throat, Beth held her mother's arm. St. Andrew's Neonatal Intensive Care Unit dwarfed Beaver Falls's nursery. Each step plunged her deeper into a shadowy world of beeping machines and unknown fates.

A nurse in colorful scrubs, tummy rounded with pregnancy, greeted Beth by name and guided them to a stainless steel sink. "I'm sure you're anxious to see your son, so we can wash while I talk. Every time you come in, you need to wash thoroughly. Not only are you providing a safer environment for your baby, but for the other babies here in Level Three." She tweaked the hot and cold handles at the same time, sending a thump of water into the sink. "I'm Tara. I'll be taking care of Isaac for the next few hours, but I'm also here to answer your questions and help with anything I can."

"Thanks, Tara." Beth's thoughts stacked one upon the other, forming a deck that constantly shuffled in priority. No—everything could wait until after she saw Isaac. Rinsing her hands, she glanced over her shoulder, searching for him. As a mother, shouldn't she be able to feel where he was?

Babies lay in tiny incubators six feet from each other in the open room, each surrounded by a variety of machines on five-pronged stands with wheels, like starfish hovering over the dark floor.

As Beth and Suzanne followed Tara, a woman in a rocking chair glanced up. Her gaze darted back to the bundle she held.

Had her baby been born early? Or did it have a birth defect? An illness? Beth didn't have time to contemplate any other possibilities—they had reached Isaac.

Clear glass edged the rectangular incubator. He was curled on his side, a rolled blanket wedged behind his back. A tube stretched his mouth unnaturally wide. A crisscross of tape held the breathing tube in place, distorting his features.

Suzanne gasped. "Why does he have a tube in his mouth?"

"It looks much worse than it is." Tara traced along the tube, pointing out the corresponding machine. "We put him on a ventilator, so he wouldn't waste any energy breathing. It may look like a setback, but it's actually for the best, and the doctors here have the most experience intubating premature babies of any in the county."

Beth scanned his body. Two new hospital IDs circled his wrist and ankle.

Tara touched her arm. "We've got a bracelet for you to wear. The numbers on it match his, a security measure. Proves you're his mother."

She stared at Isaac as Tara wrapped the plastic band around her wrist. "How is he?"

"I know it can be a little imposing to see so many things attached to your baby, but really, he's doing well. His oxygen saturation level has remained steady at ninety-two percent."

"What's on his chest?"

Tara swept her hand beside the incubator. "Those stickers send the numbers all these monitors read. We keep an eye on his vitals. For example, this—" Tara pointed at a green display "—is the oxygen saturation level I was talking about. The Velcro band around his foot monitors his heartbeat."

Beth hung back.

A little splint tucked with cotton held an IV in place on Isaac's arm. Under all the tubes and lines and monitors, he slept, unaware of the stress his early birth had caused.

"We can raise or lower the hood, depending on what Isaac needs." Tara's watch beeped. "Time for his first feeding. Are you planning to breastfeed or use formula?"

"I'm going to nurse."

Tara turned Isaac onto his back. "Obviously, he's not going to be able to nurse while he's on the ventilator. Did anyone at the other hospital show you how to pump?"

"They did, right before they released me. I brought the little bit I could get." She unsnapped the insulated bag Beaver Falls hospital had given her. Handing the four-ounce bottle to the nurse, she became painfully aware of how empty it seemed. A mere quarter inch of yellowish liquid swirled in the bottom.

"Wow." Tara held the bottle up to the light. "That's great for your first time. We've got a persistent mother in here who's been trying for weeks and has never gotten a single drop. She's not giving up yet, though."

"Good for her." *Thank you, Lord.* She couldn't handle that.

Tara threaded a tube into Isaac's nose, uncapped it, and plugged a syringe onto the end, filling it with Beth's meager offering. Milliliter by milliliter, Tara pushed the food through the feeding tube. "This is the first step. When he's breathing on his own, you'll be able to put him to breast, though he won't be able to suck very well. Babies born this early are not able to suck, swallow, and breathe at the same time, which leads either to choking or not breathing."

Beth stepped closer to the incubator. "How will he eat?"

The syringe emptied. "We'll try bottles with nipples specially designed to promote the sucking reflex. Any milk he can't take in that way, we gavage, which is what I'm doing." Tara removed the syringe and recapped the tube. "I'll show you our milk storage system, which uses color-coordinated stickers for each baby. Anything you pump overnight, bring in the next visit. We use mama milk first, but we supplement with formula if we need to." Tara bent down.

Beth stooped to see what she was doing.

A shelf under the bed held diapers the size of dainty handkerchiefs, ointment, a thermometer, and a long, tube-like pacifier.

"We check their temperature every three hours. If you're here, you can do that for the nurse, but right now, what your boy needs is a diaper change."

Straightening up, Beth looked at her mother and grimaced. How was she supposed to change him with all those things stuck to him?

Faces of all the children she'd babysat flashed through her mind. No teenager had loved babies more than she had, and the sheer number of diapers she changed must rival any parent's record, but no baby had been the size of a doll.

Beth turned to Tara. "You go ahead and do it while I watch."

"Oh, no." Tara's ponytail swayed. "You don't need to be afraid to touch him. You're his mother, and he needs you to care for him."

Sighing, she took the tiny diaper and unfolded it. "Do I do anything differently?"

"Instead of wipes, we use damp paper towels."

Suzanne wet two paper towels at the sink and brought the warm squares to Beth. "Because of allergies?"

Tara nodded. "These babies tend to have sensitive skin. They needed weeks and weeks longer in the womb to protect them from our harsh world out here. We keep the lights as low as possible for the same reason."

Beth pulled back the old diaper's strips on each side of Isaac's tummy and clasped both of his ankles in one hand.

His body lifted like a bag of cotton candy.

Beth wiped him, removed the old diaper, and slid the new one under. Yes, he was so much smaller than other babies, but the act seemed normal. Normal, yet so special to do for her own child.

"Wasn't too bad, right?" Tara took the dirty diaper. "Once he's taking milk orally, never throw these away until the nurses have weighed them. We keep track of his intake and output."

Suzanne nudged Beth. "Ask her."

Tara dropped the diaper into the trash. "Ask me what?"

Beth stared at Isaac, arms aching.

"She wants to hold him for the first time," her mother said.

Tara cocked her head at Beth. "You haven't gotten to yet?"

"No, but I don't need to." Beth stepped back. "I really think he's better off being left alone, so a monitor doesn't come off or something."

"His vitals are stable and he's tolerating touch well, so I don't see why you shouldn't." Tara unrolled the blanket that had been propped behind Isaac's back and wrapped it around him. "Can you pull that rocker a bit closer so the cords will reach?"

Legs trembling from all the standing, Beth sank into the cushioned chair. Okay, the shaking might be from the idea of actually holding her baby in her arms for the first time. Without Keith.

An alarm sounded as Tara tucked the blanket around Isaac's chest. She laid him back down, opened the blanket, and reaffixed the errant sticker.

"Tara?" Another nurse handed Tara a light-blue surgical mask. "They're ready to start."

Tara groaned. "Beth, I'm so sorry. Dr. Kendal put us on alert for another little patient's surgery. I didn't think the team would be ready so soon."

"Are you helping with the surgery?"

"No. Some babies are so fragile, they can't be moved, so the surgeons basically bring the operating room to the baby. We make it as sterile as possible."

"I can still hold Isaac, right?"

"No, I'm sorry."

Beth dropped her head back against the crown of the rocking chair and stared at the hanging ceiling, each panel of it covered with dots as profuse as her regret.

"It gets worse. All parents need to leave the unit during the surgery."

Blinking her eyes, Beth beat the tears back. She should have asked to hold him right away, should have changed the diaper without hesitating. If the monitor hadn't beeped, Isaac would have been in her arms for at least a moment. "How long will the surgery last?"

"An hour or two. Plus, the unit closes to parents for shift change from 5:45 to 6:30. We transfer our assignments to the oncoming nurses during that time. I don't think it will take longer than that."

"Okay." Beth pushed against the arms of the chair as she rose. "We'll be back at 6:30." She kissed Isaac's head and whispered, "Lord, since I can't hold him in my arms, hold him close in Yours."

Tara walked them to the door. "Get some dinner. If you have extra time, you can pump across the hall in a maternity room. And, Beth? I'm sure you'll get to hold him as soon as the next shift is ready."

The double doors shut them out, keeping Isaac in.

φφφ

Beth, weary from the birth and little sleep, walked in to the NICU reminding herself of what Tara had said—she was the mother and needed to take care of her son. After washing her hands, she wet paper towels and brought them with her to Isaac's bed.

His new nurse wore plain green scrubs. "I'll be taking care of Isaac this evening. I'm Margaret."

"Nice to meet you. I'm Isaac Harris's mom." She held out her wristband. "Elizabeth. But call me Beth."

Her lips set into a straight line. "I never shorten my name. Not Maggie, not Margo. Only Margaret."

"Okay." Beth fought the urge to shout back a "yes, ma'am." She reached for a Pampers.

"What are you doing?" Margaret grabbed the diaper.

"I'm going to change Isaac."

She crossed her arms. "I already did."

What had caused her bad mood? Beth hadn't been in the nursery long enough to contribute to it. Maybe ignoring her rudeness would be best. "Could you show me the storage system for the breast milk?"

Margaret harrumphed. "I suppose I have to."

When they got back to the incubator, Isaac's eyes were open.

Beth leaned over him. The world around her disappeared as she memorized his face. Thickly curled eyelashes like Keith's. Earlobes that connected all the way like hers. His nose could have been either of theirs.

"Excuse me." Margaret edged in between Beth and Isaac with the thermometer.

"Can I do that?"

"It's easier if I do."

"All right." Beth covered her mouth. How could she phrase her next statement? How could she get Margaret on her side? "I'm sorry. I'm not trying to get in your way, but Tara said I could change him and check his temperature, so—"

"We each do things differently. I prefer to provide the best care possible by doing it myself." Margaret slid the thermometer into its sleeve and put it on the shelf.

"I understand." The nurse was highly trained; Beth, merely the inexperienced mother. "Would it be okay if I hold him for a minute? Tara thought I could after the break since I haven't had a chance yet."

Margaret stared at the monitors. "He's a very fragile baby, not a plaything. The more he's left alone at this stage, the better off he will be." Her voice trembled at the last words. "I'm sorry." She lowered the hood, the mechanic drone of the motor shutting Isaac in behind the closed plastic.

Chapter Forty

Luke Winslow.

The name bounced around in Tony's head, reverberated in his heart. He knew the kid. Had umped for some of his baseball games during the summer, been impressed by his respectful manner. Not the kind of boy likely to do something stupid and get himself in big trouble.

He took another bite of his hamburger, savoring the grilled onions. Probably not the best choice, since he would conduct at least one interview this afternoon. He gulped his root beer and grabbed a handful of fries. An SUV sped past the restaurant window, but he chose to ignore it. There were more important things on his mind than a soccer mom hurrying to the grocery store before picking the kids up from school.

A hard slap across his shoulder and a boisterous greeting signaled Katza's arrival. "A late lunch, huh?" He slid into the opposite seat, waved down the waitress for some coffee, and added cream and sugar. "Okay, partner, bring me up to speed."

"What? Your best friend didn't give you the inside scoop? Aren't you and Chief like this?" Tony crossed his fingers and waved them at Katza.

Katza cracked a smile. "Chief didn't give much info. Only said it was about that accident the other week and you were sniffing something out."

Tony stretched his legs under the table and looked around.

No one close enough to overhear.

"Yeah, I did a bit of investigating at the tow yard yesterday. Came across a steelie that had been overlooked in the front seat. Poked around at the accident site this morning and found a slingshot with the word "sorry" carved in the handle." He pushed the ice in his drink down with his straw.

"That all you got?"

Tony kicked him under the table.

Katza winced.

"No, Barney Fife. I crossed the highway for a different perspective and discovered a bag of steelies, dropped like someone had run off in a hurry. The place was surrounded with a bunch of poison oak. And when I checked with the school, I found Luke Winslow lives out that way and had a case of poison oak last week."

"Wow, that's quite a story." Katza put his coffee mug on the table. "So what do you want to do? Go see if a parent is at the house, or wait till the boy gets off the bus?"

"Let's give him a chance to get home and relax a few minutes before we show up. Hopefully I'm wrong about all this. I mean, he's a good kid, from what I've seen."

φφφ

An hour later Tony hit his left turn blinker and pulled off the state highway onto a gravel road.

The rutted private drive, littered with fallen leaves and small branches, meandered back into the hills. The storm earlier in the day had left its mark, but the clouds had broken apart, allowing glimpses of the late afternoon sun.

Tony and Katza pulled into a circular driveway at the end of the road.

The simple white house, trimmed in green, looked freshly

washed by the rain. A pile of pumpkins and cornstalks decorated each side of the front door, and an old rocker held a scarecrow dressed in well-used overalls and a plaid flannel shirt.

A man stood in the mouth of the open garage, a hammer in hand. Luke's father, Grant. He had been at his son's baseball games during the summer. Always positive with Luke, even when he missed a fly or struck out. Never questioned the decisions made by the officials.

At least not where they could hear him.

Tony and Katza cut across the grass and headed toward the garage as Grant came to meet them.

Sawdust covered his jeans. He wiped his hand on his pants and stuck it out.

Particles of sawdust grated against Tony's hand as they shook.

"Officer Barnett, what brings you to this neck of the woods?" Grant drew a blue bandanna from his back pocket and wiped his hands. "Sorry about the mess, but I've been building a curio cabinet for my wife. Don't tell her—it's a surprise."

"I won't breathe a word. Can't promise anything for Officer Katza, here." He slapped his partner's chest. "Do you do a lot of woodworking?"

"Don't get me started. It's been a hobby nearly all my life. I'm hoping it's a love I'll pass on to Luke. So far, he doesn't seem too interested. He'd rather run around and play in the hills."

Tony exchanged a look with Katza. "Has he ever worked on a project with you, Grant?"

"Little things. Making a new broom handle for his mother

or stuff like that."

"You ever make a slingshot?"

"Yep, it was a beauty. Made from hickory wood and sanded so smooth you could run your tongue along it and not worry about picking up splinters. I'd show it to you, but it's gone missing." Grant's consternation was obvious. "Luke carried it with him all summer, but says he can't find it now. Made me pretty upset, as we spent a lot of time on it. You know how kids are."

Katza broke in. "Is Luke home? We need to speak with him. With you present, of course."

Grant glanced around as if expecting his son to appear from thin air. "He was here a few minutes ago, right before you guys arrived. Must have gone back in the house. Want to come in?"

"Sure." Katza stepped toward the house.

Tony rocked back on his heels. "I've got to get something out of the car. I'll join you in a minute." As he walked to the patrol car, the weight of dread plunged in his stomach like a roller coaster drop. He wanted to skip the coming confrontation, the pain carried in the facts he would present. Hated to bring rough news to a decent man like Grant Winslow.

When he entered the house, Grant and Katza were in the middle of a conversation that stopped when they saw him.

"So what's going on, guys?" Grant's voice sounded tense. "I take it this is more than a 'I happened to be in the neighborhood.'"

Time to get to the point, let the poor guy in the loop though he wouldn't like what he heard.

He sat on the couch without being invited, and Grant took

a seat on the chair next to it.

Katza stood at the edge of the living room, stance broad, hands clasped in front of him.

Tony laid the evidence bag on the coffee table and withdrew the slingshot.

Grant's gasped. "How'd you get this? Where'd you find it?" Grant's questions tumbled out as he ran his hands along the edges of the wood. "Wait a second—what's this?" His fingers traced the letters carved in the handle. A look of bewilderment ran across his face.

Tony crossed his arms. "I found the slingshot buried at the bottom of the roadside memorial. We think Luke was somehow involved in the accident down on the highway."

"He couldn't be. You know Luke, he's just a kid." Grant's jaw was rigid, a vein at his temple throbbing a visible rhythm.

"I need to talk to him, find out what he knows."

Grant walked toward the hall. "He's probably in his room. Been spending a lot of time in there the past week or so." He stopped and grabbed hold of the back of an overstuffed chair as if he might fall from the shock of a revelation. "You think that's why Luke's changed lately?"

"How do you mean?"

The man came around the edge of the chair and dropped into it so hard the legs creaked. "He's not talking, not going out in the forest. Hardly showers. We thought it was just because he's almost a teenager, but he just sits in his room and draws gory pictures."

"I'm sorry, Grant," Tony said.

"I can't believe it."

Katza jerked his head toward the hall.

Luke leaned against the doorframe, face ashen. A notebook dangled from his hands. "I'm so sorry. I didn't mean to hurt them." His words spewed out between sobs as he dropped to his knees in front of his father, the notebook landing next to him.

"Luke, you want to tell us what happened?" Tony kept his voice soft. "Take your time."

"I … I was out shooting at some birds that afternoon, but it was too easy. I kept hitting them. I got bored and …" He looked up at his dad as if for reassurance. "I found a spot where I could see the road. When a car came by, I aimed for it. But I never thought I'd hit it." A fresh wave of tears poured out of him.

Tony squeezed his shoulder. "Okay, Luke. Then what happened?"

Luke shrugged Tony's hand away. "The shot hit the window of the car—busted it all to pieces. And the car slammed into the truck. I was going to go down to help, but the police were there right away, and I was so scared. I didn't want them to take me to jail, so I ran home."

Grant leaned forward in the chair, pulled Luke to his chest, and rested his chin against the top of Luke's head.

Tony could almost feel the father's pain, hear him asking himself where he'd gone wrong as a parent.

"I'm sorry, so sorry." Luke's body shook, making each word vibrate.

Tony stared into Luke's eyes, saw a frightened boy who had made a terrible mistake.

"What did you do with the slingshot when you ran away, Luke?"

His tears had stopped. "I brought it home with me so I

could hide it. I put it under my bed, but it was too loud for me to sleep at night with it there."

"What do you mean, 'it was too loud?'"

Luke stood up, nearly knocking Tony over. "I could feel it pressing on my head, like it was talking, telling everyone what I did. I'd put my hands over my ears, but I could still hear it. So a few days later, I took it back to where the accident happened. Hid it under the stuff other people had left there."

Katza approached Tony, held out the dropped notebook. "Take a look."

A quick glance revealed death on every page. Dark violence. The person depicted in each drawing was the same—an obvious caricature of Luke.

The import hit. He stood and examined Grant Winslow's face, praying he would understand the meaning behind Tony's words. "Your boy needs help."

Chapter Forty-one

"Dr. Kendal, when will Beth get to take Isaac home?" Suzanne shifted closer to the incubator.

The doctor's smooth-shaven chiseled features and short blond hair made him more of a "Dr. Ken-Doll." He drew his hand over his face. "I hate to make predictions because each baby has its own timetable. Isaac's officially here for Respiratory Distress Syndrome. That's a bit equivocal—he is off oxygen, but needs the ventilator. I anticipate his graduating from the ventilator tomorrow. He'll be breathing on his own, but he still won't be able to leave."

Beth cleared her throat. "Exactly what needs to happen for him to be released?"

Suzanne grabbed a notebook from her purse. She wanted it in writing, so Beth would have proof and not be tossed around between nurses' differing opinions.

The drive back to Beaver Falls last night without Isaac had been horrible. Suzanne hadn't bothered to ask about staying the night but grabbed a throw from the love seat and stretched out on the couch. As soon as the sky had lightened, the women had driven back to the hospital.

"Well." Dr. Kendall held up a finger. "He needs to drink one and a half ounces of milk every feeding for three days—" another finger "—and his weight needs to be around five pounds."

Beth wrinkled her forehead. "He lost weight today."

"Even full term babies lose a little at first. I'd give him

seven to ten days to get up to weight."

"Thank you." Beth shook his hand.

"I'll talk to you tomorrow morning." He moved on to the next baby.

Beth flipped through Suzanne's day planner. "Mom, that's not too long. He will be home by Thanksgiving."

"Great." Suzanne peeked at the calendar. "We could stuff him into a cornucopia instead of a car seat."

They both laughed.

"What's so funny?"

"Tara!" Beth hugged the young nurse. "I'm so glad you're here this morning."

"I bet you are." Tara rubbed Beth's back and smiled at Suzanne. "I heard last night with Miss Margaret didn't go so well."

"That's one way to put it. I still haven't held Isaac."

Tara's mouth dropped open. "You are *kidding* me."

Beth shook her head so quickly the tip of her ponytail flicked her cheek.

"We are going to remedy that right now. Sit."

An obedient dog couldn't have sat faster. She looked up, the anticipation on her face like that of a young girl, squatting beside the Christmas tree, ready to pick the first present.

Tara slid a blanket under Isaac. "Margaret's been working this unit for fifteen years. A month ago, she left a mother with her baby for a few minutes. When she came back, the woman had turned off the alarms and was holding her baby without permission." She gathered the wires at the bottom of the blanket, burritoed Isaac, and lifted him out of the incubator. "The baby suffered a huge setback because of the overstimulation. He almost died. Margaret's not been the same since. She's probably close to burnout."

Beth's eyes widened. "Will it hurt him if I—"

Tara placed Isaac in Beth's arm. "Don't worry. He'll tolerate this well."

One of Beth's hands supported Isaac's bottom as his head rested in the crook of her arm, the other hand clutched at his blanket so tightly Tara might have to pry him away.

Suzanne's arms ached to know the feel of her grandson, but it was out of the question today. On another day, a day when he was stronger, she would hold him for a moment. On the day he came home, she would hold him for hours.

She glanced around the unit.

Yesterday the mood had been calm, but today the nurses seemed more subdued and the whole room held a sadness. Tara moved slowly, almost reverently, as she changed the sheet in the bed and tucked a quilt on top.

Suzanne ran her fingers along the soft stitching. "Where did the quilt come from?"

Tara turned on the warming light above the incubator. "Volunteers make them. Every baby gets one."

"Why is everyone so serious today?'

"Oh, could you tell?" Tara looked over in the corner of the room.

Suzanne followed her gaze. Several screens blocked a section of the nursery from view.

"The baby—the one who had surgery last night—" Tara smoothed a corner of the quilt again. "She didn't make it. Her parents will be here soon to hold her for the last time and say good-bye."

Every moment of life seemed now to be tainted by good-byes.

Had Beth heard? Suzanne studied her face. Her porcelain cheek looked fragile, but strength lay in her jawbone.

Remembrance hit Suzanne with the force of an out-of-control elevator plummeting down a black shaft. Beads of sweat trickled down her back, bile rose in her throat. "I think I'm going to be sick."

Before the nurse could say anything, Suzanne bolted from the room and ran into the hall. She spied the bathroom down the corridor.

Breathe. Remember to breathe.

She ran her hand along the nape of her neck, wiping away moisture. Her breath was rough, difficult to draw. Her legs shook as she burst into the restroom.

Collapsing onto the tile, she tried to gain control of her emotions.

To slow each breath.

To forget the past.

Chapter Forty-two

Glimpses of the future lay in Beth's arms, snuggled against her breast. With each passing minute, she relaxed into her role as a mother, allowed it to possess her from the inside out. She could do this. The longer she held Isaac, the more confident she became.

The warmth of the NICU and the subdued lighting made a nap sound lovely, but that would mean giving up time holding her son. She stopped rocking and shifted her weight in the chair.

Isaac's eyes popped open at the change of position.

"Yes, little one, I'm your mama." She would never get enough of staring into those baby blues.

"You doing okay, Beth?" Tara came around the edge of the curtain.

Beth smiled at the young nurse. "This is a little bit of heaven. I'm so relaxed I'm afraid I'll fall asleep and accidentally drop him. Then he'll really need to be in the hospital."

Tara scanned the monitors surrounding Isaac. "Are you ready to put him back in bed?"

"So soon?"

Tara nodded. "We don't want him to get too tired. You can hold him later today—it's so good for both of you."

"I'd love that." Beth allowed Tara to take Isaac from her arms. She stood, pulled the privacy curtain aside, and scanned the large room. "Do you know where my mother is?"

"She said she felt sick, so I'm guessing she went to the restroom. That was awhile ago, though, and she hasn't come back."

Beth yawned and stretched. "Maybe she didn't want to bring sick germs back into the nursery." She waited while Tara placed Isaac in his little bed and adjusted the bilirubin light over his body. Beth leaned down and nibbled on his ear before she left, whispering words of love.

Her mother was not in the nearby lounge. Beth walked down the long hallway and entered the restroom. The scent of lemon disinfectant stung her eyes.

The room appeared empty.

She turned to leave, but a strangled sound grabbed her attention. "Mom, is that you?"

The door of the last stall banged open, and Suzanne leaned against it, a wad of toilet paper clenched in her fist. She dabbed her eyes and tossed the tissue into the wastebasket in the corner. "Hope I didn't worry you, Beth. I felt nauseous, but I'm fine now." Her voice was thin, edgy. She stepped up to the sink, cranked the spigot to cold, and held the insides of her wrists under the miniature waterfall.

Beth gazed at her mother's reflection. Something was wrong. Of course, she had just lost her husband, but this grief seemed different. "Are you sure you're okay?" She put a hand on her mother's back.

Suzanne pulled away. "I said I'm fine. I'm going for coffee."

Beth moved out of the way as Suzanne pushed the door open. "I'll come with you." What was going on? Her mother rarely turned as spiny as a porcupine.

They took the elevator to the lobby, unspoken words

hanging between them.

A few people were scattered among the tables in the cafeteria.

Suzanne took a seat near the back of the room, facing the wall.

Beth chose the opposite chair, awkwardness and uncertainty grinding in her stomach. “Mom, please talk to me. I don’t understand what’s going on.”

Suzanne wiggled her wedding ring back and forth, gaze fixed on the golden band as if it held the secret to life. Sadness contorted her face. “Sometimes, when people are young, they make mistakes.” Her voice cracked.

Beth’s fear split open. “What do you mean? What mistakes?”

Her mother scooted closer to the table. “I just … people do things they regret for the rest of their lives.”

“But what does that have to do with you?”

“Beth, I’m not even sure where to start.” Suzanne opened her purse and excavated a packet of Kleenex. “Did you hear about the death of that baby? The one they operated on yesterday? And when I saw Isaac’s perfectly formed little body … Thousands of memories I’ve tried to forget avalanched. I couldn’t breathe.”

“Mom, what are you talking about?”

“A secret, Beth. One that’s haunted me for decades.”

This was bizarre. Her mother was not a secretive person. Melodramatics did not dovetail with her straightforward approach to life.

Suzanne sighed and lifted her head. “In high school, there was a guy named Dylan. I was crazy in love with him. Too young, too stupid, to make the right choices.” She reached her hand across the table toward Beth. "Things happened, and … I got pregnant when I was seventeen."

"I don't understand. How—" Her mom had been a pregnant teen? An unwed mother? No, she must have given the baby up for adoption.

Somewhere in the world she had a brother or sister. All those years of longing for a sibling. Too many years had gone by to share childhood bonds, but it was never too late to be reunited, to learn to love each other.

"Oh, Mom, that must have been horrible." She touched Suzanne's hand, surprised at its chilliness. "You must miss that baby so much. Was it a boy or a girl?"

Suzanne shrugged, her eyes not meeting Beth's. "I'm not sure."

"They didn't let you hold the baby, or tell you anything about it? Just took it away to give it to its new parents?" Her heart broke with pain. "They wouldn't even let you have a moment? Or a memory?"

Suzanne removed her hand from Beth's clasp and blew her nose. "I didn't give the baby up for adoption."

"What?" The syllable quivered.

"I had … your grandmother made me have …"

"An abortion?" The revelation stunned on impact, clawed a vicious path through her stomach. She wanted to plug her ears, to refuse to listen to her mother's confession. The truth was too ugly, too vile. She understood compassion for women who didn't know any better, but her mother? "How could you do that?"

"Beth, there were circumstances involved that you wouldn't understand."

Who cared? What her mother had done was wrong.

"What wouldn't I understand? I understand I have a premature baby who's fighting to breathe and eat. I understand another mother just lost her baby. What I *don't* understand is how you could possibly throw a life away. No matter what the circumstances were."

"I was young and your grandmother … I didn't think this was something you needed to know, but if you had any idea what I was going through at the time—"

"Then why did you decide to tell me?" Anger constricted Beth's heart. "You should have kept your awful secret to yourself."

"You're the one that kept after me, asking what was wrong."

Beth's chair screeched as she pushed back from the table. "So now it's my fault, huh? Don't ask, don't tell? Too bad you couldn't have held it together for a few more minutes, instead of letting the true you show through."

Suzanne rose and took a step toward her daughter. "I'm sorry, Beth. I never wanted to hurt you."

Beth put up a hand. "No, it's not over that easily. You know what, Mom? Why don't you go on home? I need some time, some space."

Tears streamed down her mother's face.

Did she really want to add to her mother's pain?

But the passion of the moment had gained so much momentum she couldn't stop herself. In an instant, her mind took her back to staring at the lifeless image of her baby in the ultrasound room.

To think her mother had purposefully chosen to snuff out a baby's heartbeat.

"Mother, I've lost two babies. My preemie's in the NICU.

I don't have the energy or desire to deal with your mess. You chose to get rid of your baby. I've had no choice over what's happened to all three of mine." Beth stalked away.

Chapter Forty-three

Back again.

Was there a cosmic magnet drawing Tony to the house? It had nothing to do with a warm reception. If Suzanne had slapped him or spit on him, she couldn't have hurt him as much as she did by questioning his ability as a police officer.

But, if she hadn't done so, he would never have spent so much time on an open-and-shut case like the accident. Slim Hardy would have continued to carry the blame for driving with low blood sugar. Luke probably would have spiraled lower and lower until life had no meaning and tried to end his life.

Suzanne's methods weren't gentle, but they got good results.

He just needed her to keep the door open long enough to hear what those results were.

The handle turned and Suzanne peeked out.

"Mrs. Corbin?" Tony stuck his foot in the door before she had a chance to close it. "You'll want to hear what I have to say."

"Why won't you leave me alone?" She stared at him for a moment, sighed, and stepped back. "Come in the kitchen, and we'll see if a different setting leads to a different outcome."

Curtains closed out the fall colors. Dishes piled up beside the sink.

The first time he had been in her kitchen—to call her pastor about the crash—the counters had sparkled.

"Coffee?"

"Sure, thanks." Tony sat on a barstool. "Last time we spoke, I—"

"Yes." Suzanne filled two mugs with coffee. "I'm sorry if I came across rude, but—"

"No, no. You don't need to apologize. I gave you false information and that's inexcusable."

Suzanne laced her fingers around the mug. "You're doing the best you can, and you were so kind to us the day of …" She drew in a breath, lips parted. "Sometimes I expect more out of people than they are able to give. Nobody's perfect. Not Jake, not you, not me, though I pretend to be." Closing her eyes, she leaned over the rising steam. "I've come to accept that the accident was Jake's fault."

"It wasn't."

Her brown eyes opened.

Their shape reminded him of Beth's. "You told me it was. If you've come to change my whole universe around again …" Tears pooled and trembled, like drops of rain clinging to a forest leaf, reluctant to fall to the muddy ground. "I can't take anymore."

She'd find out sooner or later, but did he need to be the one to put her emotions through a spin cycle?

Suzanne fingered her wedding ring as she watched him. Scratches marred the golden band. What had his mother done with her wedding band when she left his father? Had it been worn long enough to have scratches of its own? Did it end up at the bottom of a lake somewhere, replaced by a new man's promise?

Suzanne was old enough to be his mother. According to the obituary, she had no one but Beth left in her family—no son to take the protective role or care for her.

"I took your admonition to heart," Tony said. "You seemed so sure something else had to have happened. During my personal investigation, I found the cause of the accident was deeper than a distraction, stranger than I had thought possible."

"What did you find out?" Hand trembling, she took another sip.

"A boy was playing in the woods beside the highway that day. With a slingshot. He thought it might be challenging to try to hit a car."

"And he hit Jake's." She set the mug down.

"Yes. The window shattered, causing your husband to swerve as the truck approached. You were right—there was more to it."

Suzanne walked to the window, pushed the curtains apart, and yanked the blinds open. "A boy killed Jake and Keith."

"I found his slingshot, tracked him down, and he confessed."

"How old is he?"

"Twelve." Too young to have to live with the knowledge he had inadvertently killed two men.

"What's going to happen to him?"

Tony scratched an eyebrow. "They're charging him with involuntary manslaughter. He's in a juvenile facility for suicidal tendencies."

"Then they should let him go home."

"If he wasn't a danger to himself, they would."

"That's why they should let him out. Let him take care of the problem himself."

"Suzanne." Too late, he realized he'd called her by her

first name. “I mean, Mrs. Corbin, you can’t really think that. This boy was a good kid. His life’s out of control, but there’s still hope for him.”

“Oh, so you’re one of those we-can-all-be-redeemed kind of guys. I don’t think so.” Her shoulders slumped. “Some mistakes are too big to be forgiven.”

“Listen, I agree with you there. The mother of the girl you found? She’s hopeless. But this boy can be helped.”

She dumped the rest of her coffee down the drain. “You can’t have it both ways. Either everyone’s got a second chance, or nobody does.”

He stood. “Mrs. Corbin, I thought you would want to know. I would appreciate it if you’d pass this information along to your daughter.”

“Actually, we’re not talking much right now.” Sniffling, she reached for a tissue.

Weird. “You seemed to get along so well.”

“She had the baby. Six weeks early.”

Tony’s heart skipped a beat. “Are they both okay?”

“They will be. Isaac’s in the NICU, but he should come home in a week or two.”

“Beth had a boy?”

Suzanne nodded. “Want to see a picture?” She pointed at the refrigerator.

Beth and the baby. Her long brown hair parted slightly off center, she stared down at the boy. Without makeup, her skin shone.

What would it feel like to see a little part of himself mixed with a little part of someone he loved?

He swallowed hard. “They’re beautiful.”

Suzanne jotted something on a notepad and tore off the

top sheet. “Here’s her cell number. She won’t answer if she’s with Isaac. You can tell her about the kid.”

Tony took the slip of paper. “I’ll do that. Thank you.” At the door, he paused. “I don’t think I’ll need to come by anymore, so rest assured.”

“I don’t rest anymore,” Suzanne said. “I wait.”

“What are you waiting for?”

“To see if life will get better.”

φφφ

In the squad car, he unfolded the piece of paper and stared at the numbers. He grabbed his cell phone and entered them. His thumb rested over the send button.

Was she taking care of her son right now? Agonizing over his health? Or was she taking it all in stride? His dad would say he cared because he loved the underdog. If Tony saw a woman hurting or in trouble, he wanted to help. Which in Mandy’s case, hadn’t turned out so well.

Again, he thought of Isaac and his new place in Beth’s heart, about the loss of Isaac’s dad. Would she ever have room for anyone else? Maybe. Later, much later, of course.

He pressed the button. “Hello, Beth? This is Tony.”

Chapter Forty-four

On the floor beside the hospital crib, the car seat waited. After thirteen days, Isaac was leaving the NICU nest. For the first time, sunlight would warm his face. Day would change to night and stars would wink down at him. Beth could hold, change, and bathe him whenever she wanted. No more asking permission to be his mother.

Frogs hopped across Isaac's light green onesie and his hat looked like a lily pad. It slouched over his eyes, and when he curled his legs up to his belly, his feet swam upstream into the main body of fabric.

"Hey, little tadpole, don't blame me. Your daddy chose this outfit—if you were a boy—to wear home."

"Ready?" Tara. How perfect that she would be the one to see them off.

"I'm so thankful for all you've done for him. For both of us, really." She embraced the nurse. "Every time I left him with you, I felt like you would love him until I came back."

"We're going to miss him. Except, whenever I get close to Isaac, my baby has a jealous kicking fit."

Isaac squirmed. Though clothed, he seemed naked without any machines attached to him.

"Are you ready to go home, big fella?" She held his arm steady while the nurse snipped off his bracelet.

"Call us anytime, day or night, if you need to," Tara said. "We contacted your pediatrician and he wants to weigh Isaac every day for at least the first week to make sure he's keeping up on his feedings. I told him I've watched you and I know you'll make sure Isaac eats all he needs."

"Being stubborn has its advantages." Grinning, Beth tucked the cut bracelet in the outer pocket of her purse.

"And disadvantages?" asked Tara.

"Sure, but I'm too stubborn to admit them."

"Does that have to do with why your mother isn't here?" Tara handed her the rest of the preemie diaper package.

"This is my family, you know?" She tucked the leftover diapers in her bag. "Isaac and me for the next eighteen years. My mom's his grandma, not a substitute for his father."

"My suggestion? Don't shut her out. You'll need her help to raise him well."

"You don't know my mother." She scooped Isaac up and placed him in the car seat.

Even with an insert around his head, he slumped forward.

"After you get him buckled, prop a rolled blanket on each side. It will hold him in place better."

That kind of advice, Beth could take.

Tara posed Beth beside the car seat. "One last picture."

A series of strident beeps sounded from a machine across the room.

A nurse shouted Tara's name.

"I was going to walk you to the car, but this sounds serious. You'd better get out while you can."

A flurry of hugs and good-byes swept Beth and Isaac out the door and into the elevator. As the metal doors slid shut, she inhaled and closed her eyes. For the first time, she and Isaac were alone together. Quiet rang through the space.

Thank You, Lord, that he's mine now. And that he's healthy.

The elevator bounced to a stop on the ground floor.

How was she supposed to get everything to the car? It might have been easier to put up with her mother's presence than to bear the sole responsibility for carrying everything and getting Isaac home safely.

Schlepping the car seat, diaper bag, and other baby paraphernalia to the Honda, she gritted her teeth. "Your mama's not the smartest cookie in the jar, little boy."

As she drove the long road home, she alternated between watching traffic and using a double-mirror system to make sure Isaac stayed pink and content. If he had difficulty breathing, his color would fade to the gray of the wisps of fog fingering the car. By the time they reached Beaver Falls, she had a headache and fought dizziness.

"What was I thinking? Grandma would have brought us home and then left if I had made it obvious I wanted to be alone with you." She eased into her driveway and pulled the keys from the ignition.

Home. A cozy two-story house. Last night the doctors had told her that barring any unforeseen circumstances Isaac would be released the next day. She had spent last night cleaning the whole house, vacuuming Mizpah's hair off the furniture, and laundering the crib sheets in hypoallergenic soap. Hushed and anticipating, the rooms stood ready to meet Isaac.

A car pulled up next to her and Officer Tony Barnett climbed out.

Why was he here? The last time they talked—what? a week or more ago—he'd broken the news of Luke's involvement, which explained the kid's strange behavior, though it shocked Beth to know such a sweet kid, a kid in one of her own classes, had been a part of her husband's death.

A gust of wind blew Tony's baseball cap off. He tromped across the front yard chasing it. Red-faced, he opened her car door. "Welcome home." Rough lips formed a crooked smile.

Keith's straight-toothed grin flashed across her memory. "Something I can help you with, Officer?" She got out of the car.

He rubbed his hands together. "Could we talk inside? It's kind of cold out here."

Schlep again or let him help?

She wanted to walk in alone with Isaac, savor the experience of bringing her son home at last, but the pounding near her temples begged for the policeman to give her a hand. "Okay, Officer. I hope the conversation will be short, though, because Isaac and I are exhausted and need a nap."

"Will you just call me Tony?"

She opened the rear door and unsnapped the carrier from the car seat base. "You can grab the bags."

He loped ahead of her, bags already in hand, and opened the screen door.

On the narrow porch, he and the bags took up a lot of room.

She squeezed past him to unlock the door.

"Cute kid you got there." His minty breath distracted.

"Thank you." She fumbled at the lock, twisting the key. She spilled into the entryway.

Tony hulked behind her. Taller than Keith, stubbly and tough, he was too much man to have around. He made her feel short and frumpy.

"We're inside." She set the carrier down, unbuckled Isaac, and cuddled him. "So talk."

"I spoke with your pastor earlier this morning."

"Alan? What about?"

Tony wiped his feet on the doormat. "Luke Winslow. Alan thought you might be able to help with his counseling."

"Why would he think I could help?" Though Isaac hadn't complained yet, her body knew it was time for him to eat. She willed Tony to get to the point.

"It doesn't hurt that you already have a relationship with Luke, but there's more." Tony lowered the bags to the floor.

"Let me stop you there. After you called and let me know he was to blame for the accident, I pushed it away. I'm not ready to work through yet another issue right now. I've got enough on my plate, don't you think?"

"Your pastor says you can do something no one else can for him. Your mother certainly can't."

Beth put one hand on her hip. "What can I do that my mom or a professionally trained counselor can't?"

"Something I'm not too good at either." Tony's eyes darkened. "Forgive."

Chapter Forty-five

Exhaustion colored Beth's days Blurry-Eyed Red. A color every new mother could identify with. How could it be this hard? How could one little body require so much time and energy? If breathing weren't automatic, she wouldn't have time to draw a breath.

It had all been so easy when Isaac was in the hospital, where there was help available the moment she needed it. Home alone, after a couple sleepless nights, it was an entirely different situation.

The feeble sun of the November afternoon was setting, its rays drawing shadows on the wall. Dusk clung to the sun's coattails, threatening long hours of isolation and weariness. If only she could get a good night's sleep.

She rested her head against the overstuffed chair. Her back tensed, threatened to freeze into place. She rolled her shoulders, releasing as much tightness as possible.

Isaac's piercing scream rose above the lullabies playing in his room.

A part of her wanted to join him in voicing unhappiness, give in to the frustration growing in her heart. She heaved herself out of the chair and went down the hall to his nursery.

Her tiny son lay on his back, face screwed up in anger or pain—she wasn't sure which. His arms and legs churned, a miniature Bruce Lee using martial arts on an invisible foe.

"Hey, Isaac, you're all right." She kept her tone calm and gentle as she cooed to him during his diaper change.

His cries never quieted.

She wrapped him in a receiving blanket and put him up to her shoulder, gently patting his back as she paced the length of the house. Maybe it was a gas bubble or a tummy ache, but how was she to know?

He settled down, exhaling puffy baby breaths against her neck before sucking on her bare skin.

"Ooh, that tickles." She nuzzled his cheek and dropped onto the rocker so he could nurse.

It was still hard work for him to move to the natural rhythm of a newborn. Though born two weeks ago, he wasn't due for another month.

After only a few minutes, he succumbed to the lure of sleep.

Beth wiped an errant drop of milk from the corner of his mouth with the edge of his blanket and he twitched in response. Dare she try to put him back in his crib? Sleep deprivation made her arms as heavy as her eyes, and she longed to take advantage of his naptime for one of her own. Fear of waking him in the process of getting out of the chair was motivation enough to stay put.

Beth swallowed, felt rawness in her throat. Her headache from the other day was back in full force and her joints ached. She pushed those thoughts away. She couldn't be sick. Isaac depended on her for everything.

She dozed.

Darkness swaddled the room when she opened her eyes.

Isaac slept, chest rising and falling with steady accuracy.

Beth moved her hand from under his body and touched her forehead. Fever had been hiding behind her other symptoms.

Oh, dear Jesus, what am I going to do? This isn't what I had planned. I envisioned days filled with the joy of parenting, not sleeplessness and illness. I don't think I can handle this—it's too much.

There was no voice in reply, but she knew the Lord was speaking to her heart in His gentle way, telling her to swallow her pride and call her mother. The mother who'd disclosed a huge secret, thrown it in Beth's face and expected things to remain the same.

A car raced up the street, gunning its engine as it went by.

Isaac startled, his cry taking up where it had left off before the last feeding.

Beth rose and jostled him up and down as she went around the house turning on lights, trying to chase away her anxiety. Her head throbbed and tears flowed.

She walked by her phone several times before picking it up. Cradling it to her ear, she placed Isaac back in his bed and walked partway down the stairs. She sat on a step, sagging against the wall as his wail sought her out.

"Hello?" Her mother's voice brought instant solace.

"Hi, Mom. Guess who?"

"Do I hear my grandson crying?"

"I think the whole neighborhood hears him. And soon they'll hear me."

"Do you need some help?"

Beth nodded. Pain careened around her skull. "I'm coming down with the flu or something, Isaac has cried day and night since we've been home, and—as you know—I'm all by myself."

"Do you want me to come over? I could spend the night. Give you a chance to rest." Her love flowed through the mystery of satellite bounces straight to Beth's heart.

"That would be wonderful, Mom. How soon can you get here?"

When she hung up, calm descended over her spirit. Her mother, her imperfect mother, was an answer to prayer.

Beth climbed the stairs to Isaac's room, picked him up, and held him close. His head was sweaty from crying, and he smelled as if he could use a diaper change.

But his grandma would be here soon.

Until then, Beth could cling to her child and comfort him as best she could, secure in the knowledge that someone stronger would take over when she could no longer go on.

An hour later Beth sat in bed, covers tucked tightly around her, a half-empty cup of hot tea on the bedside table. Though her head ached and her throat protested with every swallow, she felt better already.

Her mother would stay as long as she was needed, taking up the slack.

Suzanne's voice filtered through the closed door as she talked and sang to Isaac.

Beth reached out to turn off the lamp and noticed her unopened Bible. Sleep beckoned, but so did God's word. She picked it up, opened it at random to the book of Isaiah, and read: "Like babies you will be nursed and held in my arms and bounced on my knees. I will comfort you as a mother comforts her child."

Chapter Forty-six

Propped against a pillow, Isaac nestled in the slant of his mother's legs. For the moment he appeared content, an innocent angel. Not the screaming banshee Suzanne had dealt with the night before. His moods changed quicker than lightning, startling cries interrupting the calm around him and charging the air with impatience.

She sat on the edge of Beth's bed and stuck her pinkie finger against Isaac's open hand.

His wee fingers wrapped around hers—an automatic response, doctors might say—but he was purposefully drawing her close, responding to her love. "He's so sweet, I could kiss his little face right off." She leaned low and nibbled his cheek, looking forward to the day when he would react with laughter. She straightened up and ran her hand over his head, playing with his dark hair.

"How can you be so chipper, Mom? Sounded like you had a rough night. Every time I got up to use the bathroom, I heard him fussing and you singing to him."

"You must not have gotten much rest either, with me waking you every three hours to feed him."

Beth yawned. "Well, he had to eat."

"I haven't been sleeping much lately anyway. If I'm going to be awake, I might as well be awake holding someone I love."

Beth coughed, sipped the hot Tang Suzanne had left on her bedside table. "Did you sing to me when I was little?"

"All the time. Especially 'You Are My Sunshine.' Isaac liked that one, too. Didn't you?" Suzanne brushed his hair forward, toward his forehead. "I hadn't noticed it before, but the hair here is longer than the rest. Looks funny."

Beth pulled the offending lock away from his head. "No it doesn't. I can gel it and make him look like he's got a Mohawk."

Isaac's eyes grew large and he kicked his feet, letting go of Suzanne's hand.

"I don't think he's fond of that particular hair style."

Beth lifted her gaze. "Thanks for coming, Mom. I know we've had a hard time getting along lately, but I do love you, and I'm really glad you're here."

"Love you too. Get yourself well. I'll take care of things." Suzanne leaned over and pressed a kiss on her daughter's forehead. "How's that sound?"

"Heavenly." Beth stretched her arms over the carved headboard. "I ache everywhere. More sleep would be divine."

"You don't think I'd let you get out of bed, do you? You're still running a fever—I can see it in your eyes. You settle back and take it easy, and I'll bring this boy to you whenever he gets hungry." She lifted Isaac from the cozy nest of his mom's legs. "We'll be downstairs."

In the kitchen, she stashed Isaac in his baby seat and put water on to boil. She searched the cupboards and came up with a packet of instant oatmeal.

Isaac fussed.

She grabbed hold of his sleeper-encased foot. "Hey, little guy," she crooned. "Life's not that bad. Let's get breakfast ready for your mama."

He spit up, sour milk rolling down his chin and into the

sweaty crevices of his neck.

"I forgot to burp you, huh?" She wiped his mouth with a dishtowel. "Well, after I make your mommy's food, let's give you a nice, warm bath."

She poured boiling water into the bowl of oatmeal and stirred, sprinkling brown sugar over the steaming mound. Dropped a handful of raisins on the swirls of melting sugar. Glanced at Isaac.

Asleep.

Perfect. She could take Beth's breakfast up while he napped. Gingerly, she moved his carrier from the kitchen table to the floor in the living room and returned for the oatmeal.

Hot, healthy comfort food. Perfect for a rainy morning and a case of the flu. Beth would understand that the offering of food and taking care of Isaac meant Suzanne would always be there for her, loving her. Heat seeped through the ceramic bowl, warming her hands.

At the head of the stairs, she set the bowl on the flat top of the banister and opened Beth's door.

Her daughter was curled on her side, comforter over her shoulder, sound asleep. So young and vulnerable with her dark hair spilling over her cheek. Beth coughed, burrowed deeper under the covers.

Suzanne tiptoed backward and shut the door without a sound. When she'd been rummaging through the kitchen, she'd noticed the contents of the cabinets were in disarray. While Isaac slept, she could put the place in order.

First, she picked up the house and started a load of laundry, throwing the dishcloth she'd used as burp rag into the mix.

In the cupboards, canned vegetables mingled with boxes

of noodles. Spices hid among the jars of spaghetti sauce and pickles, bags of chips stuffed on top. Did Beth unload her groceries by the bag instead of putting like items together? Hadn't she grown up in a house of perfect order? Maybe Keith's family had taught him to live haphazardly.

She pulled everything out of the cupboards. By the time she emptied the shelves, groceries covered the table and heaps of sorted food dotted the countertop. She mixed a bucket of bleach water, grabbed a rag, and pulled a chair over to stand on. She fell into the easy rhythm of cleaning, an action her body had known so well but felt so little of since Jake's death.

New contact paper would have to wait for another day. She dried the shelves and put the groupings of groceries away. Veggies with veggies, next to the fruit. All the cans on one shelf, boxes on another. Spices in the cupboard next to the stove. Labels facing the front.

Crumbs and flour sprinkled the floor, shrapnel from the deep cleaning episode. She swept the room and whisked the pile into the dustpan. Outdoors, she dumped the bucket of bleach water on a patch of weeds in an empty flowerbed. The mop hung in the laundry room. She snagged it as she went by and propped it against the counter while she refilled the bucket with clean water and disinfectant.

The mop handle slid along the edge of the counter, slowly at first, then gathering speed.

She lunged for it, but her hand swiped only air.

Smack. The handle slapped the floor.

Isaac woke with a scream.

She ran to pick him up. If she were fast enough, Beth wouldn't hear his cries.

Isaac quieted in her arms, gazing at her with his serious

blue eyes.

Spreading a blanket on the carpet in the living room, she maintained eye contact. She laid him on his back and sprawled next to him.

He yawned, his mouth a pink oval. There was a little of Jake in the shape of his chin.

She nuzzled him and caught a whiff of sour milk. "The kitchen's mostly clean. Why don't we see about you?"

She left him on the floor while she filled the kitchen sink with warm water and lined it with a towel from the linen closet. Isaac didn't fuss when she stripped him, though he did wave straight arms topped with fists as she took off his diaper. The last remnant of his umbilical cord fell off when she wiped it with an alcohol swab.

"Now it's okay for you to get wet, buddy."

He blinked as his feet touched the water.

She submerged his body, cupping his head with a hand and running a soapy washcloth over his tummy and neck with the other. The sweet smell of baby shampoo filled her nose.

Another towel, folded in a triangle, waited on the kitchen table.

She carried him, dripping, to the dry towel and wrapped it around him. "Let's get a diaper on you as quick as we can, huh?"

A corner of the towel fell into Isaac's mouth and he sucked at the fabric.

"Yes, we'll wake Mommy up soon, too."

In the nursery, she found a bottle of baby lotion inside the diaper bag. She diapered Isaac and squirted a dollop of lotion into her palm, rubbing her hands together to warm the cream. As she applied it, she massaged his limbs, undulating against his muscles.

Isaac's skin, firm and smooth, drank in the moisture. He kicked his feet as she dressed him in a sleeper and zipped it up.

"How does it feel to be fresh and clean?" She rubbed her cheek on his forehead, kissed him. "Time for a haircut."

Beth's barber scissors made quick work of the uneven pieces of hair. Had there ever been a more handsome boy? She rocked him in the nursery recliner, pulling him close to her heart. Soon she would wake Beth, but for now she would enjoy the warmth of holding her grandson.

A click from the hallway. Beth was up.

Rocking forward, Suzanne stood. She met Beth in the hall. "Feeling better?"

"I'm over the worst of it, I think." Beth reached for Isaac. "Thanks, Mom. I'll feed him and maybe get some lunch."

"Want a fried egg sandwich? I'll make you one if you come see what I did in the kitchen."

"Okay." Curiosity prowled over Beth's face. "What did you do?"

"Follow me." Downstairs, around the corner, into the kitchen. She threw open the cupboard doors and stepped back. "Ta-da."

"You alphabetized my soups?" Beth laughed.

"I organized your staples." She took a carton of eggs from the refrigerator and slid a frying pan onto the front element. "I could help more often if you'd let me."

"Could I handle more of your help? Wait, you can train the dog."

"Mizpah's outside, by the way. But I'm serious. Maybe we should think about living together."

Beth guffawed. "That wouldn't work."

Prickles of pride jumped up Suzanne's spine. "Why not?"

Silence suffocated the room.

Beth cuddled Isaac, burying her nose in his neck. "You smell so good, sweet boy."

"That's a perfect example of how I can help you." Suzanne cracked an egg into melted bacon grease and swirled the yolk into the white with a spatula. "I gave him a bath while you were asleep."

"You gave him a *bath*?"

"He needed one, Beth." She dashed salt and pepper over the frying egg.

"Yeah, Mom." Beth's voice sounded choked. "He needed one because I've never given him more than a sponge bath. I was waiting for his cord to fall off."

"It fell off today."

"That's not the point. I'm the one that should have given him the bath."

"I'm sorry." Suzanne flipped the egg over. Sizzling grease splashed onto her wrist. She wiped it hard against her leg. "I didn't realize it was such a big deal."

Beth jostled Isaac, though he wasn't making a sound. "No big deal. Just his first bath ever. Can never be done again."

Suzanne spun from the stove, and set the frying pan on a hot pad. "Here's your egg. Unless I'm overstepping my bounds to make you food."

"Please, Mom, get off your high horse. What else did you do?"

"Nothing really. The kitchen and his bath." She glared at Beth. How could her daughter yell at her for taking care of Isaac? For moving a few cans around? If those were seen as negatives, she'd rather not tell Beth anything else.

Beth eyes narrowed. "I don't believe you."

"Ah, fine. Since you're freaking out anyway, I'll confess. I evened out his hair."

Balancing Isaac against one shoulder, Beth jerked her hand through the air, fingers spread wide. "His first haircut? You're like the grandmother from the black lagoon." Her hand froze in mid air. "Is that the washing machine?" She turned on her heels, ran into the living room, and yanked cushions from the couch. "Where is it? Tell me you didn't."

Suzanne pictured Isaac's brain bouncing in his skull. Shaken Baby Syndrome. "If you calm down, I'll talk to you in the kitchen."

The carton of eggs needed to go back into the refrigerator. She reached for it as Beth rushed up behind her.

"You did the laundry."

She could never have imagined those words coming out as an accusation. "Yes, I did, so shoot me."

"It still smelled like him." Beth crumpled against the wall and slid to the floor, her sobs so loud Isaac started crying. "You washed his shirt, Mom. The shirt he wore the day before he died. The shirt he didn't throw in the hamper."

The old T-shirt she had found stuffed in the corner of the couch. "I was trying to help. I didn't ..." A knot twisted her vocal cords like a pretzel. Tears welled up.

Beth mumbled in the midst of her crying.

"What?" She knelt beside her daughter.

"Get out." Beth sprang up, grabbed an egg from the carton. "Get out!" She threw the egg against the clean floor.

Splat.

"I'm your mother. You can't throw me out."

Beth picked up another egg. "Leave now." The egg hit the linoleum, shell breaking into shards. "Get out of my house. Get out of my life."

Chapter Forty-seven

Mostly Honest Abe's Machine Gun Parlo.

The blue sign hung over the barred door. Barred windows flanked the entry.

Suzanne unknotted the purple scarf from her neck and let it float onto the passenger seat. She should have worn jeans and a pullover instead of a tan pantsuit, but at least she would look a little less formal without the scarf. She got out of the car and started toward the door. The crispness of her pants felt strange after spending the last few days in soft, warm sweats.

Her pump twisted on the gravel of the parking lot and she lurched forward. The very picture of class.

At least no one knew her here.

A bell jangled as she pushed the door open.

An older woman stood up behind the counter. Her gray hair hung past her shoulders. As thin as she was, she'd have to run around in the shower to get wet. "Welcome to Mostly Honest Abe's. Let me know if you need any help."

Not the type of worker she'd expected to see manning the cash register. What would the woman do if someone tried to steal from the store? Swing a granny-sized purse at him?

"Thanks. I'll look around a little bit."

Propped against the back wall, rifles stood at attention. Handguns lay on red felt in glass-topped display cases. Probably bulletproof glass. Ironic.

What was she doing? She knew nothing about guns and had never set toe, let alone foot, inside such a place. Why now?

Because she needed a gun and she needed one soon. "Actually, I want something specific, but I'm not sure what."

The woman clicked her dentures together. "You looking to buy a gun?"

"If I can."

"What for?"

"My husband passed away a month ago. I don't feel safe at night without him around."

Layers of skin pulled together at the corner of the woman's eyes, like layers of rock in a canyon wall. "I can understand. My husband, Abe—the Abe from the sign—he died near ten years ago and I still sleep with my Glock tucked underneath the pillow." Her dentures clicked again. "I'm Wilma."

"I'm Suzanne."

"Pleased to make your acquaintance. So you need a weapon for self-defense?"

"To feel secure, yes."

Wilma grabbed a long, black gun off the wall behind her. Holding it with the barrel toward the ceiling, she yanked down on the middle section and a kachunk resounded in the room. "This is a 12-gauge pump shotgun. Best for stopping intruders because, instead of seeing some nice lady like you—woke out of a dead sleep, waving a little gun around, hands a-shakin' and knees a-knockin'—they hear that sound. Already, they're thinking of the fastest way out."

How did the very weight of such a big gun not topple Wilma forward? Her stick arm jutted out at a ninety-degree angle, keeping the gun aloft.

"Shells won't go through drywall, neither. Safer to use in

a neighborhood."

"I'm not worried about that, but I'll need something smaller. A gun I can carry and learn to handle."

Wilma laid the gun on top of the counter and fingered the key ring hanging from her wrist. "You have any brand preference?"

"No, I'll buy anything. As long as it's easy to use and pretty well foolproof."

"Got exactly what you need." Wilma unlocked a cabinet and brought out a small handgun. "This would protect you right well. And it's less prone to failure than others."

"What kind is it?" Suzanne eyed the short barrel.

".38 special Smith and Wesson snub-nose. Called the Chief's Special. The ammo's cheap, the bullets are easy to load, and it's simple to use."

"Show me."

"Thumb latch is right here." Wilma depressed a button above the trigger. "Push the cylinder out with your fingers. Never try to snap it open like they do in the movies or you'll be eating a face full of ammo." She handed the gun to Suzanne. "You try it."

The weight of the small weapon surprised her. Her hand sagged and she curled her wrist to keep the weapon steady. Gripping the gun, she tipped it sideways, sliding her thumb along the latch and pushing at the cylinder with the opposite fingers. Nothing happened.

"Push harder."

A little more effort and the cylinder flopped out, spinning.

"Called a revolver 'cause of that. Fit the bullets in those spots and you got five shots."

"Can I see the bullets?"

Wilma whipped a box of ammunition out and set it before Suzanne.

Cardboard flaps folded over each other.

She laid the gun down, opened the flaps, and slid out a Styrofoam tray. Gleaming bullets nestled in five lines of ten. "All you do is put them in and pull the trigger?"

"It's single action, double action. Can cock the hammer and have an easier shot, or pull the trigger hard and shoot without touching the hammer."

"Where's the safety?" Suzanne picked up the gun and twisted it from side to side.

Grimacing, Wilma guided the barrel away from her. "You ever been around guns before?"

"Not really."

"First rule is to never, ever point them at anybody. Unless you mean to." Wilma cackled. "Revolvers don't have safeties. It's pretty obvious when they're loaded, and you shouldn't have any bullets in the chamber until you're ready to shoot."

"I'll buy it. How long do I have to wait?"

"Ten minutes, I guess."

Suzanne's jaw dropped. "You're kidding me. Don't you have a waiting period or something?"

"Welcome to the great state of Oregon. If you've got a valid driver's license and a clean record, then you're the proud new owner of a Chief's Special."

Heart pounding, Suzanne slid her license across the counter. What was she doing? Suzanne Corbin buying a gun? Jake would never have believed it possible.

Don't do it. The thought shot through her mind.

"Want to know how much it's going to cost you?"

She pulled a credit card from her wallet. "Doesn't matter.

You can't put a price on taking care of yourself, can you?"

As Wilma called in her information, Suzanne wandered around the shop.

A magazine rack held the latest copies of *Outdoor Life* and *Field & Stream*. Above them hung the head of a buck, antlers proudly raised. A Winchester clock ticked the seconds. John Wayne, frozen in time, stared back from a trio of framed pictures.

"Ma'am?"

"Yes?"

"You've been approved." Wilma perched on a stool next to the antique cash register and logged the sale in a huge, hardbound notebook.

"They had no record of my felony?"

Wilma snorted. "Don't you joke like that. Folks get rejected even if they have an unpaid parking ticket." She examined the gun and copied something off of it. "Go to the county office to get your concealed weapons permit as soon as you can."

"Am I all right taking it home?"

"Keep it in plain sight and, if you get pulled over for any reason, tell 'em right away you got a weapon in the vehicle. And don't leave it in your car in case it gets stolen." Wilma closed the book. "I bought that at an estate sale last week. Great gun. I'm sure it will serve you well."

"As long as it works, it will."

"Saddest thing, too. About the man who owned it."

Like she hadn't been around enough sad things lately. "Oh?"

"An old man diagnosed with Alzheimer's. No family. Decided to end it all. Went to a gun range, shot all day long, and blew his brains out at closing time."

Shivers darted up her shoulders.

"Horrible." Wilma waggled her head. "Just horrible."

Chapter Forty-eight

Beep ... beep ... beep.

Each swipe of the cashier's hand raised the total of Beth's loneliness. The pre-formed turkey loaf, a box of instant mashed potatoes, a small pumpkin pie from the bakery—all blatant signs of her self-imposed isolation for Thanksgiving dinner.

Her mother had called and invited Beth to join her at Nancy and Jim's, but Beth had declined. She wasn't through stewing about her mother's interference in her life and she'd rather be on her own, Isaac her only company. It'd been harder to push off Chloe's invitation—and the five others from church members—but she couldn't handle being around a happy family.

A bagger at the end of the conveyor belt refilled the shopping cart with sacks of food. Isaac slept in a front pack suspended from Beth's shoulders. The grand total appeared, and she craned her neck past Isaac's body to make sure she redeemed the correct coupons.

"Would you like help out, ma'am?" A blond, robust teenage boy wearing the store's uniform already had hold of her cart as if he knew she would say yes.

"Thanks." She put the receipt in her purse and led him toward the nearest exit.

"No problem. You single parents have it hard."

She stopped at the door. "What makes you think I'm a single parent?" She thrust her left hand in front of his face, displaying her wedding band.

"Whoa. I'm a total dork. Sorry." The boy shrugged. "My mom raised me by herself, and the food you bought reminds me of our holiday meals. When I see women by themselves with kids around town, I can usually spot which ones are on their own. I assumed you were one of them."

The automatic doors started to close.

Beth moved out to the sidewalk and tucked a blanket around the front pack, cocooning Isaac. "Assuming is a dangerous practice."

"Hey." The teenager glanced over his shoulder. "This is only my second day here. Like, if you tell my boss I said that, he might fire me."

"Then you'd have tomorrow off." The worry on his face made her smile. "No harm done. A tip, though? Stick with talking about the weather or the possibility of the mill shutting down or what brand of toilet paper they bought. Don't delve into a customer's personal business."

"Yes, ma'am." He loaded the groceries into her trunk while she buckled Isaac into his car seat. "Have a good day." He ran the cart back into the store, gathering others on his way.

Staring across the parking lot, she started the engine and let the car idle. Single mother. She was, wasn't she? Though her heart was still married to Keith, in reality she was going to raise Isaac on her own. Discipline, spiritual teaching, talks about girls—all of them were her responsibility.

She rested her head against the steering wheel, suddenly too tired to sit upright.

Isaac had slept all through the shopping and would be wide-awake when they got home. No chance for her to have any down time.

She could rustle up a quick lunch, take a long, hot bath with him, and they could nap together. The thought of her head sinking into her pillow made her straighten up and drive.

It took three trips for her to carry all the bags into the house, Isaac cozy in the front pack. She opened the cupboard and her mother's handiwork stared back at her. She and Beth hadn't talked since that day—the day she ended up with egg on her floor.

And egg on her face.

After her mom left, the mess was still there. And who had to clean it up? She did, of course. How could she allow her mother to get at her that way?

She stuffed the groceries into the cupboard, disregarding the alphabetized order, and banged the doors shut.

Beth's heart quivered. Did God expect her to forgive so soon?

Her heart was too raw. Of course distancing her mother didn't fit in with any purpose God had planned for her, but it felt good.

Beth closed the cupboard door. There was always time to do the right thing later.

Chapter Forty-nine

Suzanne cranked up the heat and looked out the kitchen window. Frost still covered the lawn this early December afternoon, but her heart had to be colder yet.

Empty soup cans spread their jaws, sharp edges as dangerous as fangs. Bread crusts littered the counter and desiccated carrot and potato peelings hung from the sides of the sink like feathers on a boa. Spilled coffee grounds gritted against the bottom of Suzanne's bare feet.

She brushed them off on the area rug. She would have to break down and clean up this mess sometime. Today had been filled with the same thing as yesterday and the day before that—hours spent hiding in bed punctuated by onslaughts of tears that drained her dry.

Yes, she had been much too busy to clean house today.

The phone rang, startling her.

Let the answering machine pick it up. She did not have the energy to converse with people. A simple "Yes" or "No" was all she could manage, and many people seemed uncomfortable with that. It was less complicated to let the machine intercept the call until she could conveniently forget to return it.

Jake's voice said, "You've reached the Corbins. Neither of us is available to take your call, but if you leave your name and number, we'll get back to you as soon as we can."

Nancy said it was macabre to use that recording, but Suzanne couldn't bear to erase Jake's message. Sometimes, in the darkest hours of the night when sleep was her enemy, she would push the button over and over, listen to him, and long for the days when he had said words meant only for her ears.

A voice intruded. "Hello, it's Pastor Alan. Calling to see how you're doing. But since you're not answering, you're probably over at Beth's, spending time with that new grandson of yours. He must have you wrapped around his little finger. I'd be over there all the time too, if I were you. Call if you need anything."

Showed how much he knew.

The weeks since her run-in with Beth had slogged by with little contact between the two. Funny—they'd had more misunderstandings in the last month than in all of Beth's life. At a time when circumstances had plotted against them, a time when she needed her daughter's love and friendship the most, Beth had let her down.

No one really cared about her anymore. The flood of sympathy cards had ceased, with only bills filling the mailbox each day. Friends stopped calling, and no one ever dropped by.

Not that she blamed them. Who wanted to spend time with her anyway?

Maybe Beth had told them about the abortion.

No wonder they were ignoring her. Everyone from God on down had turned his back on Suzanne. Or, at the very least, forgotten about her.

She had given up asking Beth's permission to go over and see Isaac. Beth offered one excuse or another as to why it wasn't a good time. Obviously, her daughter was able to manage on her own after all. Felt free to use Grandma when it was advantageous, but discarded her like expired milk afterward.

Days and nights blended into each other. Her bed was now her new best friend. How many days had she slept in this sweat suit? How long since she'd washed her hair? It didn't matter, anyway. Nothing did.

She thought of making toast, but fuzzy blue-green mold covered the loaf of bread. The garbage can under the sink reeked. It needed to be taken outside.

But not today.

She turned her back, left the kitchen. She wasn't hungry after all.

A phone book lay open on the dining table, the yellow pages catching her attention. That's right, she tried looking something up last night. Something important. Suzanne picked up the phone, found the number she was looking for, and placed the call.

"Patton Insurance—this is Stacy."

"Uh, hi." The words stuck in her throat. She was unable to go on.

"May I help you, ma'am?"

"Yeah." Suzanne rubbed her eyes, tried to concentrate on getting the information she needed. "I was wondering, do you pay out life insurance on suicides?"

"Well, … I don't know. Never had a question like that before. I'm a new receptionist here, so let me ask someone else. Hang on a minute."

Stacy's muffled voice, as if she'd put her hand over the receiver to ask her question, came into Suzanne's ear.

A moment later, a man was on the line. "You have a question about suicide?"

"Yes, does suicide void a life insurance policy?"

"What's your name, ma'am?"

"It doesn't matter. I just want an answer to my question." His prying got on her nerves.

"It matters to me, ma'am. We don't give out that kind of information to anonymous callers. Why do you want to know?"

"It's for a friend of mine. Her husband died, and she needs to know if she gets the money."

"And your name?"

The end result was worth the loss of privacy. "Suzanne. Suzanne Corbin."

"Mmm." It sounded as if he was making note of it. "Okay, this is how it works. If her husband had a policy with us for two years or longer, then yes, the monies would be paid out."

She hung up without officially ending the conversation, closed the phone book, and padded down the hall to her bedroom.

An hour later, the doorbell rang. Nancy stood on the stoop with a bag of Chinese take-out. "Jim's at a seminar in Seattle, so I thought I'd come join you for dinner tonight."

Suzanne stayed in the doorway, keeping Nancy from seeing into the house. "I'm not really feeling that well."

"Oh, Suzanne, you must have caught that flu that's going around."

Not likely, since she lived like a hermit.

Most people would take a step back at hearing someone was sick, but Nancy moved closer. "Let me come in and make you a cup of tea."

"I don't think that's a good idea." She forced a hollow cough.

"Are you sure? I brought yummy food." Nancy lifted the bag.

Delicious aromas of sweet and sour pork and fried rice wafted out. "I'm sure. I don't want you to get sick."

"But we always share our fortunes. Can we at least do that?" At Suzanne's nod, Nancy fished two fortune cookies out of the bag. She handed one to Suzanne and bit into hers. "'You will have many friends.' Well, that was certainly profound. What does yours say?"

Suzanne half-heartedly opened hers.

A wise man savors each moment, never knowing when it will be his last.

Unbidden tears welled up in her eyes and cascaded down her cheeks.

"You should leave." Suzanne moved back to shut the door. "I want to be alone."

The shocked look on her friend's face mirrored Suzanne's inner turmoil. "Suzanne, what is it? Did I do something wrong?"

"Try to understand," she pleaded. "I need to be by myself right now."

Nancy put a hand against the door, keeping it open. "Suzanne, I realize there's no way I can understand exactly what you're going through. But I care about you. Don't keep hurting so badly. Allow me close enough to help you."

"Just go."

Nancy dropped her hand. "If you really want me to, I will. But I'm going to come check on you tomorrow. And I won't accept any excuses like I did for Thanksgiving."

Suzanne watched through the picture window as her friend drove off. She locked the door, pulled the drapes, and curled up on the couch under her favorite afghan. The dampness of her collar, wet from tears, felt cool against her skin.

That fortune, what had it said? Something about never knowing when life would be over, and needing to savor it? Why hadn't she done that with Jake that last day? Instead, she had nothing to live with but regret.

φφφ

She awakened during the night. The deep sense of despair that had rocked her to sleep in its arms greeted her the second she opened her eyes. It had gained weight during the hours she slept and sat atop her bed, both feet pressing heavily on her chest. Her breath came in shallow gasps and what air she was able to inhale seemed ineffective. She turned on the bedside lamp, pushed her pillow against the headboard, and cautiously rested her back against it. Maybe the change of position would ease her breathing.

Her movement reflected in the dresser mirror across the room. For a moment it was the personification of despair. Even without her contacts in, she saw dejection in the woman looking back at her in the moonlight.

"That can't be me," she whispered. "I look like an ancient old crone. Like something from Shakespeare." She had lost weight since the accident. A skeletal face, sunken cheeks.

What should she expect? All her life juices had been inexorably leaking out. Her heart probably circulated formaldehyde.

Even Beth and Isaac weren't enough to give her a reason to enjoy life. Especially since Beth had pushed her aside.

Beth was young and attractive. She would soon find a decent man to marry and he would become a father to Isaac.

There would be even less room in her heart for Suzanne.

She forced herself out of bed, trudged to the bathroom, and splashed cold water on her face. The close-up view in the mirror showed a more pathetic scene than what she'd seen in the bedroom. Dark circles had taken up permanent residence. Dull, lackluster eyes stared back at her, a myriad of wrinkles radiating from them like African tribal markings. Her skin was sallow, hair limp and lifeless.

The moment had come. There were things to set in motion.

No more lying around.

No more killing time.

Chapter Fifty

The clock showed well after midnight.

Where the energy came from, Suzanne didn't know. She was simply aware of a powerful force sweeping through her body, giving her muscles strength she hadn't possessed in weeks. Fueled by a sense of urgency, a manic surge whipped her to a frenzy.

An unfamiliar sensation of hunger gnawed at the pit of her stomach. It didn't matter—she could eat or not eat what she wanted, when she wanted. There was no one to answer to. She headed to the kitchen.

The stench of rotting food overwhelmed. She pulled the half-full garbage can out from under the sink, afraid of finding maggots if she examined it too closely. She opened the fridge and tossed all the contents into the trash—congealed milk, bologna with curled edges, slimy zucchini, Tupperware containers filled with who knew what. Soon the refrigerator was bare. She found a TV dinner stashed in the back of the freezer, brushed the ice crystals off, and started the oven.

While her Chicken Delight baked, she attacked the rest of the kitchen, relishing the order that, inch by inch, replaced chaos. The sink sparkled, countertops shone, and linoleum glistened by the time her food was ready.

She ate while making a list of things she didn't want to overlook. It was important to cover her bases, make things as easy as possible for Beth. No sense leaving things up in the air.

When she finished her planning session, it was 3:30 in the morning. Rain fell, creating white noise that tempted her to dull her pain in the anesthetic of sleep. She shook off the inclination and went outside to stand under the overhang on the patio. Moisture carried on the cold breeze, hitting her face and wetting her hair.

After a few minutes, she turned her back on the storm. Inside, she rummaged through the bedroom closet, found a pair of jeans and a yellow pullover, and took them with her into the bathroom. Teeth chattering, she stepped into a steaming shower.

She dried off. After days and nights of wearing the same clothes, the clean garments caressed her body. She stripped her bed and started a load of wash before retrieving empty boxes from the attic. In the living room, she set them on the floor and carried armloads of clothing from her dresser drawers and closet until the boxes were filled.

She left Jake's clothes. Beth might want something of her father's.

The blue dress she and Jake had fought about the last time they spoke hung in the back of the closet. After the funeral, she'd brought it home from the dry cleaner's. She stood in the center of her room, undecided as to the fate of the dress, before laying it out on the freshly made bed. Searching through her jewelry box, she found earrings that matched the outfit. She attached them to the bodice of the dress, piercing the material with their sharp posts.

Morning dawned as she finished crating up all her clothes. Misty clouds hovered. Rays of sun broke through the gray.

She got a blanket from the linen closet and spread it on the floor. Beth had always mentioned how she would love to have the painting that hung behind the couch. Suzanne lifted the frame from its nail and wrapped it in the blanket. Not professional, but it would provide the protection she desired.

Her feet dragged as she made a final pass through the house, energy spent. She moved from room to room, remembering happier days, occasions that had brought joy and fulfillment to her heart as a wife and mother. Those days were gone, consigned only to memories.

I nearly forgot.

She hurried to her bedroom, opened the closet door one last time, and unearthed a small suitcase in the corner.

The latches opened with a gentle push.

She slid Jake's clothing along the closet rod, rejecting each piece until she came to his velour bathrobe. She slipped the maroon warmth around her body, stroked the elbows that had grown thin through the years. Buried her nose in the lush fabric, savored the Jake-ness of it.

The robe was bulky, but she crammed it in the suitcase, snapped the latches closed, and carried it out to the car. She returned to the living room for the painting. "Good bye, Jake." The whisper echoed in the quiet.

Traffic was sparse so early in the morning. She pulled against the curb in front of Beth's house, stared at the window on the second story where Isaac should be sleeping. She opened the trunk and removed the blanketed bundle.

She rapped softly on the front door. If Isaac still slept, she didn't want to wake him quite yet. There was no response, so she knocked again, louder.

Mizpah's wild bark punctured the morning's silence.

So much for being quiet.

Within a few moments the door opened. Beth blocked the

entrance with her body. “Mom? What are you doing here?”

“I was in the neighborhood and thought I’d drop by. If that’s okay.” The painting was getting heavy. She put it down on the stoop and leaned it against the lower part of her leg.

“I don’t know if that’s such a good idea.” Beth’s eyes darted to the blanket-covered package, then back to Suzanne’s face.

“Please, honey, I’m your mom.”

“Exactly. That’s the problem.”

The heat of embarrassment warmed her face. “May I come in? I won’t stay long.”

“You promise?” Beth moved aside.

She picked up the painting and scooted by. “Where’s my grandson? I thought the dog’s barking would wake him up.”

“He was beginning to stir when you knocked.” Beth started up the stairs, gathering her robe around her. “And Mizpah only barks at strangers.”

Suzanne propped the covered painting against the living room wall and awaited Beth’s return. She hadn’t expected her daughter to be so angry, to harbor such a grudge. What about Christian forgiveness, anyway?

When Beth came downstairs, Isaac was cuddled in her arms.

Suzanne automatically reached out her hands for him.

Beth held him tighter. “I’m not so sure I want him to have another haircut. I’m still recovering from the last one.”

Suzanne cringed. This wasn’t how she wanted it to end. “Beth, please. I want to hold him.”

Beth seemed to weigh her request before answering. “Okay, but only for a minute. He needs to eat, and I don’t want to get thrown off schedule. We have plans today.” She passed the baby over.

The soft weight of her grandson was too much. His innocent sweetness evoked emotions she didn't want to acknowledge, brought tears she didn't want to spill. She covered his little face with kisses, sang nonsense words he would never remember.

"So, seriously, why are you here?" Beth removed her son from Suzanne's embrace. "I don't remember inviting you for breakfast." Beth's tone was icy, the sarcasm thick.

Suzanne recoiled from the hurt. "Don't worry. I already ate. I just wanted to see you guys before I left."

"You're going someplace?"

"I'm going to the coast. To a women's retreat Pastor Alan told me about. He thought it might help me." She forced herself to sound relaxed.

"That's a bit hard to believe. You never were a retreat kind of person."

"I know, but this is an opportunity for me to take a look at my life, see where I'm going. I thought you, of all people, would approve of that."

Isaac fussed and Beth settled in the rocker, began to nurse him. "I don't know why you're suddenly concerned about my approval. You know best, as always, about everything."

"Is that how you see it?" Nerves tingled across her shoulders. "I'm sorry I—"

"I don't want to hear it anymore. You've gotten so much worse since Dad died. And without Keith here as a buffer, I can't deal with it. You're getting me so worked up I can't even nurse." Beth raised Isaac to her shoulder and patted his back. "Maybe we can talk later."

"Yeah, maybe later. I've got to go. Let me tell my

grandson good-bye." She crossed the room, crouched next to the rocker, and cupped her hand over his head, his dark hair silky to the touch. "Never forget your grandma loves you, little one." She used the rocker arm as leverage to get up, took her purse, and headed toward the door. "Take good care of him, Beth."

"It's going to take time, Mom. Give me some time."

"Sure. We have lots of time. Until then, remember that though I'm not perfect, I love you to death." Suzanne left, stepped across the slippery ground, and opened the door to her car.

Beth called out. "Wait. You forgot your package."

"No, it's for you." She pulled her door shut and fastened her seat belt. She glanced at her rear view mirror as she drove away.

Beth's beautiful, puzzled face grew smaller and smaller.

Chapter Fifty-one

"He's eaten, so he should be fine for a few hours." Beth handed Isaac across the half-door of the church nursery to Melissa, Pastor Alan's daughter.

"I'll come find you if I need to, Mrs. Harris."

Beth propped the diaper bag on the door. "It sure is nice of you to watch the kids for the Spiff-up-the-church Day."

"Is that what my dad is calling it this year?" Melissa rolled her eyes. "Anyway, babies are *so* cute and I don't like to get my hands dirty."

"That's why I brought work gloves. So my perfectly manicured fingernails would not be damaged while I serve the Lord." Beth showed off her plain, chewed-to-the-quick nails.

Melissa giggled and lifted Isaac away from her body. "He's really small and all, but I promise he's okay with me 'cause I will be *so* careful. And there's lots of other kids from the youth group helping out, too."

"I know. Your dad says you're a natural. If you hadn't been here to take care of Isaac, I'm not sure I would have come."

Melissa blushed. "Your son is *so* handsome. All the little girls in here are going to be drooling over him."

"Or maybe they're teething." Beth left the nursery and moseyed in between people to the church kitchen. She dropped a tea bag into her insulated mug emblazoned with *#1 Teacher* and filled it with hot water.

Alan walked up. "Thanks for coming, Beth. We're all

meeting in the lobby in five minutes."

"Yes, sir." She emptied three sugar packets into the cup and stirred with a white plastic spoon.

People milled around in the lobby, everyone dressed for getting dirty. A deacon who usually sported a suit and tie wore ripped jeans and a grungy sweatshirt. Much of the church crowd had on overalls and boots.

She glanced down at her outfit. Her legs were twice the size of normal because of thermals under her oldest running pants. But her mind had already been somewhat distracted from wondering why Mom had given her the painting. Thinking of helping others left less room to obsess about herself.

"Everyone, listen." Alan stood in the middle of the room. "We've got a lot of cleanup to do today. Fall sneaked by and winter surprised us. I asked you to dress warmly because most of you will be outside."

Beth unzipped her hoodie.

"The flowerbeds need cut back and mulched. Bushes need pruning. We need a couple people to caulk the siding, especially around the windows. There's a little electrical repair. Deep cleaning the church kitchen. And some lucky people get to work on Christmas decorations."

Hands shot up all over the room.

"I see we've got quite a few volunteers for the fun task. Unfortunately for you wimps, we've already assigned you according to your abilities. Or lack thereof."

Several people moaned.

"Okay, okay. Let's get to it. Your team leaders probably called you earlier this week if your job is technical, so you know who you are. If you haven't heard from anyone, a list is posted on the sanctuary door. Thanks again for giving up a whole day to make your church a more attractive place."

She waited for the crowd to disperse. If she ended up working in the kitchen, she'd need to take off a layer of clothing. She ran her finger down the work list.

Beth Harris. There she was, under Outdoor Decorations. The name right below hers jumped out.

Tony Barnett.

What? He didn't go to their church. She spun around to find a plaid shirt blocking her path. She glanced up.

Tony smiled at her. "So, we're working together." His voice surprised her with its deepness. Maybe he sounded huskier than usual from the early morning air ... or he was fighting a cold …

She stepped to the side. "What a surprise. I never thought you'd be here."

He frowned. "I hope it's not an imposition. Alan invited me the last time I talked to him."

"No." She started out the door. "It's a free country. Anyone can fix up a church, right?"

"Right." Tony followed her outside.

Brett Calvin waited on the grass. He latched on to her sleeve, dragging her across the frost-tipped lawn. The short man sniffed, his constant allergies wreaking havoc with his respiratory system. "Glad I snagged you, Beth. When Alan put me in charge of coordinating all the lights, I panicked. Then I thought, if I get Beth Harris, she'll pull it all together."

"Um, thanks. But why do you have so much confidence in me?" Beth edged her arm from his grasp and matched his stride.

"We caroled at your home last year, don't you remember?

Your yard looked like it belonged in a decorator's magazine. I'm hoping you can work that same magic with these $2.80 strings of lights." He walked with quick, nervous steps.

"Our electric bill in January wasn't so beautiful." She glanced over her shoulder.

Tony trailed behind, thumbs hooked through his belt loops, head rocking from side to side in cadence with his stride.

"I'll do my best, Brett." Her breath puffed out in front of her, breaking apart beneath the overcast sky. "Show me what I've got for raw materials."

Half an hour later, she and Tony were stringing blue lights around the bare maple tree at the entrance to the parking lot.

"Keep the cords right at the edge of the branches and it will show off the shape of the tree." She handed another string up the ladder.

"Yes, ma'am." He looped a strand over a high branch. "Have you talked to Luke Winslow yet?"

She scuffed her toe on the ground. "I'm planning to call him soon. It's just been busy." Plus she had no idea what to say to the boy.

A man with a scarf wrapped around his neck and an Elmer Fudd hat, complete with earflaps, strode over. "Looking good." Her pastor's voice.

He was right. Already, blue sparkles dappled the limbs. A festive feeling washed over her. With Christmas less than a month away, she needed to work things out with her mom. Otherwise, it would be just Isaac and she beside a scraggly pine, pretending they made a family. The day would be as pitiful as Thanksgiving had been.

"How's your mom doing, Beth?"

She stepped onto the lowest rung of the ladder and pulled on the tail end of a string Tony was trying to untangle. "I haven't been the best example of love these last few weeks. She gets on my nerves so quickly."

Tony's gaze rested on her for a moment, then returned to the lights.

"When she comes back, I need to apologize."

Alan lifted his head. "Where is she?"

"At the retreat you sent her on."

"I don't know about any retreat."

Beth hopped off the step. "The one at the coast?"

"Nope. Are you sure she said I told her? Maybe Women's Ministries set it up."

Crossing her arms, she shook her head. "She came by this morning and brought me a painting Dad had given her. Kind of like buying my love back, I think. She said she was heading to the coast overnight for a retreat *you* recommended."

Tony cleared his throat. "Is there any reason she would lie to you?"

"No. Mom never lies. This doesn't make sense." She searched the crevices of her memory for anything else her mother had said. In the dark room of her mind, she bumped against a sharp thought.

Her mother *had* lied to her.

Chapter Fifty-two

Sirens wailed in Tony's head. If he'd been in the Navy it might have been sonar beeps; a firefighter, blasts of an alarm. But as a cop, he heard sirens when Beth's face paled as soon as she'd said her mother always told the truth. He sensed a story behind the change, yet more than that bothered him.

He balanced a box of lights on the top of the ladder and climbed down. "So, neither of you knows where Suzanne is?"

They shook their heads and looked to him for help, as if his training gave him extraordinary skill to divine the whereabouts of missing persons.

"Let's start from the top." He pointed at Beth. "She came by and gave you a present. She said she was leaving?"

"Yes. For the coast."

"Did it feel like she was saying a final good-bye?"

Beth eyes grew huge. "You don't think …"

"Alan, can I talk to you for a second?" He moved away from the ladder, hoping the pastor would follow.

Alan did, but so did Beth.

"Tony, if you've got something to say about my mother, I want to hear it. If you have a reason to believe she might hurt herself, I need to know."

"Beth." He grabbed hold of both her shoulders. "I want a minute with your mother's pastor. I'm going to ask, as an officer, about anything she may have confided to him, which is protected because he's clergy. Trust me when I say I don't want you to be a witness to that."

Her brown eyes stared up at him, filled with fear.

"There's no reason to worry about your mom yet. And Alan might choose not to tell me anything."

Alan tugged on an earflap of his hat. "Tony, if I had any information, I would share it with you, but I don't. Suzanne has avoided me ever since I helped her husband see he needed new life in order to really live. That privilege you were talking about? She's never taken advantage of it."

Tony's stomach growled. Almost lunchtime, but it didn't appear food was in the short-term forecast. He rolled his neck. "So she's never discussed spiritual stuff with you?"

"Suzanne has not, as far as I know, ever accepted the love of Jesus. Anytime I bring it up, she closes down."

The opposite of Beth. She had stuck with God during a hard time instead of walking away.

He rubbed his forehead, tracing the creases with a gloved finger. "Can we take a look at the church schedule? Maybe there *is* a women's retreat at the coast. They send you brochures and stuff, right?"

"Let's check my secretary's file folders. She keeps them categorized by month."

"We could call and see if Mom's registered." Beth set off for the church building.

The nasally, mustached man who had given them the job of decorating waved his arms. "Wait, you're not done yet. I've got another crate of boxes in the car."

Beth broke into a trot and yelled back, "Sorry, Brett. Something's come up."

Alan stomped his feet on the huge rubber mat unfurled outside the double glass doors. "Melissa's got my office keys."

The heated air of the lobby hit like a wave.

Tony took off his gloves.

"I'll get the keys, grab Isaac, and meet you guys by the office." Beth disappeared down a hallway.

"I'm glad you happened to be here, Tony." Alan doffed his hat and unwrapped his scarf, walking the opposite way Beth had gone.

"'Happened' to be? Don't you preachers believe God's in control of everything?"

Alan dropped the hat and scarf beside the office door. "He most definitely is. And He's going to use you today, if you let Him."

"Why? Is there something you couldn't say in front of Beth?"

"I only hear what God tells me. And He says He'll use anyone who's willing."

Tony leaned against the wall. Willing? If he could serve God today, would he? "What is God telling you about Suzanne?"

Alan glanced up the hallway as if making sure Beth wasn't coming back yet. "I don't hear an actual voice, but I know she's in trouble. I'm praying we can reach her in time."

They stood in silence for a few minutes.

Tony's palms itched to get going. Flipping through paper work, making phone calls, anything—anything but standing around doing nothing.

Beth ran up, breathing hard, Isaac cradled in her arms. "Melissa wasn't there. She was wandering all over the place looking for me." She held a small key ring out to Alan. A fish made of two square nails twisted together hung from the ring. "Can I use the back office while you look in Carlene's desk?"

"No problem." Alan let them into the front office.

Beth vanished behind another door, leaving it open a crack. "Let me know if you find anything." Her voice carried over sounds of Isaac's fussing.

Seconds later, he quieted.

Alan tugged on a file drawer, pulled out a moss green folder marked *December*, and flipped it open. "Grab a stack."

Tony took a handful of papers and scanned them one by one. A hard copy of an email broadcasting the work party. A present-wrapping get-together announcement. A brochure for a retreat at Cannon Beach Conference Center.

"Got it." He held the pamphlet up.

Alan snatched it as Beth propped open the door, keeping part of her body hidden.

"Nope." Alan sighed. "The date's next weekend."

Tony stared at the info. When would he learn to check his facts before opening his mouth? Somehow, he always flubbed in front of Beth. She must think he made a career out of feeding her misinformation. "Sorry, Beth, I should have looked closer."

She rolled her eyes. "Keep going. Maybe there's another one." She let the door start to close. "Pastor Alan, have you checked your messages yet today?"

"I've been too busy getting everyone started with the work party. Why?"

"The red light is flashing."

"When you're done with Isaac, I'll listen to it."

They exhausted the folder's contents by the time Beth reappeared.

Alan entered his office and closed the door behind him.

Tony rocked back in the secretary's leather office chair.

"Isaac's bigger, isn't he?"

"I think that's the way it works." Beth smiled, her lips full. "But I don't have to take him to the doctor for daily weigh-ins anymore."

"You've been seeing the doctor everyday? That must have—"

Alan threw the door open. "Come listen to this."

Beth's mouth drew into a short, flat line. They crowded around the answering machine as Alan punched the playback button.

"Hi, Pastor Kearns. This is Stacy from Patton Insurance. We received a call from Suzanne Corbin a few minutes ago. We usually contact spouses in this situation, but since her husband is deceased, my supervisor recommended I let you know. We got your name from her husband's obituary. She asked, supposedly for a friend, whether or not life insurance still paid out after suicide. Please let us know if we can assist in any way."

"Friday. 4:53 PM," the machine added.

"Mom, no!" Beth doubled over the desk. "We've got to find her."

Tony wanted to comfort her, but that wasn't his place. His value came from taking action. "First, we search her house."

Chapter Fifty-three

Rocky Point. Little more than a speck on the map, devoid of personality or tourist attractions. A simple town lost in the shadow of the stone formations at Cannon Beach or the tourism of Seaside's boardwalk, the places Suzanne and Jake had haunted through the years—walking on the beach, watching the distant horizon, and planning for the future.

The word *future* didn't exist anymore—there was no such thing. The past was all that mattered, and it could not be relived. The present was empty, too painful to contemplate.

Suzanne pulled off the highway onto a side street. No brand-name motels shouted their presence. Just weather-beaten storefronts interspersed with decrepit houses. Progress had skipped town decades ago, left a tired has-been in its place.

She drove up and down the streets, searching for the right address. The town was sheathed in silvery-gray light as the sun strained to burn away the overcast. She rolled her window down partway and inhaled the wintry ocean air.

She turned back to head toward the highway and she spotted it, set back against the western end of a pot-holed street. A hand-painted sign. *Bide Awhile—Cabins for Rent.*

She turned onto a narrow, graveled road and followed it until it ended in front of a dilapidated cabin.

Wooden shutters hung askew, banging in the wind. A stack of wood rested on the front porch and smoke curled from the crooked chimney, rising into the clearing sky. A large black and white dog pawed through an overturned garbage can. He snarled at her and went back to his task.

A white-haired man, shoulders stooped, came around the back edge of the cabin carrying a load of firewood. He dropped the logs to the ground and made his way to her side of the car. "Thought I heard something." He turned to the side, spat, and wiped the back of his hand across his mouth. "You wantin' a cabin?"

Maybe she should gun the engine and peel out of the drive. The ad in the paper hadn't told the real story. Some spin-doctor had worked his magic, created a mythical tale of quaint cabins nestled in coastal forests. Hadn't said a thing about sagging shutter, a phlegmy old geezer, and his killer dog.

She rolled her window up a little further. "Actually, I called yesterday and made a reservation."

The man slapped a hand on the side of his overalls and guffawed. "That was smart of you. Yup, gotta have a reservation to get in here." He snorted and spat again.

Right. Like this was *the* place to stay on the coast. Well, she was here, and it didn't much matter what the accommodations were. She could live with them. "I asked for your most secluded cabin. One closest to the ocean."

"That would be lucky number seven. It's kinda off by itself. An easy walk to the beach." He reached into the pocket of his pants and pulled out a metal ring packed with keys. His arthritic fingers shuffled through them until he came to the right one. He unclipped it. "Here's the key. You can drive down and park right by the cabin. Should be clean towels in there. If not," he cackled, "call room service." He walked a few paces away.

"Hey, wait. Don't I need to check in?"

"Don't worry about it. Stop by the office when you're ready to leave and we'll take care of things then. Bruiser, leave that there garbage alone." He picked up a piece of firewood and threw it in the dog's general direction.

Bruiser slunk off, growling over his shoulder.

The battered, robin-egg-blue door of the cabin had a rusty handle and a dead bolt for the lock. Not too fancy, but she didn't need fancy. Or safe.

Mustiness thickened the air inside the one-bedroom cabin. She threw her lone suitcase on top of the saggy bed and inventoried her surroundings. Black mold resided in the corner of the shower, an elaborate cobweb on the bathroom window. A small radiator stood against the bedroom wall, dusty towels resting on top.

No television, no phone.

No problem. She wouldn't be spending much time here.

Outside, she listened to the distant surf. The pale-blue sky was now empty of clouds. A light wind mussed her hair.

She locked the door behind her and wandered down the path toward the ocean. A wide, sandy beach stretched out before her. She continued along the shoreline, walking close to the waves that flirted with her shoes.

Broken shells littered the sand. Her longing for Jake was so intense she might shatter into a million pieces that would never fit back together. Though the sun was bright, it couldn't penetrate the darkness of her soul. Nothing could. She sank onto a large piece of driftwood and plunged her hands into her coat pockets.

A young couple walked past, arms wrapped around each

other's waists. The woman's long hair whipped in the breeze and she lifted a graceful hand to brush it from her eyes. They looked newly wed, birdseed almost clinging to their clothes. In a burst of exuberance, the man broke the embrace, grabbed the woman's hand, and pulled her into a run along the surf. Their joy in each other was so obvious it seemed obscene.

A shriek of laughter made Suzanne glance to her right.

A toddler, bundled in layers, threw a large beach ball toward the ocean. His father rushed after it as the wind seemed to join in the game.

Farther down the beach, a group of teenagers flew multicolored kites, and a solitary man threw Frisbees to a couple of invigorated dogs.

Everywhere she looked, people were enjoying life. She didn't belong here.

Brushing sand from her pants, she walked back in the direction of her cabin.

An elderly couple came toward her, strolling arm-in-arm, talking animatedly with each other as if an invisible cord of history bound them together.

A primal scream erupted from the pit of Suzanne's stomach before she had the opportunity to stifle it.

Those nearest turned their shocked faces toward her.

For the first time in her life, she didn't care what other people thought. She ran toward the cabin, tears pouring like hot lava down her cheeks.

That should have been us. Jake and I were supposed to grow old together. We're the ones that should be walking on the beach. We're the ones that were supposed to get white hair. Why do other people get to, but not us? It's not fair! I can't stand it!

Anger, pain, and betrayal consumed her as dry heaves wracked her body. Anguished cries erupted from the core of her being, as though a dam had broken loose and nothing could hold back the flood.

By the time she arrived back at the cabin, she could barely stand. Fumbling with the key, she finally held it steady enough to insert into the lock. She closed the door behind her, locked it, and pushed the suitcase to the far edge of the bed.

Exhaustion hit with full force. It would take strength to carry out her plan. She didn't want to botch it, to leave any detail undone.

The bedsprings protested against the weight of her body.

She crawled under the covers, pulled them over her head. She would sleep for a few hours, wake one last time.

Chapter Fifty-four

Beth spotted the fake rock under the camellia bush. She flipped the stone over and retrieved the spare key. “This decoy’s been around since junior high.”

Alan held Isaac.

Thankfully he had offered instead of Tony, who still seemed like a stranger. Something about him kept her from letting down her guard. He’d been the messenger who told her about Keith’s accident. His lips had shaped the words informing her of her father’s death. Though their paths had twisted together in a bizarre way—the accident, the investigation, and involvement with both Britney and Luke—they led separate lives. To forge a friendship with a man so soon after losing Keith seemed disrespectful.

Yes, even a friendship would be out of place.

Who knew if that was all Tony wanted, anyway? A nice man like him, compassionate and committed, could be in the market for a wife. If she allowed him to become involved in her life, how would she insure his sense of duty would remain only that?

“Shall we?” Tony gestured at the lock, impatience evident in his movement.

Shaking off her uncertainty, she let them into her childhood home.

Boxes lined the foyer, each labeled *Goodwill* with a black marker. Another army of boxes circled the dining room table. The scent of Lemon Pinesol, overlaid with a hint of Windex, filled the air. The house had no smell of its own. Both her parents' presence had been wiped away.

"Wow." Tony slowly turned in the middle of the living room, surveying the entire area. "Last time I was here, magazines were piling up, dishes were strewn around. Now it looks as if a germaphobe from the CDC lives here."

"It's empty." A ridiculous statement. Boxes and furniture surrounded them, but her mother was missing. "She's definitely gone."

Tony raised a hand. "Stay here. I'll search the bedrooms."

She closed her eyes. *Please, Lord, lead us to Mom. Protect her.*

When Tony ambled back, shaking his head, Beth exhaled the breath she'd been holding. At least they knew Suzanne had not harmed herself at home, even if they were no closer to finding her.

"These were on her bed, Beth." Tony held out two envelopes. One labeled *Beth*, one *Isaac*.

Whatever words they secured were words that would kill hope. "I won't open them. Not unless I have to."

"She's also got a dress laid out, accessories and all."

A sword lopped off a huge chunk of that hope.

Alan handed Isaac to Beth and walked into the kitchen. "I'm no cop, but I think we should start by going through her garbage. She might have thrown away a clue."

Tony arched his eyebrows.

"Hey, it works in the movies." Alan opened the cupboard door under the sink and pulled out the trashcan. A fresh liner billowed in the rectangle. "Okay, maybe the bathroom trash. Or the garbage can outside."

"Won't work," Tony said. "I checked the can at the curb

when we pulled in. Either it got picked up this morning, or Suzanne made a run to a Dumpster."

"Mom cleaned everything out." The finality of what her mother might have done sucker-punched her stomach. She sank onto the couch and laid her cheek on Isaac's head. He felt hot.

"Oh." Alan grabbed the notepad by the phone, tipped a pencil against it, and rubbed. "If she wrote down a phone number, we can call it."

Tony crossed his arms, leaned against the counter, and shook his head. "That would be too easy."

"You're right. Nothing." Alan balled up the piece of paper, threw it into the trashcan, and shoved it back under the sink.

Beth laid Isaac on her lap. "Play her messages, if she has any." It worked in Alan's office. Maybe it would provide direction for them now.

"There's an old one." Tony hit the button.

"Hi, Suzanne. Nancy again. I'm calling to tell you that you're meeting me for a late lunch today at CJ's Coffee Shop. I'm not asking anymore, because you'll say no anyway. So I'll see you at 1:30. And …" her voice changed to a more intimate tone "… I think it's real progress to take Jake's message off the machine. See you then."

The phone rang as the machine beeped.

Beth jumped up. "Should I answer it?"

"Sure." Tony moved aside.

"Hello?"

There was a pause. "Beth? Is that you?"

"Yes."

"It's Nancy."

Clenching the phone between her cheek and shoulder, Beth pulled Isaac's blanket back and fanned him with it. "We were just listening to your message."

"So your mom is with you? I've been waiting for her to join me for the last half hour."

"Actually, I'm with Pastor Alan and a … friend." She could kick herself. That was exactly what she determined Tony wouldn't be. "Do you have any idea where Mom might be? Did she mention going on a retreat to you?"

"No. What's going on?"

Isaac's forehead felt hotter. "We're trying to figure it out."

"I stopped by yesterday, but she wouldn't let me in the house."

"She's in trouble, Nancy."

"I get that feeling, too, Beth. Let me know what you find out. I'll be praying. Bye."

Beth hung up.

Tony snapped his fingers. "Give me the phone. I can't believe I didn't think of this right away."

"What are you doing?"

He brushed against Beth's hand as she passed him the phone. "It doesn't sound like Suzanne's been too talkative lately. Her last phone call might give us a clue to where she's gone."

"Great idea." Alan clapped his hands together.

The tones of redialing streamed from the phone. Tony put the receiver to his ear and grabbed the notepad Alan had used for his detective work. He waited, mouth open as though ready to speak. Instead, he scribbled for a moment, then held the paper up as he dropped the phone back into place.

Bide Awhile Cabins. Rocky Point.

"Some old guy saying to leave a message. I'm going to call the police department there and have them do a welfare check." Tony whipped out his cell.

Alan held up a hand. "This might not make sense, but I have the feeling we need to go in person. Suzanne might respond to someone she trusts. A uniformed police officer could push her to act more recklessly." Alan strode toward the door. "I'll drive you there, Beth. I'll have Melissa go home with a friend."

Isaac yawned. His cheeks sported red blotches and his eyes were unnaturally glassy.

"I think Isaac's coming down with something. Alan, I can't take him if he's sick. And I won't leave him with anybody else."

Tony pushed his sleeves up. "I could case the joint. See if Suzanne's car is there, try to find her."

"That's nice of you to offer, but she won't talk to you and you know it." Beth tugged at a piece of her hair.

"I'll go by myself." Alan checked his watch. "I could make it in about two and a half, three hours?"

"You would do that?"

"For one lost sheep, a shepherd leaves the flock."

Tony crossed the tile and opened the door. "Alan, I don't think you have a minute to waste."

They climbed into Beth's car and headed to the church. Beth sat in back, next to the car seat, staring out the passenger-side window as Alan drove. Would he be in time to save her mother? If only Isaac weren't sick.

Lord, I've been so horrible to Mom. Instead of offering her comfort, I've shown anger and impatience. I've made her believe I'd be better off without her. Forgive me. I can't handle losing her, too.

Alan pulled into the parking lot. "I'm hoping Suzanne will open up to me, Beth. Maybe the depth of my relationship with Jake will carry some weight. I'll do everything I can to bring her back to you."

She nodded.

"Tony, can you drive Beth home and stay with her until I call? She shouldn't be alone."

Tony took Alan's place behind the wheel as the pastor ran up the walk to the church, racing past the poinsettias someone had set along the pavement.

Outside the car window, blue lights twinkled in the maple tree.

Chapter Fifty-five

What was the proper thing to do when one's mother was missing? Beth had no idea. As she mulled over her options, she remembered she was stuck with an unasked-for companion.

Unasked for, but not unappreciated.

She turned to Tony. "What about your car? I can drive myself, you know."

He rolled through a stop sign.

Cop's prerogative?

"It's only a few blocks. I can walk back and get it later."

In this swirling maelstrom, his kindness steadied her.

A minute later, he parked the car in her driveway. Before she could, he reached for Isaac's baby carrier. He jiggled the fussy baby as she unlocked the front door.

Isaac squalled as they entered the house.

She went down the hall, adjusted the thermostat, and returned.

Tony had unstrapped Isaac from the carrier and held his tiny body close. The sight of her son in the arms of a man young enough to be his father didn't look right, especially since Keith had never held his son.

He seemed to sense her unease. "Here, Beth. He needs you."

She tucked a thermometer under Isaac's hot arm and swayed from side to side as the digital numbers grew. Over 102 degrees. "Would you mind getting the baby Tylenol from the upstairs bathroom cabinet? It's on the right-hand side."

As Tony clomped up the stairs, she spread a light blanket over her shoulder and tried to nurse Isaac.

He turned away from her offering, drawing his knees up to his tummy.

Mom would know what to do. I have no idea how to take care of a sick baby.

What a twist—her mother, who always had a suggestion, always wanted to be involved, couldn't be found when she *was* needed.

Beth's rejection had surely played a part in her mother's despondency. She groaned at the implications, guilt overwhelming her. *Oh, God, I'm so sorry. Please give me a chance to make it up to her.*

Tony's footsteps signaled his return. He handed her the bottle of medicine. "Is this the right one?"

She nodded, used the dropper to suck up the correct amount, and squirted the purple liquid into Isaac's mouth.

He sputtered.

The medicine dribbled out.

"Tony, what am I going to do?"

"Is there anything we can do to lower Isaac's temp? Like a cool bath?"

We. What a wonderful word.

"Good idea." She held Isaac in the crook of one arm as she wedged the baby tub into the kitchen sink. "Do you mind going back upstairs for his jammies? They're in the top drawer of his dresser. And his duck towel is hanging on a hook on the wall."

By the time Tony returned, Beth had undressed Isaac and lowered him into the tepid water.

Tony leaned against the counter and watched her.

She sponged Isaac's head. The rhythm of her movements calmed Isaac—the splash as she plunged the sponge under the surface, the trickle of water as she squeezed it over his skin. She dried, diapered, and dressed him. Paced until he fell into a fitful sleep.

"Will he wake up if you lay him down?" Tony whispered, gesturing at the playpen in the corner of the living room.

"I can try."

Isaac curled a fist beneath his chin as she eased him onto the mattress. He seemed more relaxed than she'd seen him in hours. She breathed a prayer of thanks. One less thing to worry about.

"You're a great mother." Tony scratched his shoulder blade as the two of them walked back into the kitchen.

"Thanks, it's easier when someone else is around." She filled the teakettle with water and set it on the stove. "I think I would have fallen to pieces if you hadn't been here, what with Isaac being sick and Mom being …" The tears took her by surprise.

His voice was deep, like a slow-moving river. "You know, I think you would have handled the situation fine if you'd been by yourself. There's a quiet strength in you."

Blushing, she put a basket of tea, apple cider, and hot chocolate packets next to a couple of mugs.

Tony stuck his head into the fridge and emerged with a jar of mayonnaise in one hand and a package of sliced ham in the other. "I'll make us some sandwiches."

Beth smiled. "Plates are up in the first cupboard on the left." She sat down on a kitchen chair, overcome with weariness.

He searched through a cupboard, making himself at home. “You got any chips around here?”

It felt too familiar. Her heart leaped in rebellion. “Tony, maybe you’d better make your sandwich to go.”

His hand froze in mid-air. “What’s the matter? I overstay my welcome?”

“Probably not.” She bent her head. “Never mind. I’m strung so tightly that everything rubs me the wrong way. Keep making the sandwiches.” She rose, rinsed the breakfast dishes in the sink, and stuck them in the dishwasher. Since her mother’s reorganization of the kitchen, she had left everything strewn about in silent mutiny against being controlled.

Tony must think she was a slob.

She closed the blinds on the window above the sink. “It’s dark already. He must be getting close by now.”

“Alan? Yeah, probably so. But that doesn’t mean he’ll be able to call right away. You understand that, don’t you?”

Her spirits sank lower at his words, at what he wasn’t saying. The unintentional clues left at the house showed a well thought-out plan. Her mother’s despair could make her capable of anything.

They ate their sandwiches, Beth’s crumbly and dry in her mouth.

Isaac whimpered from the other room.

Slow minutes ticked by, prolonging her misery. “Tony, don’t you have to work tonight?”

“I already called in sick.”

“When did you do that?”

“While you were finding the key at your mom’s. Wanted to give the department plenty of time to find someone to replace me on patrol tonight.” He dug in his pocket, brought out a knife, and wiped the blade on his pants before slicing an apple she'd left on the counter.

"Are you really sick?"

"No, but you're sick with worry." He smiled gently as he snapped his knife shut and offered her an apple wedge. "That's close enough."

Chapter Fifty-six

Suzanne tried to open her eyes, though she wasn't sure if they actually opened or not. Darkness had descended, filling the room with a blackness she couldn't see through. No light sneaked between the slats of her closed blinds, no sound penetrated her four walls. There was only the awful presence that had awakened her at home the night before.

She rolled to her side and felt for the small lamp she remembered seeing on the nightstand beside the bed. Her hand brushed against the wooden base and fingers climbed it to the switch. She pushed the toggle, inviting light into the room. A dim glow crept through the old-fashioned lampshade, creating gloomy shadows in far corners.

She sat up. What next?

Her stomach growled, complaining that she hadn't eaten for over eighteen hours. Mind, body, soul—all were full of emptiness.

She got up and went into the bathroom. The fluorescent bulb above the sink gave off a garish glow, caused her skin to look pasty, her eyes hollow. A diagonal crack ran the length of the mirror, cutting her face in two. She leaned over and ran cold water into her cupped hand, brought it to her mouth. The iron of old pipes defiled her tongue and she spat the water out. Another glimpse in the mirror spurred her on. She switched off the light, undid the bolt on the door, and stepped into the night air.

Fog slipped in and out between the trees, hiding the moon

from view.

She made her way to the car and unlocked the trunk, the small bulb inside illuminating the space. She paused and listened.

Only the far-off sound of the waves rushing to shore, the ever-present wind blowing through the trees. The isolation was ideal.

She stretched to reach the back recesses of the trunk and pulled out the canvas bag she'd stashed there several days ago. The weight of it reassured and lent approval to her plan.

Back in the cabin, the door wedged shut, Suzanne placed the bag on top of the dresser, removed her suitcase from the far side of the bed, and put it on the floor. She drew a deep breath.

I can do this. I have to do this.

The bedcovers were jumbled from her nap. Better to have them out of the way. She separated the tangled mass, folded the bedspread and sheets, and stacked them on the floor by the door.

The dirty mattress stared at her, daring her to add one more stain to its collection. That she would not do. She went to the dresser, opened the bag resting on top, and extracted the package within. Tough plastic enclosed a new tarp. Suzanne found a nail file in her purse and used it to penetrate the covering. She shook the wrinkled tarp free, the acrid chemical smell attacking her senses. Spreading the blue plastic over the bed, she smoothed the edges as carefully as if she were preparing her bridal bed. In reality, wasn't that what it was? The place where she would lie and wait to meet Jake?

The tarp crinkled beneath her as Suzanne lowered herself to the bed, feet still planted on the floor. She rubbed icy hands together. What lay ahead?

Wait for me, Jake—I'm coming.

Worrisome thoughts tumbled through her numb mind. A sense of unreality clung to the whole process, yet this was the most real thing in her universe. A conscious choice to take life and death into her own hands.

It meant more agony for Beth, but, in the long run, it was best. Beth was strong enough to grow past the pain. And Isaac? He would never know how much a part of his life his grandma had wanted to be. He couldn't miss what he never had.

The suitcase was awkward, but light, as she pulled it up beside her on the bed. She undid the clasps and spread it open, the hint of Jake's Old Spice pushing aside the stale air around her. Though she had packed it, knew what was inside, the sight of Jake's maroon bathrobe stabbed her wounded heart. He had worn it for so many years it seemed to be an extension of him.

She buried her nose in the worn fabric, inhaling memories, then stood and slipped her arms through the sleeves and tied the sash around her waist.

A couple of steps and she was standing before the dresser, the canvas bag in her hands once more. She brought it with her to the bed and withdrew the revolver. Her fingers tightened on the handle, unfamiliar but soothing.

Soothing, yes. Soon the pain would be gone.

Suzanne turned the barrel toward her, gazed at the black hole promising oblivion. The barrel was shaped like a lock—the kind opened by an old skeleton key. Indeed, it promised to be the key, the solution to her problems. She would rather die than live without Jake.

But would pulling the trigger really end the pain? What if the place she moved on to wasn't what she thought it to be?

The thought made her sick to her stomach. But she couldn't live with the anguish any longer.

The gun trembled in her hand and she laid it in her lap.

I just need a minute.

Her pulse was rapid, erratic.

But what if...

Her breathing ragged, skin sweaty.

What if Jake was right and heaven is a real place? What if he's there and I can't get in because of rejecting his Jesus? And if heaven's real, then what about hell? I might not join Jake after all.

Suzanne's stomach roiled, bile rising in her throat. She swallowed the burning acid, nausea growing with each passing moment.

She tightened her grip on the gun. Whatever waited on the threshold in the split-second after death … well, she would face it. There would be nothing she could change at that point.

She ran her finger along the barrel of the snub-nose gun, noted the Smith and Wesson imprint on the grip—an S with a W imposed on top, a circle around them both. The significance of the two letters hit her hard: the initials of her maiden name, Suzanne Whitten. She had become the woman she was—a woman sitting in a dark room, holding a gun—because of her experiences as Suzanne Whitten.

Childhood flashbacks appeared: report cards ridiculed because of one B, a ruler slapping her fingers after striking the wrong note during piano practice, being locked in her room after a boy called.

And Dylan. His eighteen-year-old face swam before her.

No. She didn't need to spend her last minutes this side of whatever thinking of him, of his bitter rejection of both her and their baby. He had haunted her enough. She wouldn't allow him to follow her to the grave.

Powerless tears, full of despair, tumbled down her cheeks. Suzanne wiped her eyes with the bathrobe's sash.

Jake would have used his fingers to absorb her tears, his compassion to ease her unrelenting sorrow. His undeserved love was the bedrock upon which she built her life.

Without it, she had nothing. No meaning, no purpose.

She centered herself on the double bed and made sure she could reach the switch on the lamp. Her hands, though still cold, no longer shook. An eerie calmness took over.

With the gun secure in one hand, Suzanne leaned over and turned off the light.

In utter darkness, she lay down on her back and lifted the smooth barrel to her mouth.

Chapter Fifty-seven

The barrel clinked against her teeth. The metallic taste gagged her. She closed her lips around the gun and counted.

Five … four …three …

Someone pounded on the door so hard she feared it might break down. She froze, finger on the trigger.

Quick. Do it now.

Inside her mind, a different voice whispered to take the gun from her mouth.

Another round of pounding. "Suzanne! It's Pastor Alan. Open the door!"

How could he know where she was? Or was it a figment of her imagination? His voice acting as the voice of God?

She placed the gun beside her on the tarp and stared at the darkened ceiling.

"I know you're in there. I see your car. And the light went off when I pulled up."

God wouldn't be so mundane. It must be Alan.

After a moment of silence, a loud thump reverberated, as if he had hit the cabin's outer wall. "Come on. All I want to do is talk."

The door rattled again, and Alan burst into the cabin.

He must not have expected the door to be unlocked because he pitched forward, his silhouette blocking the faint light from the fog-shrouded moon.

"Go away. I want to be left alone!"

Alan flipped the overhead light on, blinding her.

She ducked and huddled on the bed. Her closed eyes adjusted to the brilliance as she realized what she must look like wrapped in Jake's robe, curled on a tarp. Luckily, she'd moved the gun, hiding it from Alan's view.

He hurried to her. "Are you okay?"

She avoided his gaze. "Why did you come?"

He sank down next to her, and her body tilted into his warmth.

Even her flesh was a traitor.

It isn't too late. You can reach the gun.

And then what? Wrestle with Alan and chance having a stray bullet hurting him? He wouldn't sit back and watch her exercise her right to take her life.

He pulled her closer and stroked her hair. "I'm not going anywhere."

Silence.

His hand, rising and falling, caressed her head.

Nothing but silence.

He took her hands in his.

"Alan, I can't go on like this any longer. I hurt *so* badly." Teardrops trickled down her cheeks, and she tried to pull her hands from his grasp to wipe them away.

"No." He tightened his grip. "You need to let them flow. You keep covering up your hurts. Let them out. Don't be ashamed of them. Let me be here with you while you cry."

Could she really let go? Expose the fatal thoughts? What was there to lose? "I want to die. I want this life to be over. To feel nothing." She sobbed into his arms.

"Have you done anything yet, Suzanne? Did you take any pills?" He glanced around the room.

She wrenched her hands from his and bolted off the bed,

exposing the gun.

He reached for the weapon. “Thank You, Lord God. Thank You.” His voice trembled.

“Why would you thank Him? I’m about to blow my brains out on a tarp for easy cleanup, and you think God’s here?”

“Absolutely, because I arrived in time to stop you.” He flipped open the cylinder and let the bullets fall into his palm.

Maybe he would see how serious she was. Not one bullet, though she’d hoped that was all she’d need, but two. In case the first wasn’t completely effective.

She paced the room, lethargy replaced by anger. “I am so mad I could explode.” She grabbed a pillow from the bedding stacked by the door and sent it flying in Alan’s direction. “I want a padded cell where I can beat against the walls and scream at the top of my voice and not have to worry about anyone hearing me. And what’s with you, anyway?” Suzanne wiped her eyes. “Aren’t you a man of God? You want to say something wise that will make me feel better? God has ruined my life and there’s nothing you can say in His defense.” She yanked the door open and ran outside. In the darkness, she halted.

The crash of waves sounded in the distance.

She ran past her car and onto the broad sandy path, fog limiting her view to a few steps in front of her. Following the call of the relentless surf, she ran as if death itself were on her heels.

But no, if it had been death she would have turned and welcomed it with open arms. This was life pursuing her.

She tripped over a tussock of grass hiding in the sand.

The fog parted. Whitecaps glistened in the partial

moonlight.

Behind her, Alan called her name, panic evident in the timbre of his voice.

He would soon catch up with her. The only way of escape was to hide.

A mound pressed its way out from the smooth beach.

She darted around the far side of it and collapsed into the cool sand, letting it conform to the shape of her body as plaster to a mold.

Loud, rapid breathing, her arms stiffening.

Her nightmare had come alive. Running on the beach, chased by a man, falling on the sand. Moonlight, fog, and fear.

This is what she'd been scared of, run away from? A kind man wanting to help her?

Alan zeroed in on her hiding spot as if he held a metal detector. "Please, let's talk."

"I should have known I couldn't hide from you."

Alan squatted. "Are you talking to me or to God?"

"What do you mean? Of course I'm talking to you."

"I keep praying for the day when you'll acknowledge that about God. He's the One who's after you—the One who's not giving up. No matter where you go, He's already there."

"And you find that comforting?"

"It means I'm not alone even when I feel like I am." He held out his hand.

She let him pull her up. "Guess what?" Suzanne walked to where the sand met the sea. "I want to find a place away from a deity who's always waiting for me. Who knows what horrible thing He'll do to me next?"

"Have you told God how you feel? How angry you are at Him?"

"If He's really there and really God, He already knows, doesn't He?" She paced a patch of sand, robe blowing out around her.

"For your sake, you need to verbalize it—say it right out loud. Exactly how you feel."

"No, I don't think so." She stood out of reach of the lapping waves. "He'd probably strike me with lightning."

"God's big enough to handle what you think of Him. You think He'll zap you for your honesty?" Alan pointed a finger in her face. "Why don't you have some guts and find out? He's already told you what He thinks about you. Sermon after sermon, you sat next to Jake and heard how the Lord loves you no matter what, how you can come to Him just as you are. It's about time you tell Him what *you* feel."

"I can't." She dug her bare toes into the sand, hoping to find some hidden warmth. "I wouldn't know how to start."

"Let me help you." Alan tipped his head back. "Father," he yelled, "Suzanne's got something to tell You." He sat down. "It's your turn. Tell Him."

"This is insane."

"And you don't do crazy things? Like plan to use a gun to—"

"Fine," she snapped.

"You've got all these pent-up feelings. A lifetime's worth. The last few months brought them to a head. So shout them out to God."

Not one word emerged from her mouth. The pounding waves punctuated the fog-draped stillness of the night.

Alan lifted his face toward the heavens again. "Lord, Suzanne's kind of shy about this, but she's angry at You. In fact, maybe 'angry' is too gentle a word."

At that moment, she didn't care if she made a fool of herself. She spoke, unable to stop the flow of venomous words. "That's right. I don't like anything You've done to me. You're cruel and uncaring. How dare You take my husband?" she screeched. "What did he ever do that You would treat him this way? And me. I don't deserve this pain, this ... this desolation of my soul."

"The Lord knows about pain, Suzanne. He can take it away."

"Easy for you to say." Her words were edged with gall.

"It wasn't easy to watch my wife die of cancer. God carried me through many moments of despair."

She trembled. How could her heart continue to beat in such a harsh environment?

"What else are you mad about? What's at the bottom of the rage? Why won't you let God's love penetrate your heart?" He fed her the questions in rapid succession.

She trod the same stretch of sand over and over, a captured lion testing the confines of her cage.

The ocean wind roared.

She clutched both hands to her head, entangling fingers in her hair. Deep-seated emotions, like silt in the river of the past, came pouring out, an uncontrollable torrent.

"Beth abandoned me."

"Did she?"

"She pushed me away, tore me down."

Alan stretched out his legs, apparently in no hurry to go anywhere. "Did you have a good relationship with *your* mother?"

Suzanne's voice rose above the sound of the crashing surf. "She was a cold-hearted, controlling woman who never loved me. I'm nothing like her."

"Is it time to grant her forgiveness?"

"Alan, if you knew what she did … Monsters don't deserve forgiveness." Disgust colored Suzanne's words. "Her or Dylan."

"This Dylan, he's a monster, too?"

"I can't tell you why, but, yes. If you knew what they made me do, you'd walk away and leave me alone on this beach."

"Try me."

Suzanne scoffed.

Alan chuckled. "You wanted to be left alone, right?"

"Beth knows, and she hates me because of it."

"God knows, Suzanne. And He still loves you."

Tears evaporated and hot fury filled her bones. "Dylan made me promises he never intended to keep, like marriage and a family. As soon as he found out I was pregnant, he dropped me. But only after he made one more promise."

"What was the promise, Suzanne?"

"If I got rid of the baby, he'd come back. I wasn't going to do it, but my mother forced me to. She thought Dylan and his money and his prestigious parents were the best thing that would ever happen to me. She arranged for me to kill my child. She sacrificed what I wanted for what she wanted."

"That's not love, Suzanne. Jesus loves you. He sacrificed himself to save you."

Righteous anger burned through her, leaving an empty shell.

The wind had driven the fog away.

On the moon-washed sand, body shaking , she glimpsed a future free of burdens, with no condemnation. Was there more to life than what her physical eyes saw? Jake had found a hope, an expectancy of greater things, hadn't he?

The choice lay before her. Either she would have to face the hurt, or she would shrivel up and waste away.

φφφ

A little after nine, the telephone rang.

Beth started at the anticipated sound.

Tony came to her side and placed a companionable hand on her shoulder.

"Hello?" She held her breath.

"She's okay, Beth. She's okay."

"Thank You, Lord." Gratitude flowed over her. "Oh, I'm so glad. Let me talk to her."

"She's pretty exhausted." Alan's voice was soft, full of emotion. "It would be better if you wait. She's agreed to get something to eat with me. But listen, I need you to pray as hard as you've ever prayed before. God is working on her, and I don't want anything to stop that."

The conversation over, Beth walked to the living room, dropped to her knees before the couch, and bent her head. Before she closed her eyes, she glimpsed the painting her mother had brought. It still leaned against the wall, mocking her with its beauty, reminding her of her ugly spirit.

Chapter Fifty-eight

Tony stuffed his hands in his back pockets as Beth propped her elbows on the seat cushions and closed her eyes.

Should he leave? If she shared what Alan had said on the phone, maybe he could. Beth's exclamation of joy provided a good clue that Suzanne had not harmed herself, but what condition was she in?

If you can't beat 'em ... aw, why not?

He folded his long legs underneath him and squatted beside Beth.

God, thank You for whatever good news Beth received. I ask You to keep Your powerful hand of protection on Suzanne and heal this mother-daughter relationship. Amen.

He opened his eyes.

Whoa. That was easy. He could have been praying short things like that for years. Maybe it would have helped him not worry about his mom and sisters and their new life. About Mandy. Especially about Britney.

And let me know Britney's okay. Amen. Again.

"Do you believe in Jesus?" Beth's hair fell like a silky brown waterfall as she tilted her head to the side and looked at him.

"I do. But I have a lot to learn. He and I haven't been close for years."

"How did you come to believe?"

His knees cried out for relief. Must be getting old. He shifted and leaned his back against the sofa. "My dad used to take me to mass. We went every week when I was a little kid. In fact, I'm named after St. Anthony."

"What is he the patron saint of?" Her eyes stared right into his soul.

He blinked. "Of lost things, the poor, travelers." He dropped his gaze and focused on lacing his fingers together.

"It makes sense."

"What does?"

"Your need to help people, to protect them. Your wanting to get to the bottom of any situation. It's like helping the poor in spirit."

"Maybe that's why I took Mandy in."

Beth twisted a strand of hair around her forefinger. "I wondered, but I didn't want to stick my nose in where it didn't belong. When she knew who you were there at the store, it surprised me."

Did Beth think they'd had a thing? Please, no. "Blondes aren't my type."

Beth stopped toying with her hair.

"She needed somewhere to crash, so I offered my apartment. I didn't expect to get tied up with her life, but when there's a kid involved …"

Beth crossed her arms. "So Britney *is* your daughter? I thought you said she wasn't."

"No." He drew the word out. "I mean involved in all of Mandy's drama. It is completely platonic. Even less than that."

Beth fiddled with her earring and looked away from him. She seemed to be seeing much more than the entertainment center across from them. "Caring about people is usually pretty messy."

Alan had asked him to stay with Beth to be a help to her, not to drag her down. "Beth, you are so strong."

She dropped her hand. "If you knew the condition of my heart …"

"No, you live God, you show Him in everything you do. That's why I want to be around you, to learn how to be a better man."

"Tony." She turned away.

"I didn't mean it like that." He sucked in a deep breath. "I'm not good with words. I'm not trying to come on to you, I swear, but I want to hang around for a while, be part of your life. Give you a break from the baby every now and then."

Anger sparked in Beth's eyes. "Why are you always trying to be someone's dad? You lost Britney, now you've latched on to Isaac."

Anger? Or protectiveness?

He spread his hands. "No hidden motives." How could he make her understand what he didn't? "When my mom left, it was just me and my dad. We made it through somehow, but I've always believed kids are better off with both parents. If it's at all possible, I mean."

"I'm sorry, Tony. I didn't know." Beth laid a hand on his arm, then jerked it back as if she'd been burnt.

"Hey." He wrestled his large frame to its feet. "I'm going to get out of your hair. Call me if you need anything."

She didn't protest.

He grabbed his coat off the hook in the entryway and opened the door. "I hope Isaac feels better soon."

The storm door slapped behind him and he jogged down the steps. Brisk air filtered through his jacket. The world was a cold place. Without a warm, bright hearth to call his own, a man's marrow slowed in his bones, his life lost its zest.

He needed to start praying for himself. For a home of his own.

Chapter Fifty-nine

"Come on in." Suzanne stood just inside the cabin, motioning Alan to enter.

"Actually, there's a nice restaurant up the road a little. Not very fancy, but we can probably get a bowl of soup and a sandwich."

"I was thinking take out. I'm not really dressed for going out." She panned up from her sandy bare feet to the sandy bathrobe.

"I'll wait." He picked up the gun slowly and raised his eyebrows. "And I'll be taking this." He pulled the door shut, closing himself out.

Oh. Alone in a beach cabin with a single woman. Those tricky appearances of evil.

She captured her hair in a clip, replaced the robe with a coat, brushed off her feet, and slipped on shoes. She'd pack up things and head home after dinner no matter how late it was. The plans she had laid out to accomplish in the cabin no longer made sense. She left them behind, though what was ahead remained a mystery.

Alan drove and pulled into the small parking lot of an old-fashioned diner.

Steamy warmth enveloped her when he opened the restaurant door.

A gray-haired waitress wielded a long knife as she cut a slice of chocolate cream pie for the only customer in the place. He swiveled on a red vinyl stool, his lumberjack shirt straining across his shoulders.

The waitress placed a plate before the man and wiped her hands on her well-used apron, the chocolate smear creating an abstract design with the already-present stains. "Sit anywhere you want. I'll be right with you," she called.

Sounds of banging pots and pans collided with Golden Oldies on the radio.

Suzanne scanned the restaurant. "How about that booth in the back?" It might conceal how she looked—red, puffy eyes, mascara running everywhere, hair windblown to kingdom come.

They made their way to the far table, and Alan hung his jacket over the back of the booth.

She shivered. "I'm freezing."

"You want my coat?"

"Sure." She draped it over her legs. "Thanks."

The waitress brought them menus. "Can I get you something to drink while you're deciding?"

"Two coffees." Alan flipped both mugs right-side up.

The lumberjack strode to the register, working a toothpick back and forth between his teeth. He paid his bill and left.

Alan opened a menu. "What's your pleasure? My treat."

"Oh, thank you. I hadn't even thought of money." She bit her lip. "I left my purse in the cabin."

The waitress returned and poured two mugs of steaming coffee.

Suzanne wrapped her chilled fingers around the cup.

The waitress pulled a pen and order pad from her apron pocket. "So, what can I get for you guys?"

Suzanne pointed at the menu. "I'd like a bowl of clam chowder and some garlic toast."

The woman looked at Suzanne as if seeing her for the first time. “Hey, you okay?” She glanced at Alan, then back at Suzanne and spoke as if using a secret code. “You need any help?”

“Oh, no, he’s my pastor. He’s helping me work through some things.”

Alan smiled as she rose to his defense. Maybe because she had said “my pastor” instead of “Jake’s pastor.”

“Thought you were a couple having some trouble.” The waitress nodded in his direction. “Sorry. What’ll it be?”

“Hot meatloaf sandwich, please.”

“Ned will have it ready for you in a few minutes.” She walked toward the kitchen, hung the order on the carousel, and hit the bell. “Order in.”

Lost in thought, Suzanne traced the outline of her mug. What had happened to her on the beach? She felt a crack in the wall she’d built between herself and God. A small crack, but one with the potential of widening, of changing her life forever.

A few minutes later, the waitress set soup in front of Suzanne and a heaping plate before Alan. “Hope you don’t mind, but I asked Ned to pile extra meat and potatoes on. They’ll go to waste otherwise. No extra charge, of course.”

He whistled while staring wide-eyed at the plate. “Thank you, ma’am. Looks delicious.”

“I’ll be right back with more coffee.” Smiling, she headed to the front of the café.

“She must feel guilty for thinking I was a wife beater. I’ve never seen so much food in my life.”

A moment later, the waitress placed a coffee carafe on their table. “You two look like you need to do a lot of talking, so I'm going to leave you alone. This is full of fresh, strong coffee." She pointed to her name tag. "You call me—Delores—if you need anything else, okay?" She bustled over to the front counter and filled a sugar dispenser.

Suzanne picked up her spoon and blew on the hot soup before tasting it.

"Is it good?" Alan scooped a forkful of potatoes.

"It's too hot to tell." She munched a piece of toast. "Aren't you going to say something about my breakdown on the beach?"

"Not until you indicate what direction you want the conversation to take."

She released a heavy sigh. "In some ways, I feel all talked out. But, at the same time, I feel like there's a lot yet to be said." She swallowed another bite of soup. "I still don't understand what happened to me out there tonight. And how did you know I was here, anyway?"

He wiped his mouth with a napkin. "At the church work party today, Beth said something about the women's retreat you were going to. Thanked me for suggesting it to you."

She bent her head, unable to look him in the eye.

"At least you have enough sense to be embarrassed." He laughed. "Next time you lie, you ought to pick something a little less obvious."

She peeked at him, saw good humor on his face. "But how did you know I'd be at Bide Awhile?"

"It took some detective work, but once we got into your house and saw things boxed up and your dress lying out, we knew you were in serious trouble."

"So you and Beth figured that out, did you?"

"Actually, Tony helped."

"Tony?" Certainly he didn't mean—

"Officer Barnett. He was at the work party, too." He squirted ketchup onto the meatloaf. "Listen, we can discuss the details later. Right now I think we need to talk about you. And the Lord."

She pulled the crust from her toast, put the pieces on the edge of her plate, keeping her hands occupied while her heart wrestled with the decision before her. "Alan, I don't know where to begin. How to put God and me together in the same sentence. It's hard to believe He's interested in someone like me."

"Suzanne, He sent His son to save you. I know these aren't new words to you—you've heard them for years. But for some reason you've never believed them, have you?"

"Sure I have. I believe in God and Jesus and all that stuff. I'm not a heathen, you know."

"I'm meaning the kind of belief which changes your life. There's a huge difference between believing in the existence of something and actually putting your trust and faith in it."

She flushed. "But what's happened to the God of love you talk about? All I've seen of Him these past months is His dark side, His I'm-out-to-get-you side."

"God has no dark side, Suzanne. He is light and truth." He leaned forward and rested his elbows on the table. "I know you've tried to live a good life, but you would have to admit you've sinned, wouldn't you?"

Tears trickled down her cheeks. "Oh, Alan." She grabbed a napkin from the dispenser on the table and wiped her face. "I was such a disappointment to my mother, and now to Beth. Jake was the only person who knew all my past and loved me anyway. In my heart I know I'm a big disappointment to God, too. But I thought if I tried harder, He would love me more. Maybe overlook the choices I made in my early years." She pushed the bowl of chowder to the edge of the table, turned sideways on the seat, and rested her back against the wall.

Delores hit a switch at the front of the restaurant and the neon sign outside went dark. She sauntered over and began stacking some of the dishes. "Don't worry, I'm not trying to rush you. It'll take awhile for Ned and me to be ready to walk out of here. You want any dessert?"

Suzanne shook her head and added the crumpled, tear-stained napkin to the pile.

"No thanks, Delores." Alan arched his back and rubbed his stomach with one hand. "That was enough food to last me for a week. If it's okay to sit here and talk, that would be great."

"No problem. Let me know if you change your mind about dessert." She tucked the check under the cup of creamers and carried the dirty dishes to the kitchen.

Alan stretched his legs in front of him. "You were honest tonight. That's what God wants from you, Suzanne. He wants you to own up to the fact that you're a sinner. It's part of the human condition." He leaned back and folded his arms across his chest. "But the neat thing is it doesn't stop there. He sent Jesus as a sacrifice for our sin and to give us new life. Not a life of trying to keep a list of do's and don'ts, but an eternity of a personal relationship with God."

"I want that relationship, Alan, I really do. But I've run out of energy to go through life striving to make God happy."

"That's what's so great about God's plan—He's already done all the work."

"But it's too simple. It makes more sense to be good and

try to please God."

"If it doesn't meet His standards, what's the point, Suzanne? Who are you to change the way God does things? Don't reject it because of its simplicity. You can be free from guilt and shame. Free of the drive to be perfect. Even free from feeling you can never measure up. Suzanne, God is offering you a life of forgiveness and acceptance. You need to quit running from Him and settle things tonight, right now."

"But I still have questions."

"So what? Do you really have to have all the answers right now? Isn't it enough to know He'll show you?"

"But where do I start?"

"You already have. Just keep talking to Him."

"Here?"

"I can get you started." Alan closed his eyes and bowed his head. "Lord, Suzanne has come a long way, and she's ready to ask You to walk with her through the rest."

Easing her legs off the seat and back under the table, Suzanne lowered her head. Words welled up and spilled over. "God, all of a sudden the things Jake tried to explain to me and the things I've heard at church seem right. I don't understand why, but somehow I believe You love me." She wiped her cheek with her shoulder.

Was she actually doing this?

In a quiet, broken voice, she forged ahead. "I need you, Jesus. I need Your forgiveness. Please take control of my life. I won't run from You anymore. I promise." She opened her eyes.

Alan raised his head and smiled across the table at her. He reached into his pocket and handed her a clean, but wrinkled, handkerchief.

Sniffling, she accepted it with a tentative smile.

"You look different already, Suzanne."

"What do you mean?" Her hand crept up to her cheek.

"I see peace rather than the bitterness you've been wearing."

Suzanne's heart expanded. "It's real, isn't it? I don't know exactly what happened, but the peace is real."

"I think you'll be feeling a lot of things you've never felt before."

She stuffed Alan's handkerchief into her coat pocket. "I can't sit any longer. Let's go."

Delores came through the swinging doors of the kitchen as they reached the cash register. "Perfect timing. Ned's finishing up, and we're ready to close shop for the night."

Alan waited while she rang up their bill and counted out his change. "Hey, thanks for everything, Delores. You've been great."

"No problem. Good night, and God bless."

Alan ushered Suzanne out the door, the bell tinkling in the background. "He already has."

Chapter Sixty

Headlights from cars driving by arced across the ceiling.

A dog barked and Mizpah lifted her head from the green comforter.

"No, girl. Lie down."

Mizpah's tail thumped against the mattress, but she lowered her head and closed her eyes.

Dogs passed barks like humans passed yawns. Thinking about it made Beth yawn. She was definitely tired. Concern about her mother had taken all her energy. Why couldn't she fall asleep?

Because her mind kept going to Tony, though he'd been gone for a few hours. Tony? That wasn't right. Keith had been gone hardly more weeks than she could count on one hand. She'd still be pregnant if Isaac had taken his time, not rushed out like a linebacker after a tackle.

Yet someone other than Keith kept her awake tonight.

How can I possibly be thinking of another man? I'm disgusted. Lord, why can't I control my thoughts?

Tony had said blondes weren't his type. Well, her tastes ran toward more refined men—men that watched sports instead of played them.

In high school, Tony Barnett had been the big thing, all the girls simpering over him and his baseball prowess. But not her. She'd been too busy running track, winning meet after meet. He wouldn't have looked her way twice back then.

Was he looking her way now?

He says he's not, God, but why does he pop up wherever I am?

God works in mysterious ways. Pastor Alan preached it again and again. Could Tony be sent by God? Isaac would need a father figure, but plenty of men in the church could provide that. Like Alan himself. What made Tony so special?

He was just a man—a man with more feelings inside than those junior high girls would have imagined, open and honest, available to be part of a family.

Maybe they *could* help each other.

But she needed to find a way to make sure a physical spark would not flame into an emotional connection. Guilty as she was about her fledgling feelings, her senses had not died with Keith. She was used to having a warm body beside her in bed, a hand to caress whenever she wanted. With Isaac her sole source of physical contact, she'd been amazed by how long a person could go without a hug from another adult. Life as a single was already proving lonely.

Which was why Mizpah now slept on the foot of her bed instead of in the laundry room.

She wasn't seeking a replacement man. Her loneliness, her longing for companionship, centered on who Keith had been. He was the one she missed. His whispers of love, his goofy laugh, his passion for the junior high kids they worked with …

She flipped the bedside lamp on and opened her Bible.

Aha. Job 31:1. "I made a covenant with my eyes not to look lustfully at a girl." She closed her eyes. *Okay, Father.* If it worked for Job, it'd work for her—with a twist.

"Stay," Beth told Mizpah. She threw off the covers and tiptoed past Isaac's room, crept down the stairs, and found her purse. At the store, after he'd interviewed her about Britney, Tony held his card out between two fingers. Beth had slipped it into her purse, sure she would never have to use it but too polite to refuse.

ChapStick. Floss. A sample of perfume. Kleenex. A pacifier. Three empty gum packets. Where was the card?

She dumped the contents onto the coffee table and slid them around. There it was, caught in the teeth of a comb. She climbed back up the stairs, card in hand, and slid under the covers The blankets retained some warmth from before, but she tucked her feet underneath the weight of Mizpah's body for additional heat.

The letters comprising Tony's e-mail address jumped off the paper as if they had neon signs around them.

She grabbed her laptop from the nightstand and typed in his e-mail.

Tony, this is Beth.

It was good to have you here while I was waiting to hear about Mom, but I was glad when you left. That sounds rude, but having you here felt awkward. Then I got lonely, which I'm pretty much used to by now. I guess that's a normal feeling to have with what I've gone through, but I wasn't lonely when you were here.

Thing is I don't want to be anything more than friends and I'm afraid you are looking for more. Keith has all of my heart. I hope you understand that.

Are you up for being more of an uncle-type to Isaac? I've never had a brother and it would be pretty cool to have a guy be protective and supportive in that kind of role.

Since she sent it to his work e-mail, he wouldn't read it until tomorrow. She pushed the laptop to the empty side of the bed, tugged the comforter back up, and switched off the light.

A few minutes later, just as she dozed off, her phone rang.

An unfamiliar number.

Should she take the call? Who would call this late? "Hello?"

"Yello." A husky voice.

Tony? Should she hang up? Then she'd have to avoid answering her phone for who knew how long. "Who is this?"

"Tony. You probably didn't expect me to call you, right?"

"It's pretty late."

"I got your e-mail." Tony coughed, though it sounded as if he were muffling it. "Wanted to reassure you right away. I have no ulterior motives."

"Honestly? You're willing to stick around just as a friend?"

"Yep. Just friends."

Beth wiggled her toes under the down comforter and Mizpah's ears perked up. "Good. Because I made a vow before God, and I won't break it."

"Like Samson? You're never going to cut your hair?"

"Not quite." Beth laughed. "I'm not going to allow myself to be interested in anyone for a year."

"One year from when Keith …"

"No, I'm not fudging. One year from today."

"Good." Tony sounded sincere. "You need time, a whole lot of it, before you do. That's not what I'm after."

"Good." *Brilliant. Repeat whatever he says, huh?* Beth fiddled with the comforter.

"Since you seem to be contemplating important decisions, how about Luke? Have you figured out that part of your life yet?"

"He's only a kid who didn't think through all the possible ramifications of aiming at the car. I keep asking myself what Keith would do." She took a deep breath. "I'm not holding the accident against him. Look how I treated Mom, how I drove her away. I think it's important that Luke know he's forgiven."

"I understand. Knowing you're forgiven can change your life."

Chapter Sixty-one

Her own clean, comfortable bed.

Suzanne shut off her alarm and flopped back onto the pillow, her heart filled with anticipation of this new day. She stretched, wriggling her toes before forcing them out from under the covers and onto the rug.

A burst of laughter escaped her lips as she saw her reflection in the dresser mirror. What a mess. If Delores could only see her now. Smeared mascara raccooned her eyes. Her hair exploded in every direction, as if a small hurricane had blown over the bed while she was sleeping.

The late night trip back to Beaver Falls had seemed to last forever as she drove behind the mesmerizing red glow of Alan's taillights. It felt good to follow someone, to rely on him to lead the way and get her safely home. By the time he had pulled into her driveway, she'd been on autopilot, able only to stumble in the front door. After promising she wouldn't hurt herself, she had found her way to bed.

Now she hummed under her breath as she turned on water for a shower. She stepped in. Hot water pummeled her body as she lathered up. Minutes later, towel wrapped around her, she opened the closet door. Her closet was empty, vacant hangers where her wardrobe had been. Memories of Friday night filled her mind—reckless cleaning and boxing up clothes she knew she would never use again. Her blue dress lay in a crumpled heap at the foot of the bed, the neat pressing by the dry cleaner a thing of the past. She hadn't even noticed it last night.

She walked to the entryway, where boxes waited in a tidy row. She opened the nearest carton and pulled out a navy pantsuit. The few wrinkles shook out with little effort. She dressed, hurried to do her hair and makeup, grabbed her car keys, and headed out the door.

φφφ

Beth yawned, stooped, and poured dog food into Mizpah's bowl next to the back door. A long night with little rest. Who could sleep when her mother was suicidal, her infant sick, and her relationship with a particular policeman uncertain?

Pastor Alan had called one more time last night to say he was escorting Suzanne home and she planned to call Beth first thing in the morning.

Mizpah stuck her muzzle in the bowl, sending bits of food over the kitchen floor.

"Look what you've done." She grabbed the broom from the laundry room and swept the morsels into the dustpan. "You're going to have to eat outside once Isaac starts crawling, so enjoy the spoiling while it lasts."

The dog's long black tail whipped back and forth like a flag on a windy day.

She put the broom away and kneaded the small of her back.

Isaac swung in his baby swing. Since his fever had broken around 6 A.M., his eyes had brightened and his mood was vastly improved.

"If you're happy, I'm happy."

A car door slammed, drawing her attention to the living room window.

Her mother strode up the walkway.

Beth's heart trembled as she ran to the door, threw it open, and drew her mother into her arms.

Suzanne clutched at her, rapid breaths puffing heat onto Beth's neck.

She had no idea how much time passed as they stood there, souls mending, spirits healing, before words were even shared.

"I'm so glad you're here," Beth whispered.

"I'm so sorry."

They broke apart when Mizpah weaseled her way between them, beating their legs with her dancing tail.

"You troublemaker. Outside with you." Beth led the dog through the laundry room and pushed her into the fenced backyard. She joined her mother in the living room, stood hip to hip as they gazed down at Isaac, asleep in the swing.

"He's so precious, Beth."

"So are you, Mom. I never knew how much you meant to me until I was afraid I was losing you forever. Promise you'll never do something like that again."

"Oh, Beth, you don't have to worry. That's no longer an option."

Isaac stirred and his head fell forward, making a sharp bend in his neck.

Beth tipped his head back and wedged a burp rag under his chin for support.

His eyes opened for a moment, crossed, and closed again.

"Do you want to tell me about it?" Beth sat on the couch and patted next to her.

"Promise you'll still love me?"

"I don't know why I couldn't give you a chance to explain. I'm ready to listen this time. Were you really going to

… to kill yourself?"

"It's been so hard since your father died, Beth. I'd been able to ignore it for years, but an empty space inside me mushroomed and pushed everything else out of its way." Suzanne unbuttoned her coat. "Since childhood, I've felt the need to prove myself to those closest to me. I was never able to do that with your grandmother, to meet her expectations."

"And then you got pregnant?"

"The abortion was only one way she tried to control me. My dad refused to get involved in her games. So that was that—take care of the problem and pretend it never happened. Your dad was the best thing to happen to me. Besides you, of course. He gave me love and acceptance I'd never had, but always wanted. He was so gentle and understanding. I knew that together we could handle anything that came along."

Beth nodded. "And then the accident happened, and your security was taken away."

"Yes, there was nothing left. You had Isaac and God and that seemed to be enough. I wasn't needed."

Of course her mother felt that. Beth had done nothing but push her away, rejecting her sincere, though misguided, attempts to show love. "I shouldn't have let you think I didn't need you, Mom. I want you to be a big part of my life. But I don't want you to try to control me."

Suzanne smiled. "If anyone should understand, it should be me. I don't know why I thought you'd like it any better than I did."

"Mom, I also need you to forgive me for how I acted when you told me about the abortion. It was wrong of me to judge you, to pretend like I'm so much better than you. I'm not."

Suzanne fingered the arm of the couch. "Let me tell you what happened last night when Alan got there. God sent him at the right time. A minute more, and he would have been too late."

Beth gasped.

"I tried to run away from him. I didn't want to listen, to hear what he had to say. I thought it would be religious mumbo-jumbo. Memorized words of condemnation. But it wasn't. Alan showed me how to be honest with myself and with the Lord. It wasn't a pretty sight."

"Then what?"

"While we were having dinner, we talked about what God was offering me. I prayed and Jesus gave me peace. Like God just washed the past away."

Beth shrieked, waking Isaac. She ignored him and met her mother in an embrace. "Yes! I've prayed for this for years. Oh, Mom." A geyser of joy flooded her heart.

Suzanne broke free and rescued a screaming Isaac from the swing.

He quieted immediately, as if glad to be in his grandma's arms.

"You know what else I figured out last night? That dream I've had of being chased on the beach? It's God I've been running from all these years."

"But you're not running anymore." Beth threw her arms into the air, like a cheerleader whose team had just scored.

Suzanne grinned. "If it's okay with you, I'll get Isaac ready for church while you take a shower. If Alan can preach after his late night, I want to be there to hear him. And I want you beside me."

"Going to church? Together?" She bounded toward the

stairs. "You want to come back here for lunch afterward?"

"No, let's go out and celebrate. Then I've got to go home. There are a lot of boxes to unpack."

"Hold on a sec." Beth slid the painting her mother had dropped off out from behind the couch. "I know Dad surprised you with this. That you met in front of this picture in a little museum in Maine. You need to take it home and hang it back up. Where it belongs."

Suzanne gazed at the pioneer woman, whose arm was tight around the girl as they looked toward the horizon, grass blowing in the brilliant sun. "It's called *Completion.* I've always pictured it as a mother holding her daughter close and looking into the future."

An hour later, the three of them—Isaac, Beth, and her mother—sat in a pew listening to Alan.

To look at him, Beth would never guess he'd been up half the night. The vibrancy of his voice belied how tired he must be.

"Our Lord," Alan declared, "has come that *all* might have life, and life abundantly."

Chapter Sixty-two

"Abundant life!" Alan repeated, lifting his arms toward the ceiling.

Tony stifled an "Amen!" The man could preach it, though Tony found himself somewhat distracted.

Suzanne and Beth sat next to each other a few rows up. Every now and then, Beth would hold Isaac so his head peeked over her shoulder. His huge blue eyes seemed to spot Tony. Last night's conversation played through his mind. He was going to be a part of that little boy's life, yet Beth's vow gave him freedom from any expectations. After Mandy's manipulations, he wanted to steer clear of women who wanted more than he could give them.

Beth was different. She wanted less.

At least for now. Later, who knew?

He slipped out a side door right after the service and hurried home. Pastor Alan's sermon presented Tony with an empowering course of action. Beth had shown him a different way to live, but Alan gave concrete ways to make it his own. If he waited much longer to get it down on paper, it would disappear like whipped cream on hot chocolate.

He grabbed his black notebook—the same one in which he'd written Beth's name and number that first day at the store when she'd found Britney—and jotted his thoughts.

φφφ

Another hectic Monday morning in the courthouse. Tony emptied his change into a little bowl, threw in his keys, and topped the pile with his wallet. On the other side of the metal detector, he collected his possessions.

Behind him, a woman set off the alarms and argued with the security guards about not being allowed to take her metal fingernail file in. "I got jury duty," she said. "What am I supposed to do if I can't finish my nails?"

Tony smirked and stashed everything back into his pocket, heading up the stairs to the second-story courtroom.

Lawyers milled around, clients or their family members dragging behind. A few men hid their faces as he passed. He'd probably arrested them at some time or another.

"Hi." He waved at the next man he recognized as a past arrestee. "How's it going?"

The man dipped his head, then seemed to catch the sincerity ringing in his greeting. "I'm staying clean, sir. You won't see me going to jail again."

"Good luck." He patted his back and continued down the hall. Courtroom Five, on the right.

Britney broke free of the caseworker's hand and ran to him.

He swooped her up, swung her around in a tight circle. "Morning, Little Princess. I didn't know if I'd get to see you today or not." He leaned his forehead to hers and they rubbed noses. "Are you having fun where you're staying? They're nice to you?"

"Tony, they have a tramoline! I can bounce all by myself, but I have to sit if somebody else jumps."

"Good job being safe. Did you see your mommy yet?"

"Nope. But maybe I get to go home with her. Think I

can?"

What home? Wherever Mandy was living, it probably wasn't better for Britney than her foster home. Mandy would need a job, a place to stay. That was a lot to expect of her.

He gave Britney a hug. "I'm not sure what's going to happen. Let's wait and see, okay?"

"'Kay." Her eyes grew big and she slid down his legs. "Mommy!"

Mandy walked up with her lawyer. Dressed in a demure black skirt and a sweater set, she seemed years older than he remembered. Two clips held her hair back from her fresh-scrubbed face. She crouched in front of Britney. "Baby, I've missed you so much."

Britney's child advocate volunteer, Attorney Spencer Chee, appeared at Tony's elbow. "You reviewed your deposition?"

"I did."

"We're up in a few minutes."

Mandy clutched Britney's blouse, seemingly unaware of his gaze.

He pulled Spencer aside. "Why do they want the kids to come to these things? I don't think they should hear everything that's said about their parents. Haven't they been through enough without all the details being hashed out in front of them?"

Spencer checked his watch. "She'll be supervised in the hall until the decision is made, unless the judge wants to talk to her. Why don't we head in and get started."

Mandy's lawyer leaned down, whispered in her ear, and waited for her to extricate herself from Britney's arms.

Tony followed them into the courtroom and took a seat in

the front row.

"All rise, the honorable Judge Carter presiding."

Tony stood, waited for the judge to take her seat, and sat back down.

Spencer rose and addressed the judge. "We'd like to begin with Officer Tony Barnett. You're familiar with his deposition."

Up again, Tony raised his right hand and swore to tell the truth, the whole truth, and nothing but the truth.

From his seat near the judge, he had a perfect view of Mandy and her lawyer conferring over a piece of paper.

Mandy crossed her legs. She had on black pumps. Pumps! Not strappy high-heeled sandals or black leather boots to her knees, but pumps like the ones he'd seen the old ladies wearing at church yesterday.

Spencer started in, reviewing the occurrences of October 15. It felt like a lifetime ago to Tony, but he answered all the factual questions with precision.

Spencer moved on. "What happened when you approached Ms. Erikson after her arrest?"

"She came at me, screaming and flailing her arms. She clawed my face. Knocked me to the ground. Other officers had to pull her off."

"And she was on methamphetamines at this time?"

"Yes."

As Tony spoke, Spencer showed a picture of Tony's injured face.

"I talked to her later, when the drug was out of her system, and she was much more subdued."

"According to your deposition, you stated that Britney, Ms. Erikson's daughter, would be safer away from her mother?"

"Yes, especially after I heard burglary was added to Ms. Erikson's charges."

Spencer gestured to Mandy's representative and returned to his table.

The other lawyer approached. "I find it interesting that my client, who, the court will note, is very petite, could overcome your strength, causing you to fall to the ground, but if you say so, of course we believe you, Officer Barnett."

Or not.

"As for the charge of burglary, that was dropped within days, was it not?"

"It was." He swept his tongue across his dry teeth.

"My client has been in a recovery program, has put herself under the authority of a sponsor, and has been drug-free since her incarceration. Were you aware of that?"

His pulse thumped in his neck. "I was not, but it doesn't matter."

"You recommended that Britney not be returned to her mother's care?"

"I did."

"That's an extremely serious issue, Officer, advocating permanent removal of a child from her only known family member because of a single period of drug-use."

"It is. And that's why I disagree." Tony glanced at the judge.

The lawyer cocked his head. "With the seriousness of your recommendation?"

No, with my first opinion."

Dropping his defensive air, the lawyer stepped closer. "Are you saying you would now recommend Britney be returned to Ms. Erikson?"

Mandy stared up at him, hope shining in her eyes.

He swallowed. "I would, with certain conditions. As long as she continues her program and remains drug-free, I believe the best place for Britney is with Mandy. I've come to understand in the last few months that we all mess up. We all need a second chance."

Chapter Sixty-three

Christmas Eve

"You sure I look decent enough for the occasion?"

"Pops, I've never seen you look so nice. I can even see my reflection in your boots, I think."

Tony's father ran a hand over his smooth-shaven jaw. "I guess the worse that can happen is they throw me out for being the old coot I am."

"They're not going to throw you out. Suzanne invited you because she wants to get to know you." He shoved his dad's shoulder. "Go on. I'm right behind you."

Lester ambled up the sidewalk. "Don't run off on me, boy. I'll tan your hide if you disappear and leave me around a bunch of church folk."

"Hey."

"No offense to you, of course. You findin' religion and all."

The edge of Tony's mouth rose against his will. His dad could bluster all he wanted, but his tone of voice gave his true feelings away.

Tony rapped on the door. Waiting for Suzanne to open it, he couldn't help but remember the first time he'd stood there. So much had changed in those short months. It had looked pretty bad for a while, but everyone seemed to be pulling it together. Even Mandy, who had been allowed to have Britney for the holidays.

"You think Brit will like the doll we sent her?"

Lester hoisted up his pants. "I'm sure she will."

The door swung open.

"Tony! I'm so glad you're here. I was just basting the turkey when you knocked." Suzanne stuck her hand out. "You must be Lester."

"Yes, ma'am." His father pumped her arm. "Thank you much for inviting us. A couple of bachelors don't get a sizable spread put together on their own."

Tony flashed a grin at his dad. "Speaking of food, I left the apple pie in the car. I'll run out and get it." He glanced at Lester right before he stepped out.

His father was looking around the room, wringing his hat.

Chuckling, Tony loped down the frosty sidewalk and popped the trunk of the Nova.

Headlights lit the road, illuminating his view.

A car pulled in to Suzanne's driveway and parked alongside Tony.

Beth. She stepped out of the car, long hair glistening red and green reflections from the Christmas lights strung along the front of the house.

"Hey." He grabbed the pie, shoved the trunk closed, and walked around to her side of the car.

"Hey, yourself." She smiled. "Merry Christmas."

"Merry Christmas." He switched the boxed pie to the other hand. "Can I help you carry anything in?"

"I have the usual carful of baby things and a few dishes. Do you mind?" She opened the rear door.

"Not at all." He reached for the most easily accessible item, a bouncer.

In the middle of the bench seat, facing backward, Isaac

kicked in his car seat and his feet jingled.

"Ho, ho, ho, big fella."

"I brought a little Santa hat, too." Beth unbuckled Isaac, scooped him up, and wrapped a snowflake-patterned blanket around him. "And I got reindeer antlers for Mizpah to wear tomorrow morning. I'm going to try to get a good picture of them together under the tree."

"Sounds wonderful." Tony gazed up at the stars twinkling in the sharp night air. "Look at that sky."

She tipped her head back, joining him in searching the heavens.

Covertly, he memorized the jut of her creamy white chin against the dark backdrop of the night.

Isaac made a baby noise, bounced his head against his mother's chest.

"I should probably get him inside."

"Yeah." Tony looped a few more bags from her car over his wrists. "Did you hear that Luke was released to his parents?"

"I did. Just in time for Christmas."

"So you've talked with them?"

"I visited him last week. Took Isaac in after I showed him to the rest of the class on the last day of school before break. I thought Luke was missing enough stuff and that seeing my baby would give him a taste of something normal."

"I've seen him a few times, too."

"I know. He told me." She bumped the door shut with her hip.

"I can't believe how well he's doing."

"He might come out of this okay after all." Beth slipped on an icy patch of sidewalk.

Tony steadied her arm.

"Thanks." She blushed. "He's seeing the same family counselor as my mom and me."

They made it to the front door as another car pulled into the driveway, blocking Beth in.

Beth turned. "Alan and Melissa. I'm so glad they could come too. If it weren't for him finding Mom …"

"But he did. That's what matters." Tony struggled to get a good grasp on the doorknob with all he was holding. His fingers locked around the metal and he pushed the door open. "After you." He stood to the side as Beth stepped over the threshold.

Acknowledgments

We would like to thank the people who have given of themselves to help this book come to life.
Redeemed Writers Critique Group: Miriam Cheney and Kristen Johnson, who have so freely given of their time and writing ability to raise this book to a higher level than when it was first written. They've been through early drafts, late drafts, and we've-got-to-make-this-deadline drafts with equal unflappability. Their prayers and encouragement have carried us through the whole process.

Angela Ruth Strong, for always being there during the good and the bad. Shirley Wright, for being our patron of the arts. Donna Fleisher, who opened our eyes to the editing process.

Our test readers: Cassandra Ashcraft, Shirley Smith, John Ashcraft, Jaime Petersen, Karen Fordyce, and Jeanine Rieff. Your sharp-sightedness caught many an embarrassing typo and grammatical error. We claim sole responsibility for any that might still exist.

Early readers who graciously allowed us to share "our baby" with them before it should have seen the light of day, yet affirmed we were on the right track. Thanks to authors Jane Kirkpatrick, Nancy Turner, Karen Kingsbury, Bonnie Leon, Eva Marie Everson, and James Scott Bell. To Nikki Raichart who, though not an author, is an artist in her own right. To former members of critique: Debbie McMillin, Ernie Wenk, and Laurie Boyd. To Sarah and David Van Diest, who first believed in the power of this story.

Julie Bronleewe at Pacific Northwest Transplant Bank, thank you for the organ donation information.

We owe much to Oregon Christian Writers and American Christian Fiction Writers, who have provided stellar writing conferences through the years. From various teachers within both these organizations, we learned how to craft a story from start to finish.

Mother/daughter writing team Sherrie Ashcraft and Christina Berry Tarabochia bring a voice of authenticity to this novel as they have experienced some of the same issues faced by these characters. They like to say they were separated at birth but share one brain, which allows them to write in a seamless stream. Both live in NW Oregon and love spending time together.

Sherrie is the Women's Ministry Director at her church, and loves being the grandma of eight and great-grandma of one.

Christina is also the author of *The Familiar Stranger*, a Christy finalist and Carol Award winner, and runs a thriving editing business.

Please sign up for their Infrequent, Humorous Newsletter at Ashberry Lane for a chance to win cool prizes. Email comments, questions, or typos to Christina@ashberrylane.net

Connect Online

www.ashberrylane.net
www.twitter.com/authorchristina
www.facebook.com/sherrie.ashcraft
www.facebook.com/authorchristina
www.christinaberry.net/

Oh-so-easy Cinnamon Rolls

1 package Rhodes frozen cinnamon rolls, 12-count
1 stick butter or margarine
½ cup sugar
½ cup brown sugar
1 teaspoon cinnamon
1 cup chopped pecans, divided (optional)

Heat oven to 350°. Spray a 13x9 pan with non-stick spray.
Place frozen dough in evenly-spaced rows in pan.
Melt butter and pour over the rolls.
Mix together sugar, brown sugar, and cinnamon. Sprinkle evenly over the rolls.
Add ½ cup of chopped pecans. (optional)
Cover with plastic wrap and set on countertop to rise overnight. (If it's warm and the rolls rise quickly, set them in the refrigerator for the rest of the night, then take them out 30 minutes before baking in the morning.)
Add another ½ cup chopped pecans (optional) and bake for 20-25 minutes, until rolls begin to brown.
Drizzle on the frosting provided in the package.

This recipe is provided by Janet George, cook-extraordinaire. These rolls are served every year at the women's retreat for Wapato Valley Church of Gaston, Oregon.

Shirley's Loafing Around Meatloaf

2 pounds hamburger
2 eggs
2 small (8-ounce) cans tomato sauce
2 packages dry onion soup mix
Salt and pepper
Dry oatmeal to make the meatloaf the desired consistency

Heat oven to 400°
Combine all the ingredients in a large mixing bowl.
Spray a 9x13-inch pan with non-stick spray, then place meat in it and shape into a loaf. Bake for 1 hour. Pour off grease and let meat set for 10 minutes before slicing.

Recipe from Shirley Smith, mother and grandmother to the authors.

Also by Christina Berry Tarabochia

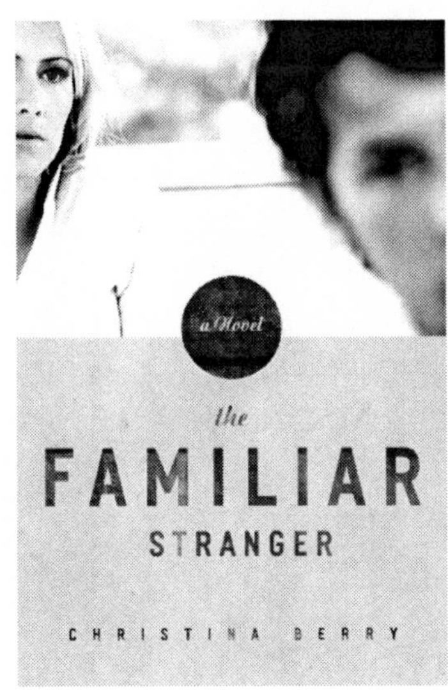

Craig Littleton's decision to end his marriage would shock his wife, Denise... if she only knew what he was up to. When an accident lands Craig in the ICU, with fuzzy memories of his own life and plans, Denise rushes to his side, ready to care for him.

They embark on a quest to help Craig remember who he is and, in the process, they discover dark secrets: An affair? An emptied bank account? A hidden identity? An illegitimate child?

But what will she do when she realizes he's not the man she thought he was? Is this trauma a blessing in disguise, a chance for a fresh start? Or will his secrets destroy the life they built together?

Moody Publishers (August 25, 2009)
Christy Award Nominee and Carol Award Winner

CPSIA information can be obtained at www.ICGtesting.com
Printed in the USA
BVOW041711190513

321092BV00002B/7/P